Spinster AND Spice

Spinster AND Spice

REBECCA CONNOLLY

Phase Publishing, LLC
Seattle

Text copyright © 2019 by Rebecca Connolly
Cover art copyright © 2019 by Rebecca Connolly

Cover art by Tugboat Design
http://www.tugboatdesign.net

Phase Publishing, LLC first paperback edition
May 2019

ISBN 978-1-943048-80-9
Library of Congress Control Number 2019938973

Cataloging-in-Publication Data on file.

Acknowledgements

For Ashley, arguably the nicest person I have ever met in my entire life, and the only person I can honestly suspect of being made out of sunshine. I consider myself so very blessed to be counted among your friends, and there are not enough blossoms in the entire world for those feelings. I'll go to Cheesecake Factory with you any time to plot randomly again. Worked out super well last time, didn't it?

And to Dark Chocolate Oreos. Life was a blank before I found you. Don't ever leave me. Ever.

Want to hear about future releases and upcoming events for Rebecca Connolly?

Sign up for the monthly Wit and Whimsy at:

www.rebeccaconnolly.com

Prologue
Mayfair, 1815

"I don't know about this, Georgie…"

"It will be fine, Izzy, trust me."

Isabella Lambert sighed as her older and more beautiful cousin grinned and practically bounced away from her, completely unconcerned about the path she was leading them all down.

It was a thoughtless idea, aside from the fact that Georgie *had*, in fact, put some thought into it. But the complications were real and legitimate, even if only Izzy could see them.

And see them she could.

They sprang into her mind with an alarming frequency, and each grew more terrifying or imposing or shocking by the moment. Imagine, a group of women gathering themselves together and embracing the title they had been given by the less than complimentary members of Society, all in the name of trying to save other girls from suffering the same fate with the same apprehension, or, even worse, behaving drastically merely to avoid it!

Being a spinster wasn't *that* dreadful, and Georgie intended to prove it.

Izzy was less convinced. Much, much less.

But she had been the one to prompt Georgie's swift actions, drastic though they were, and so she could not very well refuse her cousin in this. Or anything. Between the two of them, Georgie had always been the leader, while Izzy happily followed.

Not blindly, just happily.

That was who Izzy was, and how she was. The happy follower.

The soft-spoken cousin. The one who never said no.

The nice one.

She couldn't stop Georgie, and she couldn't let her go alone.

There was only one thing to do; the same thing she had always done.

"Be nice and act excited, Isabella," she told herself as she followed her intrepid cousin. "Be nice and act excited."

Chapter One
London, 1819

———— ❦ ————

A soft-spoken woman can be a powerful force for good. Provided anyone cares to listen.

-The Spinster Chronicles, 9 April 1817

"Izzy, where did I put the ribbons I bought last week?"

"At your toilette, Mama, by your hairbrush."

"I was just at my toilette, and they were not there."

"Are you sure?"

"Of course I'm sure, Isabella, I know what I saw."

Izzy laid her book in her lap, keeping her finger on the page, not bothering to avoid rolling her eyes. "Try under the hairbrush, Mama."

There was a moment's pause from upstairs, and then a faint humming that spoke of her mother's success in the ribbon hunt.

Izzy nodded to herself and returned to her book, not actually reading a single word.

She had been faux reading for twenty minutes now, waiting for her mother to finish preparing herself for her outing. It had taken almost twice as long as usual for her to actually leave the house, which was utterly maddening, but fairly typical for recent days.

It wasn't like her mother to be so fussy, but in the last few months, she had grown increasingly so, and her fussiness tended to be directed at Izzy whenever possible. There was only one explanation for that: Izzy was not married. It wasn't fair, and it was not kind, but there it was.

How was it possible, her mother had wondered, for the less likable of two cousins to marry rather than the other?

Izzy hadn't wondered that at all, for her cousin Georgie was very likable, under the right circumstances and with the right individuals. And in the months since her marriage, she had even grown quite cheery and sentimental when compared with her original state. Besides, Georgie was far and away more beautiful than Izzy.

Her mother would never be so coarse as to admit such a notion, but neither was she making any effort to refute it. Or convince anyone otherwise. It would never have been believed anyway. Everyone in London had eyes, and those eyes had seen Izzy often enough to know the truth.

Isabella Lambert was plain. And she was nice. And therein lay the problem.

She had other charms, and she had a decent enough fortune, to be sure, but it wasn't enough to necessarily tempt anyone to take her as she was, should they have wanted any such thing in the first place. No one had ever wanted her before, and she saw no sign of that changing, much to her mother's dismay.

"All right, dear, I am off to visit Lady Chesterton," her mother announced as she entered the parlor, adjusting her gloves.

Izzy closed her book on a finger and smiled as warmly as she could. "Yes, Mama. Do give her ladyship my warmest regards. She has invited the Spinsters to her dinner party next week, and I believe we are all to attend."

Her mother barely avoided giving a harrumph of her own disbelief. "I don't know why she encourages you. I've never found the status of spinster to be anything praiseworthy, and it will only make you all the more notorious."

"Mama," Izzy groaned, rolling her eyes dramatically. "You know how important the Spinsters are to me, and to Georgie as well. You did give your permission for me to write with them when we started four years ago."

"I know, I know," her mother admitted hastily, huffing a little. "And it really is very diverting, dear. But must it emphasize being spinsters so often?" She shook her head and pretended to fix her gloves again. "They're all coming over soon, are they not?"

Izzy nodded, trying not to smile. "They are, yes. Prue and Camden are back in London, so we thought…"

Her mother harrumphed an uncomfortable exhale. "In the future, dear, refer to him as Mr. Vale, at least to me. Would you mind?"

Izzy smiled and shook her head. "Not at all, Mama. I would be happy to. Now, don't be late for Lady Chesterton, it wouldn't be proper."

Her mother smiled and nodded. "And despite what you may think, dear, you are perfectly, exactly, as I would wish you to be."

"Yes, Mama," Izzy told her, the phrase so familiar it had lost its meaning, but was quite nice, nonetheless. "I know."

Her smile deepened, and then her mother rushed out of the room.

The butler intoned something Izzy couldn't make out but could well imagine. The door opened, closed, and then there was silence except for the butler's footsteps.

She waited until those footsteps retreated, just to be safe, and only when silence prevailed did she move to the writing desk in the corner. She moved aside the stack of books and notes from her friends that she had laid out to cover any and all evidence, not that anyone but the servants came into this parlor. If her mother had any idea, she would scour the entire room, and Izzy's bedchamber, and possibly some of the spare rooms.

But she didn't, and the rooms were left alone, and this particular parlor was unofficially designated as Izzy's. It was the one in which the Spinsters always met when they were together, and it contained more secrets than anyone knew.

Including the Spinsters.

She couldn't tell them this, or let it be up for discussion. Charlotte, for one, would have something to say about it, and it was entirely possible she would refer to it in some way in the next edition of the Chronicles. With the growing fascination over the Spinsters, and the scrutiny of them, it could actually be drawn back to Izzy, depending on how it was phrased. That was a risk she could not and would not take.

Glancing back at the door to the parlor, though no one was home to care what she did, Izzy slid the still-sealed letter out from the back of the desk.

She swallowed as her heart suddenly pounded in her chest, and a shaking hand moved a glinting strand of coppery hair behind her ear. It slid back into her eye line at once, but she would ignore it. For now.

She exhaled shortly and broke the seal, fingers trembling. She had been on edge for three days waiting for this letter, and now…

Dear Miss Lambert,

Having received your manuscript portion last week, I have taken the liberty of reading it thoroughly. While the prose is quite good and does lend itself to a story for children, I remain hesitant for reasons I cannot entirely express. But I do not wish to discourage you, nor should this in any way demean your writing. I had my doubts, as I said before you sent the selection to me, but it was more impressive than I anticipated. I had, of course, known you had some skill, given our success with the Spinster Chronicles, but it is clear that your imagination also runs in other courses.

Please submit further stories for my review, and perhaps we may meet to discuss what options and opportunities are before us. I am not convinced that I know the avenue for such works, nor where the production of it could lead, but I am willing to be persuaded otherwise should your writing prove different.

I am, cousin, most pleased by our further professional interaction, and hope for a good deal more in the future.

Your obedient servant,
Frank T. Lambert

The words reverberated in her mind, and while the letter held several words of praise and encouragement, there was only one thing that stood out to Izzy.

He'd rejected her.

He'd said no.

He…

Izzy sighed and dropped the letter into her lap. Cousin Frank was a good man, and very wise in the field of literature and publication. He had taken a very great risk with the Spinster Chronicles four years ago, and it was only right that he should have reservations about Izzy's stories.

But rejection was a bitter draught for her, and she had been so very proud of the story she had sent him. The Snail and the Salmon had been a favorite with her nieces, nephews, and cousins, and she'd thought it might have the same effect on her potential printer. However, it appeared that adults took more convincing than children to imagine these sorts of things.

She glanced down at the letter again.

Submit more stories, he'd said. Well, she could certainly do that. She had a dozen or so written out in various diaries and stuffed into bureaus in her room. Once she had written down the first two, at her sister's request, she could not seem to stop doing so. Why, half of the stories she had written had never been told to the children, and she knew very well there were several stories she had told that had yet to be written down.

Perhaps she ought to try for Robin Red-Breast and the Very Merry Tune. But she doubted it would be the same without the actual whistling, particularly when there were no children to encourage it. Still, it was worth trying for. Or perhaps Petunia the Turtle and the Muddy Puddle. That one was always entertaining. Tiberius T. Tiger's Terrible Tuesday? There was quite a clever rhyming pattern in that one. The unnamed one about the fox twins? They sang a song. Or perhaps a new one she hadn't thought up yet?

Stories she had told and stories she had yet to tell all swirled about in her mind, overwhelming and exhilarating her all at the same time. Where should she begin? What if she chose the wrong story and Cousin Frank hated it? What if she sent too many and irritated him?

What if…?

Her still trembling hand moved to her throat as she swallowed painfully.

What if it all worked and she got published, but no one wanted to read what she had written?

Her eyes widened. She had never considered that before, but it was entirely possible that she would achieve her dream but not succeed in it. All of her hard work and creative efforts, and she could be a laughingstock in the literary world. She could spend a fortune in publication and never earn a farthing for it.

What would she do then?

What would be worse?

Izzy inhaled slowly, then exhaled slowly. "Steady on, Isabella," she whispered to herself. "Let's not worry about things that have not occurred yet."

Nodding to herself, she refolded the letter and tucked it into one of her half-filled journals. She would need to consider the stories that might persuade Cousin Frank to publish her, despite his reservations, and despite the apparent misfortune of her sex.

Women were not writers, he had said when they'd brought the Spinster Chronicles to him. Not because they could not, but because it simply was not done. Izzy had barely avoided reminding him of the works of Mrs. Radcliffe and Miss Austen for her argument, knowing it wouldn't do any good to contend with him, whether in the right or not.

Then he'd defied his own words by publishing them anyway.

If anyone would see Izzy's stories turned into a collection, it was him.

But would he?

She drummed her fingers on the dark wood of the worn desk, chewing the inside of her lip in thought. She would have to assemble all of her journals with stories in them and compile them all into one. She'd need to see what she had and what she did not, what might be convincing and what might not.

And all of it with the utmost discretion.

It would be the most terrifying, vulnerable thing she had ever done, being less than bold and daring in her everyday life. She was the sort to sit still and let life pass her by, and that would not do at all for something like this.

Writing a collection of stories for children wasn't necessarily a great accomplishment or a bold adventure, but it certainly felt close.

"Miss Lambert?"

Izzy whirled in her seat, one arm flying to the desk to cover the papers there, though nothing incriminating would be visible anyway.

"Yes?" she cried, not hiding her anxiety in any way.

Collins, their warm and surprisingly affectionate butler, stood there, not bothering to hide his surprised and sardonic look.

"You have a letter."

She blinked slowly in response. "Another one?"

"Indeed, Miss Lambert." His mouth curved to one side. "This one came by express from Mrs. Northfield."

"Catherine?" Izzy blurted out. "My sister?"

Collins raised a dark brow. "Unless you expect to receive express messages from her mother-in-law, Miss Lambert, I would safely assume all references to Mrs. Northfield regard your sister."

That earned the butler a scowl as Izzy held out her hand for the note. "That's enough out of you, I should think."

"Indeed, Miss Lambert." He chuckled and handed over the note, bowing over her hand.

Izzy shook her head as she broke the seal, sighing as the butler left the room. He was one of the very few people on earth that she could be impudent with and not feel guilt, and she was now wondering if she had been unwise in doing so.

Still, he kept her secrets, so that must be worth something.

She scanned the letter quickly, smiling ruefully that her sister's penmanship was as perfect as it ever was, though more words had been crossed out than was usual in her correspondence.

Rose refuses to sleep without the story of the canary or the bluebird or what have you. She has been exasperating Northfield and myself to within an inch of our very sanity, and unless you wish to take up residence with us and be her nanny until this foolishness has passed, I desperately need a copy for myself. We never had this trouble with Cecelia, or either of the boys, so do save us, darling Izzy. My head aches even now, I don't know what I shall do if you refuse me.

Izzy scanned the lines a few more times, wondering what was possibly so urgent about this that it warranted the additional expense of sending it express.

"Well now, that is a promising expression on your face, dear. What's the note?"

9

Izzy looked up, already smiling, at the sound of her cousin's amusement. Georgie looked radiant, as she had done for the past few months. Marriage, it seemed, agreed with her, and her bright emerald eyes sparkled with a never-before-seen light.

"What are you doing here?" Izzy exclaimed, rising and going to hug her. "I thought you were not due back for another week at least!"

Georgie grinned and kissed her cheek, a fair lock of her hair unraveling from its pins. "Well, the weather has been so mild, and Hazelwood Park is delightful, but rather large for just the pair of us. We decided to come up early, particularly with winter keeping many people out of London. It really is the best time to be here."

Izzy gave her cousin a quizzical look. "Is it? No one is here after Christmas."

"Which is precisely how I like it," Georgie quipped without reservation. She glanced down at the note Izzy still held and brought her gaze back up to scan her cousin's face. "That looks like Catherine's handwriting."

"It is." Izzy held the note out for her, knowing her cousin would take it from her anyway.

Georgie snatched the paper and gleefully read the words, her lips moving as she did so. "My, my, having trouble with our word choice, are we? Decisions, decisions..." Then she snorted a laugh. "Refuse? When do you ever refuse Catherine anything?"

"Excuse me," Izzy protested, taking the letter back. "I am perfectly capable of standing up to my sister."

Georgie sighed, knowing that was a lie, and shook her head. "So, I imagine after the meeting today, you will be recording whatever story it is she wants and having it sent over?"

"More than likely," Izzy admitted, setting the letter back down on the desk and tidying up the surface. There would be no more thinking or talking of writing while Georgie and the others were here. They were too intuitive, and Izzy was too poor an actress.

She glanced at the mantle clock on the other side of the room. "Unless I can start it now..."

"Don't you dare!" Georgie took Izzy by the arm and tugged her away from the desk. "Just because your sister sent her ridiculous request by express unnecessarily does not mean that..."

10

"What was sent by express by Catherine the Terrible and why are we rationalizing it?"

The cousins groaned in a very soft distress even as they smiled and turned to face Charlotte Wright, the most outspoken of the Spinsters, and by far the wealthiest of the group.

Charlotte had her hands on her hips, full lips curved in her typical mischievous smile, her dark hair just the faintest bit mussed by the bonnet that had so recently been removed.

"My sister is not terrible, Charlotte," Izzy reminded her, though it was rather weak by way of defense.

"No, she's not," Charlotte allowed, making a face of consideration that surprised Izzy immensely. Then Charlotte made the most perfectly derogatory expression that she had ever been capable of. "She's spoiled and helpless and constantly enabled by her family members, and I am terrified of the fact that she is raising offspring of her own when she is so clearly a child herself."

Georgie burst into a fit of giggles and coughs, gasping odd choking sounds in between, while Izzy stared at one of her oldest friends, her lips twitching.

"Why didn't you say that instead of terrible?" Izzy finally inquired, feeling rather impish at the moment.

Charlotte sighed heavily. "It is such a mouthful, so I summarized with terrible." She rubbed her hands together and moved over to Georgie, bending down to kiss her cheek. "Lovely to see you. How was your Christmas?"

"Delightful, thank you," Georgie replied with a smile. "And yours?"

"Dreadful, thank you." Charlotte rolled her eyes and sat next to Georgie without any of the same elegance. "I hate siblings."

Izzy sat back down in her chair, grinning helplessly. "What did they do?"

"Don't encourage her!" Grace Morledge snapped as she strode into the room, cheeks tinged pink from the cold. "I had to listen to the entire saga of the Wright Family Christmas, and I went home and almost hugged my brother!"

Charlotte cackled in delight and clapped her hands. "Brava, we have finally succeeded! I cannot wait to tell Mama."

Georgie looked at Charlotte in confusion. "Is that something she would be proud of?"

"In a very twisted way, yes," Charlotte answered, still smiling. She turned to Izzy. "What are we refusing Catherine?"

"We're *not*," Izzy insisted, more bemused than upset. Charlotte had that effect on people.

"Of course we're not," Charlotte sighed. "We never do."

Georgie looked at Izzy with the most triumphant expression known to man.

Izzy ignored her.

Grace sat down in the chair beside Izzy, shaking her head. "Does anybody know if Edith is coming today? I didn't hear if she had gone to Scotland for Christmas or not."

"She didn't," Izzy said, barely avoiding a sad sigh. "I invited her to spend Christmas with us, but she politely declined. I'm afraid she spent it alone in that drafty house of hers."

There was an uneasy silence among the four of them at that. Lady Edith Leveson was full of surprises and secrets, and she did not share much of either, despite now being an official part of their group. They all liked her immensely, even Charlotte, but her diminished circumstances and lack of public appearances tended to worry them all.

A loud crash from the front of the house broke the moment, and they all chuckled at the hasty "Sorry!" they could hear following.

"Elinor Asheley, what is your h-hurry?" Prudence Vale stammered in her usual way, though the tone was filled with laughter.

"You'll hear in a minute, Prue! Come on!"

Scant moments later, Elinor and Prue were in the doorway, Elinor panting, Prue smiling.

"This is going to be good," Charlotte muttered as she rose to greet them.

Elinor nodded and strode further into the room, still tugging Prue behind her. "Ladies, you will never guess."

"Let Prue go, for pity's sake," Grace told the younger girl, taking Prue's other arm and hugging her. "She's not a child."

"Right, right, sorry," Elinor said, her distraction clear as she released her friend and sank into a chair. "I'm just so overcome."

"Really?" Charlotte asked as she greeted Prue. "I had no idea."

Elinor looked around the room, eyeing each of them. "Is Edith coming?"

"We don't know," at least three of them said.

"I can't wait." Elinor sat up and looked directly at Izzy, taking her by surprise. Her gaze was direct and at least partially in accusation.

Izzy swallowed with difficulty. Elinor was a clever girl, but could she really know what Izzy was hiding?

"Someone here has been keeping secrets from the rest of us," Elinor intoned with the sort of formality one would have expected from her mother.

Even Charlotte seemed surprised by that, and the silence of the room stretched on. "Besides Edith?" Charlotte pressed carefully.

Elinor shushed her with a vicious sound, and Izzy felt her face grow warm with anxiety.

It wasn't possible. It *could* not be possible. No one knew, and no one could possibly...

Elinor shifted her gaze to Georgie with a sharp jerk of her head. "Why didn't you tell us that Lord Sterling and Horrid Hugh have a sister?"

Chapter Two

—◦◦❦◦◦—

A gentleman should always be alert, active, and aware of his surroundings. One never knows when opportunities for heroism may arise.

-*The Spinster Chronicles, 22 October 1818*

"I don't think he's listening. It won't do to ask him. Anyway, he won't know."

"That's what happens when one is a perfect gentleman."

"Well, we know he isn't perfect."

"Is he asleep?"

Sebastian Morton was not asleep, and he *was* listening, but rather against his will. His friends had, for some unknown reason, decided that he should be the target of their games, and it had not yet grown old for either of them, although it had for Sebastian.

But he had remarkable endurance for things such as this and years of practice with these two would-be jesters.

"Ah ha! He twitched!"

"Twitching happens. Means nothing. Poke him."

"Don't touch me," Sebastian said without opening his eyes.

Henshaw snickered and nudged him instead. "So, you are awake! What was the last thing you heard?"

Sebastian exhaled roughly. "I have heard everything, Henshaw. You weren't exactly keeping your voice down. And Sterling doesn't know how to do so regardless, so…"

"I beg your pardon!" Tony Sterling barked with a half laugh.

"Insubordination, Morton?"

"You resigned your commission, Captain," Sebastian reminded him, finally cracking an eye open. "Forgive me for not respecting your no-longer-applicable uniform."

Sterling grinned at him from his corner of the coach, then turned his attention to Henshaw. "Poke him, would you? Hard."

Ever the obedient one, Henshaw turned to comply, but Sebastian edged into the furthest corner of the coach and held up his hands defensively.

"I will break that finger off, I promise."

Henshaw seemed to consider that for a moment, his finger inching closer.

Sebastian threw him a glare, batting at it. "Would you kindly remind me why we are riding off to a ball in the carriage like three boring bachelors when you, Sterling, have a wife? A new one, in fact, whom you happen to like very much."

"Love," Sterling clarified, raising a finger in the air. He cleared his throat and nodded firmly. "Love, Morton. I *love* her very much."

Henshaw groaned good-naturedly. "We know, man. Calm yourself." He shook his head and muttered, "Man gets himself a wife and turns into a sonnet."

Sebastian waved his friend off briefly. "Right, whatever you say, Sterling. Henshaw and I like Georgie immensely, so the question stands; why are you riding with us and not with her?"

Sterling frowned at his apparent lack of enthusiasm about his beloved wife. "She insisted she had to ride over with the Spinsters to finish catching up and told me to come with the pair of you, though I have no idea why. I can assure you, it won't happen again. She's far better company."

"I should hope so," Henshaw grunted. "She is your *wife*, after all."

Sterling's foot kicked out with lightning speed and whacked Henshaw across the shins, eliciting a grunt of pain from the larger man. Wisely, he refrained from returning the favor, which would have resulted in an all-out war in a moving carriage wherein two grown men turned into misbehaving ten-year-olds.

Ridiculous.

There really was no explaining his friends, and he had never attempted to try. They were excellent men, there was no question of that, and he would have laid down his life for either of them. In fact, he had come close to doing so in their battling days. At times, they were impeccable gentlemen and fine examples.

Other times they were more like this, and he could only shake his head.

"Don't shake your head at us, Sebastian Morton," Sterling suddenly broke in. "You can't be proper and disapproving of us for a few moments in here when you will be practically clinging to us when we get to Stanworth's, and you are surrounded by females."

Henshaw fairly howled with laughter at that, which was not appreciated.

"I'm reserved," Sebastian reminded him, "and not particularly comfortable in formal social occasions."

"That is not an excuse," Henshaw insisted firmly, shaking his head. "The whole idea behind formal social occasions is to break down reserve and improve on closer acquaintance. And you do want to find a wife, do you not?"

Sebastian reared back in shock, cheeks heating at once. "Well, I mean, eventually… Of course, yes…"

Sterling chuckled into his fist. "The panic, Henshaw… the panic!"

"Then to balls and parties we will go," Henshaw went on, ignoring Sterling's hysterics. "Again and again until we find that most fortunate of women for you."

Sebastian rolled his eyes with a groan, and looked out the window of the coach, shaking his head. Henshaw was clearly in one of his more immature moods, which Sebastian would simply have to endure until his adult version decided to reappear.

It wasn't always like this. More often than not, Henshaw was honorable and sincere, respectable and serious, though not quite to Sebastian's extremes. He was the best of companions and an excellent soldier, reliable to a fault, and wildly overprotective of his seven sisters. The fact that he saw Sebastian as a brother ought to have been a mark of great honor, but most of the time, it only led to moments such as this.

Sebastian couldn't say he minded all the time. He might be a reserved man, but he wasn't stuffy or puffed up. At least, he hoped he wasn't. He had no intention of being the sort of man that spent his time standing in the corner disapproving of everyone and everything that did not meet with his standards or approval. He just didn't find any use for being frivolous, and he did find comfort in being consistent.

His sister was always reminding him that a little fun wouldn't be remiss for anyone, but Kitty had no idea what he had weighing on his shoulders, the pressure he felt towards her, and the respectability she would need to make a good match herself. He had to be the example, he had to take care of her, and he had to be impeccable in the eyes of Society.

His friends, for all their good qualities, would never understand that. Sebastian took great pride in being a man of sound mind and firm understanding, reserve or no reserve. He could lay out a well-thought-out plan with precision and execute it flawlessly, whether on the battlefield or in other aspects of his life.

Except, perhaps, for the treacherous landscape of a London ballroom. That was a far more dangerous venue, and he was completely at sea there.

The only reason he felt comfortable at all was that his friends were in attendance, and the very few acquaintances he had of any real value would keep him grounded. Add in the fact that it was still winter in London, so the number of guests would be diminished, and Sebastian's comfort level increased.

"Did you just sigh, Morton?" Henshaw guffawed with another nudge. "What's so dreadful about spending the evening at a ball?"

"Only the prospect of watching you dance," Sebastian admitted, truly sighing in despair this time. "It's simply agony to witness."

Sterling immediately picked up the gauntlet and joined in, much to Henshaw's distress, leaving Sebastian to smile slightly to himself.

He couldn't let his friends have all the fun, after all.

17

"Oh, come now, Morton. Things aren't so glum as all that, are they?"

Sebastian turned to face the lovely figure of Georgie Sterling, smiling up at him in her usual mischievous way. She took a great delight in teasing him, though never to the same extremes that her husband and Henshaw did. He had never been certain if that was due to their only recent association or some sympathetic streak she had within her, but he was grateful for her restraint where he was concerned.

"Not at all, Mrs. Sterling," he informed her, bowing politely. "Particularly now that you are speaking with me."

Her full lips spread into a broad grin, her green eyes dancing. "Flattery from Mr. Morton must always be treasured, I thank you. But you know how I feel about being Mrs. Sterling."

"Yes, ma'am. My condolences."

Georgie burst out laughing and rapped him on the arm with her fan. "That is not what I meant!"

Sebastian shrugged. "Nevertheless, that is what you said."

She rolled her eyes, groaning faintly. "Morton, don't call me Mrs. Sterling. I adore my married state and my married name. You hear me? Adore. To the extreme."

Now he rolled his eyes but smiled. "I hear you, yes. No need to emphasize it."

"Uncomfortable?" She chuckled softly and sipped the lemonade she held. "Apologies. Just call me Georgie, will you? I can't stand being formal."

"In private, I will naturally call you Georgie," Sebastian allowed. "In public, I believe I must pay respect where respect is due."

Georgie seemed surprised, or perhaps simply bemused. "You respect me, Morton? Really?"

He, himself, was surprised by her surprise, hoping his behavior had not led her to believe otherwise. "Of course I do. You're a singular woman, Mrs. Sterling, and far too good for the likes of Captain Sterling."

She smiled still, something softer and possibly even more delighted. "That may be the nicest thing anyone has ever said to me,

Mr. Morton." Then she leaned closer. "And I do hope you inform my husband of that particular aspect of your opinion with some regularity."

"It's at the forefront of my mind at all times these days," Sebastian assured her in the same low tone. "He knows it quite well, if only because I tell him so."

"For that, Morton," Georgie announced, looking almost gleeful, "I insist you dance the next with me."

Sebastian smiled a wry grin as he held out his hand. "I am not the most graceful of dancers, Mrs. Sterling, but let it never be said that I stood in the way of a woman insisting I behave in a gentlemanly manner."

Georgie placed her hand in his and set her beverage aside. "Be gentlemanly, by all means, but not all gentleman. I want you to smile, or perhaps even go so far as to laugh. At least a little."

"If I must," he sighed, smiling at her again.

She nodded once, her fair hair dancing. "You must."

Sebastian led her to the dance floor, already smiling, and not entirely against his will.

Whatever doubts he'd had about Tony marrying one of the so-called Spinsters, and he'd surely had them, they'd faded upon truly getting to know Georgie. While she would never have done for a match for him, she was more than perfect for his friend Tony Sterling.

What's more, he actually enjoyed dancing with her.

He bowed with the other gentlemen, and then they joined hands with the couple to his left and proceeded in the circle, Georgie still seeming amused.

"And what could possibly amuse you about my dancing abilities this early in the dance, Mrs. Sterling?" Sebastian inquired dubiously. "I can assure you, the worst is yet to come."

"Oh, stop, Morton," Georgie laughed as she proceeded down the line with her hand lightly in his. "You are dancing beautifully, and you even seem to be enjoying yourself."

He gaped as best he could without being obvious about it. "Do I? How distressing, I shall rearrange my features accordingly."

"Don't be so droll!"

"Don't pester me."

"I do not pester!"

Sebastian gave his partner a look, which wasn't easy since he was spinning her about. "No?"

"No," she told him, though her tone was not nearly as certain as it should have been. "I am not a pestering person."

"Hmm," he mused, spinning her again. "And I am not a lying person."

Georgie's brow furrowed, and her eyes seemed to have trouble focusing. "And I... need some air..."

Sebastian jerked back, suddenly eyeing Georgie up and down with concern. "Pardon?"

"Air," Georgie gulped, suddenly a pale shade that was rapidly turning green. "Air."

"Right, right," Sebastian muttered, taking her out of the dance and moving as swiftly as he could for the doors to the gardens. "Steady, Georgie, it's all right..."

She swallowed harshly and seemed to have trouble blinking. "Don't want to make a scene."

Sebastian laughed once as he took more of her weight in his grasp. "Not at all, we're merely promenading, yes?"

"Something like that," she mumbled, as her body lurched slightly.

"Georgie? Georgie!" Sterling suddenly appeared by Sebastian's side, gingerly patting his wife's arm.

Sebastian nudged his head towards the door. "Sterling, get the door, and then you can take her."

The doors were flung open, and then Sterling was on Georgie's other side, and the pair of them hauled her over to a poorly lit corner of the garden.

"Georgie? Oh, Georgie, what is it?"

Sebastian turned to see Georgie's copper-haired cousin dashing towards them, completely ignoring him, and Tony, and the awkwardness of the situation.

"Miss Lambert..." Sebastian tried, shaking his head and wincing.

But she had already reached Georgie and brushed her cousin's hair away from her damp brow just as Georgie retched, and continued to do so again and again.

Sebastian turned slightly away, somewhat nauseated by the sight, particularly now that he had no protective instincts to contend with. Georgie's husband could take those on, and while he was certainly not going to abandon his friends in this unusual hour of need, he didn't necessarily need to witness it for himself.

"Well, that's what you get for eating fish and then spinning a great deal," Miss Lambert scolded, somehow still sounding playful despite the situation. "I tried to warn you."

"Izzy," Sterling broke in, smiling ruefully, "is this really the time?"

Georgie waved a weak hand at her husband. "It's always time. I'm all right now. It's passed, I think." She sat back, exhaling roughly and wiping a hand across her mouth. "I am so sorry. I haven't done that in... years, I think."

Sterling rubbed his wife's back, his brow furrowing. "What do you have to be sorry about, love? You are the one who is ill."

Georgie patted Sterling's chest. "It's fine. I'm fine." She turned to smile sadly up at Sebastian. "I am so sorry, Mr. Morton."

Sebastian folded his arms and returned her smile. "I'm siding with your husband on this, Georgie. There is nothing to be sorry for."

"I should say not," Miss Lambert added, dabbing her sleeve along Georgie's brow and cheeks. "Just a bit of sick. No harm done."

Georgie looked at her cousin, then snorted softly. "Tell that to your dress, dear. And give it my apologies."

Miss Lambert looked down at herself, and then waved a dismissive hand. "It never flattered me anyway. Can you stand, Georgie?"

She nodded, and Sebastian moved over to assist, though Miss Lambert and Sterling had her by each arm as she rose. She didn't seem quite steady, but she no longer looked pale or green, which he supposed was enough of an improvement.

"Tony, perhaps you should take her home," Miss Lambert suggested. "There's a path that leads around to the front of the house, so the rest of the guests needn't see Georgie in this state. Mr. Morton and I can let the house staff know your carriage is needed, and no one else will be the wiser."

Sebastian nodded, admiring Miss Lambert's plan for what it was.

Adapting to an unforeseen situation without a tremor of hesitation and taking charge quite efficiently. That was something he could certainly admire and go along with.

Sterling nodded and put an arm around Georgie, helping her towards the path indicated. "Thank you both," he called over his shoulder.

"Not at all, Sterling," Sebastian assured him. "We will take care of things here."

He watched as the couple moved out of sight, then turned to the woman standing on the terrace with him.

Miss Lambert looked somehow worse than her cousin had, her copper hair not quite as put together as it had been before, her dress rumpled and soiled, in some places quite obviously so.

She looked down at herself as well, then laughed once. "It really is ruined, isn't it? Oh well." She smiled as if it made no difference.

"Is it really as simple as that?" he inquired, tilting his head. " 'Oh well', and that's the end of it?"

Miss Lambert nodded and shrugged. "It really isn't that flattering at all. Or wasn't, at least. And it certainly isn't now."

"You look lovely, Miss Lambert," he dutifully replied.

She gave him a baffled look, then smiled, shaking her head. "No, that wasn't what I was looking for. I'm not one of those women that traps a man into giving a compliment at the risk of appearing ungentlemanly. Take it back."

Sebastian laughed at that and shook his head in return. "I cannot take it back, you will just have to accept it for what it's worth."

"Which isn't much, considering I do not look lovely at this moment," she offered with a snort. "But it was a valiant effort."

"Thank you, I do try." He bowed politely, letting himself smile ever so slightly.

Miss Lambert twisted her lip in thought, then snapped open her fan and held it in front of her. "There, does that hide the worst of it?" She looked back at Sebastian, head cocked in question.

"It does, yes." He glanced down at her hem and smiled again. "Though it does not, I'm afraid, help there."

She followed his gaze, then snickered softly. "No, not at all." She looked up and the brilliant blue-green of her eyes suddenly seemed to dance with the stars. "You'll have to walk in front of me when we proceed through."

Sebastian bowed again, keeping his eyes on hers. "Of course, Miss Lambert."

"Izzy," she told him, wrinkling up her nose. "I've never cared much for formality."

"Alas, I *do* care for formality," he replied with an apologetic wince. "Bit of a stickler for it."

Miss Lambert hummed softly in thought. "Can I be an exception?"

He grinned briefly. "And this is where I see the resemblance to your cousin, Miss Lambert."

She laughed now and looked in the direction Georgie and Sterling had gone. "Yes, that would be it. We'd better be off, or their carriage will not be prepared. If we keep to the outskirts of the room and proceed leisurely, no one will suspect."

Sebastian nodded and offered his arm to her, making sure to keep her behind him enough to hide the state of her dress. "What do you think that was, anyway?"

Miss Lambert hummed again, this time with a laugh, and it seemed to reverberate somewhere in his chest. "If I were to wager, Mr. Morton, I would say that in a matter of weeks, Captain and Mrs. Sterling will be announcing an addition to their family."

He looked at her in surprise as they reentered the ballroom, then away in thought. A child. That had not crossed his mind in the slightest, but he supposed...

He turned back to Miss Lambert, suddenly feeling more curious about her. "Do you wager, Miss Lambert?"

She smiled a little. "Only when I know I can win. I am not the bold and reckless sort, Mr. Morton."

"Ah, yes," he mused. "I'd once heard you described as shy."

Her brow wrinkled slightly. "Mmm... No, not shy, really. I have no fears talking to anyone, certainly not the way Mrs. Vale does, but neither am I particularly boisterous. If there were a word between reserved and sociable, I would be it."

Sebastian nodded in thought, intrigued by the idea of the elusive word to describe her. He couldn't say he had spent a great deal of

23

time with her, nor necessarily with any of the Spinsters as a whole, but their paths certainly had crossed. Until this moment, he was not sure that he could have said anything much about Miss Lambert at all.

But she was not shy, that he now knew. And she concocted plans, was unfazed by illness or emergency, and was entirely unruffled by a distressing situation.

He would have to pay more attention to Miss Isabella Lambert in the future.

"It was rather heroic, you know," she suddenly said, breaking into his thoughts. "The way you swooped Georgie away from the dance floor and out into the night in her moment of need."

He scoffed softly. "Not at all, only timely and gentlemanly. Nothing out of the ordinary, or at all heroic, as it were."

"Are gentlemanly deeds not heroic to the lady in need?" she returned, raising a brow. "I'd venture to say they are, sir."

"Venture elsewhere, if you please. I am no hero."

"You shouldn't deny it, any more than you would deny being a gentleman. I'll not venture elsewhere, and nor would Georgie, and you know it."

He sighed, half in irritation, half amusement. "Very well. As a gentleman, I now ask you to dance, Miss Lambert, though given the state of your dress at the moment, I imagine you must wish to be off soon to remedy it. And as we are avoiding scenes by our leisurely stroll, I imagine you would not wish to negate it with a dance in a gown so soiled."

"You imagine correctly, Mr. Morton," she murmured back, a teasing note to her voice. "But I grant you a dance of your request at any event in the future. You need only ask." She patted his arm as they exited the ballroom and hurried over to the footman to request the Sterlings' coach, and her own.

"Good evening then, Miss Lambert," he said rather unnecessarily, bowing yet again. "I look forward to our forthcoming dance."

She smiled at him in surprise and inclined her head. "So do I, Mr. Morton. Gentleman and hero of the weak."

"Not a hero, Miss Lambert."

"But a gentleman still."

He grinned without reserve at that. "Always that, Miss Lambert. Always." He nodded again and turned to the ballroom, then thought better of it and headed for the card room.

He rather felt like wagering at the moment.

Chapter Three

―――――◦⧉⧈◦―――――

A lady with a good character must always be appreciated. A spinster with a good character must always be pitied. It is not entirely clear why one's marital status changes things, but one cannot deny that it does.

-The Spinster Chronicles, 22 February 1816

"Oh, that's lovely. Your mother's taste in tea remains exactly as it was before."

"You don't have to drink it, Edith, really."

Edith swallowed harshly and shuddered, setting the cup aside. "Thank you, I won't."

Izzy chuckled and went back to her writing, chewing her lip thoughtfully as she debated her word choice.

"Working on the next edition, are you?" Edith queried gently, her brogue ringing out. "A bit early, we've only just released one."

"I know," Izzy replied, smiling over at her. "But I wanted to get started early. I'm just jotting down some thoughts and phrases now while it's fresh. I've been so busy lately, it's becoming more difficult to find the time."

Edith quirked her brows, her lips curving as she picked up the embroidery she'd brought with her. "Busy? Lass, what are you busy with? I was not aware that the Spinster Chronicles was becoming such a rigorous commitment."

Izzy bit down on her lip hard, hesitating. Edith was one of the more trustworthy Spinsters, it was true, but she didn't dare reveal the truth yet. Surely, she would know something soon, and then she would have news to share.

"Oh, it's not that," Izzy finally assured her. "I have just been doing a lot for my mother, and now my sister..."

"Ah, yes, I heard about that. A children's story, was it?" Edith asked, tightening her wrap around her.

Izzy smiled thinly, pressing her tongue against her teeth. "Yes. You wouldn't know this, but I tell stories to my nieces, nephews, and young cousins every time we get together. It's become a bit of a routine, and my niece Rose has apparently demanded her favorite story before she goes to bed. I've sent over a copy as best I can recall it, but it seems it's been missing something every time."

Edith nodded slowly, taking a biscuit from the tray and nibbling on it. "Stories from memory are much harder to record than people think."

"Yes," Izzy sighed heavily, rubbing at her brow. "It's different, too, when the children aren't here to prompt me. I can't remember everything about their favorite stories on my own, not with... everything else."

"I certainly understand that." Edith chuckled under her breath and shifted in her chair. "I'm Scottish, remember? More than half of our stories are told over generations, and they're told differently each time, and no one really knows what the truth of it actually was."

Izzy exhaled silently and turned back to her writing, hoping that Edith would take up that particular tangent and leave the topic of Izzy's writing alone.

The truth of the matter was that half of the sentences and phrases she had written down were from the children's stories, and not potential articles. And while she was busy with all of the stories and writing them down, it was true she was also constantly being flooded with ideas for the Spinster Chronicles and new angles to take with their articles.

And then there was the anxiety of waiting to hear back from Cousin Frank about pursuing publication. And wondering if her secret was going to come out in front of all her family, or friends, or both. And her fears for the future, her insecurities about writing at all, and her fear that her niceness was going to ruin this and everything else for her.

Oh, and she was a spinster. Still.

"When you want to tell me what is really going on in that lovely head of yours, I would be delighted to hear it."

Izzy slowly dragged her gaze back to Edith, whose eyes shone with a knowing light. Despite only being a year older than Izzy, Edith seemed to possess wisdom beyond her years, and appeared almost matronly just now.

She supposed being a widow would have that effect on a woman.

Sensing Edith was still waiting for a response, Izzy swallowed once. "I will. When I'm ready."

Edith nodded and smiled gently, which only enhanced her staggering beauty, and winked before going back to her needlework.

And that, it seemed, was that.

No questioning looks, no prodding inquiries, no hounding until more information was drawn from her in surrender. Edith truly was not going to ask any more on the subject.

What a refreshing notion.

"You are telling me that Alice Sterling is coming to London? *Before* the Season?"

Izzy rolled her eyes and saw Edith do the same as they heard Elinor now just down the corridor.

"Yes, Elinor, she is," Georgie said in a carefully patient tone. "Francis and Janet brought her back for Christmas, and she is staying. So, when they come up from the country, Alice will come as well."

They finally appeared in the parlor, and Georgie, for all her tolerance of Elinor, looked done for. She widened her eyes meaningfully at Izzy, but Izzy had no help to give. She needed to avoid the intuition of curious women to escape unscathed from this whole ordeal.

She had to avoid Elinor like the plague. Without actually avoiding her, of course. No need to be obvious.

"Tell me she is better than her wretched brother," Elinor begged with all the dramatics she had ever employed. "I could not bear having two horrid Sterlings in our midst."

Georgie heaved a sigh and turned to the younger girl, her expression firm. "Alice is the female version of Francis. Headstrong, witty, willful, but sweet. And not at all like Hugh."

"Thank the Lord," Elinor groaned, dramatic still as she flung herself down on the couch nearby. "Then perhaps I will be friends with her."

"Yes, because that is exactly what she wants from her time in London, dear," Grace commented as she and Charlotte appeared, Prue in tow, "to know you."

Charlotte snickered and nudged Elinor aside on the couch, then sat down beside her. "Introduce her to Amelia Perry. She's a much better influence."

"I beg your pardon!" Elinor coughed, flopping her hands into her lap.

"Amelia would love that!" Prue exclaimed as much as Prue ever exclaimed anything. "She has so f-few friends, despite being delightful, and I am not n-nearly as available as I once was."

Charlotte grunted softly. "I wonder why that is."

Grace sharply slapped a gloved hand across Charlotte's wrist, her polite expression never changing. "Sounds like a lovely idea. Amelia would be able to guide her and be a companion of sorts in Society."

"So would I!" Elinor insisted, looking around wildly, though no one marked her.

"Well, she will have Janet, you know," Georgie pointed out as she poured herself some tea.

"And me!" Elinor cried.

Izzy nodded thoughtfully, warming to the game they were unofficially playing. "Edith, would you have any interest in assisting her? You are such a wonderful, gentle soul."

"So am I!" Elinor whined.

"I am not that gentle," Edith protested with a laugh. "But I would be happy to help Miss Sterling, if I can. Lord Sterling is a good man, and an amusing one, so I must assume his sister will be the same."

Elinor snorted loudly and shook her head. "Don't assume *anything* with the Sterlings, Edith. Ever."

"Excuse me," Georgie murmured, raising a finger in the air. "Sterling sitting here."

Elinor made a face at her. "You don't count, Georgie. Not

really."

Izzy put a hand over her eyes, and she was quite sure she wasn't the only one doing so.

"Oh, well, there's a relief," Georgie quipped. "Would you care to tell me if my child counts as a Sterling? I would rather know before it arrives this summer."

"Well, I suppose it would..." Elinor began before trailing off as her eyes went wide.

Izzy smiled at her cousin, who now seemed to be glowing, not entirely surprised by the revelation.

Georgie colored in delight and shrugged once. "I am with child. Confirmed by the physician just this morning."

The Spinsters squealed in an odd chorus and hugged Georgie in turn. Izzy was last and held her cousin even longer than the others.

"You must have suspected," Georgie said as she pulled back from Izzy, meeting her eyes. "After I was sick all over you the other night and ruined your gown."

"Which gown?" Charlotte demanded as she took her seat again. "Not the one I gave you, I hope!"

Izzy shook her head and gave Charlotte a look. "No, Charlotte. It was my lavender muslin, and it's three seasons old."

"Oh, that's all right then." Charlotte sat back with a biscuit in hand. "No harm done."

"Not everybody can afford new dresses on the regular, Charlotte," Grace reminded her none too gently. "Don't be a snob."

Izzy gave her cousin a look. "Why have children when you have us? It's practically the same thing."

Georgie scoffed softly, then smirked as she moved to her seat once more. "Well, the thing is done. And now you all know. And Mr. Morton."

That made Elinor perk up somehow. "Mr. Morton? How does he know?"

"Oh, I was dancing with him at the Stanworth party when I became ill," Georgie explained, lounging a little in her seat. "He was quite heroic, the way he swept me off of the dance floor and out to the garden before I truly... you know..."

"I tried to tell him it was heroic after you and Tony left," Izzy added, rushing over what Georgie was hedging about. "He completely disagreed, said he was only a gentleman." She shrugged at that, smiling at the memory.

Charlotte looked slightly disgruntled and shook her head very slightly. "Only a gentleman?"

Izzy shrugged a shoulder. "That's what he said."

Charlotte gaped and turned to look at the others. "Does Mr. Morton know how rare a real gentleman is in today's society? Not just the categorization, but the manner."

"Apparently not," Grace lamented, leaning her head on Charlotte's shoulder. "But I would love to find someone who was 'only a gentleman' who would take an interest in me."

Izzy felt her smile spread at that.

Despite what had been claimed in the past, the Spinsters were not matchmakers. Not entirely, though they had made some rather fortunate introductions for a few people over the last few years. She could not vouch for the others, but Izzy had no interest in the courtships and romantic interests of Society, nor was she interested in pairing them up with anyone.

Least of all Mr. Morton, gentleman though he was.

"Mr. Morton has some excellent statistics," Elinor mused, all speculation now. "Decent fortune, though not enough to be considered a catch."

"Poor man," Georgie muttered drily. "How does he sleep at night?"

Izzy choked on a laugh, and caught Prue clamping down on her lips and near to laughter herself.

That was a startling change. Since her marriage a few months ago, Prue laughed more than anyone had heard in all the years before. Camden Vale was perfect for the shy, stammering Prudence Westfall, and no one could have predicted that.

"He has a house in the country," Elinor recited, somehow from memory, "though I can't quite recall where…"

"Bedford," Georgie reminded her, watching Elinor in fascination. "You knew that at one point, I know you did."

Elinor groaned and covered her face. "I know I did! I'm losing my touch!" She dropped her hands just as quickly. "He has one sister,

31

no other relatives. He's still in possession of his commission, though not currently active, and there is absolutely nothing at all negative about his reputation." She seemed stunned by that and looked around the room. "I don't have a negative thing to say about him. Not one."

They were all silent for a moment, letting that statement sink in. It was so impossible, Elinor having nothing to say about a man she had done her research on. She was disparaging of all men these days, which was only solidifying her desire to be a spinster, though she was still too young to really be considered such.

Nothing negative to say?

It was nothing short of miraculous.

Edith stared at Elinor in outright disbelief. "You don't expect me to believe that Mr. Morton is the perfect man, do you?"

That broke the tension adequately, and there were wry chuckles all around, particularly from Georgie.

"He *is* rather handsome," Grace mused thoughtfully, pulling at her bottom lip absently.

Charlotte nodded firmly at that. "Indeed, he is. That dark hair and barely blue eyes? And such a strong, soldierly build…"

"Barely blue?" Izzy asked with a laugh. "What does that even mean, Charlotte?"

"Oh, you know, Izzy," Charlotte tittered, waving at her.

"Pretend I don't," Izzy insisted, making Georgie snicker.

Charlotte sat up formally, her lips twisting in subtle irritation. "They aren't gray, they aren't green, they aren't blue, but they tend to be more blue than any of the others. Barely blue."

Georgie slowly shook her head from side to side. "Now why didn't I know that? I have missed so much being married."

She received a sardonic look from Charlotte for that. "I did try to warn you, Georgie, but you had to have Tony."

"I don't remember hearing you complain about the marriage," Georgie shot back. "The banns were read, and you didn't object."

Charlotte sniffed loudly. "I did not wish to make a spectacle of myself."

Grace hooted a loud laugh very unlike her natural way. "Since when?"

Charlotte ignored that. "Do you think Mr. Morton would want

an heiress?" she asked Georgie.

"No," Georgie told her.

"Who doesn't want an heiress?" Charlotte asked in complete bewilderment.

"Oh, let's see... Tony, Cam..." Prue murmured almost under her breath.

Charlotte turned to glare at her. "You *are* an heiress, Prudence, dear, so you cannot include Cam."

Prue shrugged a shoulder, smiling to herself. "That's not why he loves me, or why he married me."

"Yes, but he still married an heiress," Charlotte huffed impatiently. "The loving and reason parts are irrelevant."

"Are they?" Izzy asked, feigning surprise. She looked at Georgie with wide eyes. "Did you know that?"

Georgie shook her head and sighed. "I shall have to tell my husband. Poor man, he thinks love is everything with us."

"Oh, stop that," Charlotte scolded, throwing up her hands. "The original question was would Mr. Morton want an heiress?"

"I didn't even answer that," Georgie told her. She smiled a tight smile and fluttered her eyelashes. "I was telling *you* no. You can't have him, you would eat that sweet and good man alive, and no."

Izzy snorted and covered her mouth and nose with one hand at Charlotte's suddenly aghast expression.

"Why can I not have the sweet and good man?" Charlotte retorted. "Am I not sweet and good?"

"Of course you are," Izzy assured her quickly, shifting her expression to sincere at once. "Of course, Charlotte. You are truly good and sweet. If Georgie doesn't find Mr. Morton suited for you, she must have her reasons. She knows him better than the rest of us, and you would not wish to be married to a man so perfect, would you? I would feel so terribly insecure being with such a man myself..."

Charlotte frowned in thought, then sighed with a nod. "I suppose you are right, Izzy. I would look like a sinner beyond reckoning if I were married to a perfect man." She looked at Elinor with resignation. "Find me a flawed one, dear."

"Noted," Elinor replied. "Or you could remain a spinster. An heiress can do so without losing her station and the respect of the world, you know."

"Fortunate girl," Edith murmured very softly. "Such freedom."

Charlotte looked at her, clearly confused. "You're a widow, dear. Is there not freedom in that?"

Edith smiled, but it did not reach her eyes. "If I find any, I will certainly inform you."

Izzy couldn't bear to see Edith look so unsettled, forcing a brighter countenance than what she felt, especially when she could not express it to the rest of them. She racked her mind for any other topic they could converse on, something to distract them all, and found herself singularly lacking there.

All she had were secrets and things she could not talk about, especially with them.

"Mr. Morton has asked me for a dance," she blurted out, finding it the only possibly safe topic at the moment.

Every Spinster in the room looked at her in surprise, and the combined force of their gaze was actually quite terrifying.

Apparently, she had picked the wrong thing to say, and had put herself quite squarely in a more dangerous path.

Lovely.

"Did he now?" Grace inquired in the most suggestive tone her voice had ever used.

Izzy frowned at her even as her face flushed. "Yes, but not because of anything remotely romantic or flirtatious or… whatever you might be thinking."

Grace shrugged daintily. "I am thinking that Mr. Morton might not care for an heiress, but a Spinster could do quite well."

"Stop!" Izzy insisted, trying to laugh but failing. "It's only because we were both helping Georgie in her moment of illness, and he felt duty-bound afterwards to ask me for a dance. As my gown was quite soiled at the time, he suggested that another opportunity might be more suitable. I agreed, and there it is. That is all."

"I'd have danced with him," Charlotte offered. "Soiled dress or not."

"Well, I did not," Izzy said quickly. "He was being a gentleman, and as we all know, I am too nice, so I agreed to his offer."

Elinor looked rather curious for a moment. "What does your being too nice have to do with his offer? Seems perfectly sound by your account, and I don't see a reason why you should have refused him. It was only a dance, not an offer of marriage."

Prue's face flamed on Izzy's behalf, and she cleared her throat. "In s-situations like that, o-one ought not t-to feel so d-duty bound. Circ-cumstances were ex... ex..." She frowned and looked at Izzy for help.

"Extenuating," Izzy finished with a nod. "Absolutely. My point exactly. There isn't anything wrong with it, of course not. But clearly it was a pity offering, anyone can see that. I would wager that he has a rule about dancing with wallflowers or spinsters and I happened to fit into the category."

Georgie winced audibly and sipped her tea, then made a disgusted face from it. "Lord, I forgot about Aunt Faith's tea." She set it aside and shuddered, then looked at Izzy. "I don't know that Morton would pity you your situation, but I do know that several men do dance with wallflowers and spinsters on purpose. I believe they feel safer doing so, as they are less likely to be suspected of a courtship there. Can we blame them for that?"

"I suppose not," Grace sighed, shifting a lock of her hair behind her ear. "But I do so hate to be pitied."

"It is lovely to dance, though, is it not?" Izzy asked, brightening a little. "I suppose if gentlemen did not fix it in their minds to dance with spinsters and wallflowers, I should never get any dances at all!"

Her friends laughed at that, even Charlotte.

"Not so," Georgie told her, still laughing. "You are an accomplished dancer, and always danced more than I when I was unmarried."

"Because Izzy is nicer than you are or were," Charlotte pointed out with a wry smile. "No one ever feared insult or banter from Isabella Lambert."

Georgie inclined her head at that. "Very true, very true. I am a peculiar person."

"Particular, perhaps," Izzy corrected, relaxing somewhat in her position now that the tide of conversation had shifted. "Not peculiar. You are simply very firm in your likes and dislikes and never suffer fools."

"What, and you *do* suffer fools?" Elinor chortled. The girl's smile turned mischievous. "I think you could also be very firm in your likes and dislikes, Izzy, just less vocal about it. So perhaps we should pair *you* with Mr. Morton."

"Oh, stop it now," Izzy laughed as the others giggled. "Let us not tie poor Mr. Morton to anyone until we know him better. He is reserved and will not like it."

Edith raised a brow in amusement. "Who's going to tell him that we are pairing him? Provided we ever do. He cannot dislike what he does not know."

Izzy shook her head in warning at her friend, smiling still. "No, no, I shall not allow it. Mr. Morton did Georgie a great service, and me. He will not become a gentleman for our amusement at the center of our schemes, even in private. No one deserves that, least of all him."

"A very noble defense, cousin," Georgie mused from her seat, her eyes too keen on Izzy at the moment. "Mr. Morton has clearly found a friend in you. I wonder if he knows it."

Before Izzy could offer a proper rebuttal to such words, Georgie turned to the others and began a lively conversation on what they might name their unborn child and how to go about her confinement, though it was certainly some months away and the Spinsters would have no proper idea of such things.

Izzy could not join in for a moment, could not even consider such a thing.

Mr. Morton had found a friend in her? How could that be, when they had only spent a few moments in each other's company? Surely, she was only being nice and considerate, as she had done so many times before.

She could certainly be his friend, if the opportunity arose, she supposed, and without anything suspicious at all in it. It was a thought. He was reserved, but witty, and she was generally approving of people, though not naïve about them.

He *was* very handsome…

Izzy shook her head quickly, dismissing the thought. Handsome men must have friends same as the plain ones, it made no difference at all.

But it could make things more pleasant.

Smiling at her secret joke, she rejoined the conversation, innocently suggesting that Isabella would be a fine name for a young Sterling girl.

Chapter Four

————— ⌘ —————

A party is a most excellent place to make new acquaintances and forge alliances. For is not Society a battlefield, and its events skirmishes thereupon? Let the battle commence, and may the best soldiers take the victory!

-The Spinster Chronicles, 29 May 1815

It was not customary for a party to be held following an informal announcement of a pregnancy, but it was customary for Tony and Georgie to not do things that were customary.

And Sebastian could not help smiling at the perfectly uncustomary yet customary feeling of it all, despite the confusion it settled upon one's mind.

"Oh, now what do you have to smile about?" Sterling asked as he approached Sebastian. "Surely you don't take so much joy in the prospect of my progeny."

Sebastian snorted softly and shook his head. "Not really, no, although I do offer my congratulations."

Sterling's mouth spread in a wide grin, and his obvious delight was contagious. "Thank you. I'd name you godfather for the service you rendered Georgie, but I do believe it's customary for a family member to be named for the first child."

"I wish everyone would stop treating me as though I have done something heroic," Sebastian laughed, keeping his voice down. He glanced beyond to the few other guests, then back at Sterling. "All I did was twirl your wife enough that she became ill and saw her out of doors before anyone else could notice."

Sterling shrugged easily, which was a strange sight in one so tall. "Is not the saving of a man's wife cause for heroism?"

Sebastian didn't bother hiding a dubious look. "From being ill?"

"Saving from embarrassment is still saving." Sterling smiled at the look. "If it makes you feel better, I will stop calling you a hero."

"Thank you," Sebastian sighed, truly feeling relieved. He'd never been one for attention or honorifics, and while only a handful of people knew about it, he had already grown tired of the gratitude and looks.

"So, if you were not smiling over the news," Sterling inquired in a suspiciously mild tone, "then what were you smiling about? Have you formed an attachment and not told me?"

Sebastian chortled in surprise and gave his friend a frank look. "You do realize that you are speaking with me and not Henshaw, yes?"

Sterling only smiled in response and waited.

Sebastian debated waiting as well, just to see how his friend would take it, but as the answer was not nearly as entertaining as Sterling was expecting, there wasn't much of a point to it. He turned to lean against the wall. "Kitty's coming."

His friend's brows rose, and his smile turned more natural. "To London?"

Sebastian nodded slowly, pleased with the information himself. "After Christmas, we decided it was time for her to have her coming out. She's very shy, as I've said, so we thought having her come early might be better. Get her accustomed to London and Society before she is expected to perform in it."

"Wise notion," Sterling praised softly, matching Sebastian's pose against a nearby bookshelf. "Particularly if she has no experience in it."

"That was my thought, yes." Sebastian hesitated again, then sighed once. "I'll admit, Sterling, I am out of my depth with what to do for my sister in this."

Sterling frowned and turned to look at him more fully. "How so?"

Sebastian gave him a wry glare. "You don't see how well I manage to navigate society and its traps?"

His friend coughed a surprised laugh and began to nod. "Ah…"

"Exactly." Sebastian glanced out of the window again, not seeing anything. "I am reserved and aloof, and can find my way, but I am hardly a fixture or an expert in this. Nor do I need or aspire to be. Yet my reserve and disinclination will not do Kitty any favors in her debut. Lord knows, she'd never do it on her own."

He shook his head, thinking back to the earlier days with his sister, and the struggle he'd had in drawing her out at any given time. She was never particularly shy with him, but the moment someone else entered a room, she would barely say a word.

"Morton," Sterling broke in with some hesitation, "when you describe her as shy, how dire is it? You know Prue, obviously. Is Kitty's shyness to that extreme?"

"No, no," Sebastian answered quickly, shaking his head again. "Nothing so drastic." Then he paused, considering the idea more carefully. "But in some ways, I suppose it is. She does not stammer or blush, she doesn't even grow flustered. She does have the same startled, terrified look that Prue is so familiar with. But Kitty will not say a word, will keep her eyes lowered, and will try to make herself as small as possible. A single word from her in a public setting to anyone but myself is a feat."

The description made Sterling wince, and Sebastian smiled tightly at the response. Such a reaction in only hearing about it. Sebastian lived with it. He was right; Society would not treat Kitty with care and gentleness. They would devour her like the innocent fawn she was, and there would be no saving her after that.

He would not mind having charge of Kitty for the rest of his life, and he would take care to marry a woman who would also not mind having her as part of their household, but he did not believe for one moment that Kitty would want that. She would be comfortable, it was true, but there was nothing fulfilling in being a spinster living on the generosity of her family. She deserved a life of her own, the independence of a married woman running a house, and to have a family.

"I am not the person to help her here, Sterling," he admitted aloud with real honesty. "And I don't know who is."

"Well," Sterling began as he came to stand beside him, facing the other guests, "first of all, I don't think there is a man alive that could be the one to help her. Unless you want me to pull Prue's husband Cam, who really does have a remarkable way with shy creatures."

"No," Sebastian grunted.

Sterling smirked at that. "He's a married man. Happily, I might add."

"No."

"I thought not." Sterling cleared his throat and took a drink from the glass he held. "I'd suggest Prue, but I think putting two shy girls together would be complicated. I think Miss Morton will need someone who is gentle, patient, and understanding. Someone who knows Society well, who is content on the outskirts and comfortable."

Sebastian stared at the confident visage of his friend in confusion. Then he smiled slowly. "You have someone in mind."

"I do," came the response with a nod. He gestured to the far side of the room. "I believe you need my dear cousin, Izzy."

Sebastian followed the indication with his eyes and stared, rather shamelessly, at Miss Lambert, sitting beside a woman Sebastian could not identify. She smiled at whatever it was she was hearing, and while it was not the most beautiful smile he had ever seen, there was something different about it. Something warm. It set him at ease from this distance; he could not imagine the impact it would have on the person in her direct presence.

Her hair was much more neatly fixed than when he had seen her last, the copper curls still a touch unruly, but in a charming, relaxed sort of way. She kept her attention fixed on her companion, seemingly completely invested in the conversation at hand. Focus and kindness were intriguing qualities to have in the same moment, but the evidence was before him in the person of Isabella Lambert.

"You think so?" he murmured, though he really did not need further explanation or comment from Sterling. His suggestion had already taken root, and Sebastian's mind whirled with the possibilities.

"Of course. Can you think of anyone better?"

No, he could not, but neither could he admit such a thing. His interaction with Miss Lambert was mostly in passing, though he had heard a great deal about her goodness and kindness from several others.

He watched as her mother suddenly turned and gestured for her, saw Miss Lambert excuse herself from her conversation to go to her, and then watched as her countenance tightened. Then she smiled, nodded, and took her mother's cup. She moved to the punchbowl and refilled it, then brought it back to her, only to have her mother clearly suggest she offer to do so for the others.

And, impossibly enough, she did so.

Sterling huffed an irritated sigh. "I wish she wouldn't do that."

Sebastian nodded once, his brow furrowing. It wasn't as though a wrong had been done, not at all, but there had been no need for Miss Lambert to have been pulled from her conversation to be turned into a servant for a party she was not the hostess of. The punch had been set out in such a way that it was intended for the guests to help themselves, diminishing the need for servants to attend them. Informal gatherings such as these often had such a setup, and unless Mrs. Lambert had developed an injury in the last twenty minutes, there was no reason for her to have been incapable of fetching her own drink.

Or to order her daughter to see to the drinks of the guests.

"Is it always like that?" Sebastian asked of his friend.

"Hmm?" Sterling asked, clearly having lost track of the thing. "Oh, Izzy?"

Sebastian dipped his chin in a nod. "Does her mother always do that?"

"Everybody does that," Sterling corrected.

"Does what, exactly?" Sebastian pressed without shame, turning to face him. "What do they do?"

Sterling's eyebrows rose, and his eyes widened. "Take advantage. Haven't you noticed?"

"I don't tend to make a study of a particular young lady of Society for my own amusement," he replied rather bluntly. "I cannot say that I have noticed."

His friend hummed almost in amusement. "Well, I invite you to take notice now, though I doubt it will be entertaining. Izzy is the most accommodating girl I have ever met in my entire life. She's entirely agreeable, obedient, and good. The trouble is that it is very, very easy to approach the girl who always says yes with anything, even if it is a ridiculous request. You can say anything to her without reproach. She will always accommodate."

"And her mother uses that for her own interests?" It was a horrible thing to ask, but the evidence was before him, and it baffled him.

Sterling's mouth curved ever so slightly. "Don't turn Faith Lambert into a villain based on one exposure. She's not to be confused with Mrs. Westfall. She is a very good woman and loves her family. I am telling you that everybody does this with Izzy. Even me, if I am not careful. She never refuses, and she never resents."

He couldn't know that. Nobody could know that Isabella Lambert did not resent the abuse of her niceness and indulgent nature. A lifetime of habits was a difficult thing to overcome, or even break once. He would know, though the particulars were not the same in the least.

And now he was to ask her to indulge his whim of mentoring his shy sister? He could not, in good conscience, take advantage as everyone else did simply because he was sure she would do it.

"She would say yes," Sterling reminded him, correctly guessing his expression.

"That's not what worries me," Sebastian murmured, returning to watch Miss Lambert as she finished her rounds of the room before returning to her original companion. "I cannot ask a woman to help me simply because the answer will be the one I wish. And I absolutely cannot ask a woman I do not know well to do something this important."

He felt his shoulder shoved forward hard and stumbled a bit. "Then you'd better go get to know her better, or you'll be stuck with Georgie as a mentor for Kitty, and I highly doubt that is what you had in mind."

A shudder rippled down Sebastian's spine, and spurred him to action.

Sterling was right, and there was no way he was going to leave Kitty's fate in the hands of Georgie Sterling. He liked her, and he liked her a great deal, but her direct manner was not going to suit his sister's timidity.

Isabella Lambert was the only one he could picture in this task, although he wasn't sure why, and he couldn't exactly complain about that.

He approached the sofa she was sitting on just as her companion gracefully rose and departed.

Perfect.

"Miss Lambert," he began, fixing a polite smile on his face. "May I take the now-vacated seat beside you?"

Her lips parted in a warm smile, and she nodded, gesturing to it. "Please, Mr. Morton."

"Thank you." He sat and scrambled for something to say that didn't start in a question and end in a request. "You look well."

Well, that wasn't exactly brilliant, but it was polite.

Miss Lambert's cheeks seemed brighter as the edges of her smile touched them. "Should I not?"

He managed a small laugh at her quip. "No, of course you should. Only, the last time I saw you was under some rather... um... interesting circumstances."

She giggled and glanced over at Georgie quickly, then back to him, leaning forward slightly. "Indeed, and I seem none the worse for it, thank heavens." She sat back, grinning now. "Truly, it was a very slight inconvenience to me. Nothing at all troubling."

"And your gown?" he inquired, not at all interested in the garment, but enjoying the ease with which she could converse with him.

She winced while somehow still managing to smile. "It could not be salvaged, I'm afraid."

He tsked slightly, shaking his head. "More's the pity. Such a fine gown."

Miss Lambert chuckled warmly, folding her hands in her lap. "I hate to contradict a gentleman, Mr. Morton, but it was not at all a fine gown. It is no loss to me to have it gone, I can assure you."

Sebastian felt a bemused smile cross his lips. "Are you always so cavalier with your gowns, Miss Lambert?"

She quirked a brow. "Not at all, Mr. Morton. I'm never cavalier about anything, least of all my gowns. It was old and unflattering on its good days." She leaned forward again, and he couldn't help but to match the pose. "And I really do wish you would call me Izzy, if you can bear to."

"And I do believe you know my thoughts on the matter, Miss Lambert." He shrugged in apology. "I cannot."

"Oh, in public, I understand completely," she assured him, still seeming playful. "But here?" She looked around quickly, then whispered, "I don't think anyone will mind. It's Georgie's house, after all."

That was true, and he had to chuckle at it, even reluctantly. "That's true, I suppose. And I can't refuse Georgie anything, God help me."

Izzy laughed at that, tossing her head back, her throat dancing with the laughter.

Sebastian watched, transfixed beyond anything he could express. There were simply no words.

"No one can refuse Georgie," Izzy assured him when she had recovered herself, laughter still on her lips and cheeks. "Well, not the people who know her and like her. She just has a way." She looked over at her cousin, smiling softly.

Sebastian dragged his gaze away from her to glance at Georgie as well. She was surrounded by people at the moment, laughing and smiling, truly seeming delighted to have so many about her.

"Has she always been that way, Izzy?" he asked, turning back to her. "She's your cousin, and you grew up with her…"

Izzy smirked a little. "Georgie is the one person I seem capable of saying no to."

That stunned him, and he didn't bother hiding it. "Really?"

She nodded proudly, then wrinkled up her nose. "It doesn't happen often, but…" She trailed off with a wry chuckle. "I can do it. When I want to."

"Why do I have the feeling that you don't want to very often?" he mused, finding himself relaxing more in her presence by the moment.

"I haven't the faintest idea," Izzy replied, playfully formal. Then she sipped her drink and looked at Georgie again. "Georgie tends to have the best ideas, so it was easy to follow and to agree. More often than not, I wanted to do whatever she suggested, and if I wasn't sure, I would say yes just to see where she would lead me."

Her tone had taken on a distant, reminiscing tone, and it made him smile, made him want to ask questions.

Made him want to know more.

"Did Georgie ever lead you astray?" he heard himself ask.

Izzy glanced back at him out of the corner of her eye. "Not once." Then her smile spread a touch wider. "Or should I say, not yet?"

"So, you anticipate trouble in the future?" he teased.

"It's Georgie," she retorted with a frank look, "One must always be prepared. But that is the nature of siblings, I suppose. Although Georgie and I are cousins, we were raised more as sisters. I am closer with her than any of my siblings, and my family tends to be fairly close."

Sebastian's mouth curved on one side. "Seems to be a wonderful relationship that the two of you share."

Izzy nodded, shrugging her trim shoulders in obvious delight. "It is. And it helped that we were both spinsters, without a capital S, so our mothers despaired of us in unison. It was much easier to stand together than individually. Strength in numbers, even if the number is two."

"Capital S?" Sebastian repeated. "From the Chronicles?"

"Yes." She straightened up in her place, her eyes suddenly alight. "A spinster with a lowercase S is any unmarried woman. A Spinster, with the capital S, is part of our very select group of women who write for the Chronicles. Used to be we were all unmarried, but now we have two that are. I'm told it will add a delightful perspective to the thing." She widened her eyes dramatically, and it was clear she wasn't convinced of that.

Sebastian snickered and then recovered himself as a new guest entered, rising to bow with the other gentlemen.

"Oh, please," Miranda Sterling trilled in delight. "It's only me. As you were." She strode across the room grandly, her rich green skirts trailing behind her as though she were a queen.

Tony Sterling's stepmother was an intriguing woman, and a fine one, but there was no doubt in anyone's mind that she was also the very definition of eccentric.

"Does she always do that?" Sebastian asked Izzy as he sat back down.

"Always," Izzy told him, nodding in greeting when Miranda waved her fingers at her. "She scares half of me half the time and amuses all of me all the time."

He smiled at the description. "Seems apt."

"Izzy, dear," Mrs. Lambert said, turning to them, "will you fetch Mrs. Sterling a drink?"

Izzy's hands suddenly fluttered a little in her lap and she nodded, rising. "Of course, Mama."

Sebastian frowned without thinking.

"No, don't be silly," Miranda scolded at once, waving Izzy back into her seat with a stern look. "I am perfectly capable of fetching my own beverage in my stepson's home. Or my *darling* stepson can get one *for* me." She pointedly looked at Sterling as he came over to her.

The room chuckled together as Sterling grinned without shame. "Of course, Miranda. Anything for my favorite stepmother."

She winked at him and went back to her conversation, but not before meeting Izzy's eyes again in some unspoken message.

Izzy clasped her hands tightly together in her lap and turned more towards Sebastian.

Or perhaps only further away from Miranda and her mother.

"Miranda hates when I am needlessly biddable," Izzy whispered, her cheeks flushing slightly. "She makes a point to prevent it."

Sebastian felt a burst of pride in his chest at the thought of Miranda taking an interest in Izzy in such a way and made a mental note to be equally as conscious of both Miranda and Izzy in return.

"I approve of it," he whispered back to Izzy, smiling.

Izzy swallowed with some difficulty, then managed to smile again. "It wouldn't have been so very great a trouble to fetch a drink for Miranda. I don't mind."

"That isn't the point," he insisted gently. "Your mother is not hostess, and this is not your home. You don't have to play servant here."

His words had little, if any, impact on her. "But it is Georgie's house, and…"

"And Miranda was quite right," Sebastian interrupted. "Tony can get a drink for her, and he should do so, if anyone does. Not you. It doesn't have to be you."

Izzy met his eyes, and the sweet blue and green combination struck him again, more pronounced with the blue dress she wore. She finally smiled in earnest and laughed at herself. "You must think me a very silly creature, Mr. Morton."

"I think nothing of the sort, Miss Lambert," he told her, tamping down the desire to take her hand and squeeze it in a gesture of comfort or friendship.

Friendship.

Yes, he'd quite like to pursue a friendship with Miss Isabella Lambert, if only to save her from herself.

Among other things.

"Well, I won't embarrass you by asking what you do think of me," Izzy told him with another light laugh. "Lord knows what you would say, especially if you are being a gentleman, as you so proudly informed me you were the other night."

Sebastian reared back in surprise but smiled all the same. "You object to my being a gentleman?"

She shook her head hastily. "No, not at all. I only object to their flattery."

"Compliments are flattery?"

"Compliments, no. But when a compliment is false or exaggerated? Flattery." She wrinkled up her nose in distaste. "A lady knows the difference, Mr. Morton. Believe me, we are well aware whether something is true or not."

Sebastian chewed the inside of his lip briefly, amused, fascinated, and perplexed by the woman before him. "And do you inform the gentleman of the error of his ways?"

A faint look of panic came over her. "Oh goodness, no. I wouldn't want them to feel bad for not knowing how to compliment a woman sincerely. I would smile and nod and be as gracious as possible."

For some reason, that only amused him more, and he had to smile at her. "And then?" he prodded, sensing there was more.

The panicked look vanished, and she became playful again. "And then I tell my friend Charlotte and hear what she has to say on the subject. She has such a way with words and no discretion whatsoever. I'd stay on her good side, if I were you."

He nodded sagely. "Any recommendations on how to do that?"

Izzy surprised him by reaching out and putting a hand on his arm. "Not to worry. I'll protect you from her. She adores me, Lord knows why."

Sebastian glanced down at the hand on his arm, the warmth and weight from it seeming perfect and spreading throughout his frame.

And he had his answer.

"I wonder, Izzy, if I might ask a very great favor of you."

Chapter Five

———— ⦿∽⦿∽⦿ ————

If you find yourself afraid of the gnashing teeth of the Society monsters, your best safety measure is to find a mentor to guide you through the dangers of it all. Also, this writer suggests sampling the punch for additional stamina.

-*The Spinster Chronicles, 14 March 1818*

"Ohhh, I should never have agreed to this!"

"You absolutely should have agreed to it. You are perfect for this."

"My thoughts exactly, and it's not as though you've been asked to be Anne Boleyn at a masquerade."

"Charlotte, don't be ridiculous."

"That costume would be ridiculous. How in the world are you supposed to dance with a severed head?"

"That is the least of my concerns." Izzy exhaled slowly, her breath faltering as she did so. She wasn't normally a nervous sort of person, but the idea of mentoring a young woman for her debut was intimidating. Why, she couldn't have said, but it terrified her.

"Oh, Izzy, how can you be worried about this?" Grace asked, linking her arm with Izzy's. "You have all the sweetness of Prue without her timidity. It would be wonderful for you to help Miss Morton find her way."

Izzy grunted softly and rubbed at her arms. "Yes, because I do that so well. Why shouldn't I help someone else be just as lost as I am?"

Charlotte sidled up to her other side and gave her a stern look. "There is only room for one cynic in the Spinsters, Izzy, and I wear that crown."

"I know," Izzy mumbled, rubbing her arm again. "It just seemed appropriate."

"It doesn't suit you, dear," Grace insisted, patting her hand. "Just be yourself. That's why Mr. Morton asked you to do this, isn't it?"

Izzy inhaled deeply, exhaled, and felt the tension leave her shoulders a little. "Yes. Yes, it is." She bit her lip, then looked at her friends. "What if she doesn't like me?"

Now Charlotte slapped her hand sharply. "Stop that. Every person on this planet likes you. Kitty Morton will fall at your feet the moment she gets to know you. Or else I'll toss her in the same circle as the Sterling girl and let the stronger of the two win."

Izzy frowned at her for that. "Come now, Charlotte. Alice Sterling isn't even here yet. There is no cause to treat her as though she is Hugh in the female form."

"I don't care who she is like," Charlotte retorted as she moved away from them and sat gracefully on the divan. "I am already inclined to prefer Kitty Morton to her. And I am not Elinor, I do not have a blood feud against Hugh Sterling, of all people."

Grace gave Charlotte a wary look. "Dramatic, Charlotte. Perhaps you should go home and leave the sweet girl to us. Or visit Edith and see how her house is coming along."

Charlotte returned the look without concern. "I am perfectly capable of behaving in the public eye. I am simply less strict with my behavior in the presence of my friends."

"Pretend we're in public now," Grace pleaded, squeezing Izzy's hand. "You're making Izzy feel worse."

Charlotte met Izzy's eyes, her own wide with distress. "Am I making it worse, Izzy?"

Izzy smiled a very small, shy smile. "Perhaps a little…"

She immediately sprang up and wrapped her arms around Izzy in a tight hug. "Oh, sweet dear, I'm so sorry. I only meant to set you at ease by being so perfectly myself."

"Because that is such a comfort," Grace murmured, laughing

softly.

Izzy hugged Charlotte back and then looked out of the window, gasping, "Oh, goodness, they're here. They're here!"

She broke free from her friends and put a hand on her suddenly fluttering stomach. Her blood seemed to be rushing through her entire body much too quickly, and she could feel her pulse thudding in her ears.

Is this what Prue felt like when she had one of her fits?

How did she ever survive them?

"Izzy?"

She whirled around, wide-eyed. "What?" she snapped.

Grace and Charlotte had matching smiles of bemusement, and any time those two matched in expression, one ought to be concerned.

"What?" Izzy asked again, warily this time.

The girls looked at each other quickly, then back to Izzy. "Does this rare case of nerves have anything to do with the fact that Mr. Morton will be involved?"

"What?" Izzy barked. "No! No, of course not! Mr. Morton is a gentleman, and very kind. I never feel nervous or anxious around him, not even once, and…"

"How many times have you been in his presence?" Charlotte interrupted, though her words were clearly intended to be under her breath.

Izzy silenced her with a look. "It has nothing *at all* to do with Mr. Morton. I just… I'm not much of an example for Miss Morton. I'm a spinster!"

Charlotte's eyes widened, and she gaped. "I do really wish someone had told us that before we became friends with you, Isabella. I would never want to spend my time and energies with a *spinster*." Then her expression changed swiftly to rather sardonic and superior.

There was no course but to smile at that.

Izzy was being ridiculous, and she knew it. And what she had said was true, it had nothing at all to do with Mr. Morton. He was actually the part about this whole affair she was the most comfortable with. She knew that she could converse with him, and that he would not judge her harshly.

"You do splendidly with Prue, Izzy," Grace reminded her with an easy smile. "Kitty Morton, by her brother's own account, is not so bad as that."

"Yes," Izzy murmured, rubbing her hands together, "but Prue already likes me."

"I don't have that problem with people," Charlotte mused aloud, making the others laugh in surprise.

Izzy was still laughing when Collins appeared in the doorway. "Mr. Morton and Miss Morton, Miss Lambert." He bowed and gave her a quizzical look before vanishing.

And then the Mortons were before them.

Mr. Morton smiled, but it was an uncomfortable, formal sort of smile. His dark hair was impeccable and formal, rather like his person at the moment.

Miss Morton could not manage a smile, but her lips quivered tremulously. She was a remarkably pretty girl, with hair darker than her brother's, and eyes bluer than his as well. She was pale, but in a healthy way, and she was small in stature without being considered petite.

The poor miss was utterly terrified.

At that moment, all of Izzy's fears vanished, and she felt a wave of tenderness for the young girl.

"Miss Lambert, Miss Morledge, Miss Wright," Mr. Morton intoned with the same formality his manner possessed, "my sister, Miss Catherine Morton."

They all curtsied politely, then Izzy stepped forward, smiled, and held out her hands to Miss Morton. "Miss Morton, I am so pleased to meet you. Have you had a long journey?"

Miss Morton shook her head quickly and exhaled slowly through her nose. "I arrived yesterday," she whispered in an almost whimper. "I am quite well, thank you."

Izzy tilted her head a little and squeezed Miss Morton's hands. "Miss Morton, may I call you Kitty? Your brother has told me that is your preferred name, and as we are to be friends, I should like to set you at ease."

Miss Morton nodded and tried for a smile, though it failed to fully form. "Yes."

"Then I insist on being called Izzy to you, or Isabella if you are cross with me," Izzy told her, gently keeping her smile in place. "And I don't want you to feel as though you have to say anything if you do not wish to." She leaned forward and whispered, "And you really don't have to say anything to Charlotte at all. She can be a bit domineering."

"I can hear you, Isabella," Charlotte chided, though the tone was a good deal kinder than the one Charlotte usually employed.

"Then perhaps take the hint, Charlotte," Grace suggested in a would-be innocent tone.

Izzy and Charlotte laughed, and Mr. Morton smiled, which Izzy counted as a success.

Kitty's blue eyes only grew wider.

Clearly, this was going to be more difficult than she'd anticipated.

"Kitty," Izzy said, tugging her into the room as gently as she could, "come and sit with us in here. And if you like, I can have the others go so you are more comfortable."

The girl came without any resistance and sank slowly onto the sofa, her eyes darting over to the others only briefly. "No, they can stay. It's fine."

Charlotte smiled very sweetly and chuckled a little. "Almost convincing, pet. Why don't Grace and I go see about a tea tray and let you get more comfortable with Izzy, and then we can come back?"

A very faint flash of relief crossed Kitty's face, and Izzy could have hugged Charlotte for the suggestion. Grace smiled and left with Charlotte, both curtseying briefly to Mr. Morton, who stood in the doorway.

"And what about your brother, Kitty?" Izzy asked, covering one of the girl's hands with her own. "Would you like him to stay with us or to go?"

Kitty's eyes moved to Mr. Morton with such swiftness the answer was clear.

Mr. Morton smiled at his sister fondly. "I'll sit in the corner and read, Mouse. Miss Lambert, if you could direct me to the library…"

Izzy gestured towards a pile of books on the desk. "Please, help yourself to one of those, and next time I will show you to the library.

I think Kitty would be more comfortable if you remain visible this first time."

Mr. Morton looked at his sister for a long moment, then nodded. "I think perhaps you are right. I will avail myself of the most convenient books for the time being. And if my sister turns chatterbox, I'll find the library on my own."

Kitty smiled in earnest at that, and Izzy blinked in the face of it.

The shy girl was a stunning beauty when she smiled, and any man with any sort of vision would be drawn to her side in a heartbeat, which she would find horribly overwhelming and utterly terrifying.

Izzy pushed the thoughts away and focused on the young girl beside her. "Now, Kitty, I don't know anything about you except that you are timid and that you are eighteen. Tell me about yourself."

Kitty's smile vanished, and she stared at Izzy without speaking.

Seconds passed, and then Izzy tried to give her an understanding look. "Kitty, I know it can be difficult to open up to anyone you don't know, and this must feel a bit like a forced friendship. Would it be easier for me to talk about myself first? You could ask me anything you like or say anything that comes to mind that way."

"Yes, please," Kitty answered in a rush of relief. She smiled genuinely for the first time at Izzy. "I never know what to say, and what if I say something wrong?"

Izzy blinked at the number of words expressed and hummed a very soft laugh. "I will tell you one thing right now; you will *never* say the wrong thing with me. Trust me, I'm friends with Charlotte." She rolled her eyes dramatically and grinned when Kitty giggled. "And while we won't talk about Society today, I will tell you that there is not very much you can say when talking about yourself that will ostracize you from its circle."

Kitty nodded obediently, seeming more like a girl in the schoolroom than a young woman paying a call. That would change with time, and she would not address it now. After all, it *was* a sort of schoolroom that she was in now, and it would be until she managed it.

Which made Izzy a teacher of sorts.

How utterly bizarre.

Izzy watched for a second as Mr. Morton situated himself in his designated chair, apparently perfectly content to sit in the room without participating in any way. Then she smiled at Kitty. "I will ask that the things I share with you stay between us. Not that anything I share will be particularly personal or shocking, but there is always a possibility."

Kitty nodded once, smiling a little. "I promise."

"And that goes for you, too, Mr. Morton," Izzy called, looking over at him again.

He glanced up with a crooked smile, his eyes crinkling. "I'm not even listening, Miss Lambert."

"It's Izzy when in my home, Mr. Morton," she informed him staunchly, "and I don't believe that for a moment."

He chuckled in a low rumble. "I promise that if I hear anything, I will say nothing."

She wasn't sure she believed him, so she looked back to Kitty. "Is that good enough, do you think?"

Kitty's smile flickered brighter for a moment. "Sebastian always keeps his word. Always honorable."

"Is he, indeed?" Izzy asked, glancing over to Mr. Morton again.

He held up his hands in a helpless gesture, smiling at his sister, who smiled back.

The adoration between the two siblings was touching and entertaining, and Izzy was wild to hear their story and more about their childhood, but that would come with time.

"I wish my brothers were the same," Izzy sighed, turning her full attention to Kitty. "I have three brothers, you know, and while they are perfect gentlemen for the rest of the world, the distinction did not apply to their sisters. Or to each other, for that matter."

Kitty cocked her head curiously. "Did they mistreat you?"

Izzy's smile turned coy. "Not technically, no. My eldest brother is a barrister, and he knew from his very early days how to avoid detection for crimes against his siblings. And then how to defend against the ones he was caught for."

A surprised burst of giggles escaped from Kitty, and she clamped down on her lips until they turned white.

"William was the far more mischievous brother, though," Izzy went on, warming to the entertaining descriptions now. "None of

David's tact, but twice his daring. There is a scar on my left knee from one of his more dastardly antics. Not that he intended to harm me, and he was actually quite horrified when he did. And all of this took place at our house in Kent, mind you, not here in London."

"Were you very injured?" Kitty asked, her tone not nearly so shy now.

Izzy shook her head. "Not very, no. It wasn't so bad, it only left a mark. I felt worse for my younger sister Catherine. She fainted dead away at the sight of the blood. The doctor had to tend to her longer than he had to tend to me."

Kitty giggled again, and the sound was so musical it was a delight to hear it. "I don't have any stories of injuries or rambunctious actions. Sebastian has always been very collected and careful. I have no stories to tell like that."

There was a sad, whimsical note to her voice, but she smiled just as sincerely.

"Not all brothers are like David and William," Izzy assured her, squeezing her hand. "My youngest brother Peter is all of thirteen, and when he is home from school, he hides himself away and reads for hours on end. We had to drag him from the house for his riding lessons as a child."

"Oh my," Kitty gasped, eyes somehow wider. "And now?"

Izzy shrugged. "Well, now he loves to ride, so it was worth the effort. He is destined to be my favorite brother."

Kitty nodded thoughtfully, lowering her eyes. "Well, Sebastian is also more than ten years older than me, so it was not as though there was much opportunity to play even when he was home from school. I doubt he would even want to, being a boy his age with a sister my age."

"I am sitting right here, you know," Sebastian broke in, looking between the two of them. "And I'll have you know, I did play with you, Mouse."

Izzy glared over at him in exasperation. "Excuse you, Mr. Morton, but you were not listening, and so you can have no response. If this becomes a problem, your sister and I will excuse you from the room."

His eyes narrowed at her, and she mirrored his expression and

57

position, waiting.

Kitty made the softest scoffing sound known to man, and Izzy saw her clamp on her lips once again.

Sebastian caught it, too, and his expression softened.

It had never completely occurred to Izzy until that moment just how concerned he would have been for his sister under these circumstances, how much he wanted her to be comfortable, and to be the girl he knew her to be for others as well. This task was almost as much about him as it was for her. Rather than make everything more daunting, it actually made Izzy more excited to take it on, and more determined to adopt Kitty Morton as her friend and see her well-situated in society.

"Fine," Sebastian grunted as he returned to his book. "I will say nothing, hear nothing, and do nothing."

"Yes, thank you," Izzy chirped, turning back to Kitty with a grin. "Your sister and I are well on our way to becoming friends."

Kitty returned her smile softly, but there was real delight in it.

Sebastian had no response, and both girls looked over at him.

He dutifully stared at his book, though his eyes never moved across the page. Then he looked up and feigned surprise. "Oh dear, were you addressing me? I was not listening, as I promised."

Kitty rolled her eyes, which made Izzy laugh heartily, and Sebastian grinned, then went back to his book yet again.

"Now," Izzy said, turning serious again, "I do have to ask you one question, Kitty. Are you musical?"

Kitty's eyes widened and another timid smile appeared. "I suppose…"

Izzy laughed once. "That is not an adequate answer, dear. Let me rephrase it. Are you accomplished musically?"

Again came the timidity. "I suppose."

"Do you enjoy music?" Izzy tried for a third time, playing at exasperation.

Kitty giggled softly and tucked a dark ringlet behind her ear, her cheeks turning the faintest shade of pink. She lowered her eyes and plucked at the green sprigged muslin she wore. "I love music," Kitty murmured.

Izzy smiled and waited for Kitty to meet her eyes again. When she did, Izzy nodded in approval. "In what area?" she pressed. "Vocally? Pianoforte? The harp?"

"Pianoforte," Kitty admitted, still slightly pink. "I never perform, though. Not even for Sebastian. I couldn't, it's too terrifying."

"I quite agree," Grace replied as she entered again with Charlotte, who bore the tea tray herself. "I was forced to practice for my family starting at age twelve, and I can promise you, I am not sufficiently accomplished to this day to perform, so you can only imagine what I put them through."

Sebastian rose at once to go to Charlotte, but she shook her head at him. "No, you don't, Mr. Morton, you sit back down in that chair like a statue and let the girls have a chat. I can manage my own tea tray."

That seemed to ruffle him, and he blinked, but then looked at Izzy, who stifled laughter. He eventually smiled and sat back down, nodding at Charlotte, then smiled further when she handed him a cup of tea.

Charlotte truly was extraordinary.

Kitty had a moment of appearing flustered now that the others had returned to the room, but she still smiled at them, which was an improvement.

"Charlotte is not at all musical, you know," Izzy pointed out as Charlotte took a seat in a chair to Izzy's other side. "She is very accomplished in other respects, but she never performs musically."

Kitty looked over at Charlotte in surprise. "No one asks you, Miss Wright?"

Charlotte flashed a quick grin, then tucked it back into a more reserved smile. "No, indeed. They know better. My talents lie in other areas, Miss Morton. I envy your musical abilities, though. It would be delightful to have a skill you can appreciate for yourself and your own enjoyment rather than simply for the admiration of others."

"Enjoyment for myself is all I have with my playing," Kitty murmured shyly, smiling just a little.

"And that is all you need find in it," Izzy told her. "Personally, I have no talents that others can admire with ease. My playing is only moderate, my singing is less than admirable, and I cannot draw anything identifiable."

The other girls laughed, while Kitty looked torn between concern and amusement. "I am sure you are too modest," she managed.

"Oh, no, Miss Morton," Grace corrected with the utmost gentleness. "You will soon learn that Izzy is never too modest. She is perfectly modest enough. It is quite a task to match her in goodness."

Izzy blushed at once and looked at Kitty with wide eyes. "Kindly ignore the flattery of my friends, they are too kind."

"I am never too kind," Charlotte pointed out with a toss of her hair. "It's never in my interest."

"And kindly ignore Charlotte whenever possible," Izzy added, keeping her focus on Kitty.

Kitty giggled and bit her lip quickly, then released it as she sighed. "I am so afraid of attention," she confessed, her voice sounding a good deal stronger than she had earlier in their conversation. "I always have been."

Such a confession seemed almost monumental, given her shyness, and Izzy took it as a massive step in the direction she needed to take the girl.

She leaned forward and took both of Kitty's hands. "I think you will find, Kitty, that most of the girls in Society have those exact fears. I know I do."

"Really?" the girl asked with an innocent eagerness.

Izzy nodded twice, her heart swelling. "Really."

"I am well aware that I do," Grace added with a sheepish smile. "I hate being on display beyond anything."

They all instinctively looked at Charlotte for her response. Charlotte shrugged and smirked a touch. "I have no such concerns. I don't have much by way of talent to put on display, so I don't know what they're all looking at, but that is all they seem to do."

Izzy snorted softly and rolled her eyes, and even Kitty seemed amused and somehow delighted with Charlotte's ways.

They would have to watch for that. Heaven knew, Kitty Morton did not need to admire Charlotte Wright as any sort of example for her behavior.

"I don't want you to worry about Society and attention and performing just yet, Kitty," Izzy said with a brief squeeze of the girl's hands. "That will come. What I want is for you to feel comfortable in your own self, and with us. I know what it is to be shy and intimidated by the prospects of London and gentlemen and everything else that gets built up in our minds and in tales. I know we have just met, Kitty Morton, but I already like you very much indeed, and you will not be alone for one moment in all of this. I promise."

Kitty's lip quivered very slightly as she smiled in return. "Thank you."

She seemed so small and childlike in that moment there was no course but for Izzy to lean forward and hug her. "Believe me, it will be a pleasure, dear."

"Sebastian told me you'd be good for me, Izzy," Kitty half-whispered back, "and I think he could be right."

Izzy swallowed a lump and found her eyes wandering over to Sebastian in his chair only to find that his eyes were on her, and a proud, gentle smile graced his lips.

Their eyes locked, and in his she found gratitude, pleasure, and something that caused a tickling sensation in the pit of her stomach.

And she had to smile back at him.

She couldn't help it.

"Well," Charlotte broke in, breaking the moment, "that was a beautiful moment, girls, but Kitty really must be in need of some tea and a biscuit or two." She poured tea for her, shaking her head. "Tell me how you like it, dear, I always put in too much sugar for anybody else's taste."

"Anything will be fine," Kitty told her, almost laughing at her own response.

Charlotte gave her a bewildered look. "With tea? Oh, darling, no. You do not need an opinion on many things in this world, but the way you take your tea? You must be very, very firm there, shy creature or not."

Izzy snickered, delighted at Charlotte and Grace's treatment of Kitty, and pleased beyond measure to have these women in this room, and in her life.

And then there was Sebastian.

He watched his sister as she debated her answer, waiting.

"One sugar," Kitty finally responded in a very small voice,

smiling still. "And a little cream."

Sebastian's smile deepened at that, and he glanced at Izzy. Somehow his smile changed yet again, and she watched as a slow exhale moved his chest, his eyes still on hers. Then he returned to his reading, perfectly at ease now.

Izzy couldn't say she was perfectly at ease as she returned to the conversation with the others.

But she was close.

Chapter Six

A long walk can do wonders for a body, if not the soul. Provided, of course, that one does not come across unpleasantness upon the walk. Then it really could be a waste of time, energy, and one's hem.

-The Spinster Chronicles, 3 May 1816

"I had no idea that London was a place such as this."

Sebastian looked up from his desk to his sister, standing in the doorway of his study. She was wide-eyed, as she constantly seemed to be these days, and her hair was still loose about her shoulders. She looked so much younger than her eighteen years that it made him ache inside.

But he forced a brotherly smile and sat back in his chair. "What did you expect, Mouse? What did you think London would be like?"

Her brow furrowed slightly, and she leaned against the door. "I don't know. I always thought of London as an exciting, whirlwind of a place, with people of every station and style filling it. A place of romance, adventure, and culture..."

He chuckled wryly, raising a brow. "And it isn't?"

Kitty's eyes met his, and she smiled sheepishly. "No, of course it is. But... it is all to such a higher degree than I'd imagined. And I have yet to attend a ball, concert, or real event this Season." She shivered suddenly. "It's all rather terrifying,"

She ducked her chin and rubbed at her arms, again reminding him of the child she had once been.

He hated seeing her so vulnerable.

"I should have kept Mrs. Ramsey on," he said on an exhale, shaking his head as he stared at his sister. "She would have kept you comfortable and at ease, and you might not be so terrified of London as a whole."

Kitty's head shot up and her eyes widened further. "Oh, no! I did not mean… Sebastian, Mrs. Ramsey wanted to retire and stay with her daughter. She could not be my companion and chaperone forever, you know. And I was destined to be uncomfortable in London no matter who was with me." She smiled a little and gave a small laugh. "I cannot even venture to the ruins on the estate at Lindley alone without some trepidation."

"But you go there all the time," he reminded her. "I have fetched you from those ruins so many times…"

"Yes, but there is always a bit of fear when I ride out to them," she insisted, looking almost impish at the admission.

Sebastian shook his head, smiling fully now. "A bit of fear I can live with." He sighed softly and tilted his head at his sister. "I hope you aren't too scared of London now, Kitty. Or of the people here."

"Oh, I'm quite terrified," she informed him without batting an eye. "But I adore Izzy, Sebastian. I am so grateful you asked her to help me."

There was no helping the heat that burst within his chest then, and could he have smiled further, he would have done so. But he tempered it instead into a satisfied grunt and folded his arms loosely, if only for minimal protection.

"Indeed?" he inquired as mildly as humanly possible.

Kitty seemed not to notice the awkwardness in his tone and nodded repeatedly. "Yes! Oh, Sebastian, she is so kind. She put me at ease almost at once."

He wanted to laugh in delight, but it was completely against his nature, so he settled for a barely-restrained smile and a nod of response. "Good. Good, I hoped she would suit you. And what of her friends?"

"Charlotte is as terrifying as London itself," Kitty admitted bluntly, her lips curving on one side. "But I liked her, once I grew accustomed to her. She is very pretty, and I think she would help me in different ways than Izzy can."

"No doubt," Sebastian said, hoping his sister would not wish to explore that particular idea too far.

Kitty looked down at her slippers as she twisted them absently into the rug. "And Miss Morledge is the most beautiful woman I have ever seen. So refined and accomplished…"

Sebastian cleared his throat softly. "How do you know how accomplished she is?"

His sister glanced up at him with all her natural timidity and then some. "It was clear."

"I didn't see it." He shrugged without concern. "I will grant that Miss Morledge is very refined, but none of her accomplishments were on display over tea. She could be a dreadful dancer."

"Is she?" Kitty demanded, as much as Kitty ever demanded. "You have been here, you surely will have seen."

He twisted his lips and shook his head once. "No, dear, she is not dreadful. She is quite graceful, and polite, and almost as kind as Izzy, if I understand things right."

Kitty groaned and slumped against the door further still. "I will never manage to be half so accomplished or graceful. Or so beautiful."

Sebastian groaned and pushed himself up from his chair, trying for the gentlest of scolding looks. "Catherine Morton, do you believe for one moment that Grace Morledge would wish to be a standard to measure yourself by?"

She blinked slowly, then lowered her eyes once more. "No, she would not."

"Do you think someone like, say, Isabella Lambert would do so?" he pressed.

"No, Izzy most certainly would not."

He smiled, though his sister couldn't see it.

Izzy wouldn't.

Izzy wouldn't need to.

Izzy was…

His smile faded slightly as he pondered the unfinished statement. What was Izzy? Who was she?

Why was she a spinster, with or without a capital S?

It had never occurred to him to be curious about her in any extreme regard until now. He had known that she would be perfect for Kitty after only a few moments of speaking with her privately, but anyone with a certain degree of kindness and understanding would have done as well. Why, he could have hired another companion for his sister, and one that was not close to fifty years beyond her own age, as Mrs. Ramsey has been.

But it hadn't occurred to him to do any of those things.

He'd only wanted Izzy.

He'd wanted? What a presumptuous idea!

"Do you believe Izzy will be able to assist you enough before the Season, Mouse?" Sebastian asked, jerking his attention back to his sister, who was now watching him with a curious look. "Does her nature suit you well enough?"

Kitty's expression melted into a mixture of surprise and delight. "Of course! She is very gentle, and I feel as though she is an elder sister to me, though we really have only met the once. I cannot imagine anyone else being so perfectly suited for me."

He'd been rather afraid of that.

Why, he couldn't say.

"Very good," he managed, sitting back in his chair and going back to his work.

It was not often that Sebastian was glad to be away from Lindley, much preferring the solitude of the country to the bustle of London, but for the first time in recent recollection, London was preferable.

Lindley, it seemed, had found Kitty's departure the adequate time to create needs for repairs and strife with its few tenants. According to the letter from the estate manager, it was all too fortunate that Kitty and Sebastian were in London for the foreseeable future so as to avoid the difficulties at Lindley for the present.

Which also meant that Sebastian could not easily ride off to Lindley, or really even Bedford, if he tired of London and all it had to offer.

More's the pity.

Not that he had any great desire to leave at this time, but he did tend to feel more comfortable if there were options available to him.

No, indeed, he rather did want to be in London now, and it was not because of Sterling or Henshaw, or even Kitty.

Kitty…

He glanced up once more to see her yet standing there, not quite staring at him, but not exactly looking at anything else.

"Kitty?" he prodded, setting his pen aside.

Her eyes darted up to his, and she smiled a little. "Have you ever walked Hyde Park, Sebastian?"

He frowned a touch. "Walked it, no, though I have ridden through it on occasion. Why do you ask?"

"Izzy is coming today, and she suggested we walk Hyde Park."

Sebastian nearly jumped up from his seat and managed to slam his thigh into the underside of the desk as he did so, the sound ringing through the room. With a muffled groan of pain, he straightened completely.

"In the middle of winter?" he forced out through clenched teeth.

Kitty was close to laughing, he could tell, but she contained it. Barely. "It's really very mild, Sebastian. Bedford is much colder."

"Not that much," he grumbled, rubbing at his thigh. "And what of an escort?"

It was clear his sister was as naïve about London as she was about most other things as she shrugged and seemed completely nonplussed about it. "I'm not sure. What sort of chaperone does one need in London?"

Oh, Lord.

"Never mind," he told her quickly, trying for a smile. "Suffice it to say, two women do not go out without a chaperone. Ever."

Kitty's brow wrinkled in confusion, but she nodded anyway. "All right."

Steps down the corridor stopped them from further conversation, and Kitty lowered her eyes as the housekeeper, Mrs. Jersey, approached.

Still not comfortable with her, then.

Interesting.

"Mr. Morton, Miss Morton, there's a Miss Lambert here," Mrs. Jersey intoned in her very formal way, though she bore a curious smile. "I have shown her into the parlor. Should I offer her some tea?"

"She's here already?" Kitty squeaked, forgetting to be shy. She looked to Sebastian in panic. "Sebastian!"

He bit back a laugh and nodded. "Go and finish getting ready, Mouse. I will see to our guest."

Kitty darted off with the frantic scampering of a child, and he came around the desk towards Mrs. Jersey. "Please inquire if she would like some tea, and I will be along momentarily."

"Yes, Mr. Morton," she replied, still bearing that curious smile. She bobbed a curtsey and moved back towards the parlor.

Sebastian waited for a moment, his fingers rubbing together with a very faint anxiety. He couldn't have said why, for it was not as though she made him nervous or gave him any cause for worry or concern. On the contrary, he had never felt quite so comfortable in the presence of any woman, barring his sister and their late mother.

But here he was, slightly anxious.

He moved to the looking glass in the corridor and adjusted his cravat, then smoothed his hair, and then, for some completely unknown reason, he smiled with the full intention of examining it.

He caught himself and strode away from the looking glass at once.

"Pull yourself together, Morton," he muttered to himself, shaking his head.

The parlor was before him, and he could see Izzy within, smiling out of the window, posed rather like a portrait might have been.

But no portrait would ever have seemed so alive as this.

Shaking his head again, he moved into the room, smiling politely. "Miss Lambert."

Izzy rose at once and curtseyed as he entered. "Mr. Morton."

"Please," he murmured, gesturing to the seat once more as he moved to a chair opposite.

"I am sorry to intrude," Izzy began, smiling in her warm fashion. "I do know that I am early, but the day is so lovely, I couldn't wait."

Sebastian glanced out of the window to see the sun shining brightly, belying the chill in the air. He turned his attention back to Izzy, his expression quizzical. "And the cold would not sway you to a more comfortable activity today?"

Her smile spread and turned impish. "It is not so cold today, Mr.

Morton. I am properly attired, as you see."

He did see, and he found it quite charming. Nothing in the height of fashion, if his forays into London society were any proof, but very sensible. He found her deep red, hooded cloak and cream-colored muff to be charming, and the bonnet she wore seemed to be lined with flannel, which he thought was rather ingenious.

Izzy tugged one hand out of her muff to show gloves on her fingers, as if he had questioned her still. "And I have a scarf beneath the cloak."

"I stand corrected," he said with a tilt of his head in acknowledgement.

Her lips slowly shifted into a natural, content smile. "I hope you don't mind my taking your sister out on this winter day. I find London to be confining at times myself, and as she has spent so much time in Bedford, I did not want her to feel the same."

"I don't mind at all," he replied, surprised that she would even think it. "It's a very good idea, actually."

Her brilliant eyes crinkled at the corners at that. "I do occasionally get good ideas, you know."

He groaned at the jab. "I did not mean to imply that you did otherwise."

"And yet, you sounded surprised."

Her impish look might have been the most charming one he had seen in her yet, and it made him smile. There was nothing else to do, and no other response to give.

Except one.

"I don't know you well enough to be surprised about your ideas, Miss Lambert," he murmured. "Hopefully before the end of this, I will."

He watched as her smile faded in surprise, then tucked in against her cheekbones. And there it stayed, in a smaller version that was no less potent than its previous occupant.

And he wanted to see that smile more often.

All the time, in fact.

In everything.

"Then I think, perhaps, you should call me Izzy, Mr. Morton," Izzy told him, her voice tight with some sort of amusement. "All of my friends do."

He nodded slowly, smiling still. "Perhaps I should." But he said nothing further, and only smiled.

Izzy waited, then laughed, tilting her head back to do so, just as she had done before, and it made no difference that her eyes were squeezed shut or that her hair was covered or that she was completely bundled up.

It still struck him.

She laughed so freely, so easily, and without any restraint, though there was nothing boisterous about it. It wasn't musical, but it had the sound of a song. It wasn't delicate, but there was something gentle about it. It wasn't extraordinary, but the richness in it was captivating.

A laugh was captivating? He had no idea such a thing was possible, but here he was, moved by one woman's laughter.

"You are impossible," Izzy informed him, laughter still lingering in her cheeks.

"So my friends inform me," he replied.

"Then it seems I am your friend," she returned without hesitation, setting her hand back into her muff and lifting her brows in suggestion.

Sebastian let his smile spread and linger. "So it seems."

"Izzy!" Kitty gasped as she burst into the room entirely out of character. "I am so sorry."

Both Izzy and Sebastian sprang from their seats as though they had been caught in a sin of sorts. As if it had been choreographed, they awkwardly turned as one to face Kitty.

"Sorry for what, dear?" Izzy said sounding a bit frantic. "Sebastian and I were only being social waiting for you."

Sebastian jerked at the sound of his given name from her lips and looked at her quickly, but she was completely focused on his sister, no hint of embarrassment in her cheeks.

She'd said it without meaning to say it. She'd said it easily when in a panic.

She'd called him Sebastian.

She thought of him as Sebastian.

Izzy.

"Well, shall we go?" Kitty was saying, sliding her hands into gloves. "I don't want to be out and about when there are too many others. I'll become a complete wallflower in a setting entirely devoid of walls."

Izzy chuckled and stepped forward to take Kitty's hand. "You'll be fine, dear. We won't see many people at all, I promise." She turned to bid Sebastian farewell, but he couldn't let her.

He was moving before he meant to. "I'll come with the pair of you. You must have a proper escort, after all."

"Oh, I brought a footman," Izzy replied, eyes going as wide as Kitty's always were. "There's really no need…"

"Nonsense," he overrode as he strode past them. "He can come along, certainly, for two ladies surely require double the escort."

Kitty giggled at that, but he couldn't hear if Izzy did as well. It didn't matter if she did, he would come with them regardless.

He had to.

He called for his greatcoat, gloves, scarf, and hat, wishing he had time to change, but not willing to delay the ladies further. It would be all right; he was an army man, after all. He'd been through much worse than a crisp day in improper clothing with a new and fascinating friend by his side.

"Well," he called to them when he had his things, "shall we?"

It wasn't long before their little trio with footman in tow reached Hyde Park, which was nearly empty, as Izzy had promised, which delighted Kitty to no end.

"I do realize that I will have to socialize eventually and go to events where there will be strangers," she told them both, her breath dancing on the winter air in visible puffs.

"Ideally, yes," Izzy teased, nudging the younger girl with her slender shoulders.

"Eventually," Sebastian added with a hint of a chuckle.

Kitty ignored them both. "But I would rather not do so now." She looked at Izzy, suddenly uncertain. "Is that all right?"

Sebastian opened his mouth to reply, but Izzy beat him to it.

"Dear Kitty," she stated very firmly, "you do not need to ask permission for anything at all. If you don't feel comfortable with large social gatherings as yet, then we will not take you to one. That is the point of my being here. To make you comfortable and secure, so that when it is time for you to begin in the larger and more terrifying venues, you don't feel so alone."

Kitty beamed at Izzy, and Sebastian almost felt his knees buckle just witnessing his sister's pure and unfettered joy.

It was a look he hadn't seen her wear in many years.

He'd forgotten that she could look so.

A raw lump formed in his throat, and it took several moments to clear it as he looked away from the girls to the barren trees around them.

"Oh, look! The pond is frozen at the edges!" Kitty commented, darting over to the water like a child.

"Careful, Mouse," Sebastian called to her, though it was unnecessary to warn her.

It was a brotherly habit.

"Mouse?" Izzy repeated softly, peering up at Sebastian now. "Is that your name for her?"

He nodded fondly, watching Kitty as she wandered the edges of the pond, staring at the forming ice. "I gave it to her when she was perhaps four years old. I was around fifteen or so and home from school, and she was so quiet all the time. Granted, she fussed as any child her age does, but she was still very quiet about it. So, I told her one day, 'You're not a kitty, you're a mouse!' And impossibly, she didn't argue. She loved it." He shrugged and grinned down at Izzy. "I doubt she still loves it, but I keep at it anyway."

Izzy snickered and shook her head. "Very brotherly, Mr. Morton. I approve."

"Well, that's quite a relief, Miss Lambert," he sighed with a dramatic air. "After more than ten years, I have the approval to call my sister the name I have been calling her without approval."

"Ooh." Izzy hissed, laughing still. "Now *that* was very brotherly. Well done."

Sebastian winced and looked down at the ground. "I hope you don't take offense, Miss Lambert, that was very short."

"Not at all, Mr. Morton," she insisted quickly, her laughter evaporating. "Feel free to be as short as you like with me in jest. I will never take offense at it. I never take offense."

There was an odd sort of truth in her words, though he doubted that she was aware of it. It was too soon for him to ask her about something so profound and personal, but he made a note to do so at another time.

When he knew her better.

"May I ask you a personal question, Miss Lambert?" he asked, sweeping his hands behind his back as they walked.

"Only if you call me Izzy," she returned, trying for a smile again.

He returned her look, but pointedly kept his mouth shut, and tried to look apologetic.

Izzy rolled her eyes and scoffed. "Very well, Mr. Gentleman Morton, you may ask."

He nodded once, chuckling. "Why the Spinsters?"

She reared back in surprise, then looked away in thought. "Why spinsters… That's a question for the ages, Mr. Morton. Why are any of us spinsters? Believe me, we try to figure it out every day of our lives, and there is no simple answer. I would give anything to not be a spinster, personally, but…"

"My dear Miss Lambert, I hate to interrupt…" he broke in, eyes wide.

She paused, waiting, her brow furrowed.

He smiled in another apology. "I meant the other kind of Spinsters. Capital S."

"Oh!" She clamped down on her lips, giggled, then started walking once more, her step quicker. "My apologies. You really need to specify, you see."

"Yes, I do see."

"That's a completely different matter. Entirely."

"I thought so."

She looked up at him, clearly ready to laugh again. "It's really not that entertaining. Georgie was tired of girls despairing about being spinsters in their younger years, and some taking drastic steps to avoid it. So, we gave spinsters a voice. A commentary from our point of view, and hopefully in doing so we take away the stigma of the label 'spinster'. It's enough to live with it in ourselves; we don't need it from others as well. There's nothing worse than pity, and we're really not so poorly off, any of us. Just not married. Just spinsters."

Sebastian nodded in thought, smiling at the completely

forthright explanation, devoid of any emotion or bitterness, despite the topic.

She didn't take offense, she didn't feel bitter, and she didn't pity herself.

Yes, indeed, he could be friends with Izzy Lambert.

He would very much like to be.

"Now what is this I hear about you being nice, Miss Lambert?" he asked in a teasingly formal tone.

Her groan made him grin, and it remained there for the duration of their walk.

And for some time after.

Chapter Seven

————⟨∞⟩————

Opportunity is a strange thing. We seek it out, and yet when it comes, we let it pass us by, or we are too afraid to explore it. Perhaps it would be best if nothing ever happened to us at all. But then what would we do with ourselves? Boredom is so much worse.

-*The Spinster Chronicles, 9 September 1817*

"So, the pair of you walked Hyde Park and talked the entire time? Alone?"

Izzy looked at her cousin with an abashed smile. "It was not the pair of us at all, Georgie. Kitty was right there with us the entire time."

Georgie did not look at all convinced by the clarification. "Yes. By the pond."

"True…" Izzy wrinkled up her nose and slumped her shoulders with a heaving sigh. "All right, so she was not actively engaged in the conversation very much at all. For the most part, it was just Sebastian and I, and we simply… talked."

"Sebastian?" Georgie asked in a blatantly suggestive tone. "Really?"

Izzy flushed so quickly she thought her hair might catch fire from it. "Oh, stop, Georgie… Stop, it wasn't anything like that."

"It never is, dear."

Izzy glared at her cousin fiercely. "Don't do that. Don't pretend that my inexperience with men somehow indicates that I am also naïve in all things surrounding them. Don't pretend that your married status somehow makes you all-knowing when just a year ago you were in the same position I am."

Georgie's smile turned from impish to sad, and she came to sit beside Izzy on the sofa. "You're right. I'm sorry, I shouldn't tease. But you must understand, I am very fond of Mr. Morton, and it would be only too delightful if... Well, I am happy that the two of you are coming to know each other better."

"We certainly are," Izzy sighed, looking down at her fingers absently. "It's only natural isn't it? I am mentoring and practically sponsoring Kitty, and in attempting to make her comfortable and help her, I become more closely acquainted with him."

"Yes, that does follow," Georgie agreed with an understanding nod, her eyes wide. "How could you avoid such things?"

Izzy glanced over at her, smiling a touch. "I think I can call us friends now, Georgie. Mr. Morton, I mean."

Georgie covered her hands and squeezed them gently. "I am glad for it, Izzy. Truly. Mr. Morton could use a friend like you, and he's surely known enough hardship to deserve it."

"What do you mean?" Izzy asked with a curious lurch of her heart.

Georgie reared back warily. "He didn't tell you?"

"How can I answer that when it's clear I don't know to what you're referring?" Izzy pointed out, trying for a smile she did not feel.

Her cousin chewed on her lip for a moment. "It's not my place to reveal sensitive information about other people..."

"That's never stopped you before." Izzy turned her hands to grip Georgie's tightly. "I care about them, Georgie. Both Kitty and Mr. Morton. I am their friend, surely I may know."

Georgie hesitated for a long moment, then sighed. "All right, but you must promise to never reveal to anyone that I have told you. Especially not to Tony, he would never forgive me for revealing a confidence."

Izzy nodded firmly, still holding her hands.

"Have you never wondered why Mr. Morton and his sister are in London alone?" Georgie asked softly. "Why they are so attached?"

A sinking feeling hit the pit of Izzy's stomach. "I assumed their parents were deceased, and I did not think it right to pry."

"You assume correctly, and that is fairly known to anyone acquainted with them." Georgie glanced behind her, though none of the others had appeared yet. "What is not commonly known is that the Mortons died when Kitty was only a child. Five, perhaps six years of age. Their father passed rather suddenly, and their mother a few days after from her all-consuming grief."

"Sebastian would have been at school," Izzy broke in, her voice more of a gasp. "And Kitty…"

"Kitty was alone at the house," Georgie finished softly. "She had her governess, and the servants, of course, but Sebastian had not yet returned after his father's death when his mother also passed. He arrived to find them both deceased, that he was now the heir of Lindley Hall, and that he was guardian of his very young sister. He was only sixteen years of age."

Izzy stared at Georgie without speaking. It was unfathomable that a young man should have to bear so much, that a young girl should have suffered such a loss, and that either of them should have adapted to the new life before them without residual problems. One would never know by meeting with them or speaking with them that so much pain lay in their past.

"What did they do?" Izzy heard herself whisper.

Georgie smiled almost proudly. "Morton met with the manager of the estate and the solicitor and secured his sister's inheritance despite not having a fortune therein, then he set a course for them both. He would finish at school and go into the army, though not with a commission, and hopefully bring more fortune and respectability to the family. His parents had been honorable, but hardly noteworthy, and he knew that Kitty, at least, would need more than that to be truly secure in her future. He went home whenever possible and wrote to his sister more faithfully than some men do with their wives. Tony said he's never seen anything like it. Morton is both brother and father to Kitty, and he lived his life by both."

Tears welled in Izzy's eyes without warning, and she exhaled roughly, wiping at them. "I had no idea… I knew he was a good man, and a gentleman, but I never…" She laughed once and shook her head. "He must think me a very silly creature when he is so noble and selfless."

77

"He has no cause to find you silly," Georgie said with a fond pat to Izzy's cheek. "You haven't behaved in any ridiculous way, have you?"

"No," Izzy said slowly, thinking back, "but I do tease him, and I am not sure he agrees with it. He is so serious."

Georgie's mouth curved on one side. "Morton is the sort of man to tell you if he did not agree, Izzy. Believe me, you would know."

She smiled ruefully in return, then sniffed back the last of her tears. "I suppose this tragic past would explain Kitty's shyness. If she was always at home and without friends…"

"I do believe she was shy before all that," Georgie laughed. "But I have not yet met her, so I could be wrong."

"No, I believe you're right. She has always been shy, but I am sure her seclusion compounded it." Izzy hesitated, gnawing the inside of her lip thoughtfully. "I want her to be comfortable, and to have practice before she is expected to be out mingling with the rest of Society."

Georgie nodded, sitting back and setting her hands in her lap. "Well, inviting her here today will certainly be a test for her."

Izzy looked towards the window, her mind still whirling. "It shouldn't be too much of a test. She's already met Grace and Charlotte and done very well with them."

"You introduced her to Charlotte already?" Georgie coughed, eyes round. "Good heavens, why?"

"Charlotte has a way with people, Georgie," Izzy reminded her, turning back with a smile. "You know that."

Georgie raised a fair brow. "What kind of way would that be, Isabella?" She snickered and took the opportunity to lounge against the armrest for a moment. "No, I suppose it is better to introduce Charlotte early and let the poor dear grow accustomed by degrees."

They tended to joke about Charlotte and her intimidating, outspoken ways, and Charlotte was surely the sort of person that could terrify a shy individual, but she was in possession of a good heart and a generous spirit. She was really much less frightening in an informal setting, or in a personal conversation.

Unless you were ridiculous, pompous, or insipid. There were no guarantees then.

"But then what?" Izzy asked, her feet bouncing against the rug beneath them with anxiety. "How do I help her with more than just our little group? We are not particularly formal people."

Georgie pursed her lips in thought, then brightened and sat up. "Ask your mother. Surely Aunt Faith would love to invite Kitty and Mr. Morton for a dinner party."

"A formal party?" Izzy gave a hint of a wince. "I don't know… Those tend to have dancing, and…"

"A family party, then," Georgie clarified. She began to smile, and Izzy could see her thoughts racing around in her eyes. "Just your siblings and the children, and perhaps Tony and me. No dancing, no performances, only dinner and some games, everything easy. Perfectly comfortable."

Izzy grunted softly and rose, pushing a strand of hair out of her face. "I don't know how comfortable anyone outside of the family would be within the family for an entire evening."

Georgie laughed from her seat and rubbed her hands together. "Izzy, since marrying Tony, I have been subjected to more formal family dinners than ever before, and I can assure you from personal experience that Kitty Morton will be much more comfortable at one of your family dinners than at someone else's."

That was a thought Izzy hadn't considered, and it seemed somehow significant in a way.

Could her family, as unconventional and relaxed as they were, be helpful to Kitty in her preparation for the Season?

But what would Sebastian say about it? Coming to a family's home for dinner when they were neither neighbors nor particularly well acquainted was certainly unusual, though not unheard of. He was reserved and proper, and there was no telling what might compromise his sensibilities.

And to see Izzy when she was around her family…

Why would he want to be privy to that?

Why would he want his sister to see that?

But they didn't know, couldn't know, and there was a chance that everything would be different this time.

If he thought she was nice in public and social settings, he would be very surprised to see how she was in private with her family.

"I'll mention it to her," Izzy finally said turning to face Georgie again. "I will leave the decision up to Mother. Don't say anything to Kitty today. Or to Sebastian."

Georgie nodded and folded her shawl around her more securely. "I won't say anything. I won't even tell Tony, on the off-chance Aunt Faith doesn't invite us."

Izzy snorted once. "She'll invite you, I promise. She likes you more than me."

"Not true!" Georgie protested, laughing again. "I have never been more favored than you."

"Lies." Izzy shook her head in mock-despair, moving out to the corridor to request a tea tray. The Spinsters and Kitty would be arriving soon, and she needed to have all prepared for them.

Normally, she was not at all concerned about the details of their Spinster meetings, and any of them could have asked for a tea tray or sandwiches or anything else they could have wanted without any trouble.

But with Kitty Morton coming, she needed things to be a little more perfect than normal.

Kitty wouldn't care, she was perfectly unassuming.

But if she should confide in her brother...

Well, *that* needed to be perfect.

"Miss Lambert," Collins intoned as he stepped into view from the front of the house. "A letter for you."

"Oh, from Kitty Morton?" she asked out of habit, reaching out for the letter on the tray.

Collins shook his head, smiling just a little. "No, Miss. I believe it is from Mr. Frank Lambert."

Izzy's heart stopped for the space of several moments, then restarted again with a vengeance. Her chest and ribs ached while her fingers hovered over the parchment for longer than they should have.

What had he said? What had he thought? She had only sent him two more stories with the promise of more to come, but then she'd begun helping Kitty Morton, and her time had been taken up there.

She hadn't forgotten about her stories and her promise, but for the first time in ages, it hadn't been at the forefront of her mind.

She certainly had not expected a response already.

"Miss Lambert?"

Izzy raised her eyes to those of Collins, and she exhaled shortly before plucking the letter from the tray. "Apologies, Collins. I was lost in my thoughts."

He smiled knowingly, inclining his head. "Of course, Miss Lambert." He bowed slightly, then vanished, as he was wont to do.

She watched him go, then glanced down at the letter in her hands, fully aware of her cousin waiting in the parlor and her friends' imminent arrival.

But she had to know.

She stepped into her mother's parlor, which was rarely used anymore, and broke the seal, her pulse pounding in her ears as her eyes darted across the page.

Dear cousin,

I am pleased to inform you that the two additional stories you have submitted are some of your finest work yet. I would greatly appreciate seeing more work of this quality, and then, perhaps, we will be able to discuss our options moving forward.

Regardless, I would like to meet with you in a professional capacity in the next week or so to go over matters, including the Spinster Chronicles. Kindly respond with your availability.

Yours,
Frank T. Lambert

Izzy stared at the note, grinning without reserve, fearing her cheeks would crack from the force of her smile.

He wanted to see more? The stories she had sent him had been particularly good ones, but she could certainly create more of the same quality. She had dozens stored up, just waiting for a moment to be written down.

She wanted to start now! This very moment, there was a story she could put down and send off to him that he would love! Or that he could love, at any rate.

Then again, it was entirely possible that the next story would not be as appealing to him. He hadn't agreed to publish her yet. He had to have more proof, and he wanted to discuss options.

What options were there? Either he published her, or he did not publish her.

Two options.

Discussion could only mean he did not want to publish her, and he could not bear to tell her in writing.

Her next stories for him had to be nothing less than the absolute best she had to offer. She *had* to convince him that her stories were good enough, that she was worth the risk, and that this really could work in his favor. How she was going to do any of that was still unclear, but she had to try.

And for the first time, she dearly wished that the Spinsters were not coming to meet at her house.

The bell rang below, and she jerked out of her half-delirious stupor, refolding the letter and stuffing it into her neckline before going to request the tea tray as she had planned.

She had to keep up appearances for her friends. They could not find out about this, and if she were distracted in any way, that might provoke Charlotte or Georgie to ask too many questions…

This needed to be her secret for a bit longer.

And right now, she had to focus on Kitty.

Once the tea tray had been ordered, she returned to the parlor. Edith had joined Georgie and was now sitting beside her.

The two of them were completely different in coloring, with Edith's very dark hair and Georgie's being very fair, but there was no denying that they were both exceptionally beautiful.

Once Grace arrived, there would be another, and while Izzy had never felt particularly jealous of any of them, she could not deny that there was a slight twinge in her heart of something sad when she saw them. She was not in the habit of pitying herself, but surely a bit more attractiveness in her features could not be amiss?

Edith saw her then and smiled widely, enhancing her stunning beauty even more. "Good morning, Izzy. I hear we will be having a guest today."

Izzy smiled and nodded as she came further into the room and took a seat. "Yes, and I am expecting the two of you to be on your best behavior."

Georgie rolled her eyes, while Edith only maintained her perfect smile. "I only ever have best behavior," Edith told her with a twinkle in her eye. "It's all I know."

"Why do I doubt that?" Izzy wondered aloud with a curious tilt of her head.

"I'm sure I haven't the faintest idea," Edith replied, suddenly looking as proper and refined as royalty.

The sound of footsteps in the corridor brought them all up and Izzy smiled when Kitty Morton appeared in the door, looking more like the timid creature Izzy had first met than the girl she had walked with only yesterday.

Izzy rose and went to her, taking her hand. "Kitty dear, welcome. Let me introduce you. This is my cousin, Mrs. Sterling, but she will insist you call her Georgie."

Georgie inclined her head, smiling warmly. "Good morning, dear."

"It's a pleasure," Kitty whimpered, smiling weakly.

"Oh, lass, such a terrified sound," Edith murmured tenderly. "It's not as bad as all that. You already know Charlotte, and the rest of us are quite tame by comparison."

That steadied Kitty's smile creditably, and Izzy felt the tremors in Kitty's hand cease. "And this is Lady Edith Leveson," Izzy went on, smiling her appreciation at her friends. "You may call her Lady Edith if you wish, but the title is not necessary."

"A pleasure," Kitty said again, her voice stronger.

"Whatever makes you more comfortable, dear," Edith said, patting the chair beside her. "Come, sit here, if you can bear to."

Izzy chuckled wryly. "Why would she not be able to bear sitting by you? You are beautiful and lovely and charming and kind…"

Edith's lips curved and she winked at Kitty. "She's earning herself a fiver for the compliments." Then she sighed dramatically. "But alas, I am a Scot, lass, despite my marriage to an Englishman. Can you bear to sit beside me as such?"

Kitty delighted Izzy by releasing her hand and moving almost confidently to the chair. "I certainly can, Lady Edith," she stated before sitting very firmly in the indicated chair.

"Brava, dear," Izzy whispered with a wink as she sat in her previous chair.

"Did I hear a new voice being particularly decisive?" Charlotte's voice called from the corridor. She appeared then, her gown a rich green velvet, and her eyes sparkling with the same mischief her lips had in their curve. "Good morning, all." She brightened when she caught sight of Kitty. "Kitty, my pet! What a lovely surprise!" She swept into the room and took the seat closest to the girl. "Are we turning you into a Spinster with a capital S, darling?"

Kitty looked at her in outright bewilderment. "A what?"

A loud scoffing sound turned them all to the doorway where Grace and Elinor were entering, and Elinor rolled her eyes.

"Please, Charlotte," the younger woman groaned. "She's only just met us, she can't possibly be joining us already."

Grace looked at Elinor in derision. "Excuse me, but I would take Kitty Morton in a heartbeat, if I thought it would suit her to join." She looked over at Kitty and smiled at her. "Good morning, dear. That dress is so lovely with your complexion."

Kitty smiled, but her face flushed a little, and she was clearly overwhelmed with the number of people in attendance.

"Is anyone going to introduce me?" Elinor demanded as she plopped herself down into a chair by Izzy's desk, which made Izzy particularly nervous. Elinor was conniving and admired Charlotte to an unsafe degree.

Charlotte glanced at Elinor without much concern. "Calm yourself, child, you are not being replaced by our sweet Kitty here." She looked at Kitty with widened eyes. "Kitty, that's Elinor Asheley, who is closer to your age than any of us but is determined to be a spinster despite not actually qualifying for the status."

"I wonder where she got that idea from," Georgie murmured as the tea tray was brought in. "Determined to be a spinster…"

That earned Georgie a hard look, but everyone else laughed.

Kitty seemed torn between laughter and owlish staring, but then lowered her eyes as her fingers twisted in her lap.

"Charlotte," Izzy murmured so only she could hear, nudging her.

Charlotte saw the same thing and cleared her throat in the gentlest way. "Kitty, is there anything you wish to ask anyone? You don't have to, by any means, but you certainly can. We don't ask permission here, and your sweet little voice could get lost in the noise. I would ask now, if I were you."

Kitty's face lost its color, and her eyes met Izzy's in wide-eyed panic.

"It's all right, dear," Izzy told her, smiling in encouragement. "I promise you, we are all friends here. Every one of us."

Kitty wet her lips before meekly asking, "I was told that one of you was shy like me. Is that true?"

"It certainly is," Elinor laughed, sounding less cynical than she had in months.

"And h-here I am," a familiar stammer said from the doorway.

They all turned to grin at Prue, but Prue only had eyes for Kitty, and came straight to her. "Kitty Morton, it is a p-pleasure to meet you." She smiled and took Kitty's hand in hers. "I'm Prudence Vale, and I am possibly as scared as you are about the upcoming Season."

"But you're married," Kitty commented softly, visibly relaxing the longer she was in Prue's presence.

Prue grinned in a way that Prue rarely grinned. "I am, my dear. But it t-took me long enough to g-get there. I have no idea what this Season will bring."

"That makes seven of us," Grace moaned as she reached for her tea. "I hate this time of year."

"Oh, it's exciting!" Charlotte insisted.

"No, it isn't!" the room chorused together.

Including Kitty Morton.

Chapter Eight

———————⟨∞⟩———————

There is nothing so unpredictable as family, and nothing so unpredictable about families as when they are on display.

-*The Spinster Chronicles, 19 January 1818*

"Why are we doing this again?"

"Because when respectable families invite you for dinner, you accept with gratitude."

"Do you know Mrs. Lambert? Because I know I do not."

Sebastian looked at his sister in surprise, confused that she was now expressing her fears and discomfort instead of mulling in it silently. It was not a problem by any stretch, as it was now possible to address them directly, but it was different, and would take some getting used to.

"I have met her once, yes," he informed his sister, "and she is a kind woman. She is Izzy's mother, and I believe felt a desire to offer hospitality to you as Izzy is an unofficial sponsor for you."

Kitty looked up at him as the carriage approached the house, her bright blue eyes wide, but her expression scowling. "I hear the scolding you are not giving me, you know."

"Good," he grunted. "I did not want to get into particulars."

She scoffed quietly, but her lips curved into a wry smile.

Sebastian chuckled and kissed his sister's brow. "You'll be fine, Mouse. And you look lovely."

Kitty brightened at that. "Truly? I had Molly try a new style with my hair today. Charlotte thought it would suit my face, so she lent me the hair combs." She turned her impeccably curled and plaited hair to show him the amethyst encrusted silver combs that flawlessly matched her gown.

He smiled at the sight. "Perfect, Mouse. You look so much older than I think you should, but it does suit you very well."

"Yes, well, I am still a girl of ten in your eyes." She giggled and linked her arm through his. "I will never be old to you."

"Never," he vowed. He peered out of the window as the carriage stopped, then glanced back at Kitty. "Are you ready?"

She bit her lip, then shook her head. "No. Can we leave now?" She offered the barest hint of a smile.

He wasn't sure if it was a smile of hope or in jest. Either way, his answer was the same.

"Come on," he told her, tugging her gently.

They disembarked and made their way to the house, where the door was flung open before they could ring the bell, and Collins welcomed them in with more warmth than Sebastian had ever seen in a butler before.

Their coats and other things were taken, and they followed him to the drawing room.

He heard a soft muttering and glanced at Kitty only to see her lips moving at an almost frantic pace as her eyes grew rounder with each step.

"What are you saying, Mouse?" he teased under his breath.

"I'm running through the Lambert family names," she told him absently. "Izzy wrote it out for me in an attempt to make me feel better."

Sebastian bit back a smile and nodded in thought. "And did it?"

They reached the parlor and everyone within who had been sitting rose. Even Sebastian, who was not usually intimidated easily, felt his palms begin to perspire.

"No," Kitty whispered through a forced smile. "No, it did not."

Sebastian would have smiled had he not currently been on display.

Izzy was suddenly rushing to them and curtseyed quickly. "Mr. Morton, Miss Morton, welcome to our home. Let me introduce you to the rest of my family." She smiled at them both, and he suspected she would have been beaming had she not restrained herself for Kitty's sake.

She led them to the others in the room, and Sebastian bowed at least three times as he was introduced to two brothers, two sisters-in-law, a sister, a brother-in-law, and their hosts, Izzy's parents. It was all a blur to him, and he doubted he would remember their names or specifics about them, apart from her parents.

He was partly distracted by his concern for Kitty, though she seemed to be faring well enough, and partly distracted by Izzy herself. Her gown was an elegant shade of green that contrasted with her hair in a fascinating way, and her eyes seemed greener for it. The copper tones in her hair glinted in the candlelight of the room, and her smile seemed to create more on the faces of the others.

As formal as the introductions had seemed, it only took him a few additional minutes to realize that that would be as far as the formalities would extend.

Georgie waved at them all, and Kitty smiled a true smile for the first time. Tony met eyes with Sebastian, and he felt a sense of relief at having a friend and ally here.

Aside from Izzy, of course.

But he could hardly ask her to take sides against her family, should the need arise.

"Izzy," her oldest brother called as she finished the introductions with their parents, moving the pair of them over to Georgie and Tony, "stop being so proper and relax. Mr. Morton could surely use a drink, and Miss Morton might wish for one as well!"

Sebastian watched as Izzy's face colored, though she smiled with what seemed to be real amusement, and she rolled her eyes before moving to the sideboard.

He ought to intercept her, ought to tell her no, that he could get it himself...

"Dinner is served," Collins intoned, seeming to appear out of thin air.

Izzy stopped in her place, then changed direction to come back towards them. She widened her eyes at Kitty and Sebastian even as she smiled, which made him relax slightly.

He couldn't possibly have corrected her or her family in their own home, and it certainly was not the same as her being asked to fetch a drink in her cousin's home, but... There was something unsettling beginning to stir within him, and he wasn't entirely sure what to do with it.

Mr. and Mrs. Lambert led the way into dinner, followed by their sons and their wives, Izzy's younger sister and her husband, and Georgie and Tony. Sebastian followed with Kitty, though he looked at Izzy, unsure if he should be escorting her instead.

She shook her head quickly, obviously knowing his thoughts. "It's fine," she whispered, smiling with ease. "Go on."

It was deuced awkward to be followed by one's friend in her own home, but he supposed there was nothing for it. Formal processions were difficult businesses.

The dining room was well furnished, with all the finery a family of station could wish for without any of the excesses that would put off visitors or shy girls already terrified of being present. There didn't seem to be much order to how they would all be sitting for dinner, despite the formality of their entrance, and Georgie was quick to take the seat beside Sebastian while Tony acted as a buffer between Kitty and Mrs. Lambert, who sat at the end.

The gentleman who had to be husband to Izzy's sister sat to Mrs. Lambert's left, next to Sebastian, surprising him.

Where was...?

"Oh dear," Mrs. Lambert gasped, eyes wide. She looked down the table twice, then up at Izzy, who stood helplessly in the room without a seat or place setting.

"Oh, not again," one of the Lambert brothers said, tugging at his cravat.

Again? There was a habit of forgetting place settings?

Mrs. Lambert's face pinkened and she wrung her fingers together in obvious discomfort. "Izzy, dear, would you mind terribly going to eat with the children? We'll fetch you when we're finished here to rejoin us."

Sebastian stared at the woman for a moment, then turned to look at Izzy, who matched her mother's discomfort to the same shade of pink.

Surely she wasn't suggesting...

"Not at all," Izzy replied, though her smiled was the picture of a forced one.

"Aunt Faith," Georgie protested at once. "Do let me, won't you? The children..."

Mrs. Lambert shook her head. "Oh, don't be silly, Georgie, you're our guest."

"Georgie's a guest?" the oldest brother scoffed without politeness. "Since when?"

Georgie turned to glare at him fiercely. "Shove it, David, or I will crown you with your own dinner plate." She turned back to her aunt, her look pleading. "Aunt Faith..."

But Mrs. Lambert was firm, shaking her head once more. "Izzy is fine, dear, I promise. Izzy doesn't mind, and she adores the children."

"That wasn't exactly my concern," Georgie muttered so only Sebastian could hear her, her gaze darting to Kitty, who watched the whole thing with panicked eyes.

Izzy smiled a very thin, very tight smile, as she turned to leave the room, glancing at Kitty with some apprehension. Then her eyes met Sebastian's, and her forced smile suddenly became much closer to natural, no doubt trying for reassurance.

It did not convince him.

To be cast out of her own dining room because there weren't enough place settings? It was ridiculous, surely an additional chair and place setting could have been brought out, especially for a family dinner.

He looked around to see if anyone else would bring up the obvious lapse of judgment, but only a stewing Georgie by his side and a resolutely blank-faced Tony seemed affected by it.

And then there was Kitty...

"Don't worry, Miss Morton," Mrs. Lambert told her as they all sat, "you will be perfectly comfortable with my daughter Catherine beside you."

"I doubt that," Georgie grumbled as Sebastian helped her into her seat.

Sebastian flicked a wan smile at her before taking his own place.

"Is she really so bad?"

Georgie glanced at him slyly, a ringlet near her ear dancing in time with her earring. "Not at all. She's far tamer than Charlotte. Catherine is simply not as likable. You'll see." She cleared her throat and smiled at her cousins, before whispering, "Her husband is quite wonderful. You'll like him."

"I'd rather just talk with you, if it's all the same," he replied in the same tone, smiling at Izzy's sister, who was no doubt classically prettier, but did not have quite the same charm.

Georgie gave him a half wink and patted his knee before looking past him. "And how are the children, Mr. Northfield? I dare not ask Catherine, I know how she describes things."

"Well, I don't know where Izzy would have got to," Mrs. Lambert huffed as the gentlemen rejoined the ladies after dinner. "I sent for her ages ago."

Catherine shook her head slowly, frowning. "To abandon poor Miss Morton like this."

"I think being forced out of her own dinner might have something to do with it," Georgie mused, not bothering to lower her voice.

Anna Lambert bit her lip on a laugh and looked to her sister-in-law Jane, who did not react fondly.

Sebastian would count Anna in his favor for that, while Jane was obviously the more ridiculous of the set.

Which was strange, as she seemed more formal than ridiculous, but she had married a Lambert brother, so clearly, she was not so very proper.

"Think we can escape with her?" Tony inquired very low behind him.

If only.

Kitty sat beside Georgie without speaking, though she no longer looked as terrified or panicked as she had earlier. Tony's sitting by her and engaging her in conversation throughout dinner seemed to have gone a long way to setting her at ease. Lord only knew how she had done with the ladies, but Georgie seemed fiercely protective of her now, so that would suffice.

But it was Izzy that he had wanted for Kitty. It was Izzy whose temperament would suit. It was Izzy who had already made great strides with Kitty's comfort. It was for Izzy that they had accepted this invitation.

It was Izzy he had wanted to see.

And Kitty, of course, had wanted to see her. There was just something about Izzy that made him comfortable, that put him at ease, and made him want to smile. *Did* make him smile more often than not, it seemed, and for a man who was known for his reserve, that was certainly something. Not that he was unpleasant or disinclined to jovial things or expressions, he simply... wasn't prone to them.

It was far too soon to say, but it was entirely possible that Izzy could change all of that.

And he did not want to be in here with her family talking of everything and nothing in all politeness.

Collins suddenly appeared in the doorway and bowed to the group. "Miss Lambert is in the children's parlor, madam. She will be here momentarily."

Mrs. Lambert smiled in response, and there was something very matronly and almost proud in that smile, and Sebastian wondered at it. Despite having sent her daughter to eat with the children rather than sit with the guests, her mother knew her well enough to know exactly what Izzy was up to, and she loved whatever it was.

Curious.

Catherine had no such expression. "What is she doing in there, Collins?" she demanded with an exasperated look at Kitty, as though the girl should have agreed with her. "We have guests!"

"Catherine," her mother murmured softly, but with warning.

"I believe she is telling the children a story, Mrs. Northfield," Collins informed her formally. "As they are off to bed soon, she acquiesced to their request for one."

The family in the room all seemed to make the same sound of acknowledgement and understanding, while Tony, Kitty, and Sebastian all looked resolutely clueless.

Georgie took pity on them all. "Izzy has a gift for making up and telling stories to the children. It's become a bit of a tradition whenever they are all together."

Kitty looked at Sebastian in surprise, but smiled at the revelation. He tried to smile back but couldn't quite manage to.

His imagination was already up in the children's parlor, watching Izzy tell a story to her utterly rapt nieces and nephews. Their eyes would be wide and fixed on her, their bodies eagerly canting towards her, desperate for more. Izzy would drink it all in and channel their energy back into the telling, using her hands in broad gestures, her voice taking on new qualities with each character, dipping for effect and drawing the children further and further in…

He could see it all so clearly that the story was almost audible to him.

How could he know something so perfectly so soon?

He swallowed once and tried to engage with the room again, but it was utterly impossible. His mind was too filled with other, more engaging things, and it would be enough if he could maintain a polite, listening façade.

It should be enough; not many of them had engaged Sebastian in conversation at dinner, aside from Mr. Lambert, who seemed poised to be his favorite member of Izzy's immediate family. Even now, he was sitting in the corner of the room in a chair that was clearly well-loved, watching the conversations around him rather than participating in them.

Rather as Sebastian was prone to do at this moment.

"Do you remember that story Izzy told the children at Christmas?" Anna asked of the room, smiling warmly. "Something about a puppy, wasn't it?"

For the first time that evening, Jane laughed and nodded. "A puppy and a kitten roaming about London on Christmas. The boys couldn't stop talking about it."

William laughed as well. "Sophie still asks for Petunia Puppy and Kitty Kitten before bed. Anna and I try, but we just cannot tell it right."

Kitty was as engaged in this conversation as he imagined the children were in Izzy's story. "What was the story about?" she asked them, forgetting to be shy and afraid.

David chuckled and sipped his port before responding. "None of us are quite sure, but the animals are roaming about London and somehow they save Christmas."

"That sounds enchanting," Kitty said with a smile. "The children must love it."

"Oh, they do," Catherine assured her, partly in amusement, partly in annoyance. "And they seem to remember every detail, so our attempts at retelling always falls short. We can never get it right."

"Only Izzy," David cried, mimicking the children. "Only Izzy, Papa!"

"Izzy knows," William continued in the same tone. "Izzy can tell it right!"

Sebastian found himself smiling despite his previous disinclination. His sister, on the other hand, was beaming in a way that surprised him.

"Oh, I would love to hear her tell one," Kitty said with some longing, clasping her hands in her lap.

"Tell one what?" Izzy asked as she came into the room, her complexion rosy and filled with light. "I hope you haven't been deceived by my family into thinking that I'm somehow an actress or possess an abundance of wit."

"No worries there," David muttered with a playful look.

Izzy rolled her eyes and sat beside Kitty with a huff. "Remember what I told you about brothers, Kitty? This is exactly what I mean."

"What did you say?" her brothers asked in chorus.

"Oh, please, you lot," Catherine groaned dramatically. "What will the Mortons think of us?" She turned to the pair of them with wide eyes. "I do apologize for them, truly."

Tony looked at Catherine with a frown. "You don't care what I think of you all?"

"Not even a little bit," she shot back, making him and the others laugh. "You're in the family, Tony Sterling, so you're stuck with this."

"Pity he's actually stuck with Henry and Lawrence as family," William commented with a screwed-up face of distaste.

"I beg your pardon!" Georgie protested with a laugh, failing at mock outrage.

Kitty looked up at Sebastian in bemusement, and he knew her thoughts exactly.

This was clearly an insane family, and yet there was a charm to them. Something engaging and filled with love, even if they were not quite sure what to do with Izzy and her goodness, and while he could not say he necessarily felt drawn to them, he would admit to having his eyes opened.

And it was strangely refreshing. The only families he had ever seen, aside from Tony's brother and stepmother, had been very formal and almost distant.

This was completely opposite.

What might Kitty have grown into had their family been more like this? What would he himself have become?

"Mama," Izzy suddenly said, turning to her mother with wide eyes. "Did you see that it has begun to snow again? It seems to be falling quite hard."

Sebastian straightened and glanced out of the window himself, his mind shifting completely. The carriage would need to be called as soon as possible, and he should be able to take Kitty home without too much difficulty. Their home wasn't too far, and he doubted the weather was bad enough to truly affect anything. It was London, after all, not Northumberland.

"Well, I suppose my sister and I must return home, then," he announced, trying to sound politely forlorn, which wasn't much of a stretch for him. "We mustn't let the snow pile up."

The entire family, apart from Izzy and Georgie and Tony, looked at him in bewilderment, and it only occurred to him then that none of the others seemed remotely concerned about the weather, nor had they considered leaving.

Just him.

"Nonsense," Mrs. Lambert told him with a wave and a knowing light in her eye. "We have plenty of room here, and no need to rush you off. You will both stay here this evening."

He blinked at the statement and glanced at Izzy. She looked as stunned as he felt, which made him smile.

And agree.

Chapter Nine

———— ⸙ ————

Eventually, all secrets come to light. Even if that light is only one tiny flickering flame.

-*The Spinster Chronicles, 6 December 1817*

There was no possible way of sleeping with two unexpected guests in the house along with the rest of the family.

Was her mother actually *insane*? To invite the Mortons to stay in their house when the weather was perfectly fine for travelling... It was madness! Izzy hadn't brought up the weather as a hint to encourage an invitation for Kitty and Sebastian; she'd only said it because it was so perfectly wintery!

Why in the world would she want them to stay? After the embarrassment of being summarily dismissed to sit with the children, when it was Izzy alone who had suggested the Mortons come to dinner. She had been forced to abandon Kitty in her hour of need, unable to temper anything her family said or did, or explain anything to Sebastian, who would have undoubtedly been shocked by the Lambert family antics.

But her mother wouldn't be put off, and so Sebastian and Kitty had stayed the night.

There was only one problem.

Despite what her mother had claimed, they did not have plenty of room for everyone, and there had been no rooms to spare.

Oh, there were rooms for David and Jane, and for William and

Anna, and for Catherine and Daniel, as those rooms were always prepared for them and occasions to stay at the Lambert family home tended to be fairly frequent. With all of that, however, there were only two guest rooms to spare, leaving either Sebastian or Kitty without a room.

Enter her mother yet again, who had been quick to suggest that Miss Morton stay in Izzy's room, while they would make something up for Izzy.

Polite protestations had been made, of course, but everyone had chimed in that Izzy would be fine, and that this was a regular occurrence when guests were staying with them.

Unfortunately, that was all too true, and in these particular circumstances, that meant that Izzy was in the nursery with the children. At this moment, that also meant there was a small pair of feet pressing into her back at just the wrong spot. It wasn't uncommon for her to be in these situations, but on all the other occasions she was in a bed fitted to her size and the children were the intruders, not the reverse.

Oh, but Sebastian's face when he had found out!

It would haunt Izzy's mind for a while, and her embarrassment had been so extreme that even Prue would have been startled by it. She had never thought that her nature with her family should be so drastically on display so early in their acquaintance, and she was not particularly giving or good therein. It was simply easier to acquiesce and obey, to avoid anger and temper, or any kind of show.

Catherine had been only too skilled in her demands for this or that, and Izzy saw how it wore on her parents, so she'd determined to never follow suit.

And she never had.

Georgie had given up trying to change anything, and occasionally took a stand for her, as she had done in the dining room, but even she had been worn down by it all.

Within the family, at least. Georgie still had quite a great deal to say when Izzy was too accommodating in the public or social realms.

It wasn't often than Izzy was ashamed of her behavior, or embarrassed by it, but seeing Sebastian's reaction made it all too real, and now she was thinking too much and feeling too much about matters and details that had never really bothered her before.

Ridiculous business.

She shifted on her too-small mattress and lifted little Rose's feet from out of her back, tucking them back under the covers. The girl's blonde hair was strewn all about the pillow and rapidly tangling further still, as she was not a quiet or immobile sleeper. Her breathing was loud and almost whistled with every exhale through her perfectly formed, little-girl lips. She had insisted, with all the tenacity she had inherited from her mother, that Izzy *had* to sleep with her, and tell her a whole new story just for her as they fell asleep.

Molly Moose had been created then, and it had the potential to be one of her best stories yet. An uncoordinated moose who could not do anything without tripping over her own feet? Rose had loved it, and Izzy predicted that Rose would intentionally be stumbling around her own house for a great many days to come.

She would have to warn Daniel and Catherine about that one.

Izzy exhaled and looked up at the ceiling of the nursery, listened to the six different sounds of sleeping children around her, and shook her head.

There would be no sleeping for now.

She pushed herself gently out of bed, careful not to jostle the mattress or Rose, then grabbed her wool shawl from the bedpost and slid her feet into slippers. The candle she had brought in with her sat on the table by the door, and she picked it up, slipping out into the corridor and lighting the wick with the lone candle at the end of the hall.

If she couldn't sleep, she might as well be productive.

She was used to working while the house was silent, and while she usually wrote at the desk in her room in the middle of the night, her parlor would suffice this once.

The stairs were more than unusually accommodating in their silence, and she tiptoed into her parlor, shivering in the darkened room. The fire had gone out, but there were still some embers remaining. She raced over to build the fire back up. She didn't need it to be roaring, but she did require some light and warmth.

When the flames were dancing merrily, she darted over to her desk and set the candle on it, pulling out the manuscript she hadn't finished the other day and a few fresh sheets of parchment. She bit her lip in thought, trying to remember how she had begun the story with Rose. It wouldn't make much difference to Cousin Frank, but if her niece ever read the story, or heard it, she would throw a fit, and it seemed that would have some effect on the story for others.

The phrase came back to her, and she smiled at it.

"An uncoordinated moose is an unconventional moose," she murmured aloud as she dipped her pen into the inkwell and jotted down the words on the page. The rest of the words seemed to flow out of her as a stream over rocks, easier than ever before, her mind twice as clear.

But Molly Moose was not afraid of being different. Nor did she feel the need to compare herself with the other moose who could walk with ease, in perfect motion, and at times in perfect formation. Molly Moose had never walked a straight line without falling on her face after exactly seven paces. Always seven, and always on her face. But Molly Moose was determined that she could do everything that other moose could do, even if she fell…

"Couldn't sleep?"

Izzy gasped loudly and whirled, flinging her arms over the pages and nearly knocking over her inkwell.

Sebastian stood in the doorway in his shirtsleeves and trousers, his dark hair far more rumpled than seemed possible for him, yet without being indecent or shocking. On the contrary, he seemed somehow more human than she had ever seen him before. She hadn't even realized that he had seemed somehow above mortality until this moment when he was so solidly in it.

And now his mouth was curved up in a crooked smile, and he had clearly seen her entire reaction.

"Sebastian," she managed, her voice quivering as her heart raced frantically within her.

He held up his hands in surrender, eyes widening. "Apologies. I didn't mean to startle you. I thought perhaps you'd heard me coming down the stairs. They creak."

Izzy swallowed harshly and pressed a hand to her chest. "They don't if you know where to step."

"Are you in the habit of sneaking downstairs in the middle of the night, Izzy?" he asked, smiling again, his voice low.

Izzy. Her name on his lips sounded like the humming of a particularly lovely song, though one whose tune she didn't recognize. But one she found herself desperate to sing.

"Sometimes," she heard herself reply, smiling now herself. "But only with very good reason."

Sebastian grinned briefly then gestured to the room. "May I?"

Izzy snorted softly and mimicked the motion. "Please do."

He nodded with all politeness, though his smile was still teasing. He sat on a couch in the room, then looked over at her, his look still far more teasing than she had expected from him. "May I ask what you are hiding over there? Or should I ignore the very frantic covering you were doing?"

Izzy's eyes widened, and she gaped for a moment. "Ignore it, as any perfect gentleman would!" She gave him a scolding look.

"I never said I was a *perfect* gentleman," Sebastian told her as he settled in his seat, looking far too relaxed. "Just a gentleman." He smiled warmly, then let it fade. "I won't ask about your private affairs, Izzy. If you don't wish to discuss it, that will be the end of it. I was hoping to sit here by the light of the fire and sketch, but since you are already here..."

Sketch? There was no possible way he truly sketched, but the notepad in his left hand seemed real enough.

He turned to leave, and her natural instinct took over. "Please, don't go. I can just as easily move my work elsewhere."

"Nonsense," he disagreed.

"Perhaps we could both stay," she suggested, surprised by her own boldness. "No one is awake to complain. You simply sit by the fire, and I'll just remain here. Will that suit?"

Sebastian looked thoughtful for a moment, then smiled and nodded.

Izzy returned his smile, then turned back to her writing, but she couldn't help sneaking a peek at him. Surprisingly, he was not watching her. He sat with his knee bent, the notepad propped upon it, sketching. No inquiries into her work, no suspicious looks, no taunting until she relented.

That was really it? She protested and asked him to ignore it, and he respected that?

She turned back to her desk and the pages on it, jotted down a few more lines, and glanced behind her at Sebastian, curious and wary.

He seemed as content as he could be, sketching away in his notepad, his brow knitting slightly as he focused.

Izzy turned back around, frowning and writing another word or two, before turning back to Sebastian. "Is there enough light for you to really sketch properly? I can light more candles."

"No, this is sufficient," he told her without looking up.

"Is it?" she persisted, looking around. "Let me light more candles, Sebastian."

He glanced up at her with a shockingly pointed look. "If I wanted more light or more candles, Izzy, I would light them myself. No need for you to do so." He quirked a brow and went back to his sketch.

Now Izzy frowned at him, not bothering to pretend otherwise, and she drummed her fingers on the back of the chair.

"I can feel you staring, Izzy," Sebastian said calmly.

She frowned further still. "Why did it sound as though you were criticizing my offer to help you?"

He shook his head once. "I did no such thing. I said I would do it."

"Your tone implied displeasure."

"Did it?"

"Don't be intentionally evasive, Sebastian," she insisted, gripping the chair. "Tell me if I was right, and there was something you did not like about what I said."

The pencil stopped scratching against the page, and then Sebastian sighed, lowering the pad and giving her a very frank, but not unkind look. "Your offering to light the candles did not upset me in any way. It is a perfectly kind and generous offer, and very thoughtful."

Izzy blinked twice before asking, "And the trouble there is…?"

He hesitated, then narrowed his eyes a little. "I was here for dinner and for the arrangement of sleeping quarters, Izzy. I saw what happened to you, and how you were treated."

"You needn't make it sound as though I am abused by my family," Izzy retorted, her cheeks beginning to heat. "I am no victim here."

"Perhaps not," he considered, keeping his tone mild. "But there is a significant amount of taking you for granted, and overindulgence of your good nature. To dismiss you from dinner simply because there was not another chair?"

"Oh, but…"

"And where are you sleeping, anyway?" he overrode, raising his voice only enough to be heard over her. "I know my sister is in your room."

Izzy swallowed her retort and scowled. "The nursery."

Sebastian stared at her for a too-long moment. "You cannot be serious."

There was nothing to do but force a tight smile and shrug, wrapping her shawl more securely around her. "If we did not have guests, I could have made do on a sofa in the library."

"Surely not."

"I have done it before," she said simply.

"In your own home?"

His incredulity amused her more than anything else. "Where else should I do it, Sebastian? As a guest at someone else's home?"

The furrows in his brows deepened. "Ideally, never."

"But it happens," she insisted, shrugging a shoulder one more time. "I am not bothered by it now."

His furrows cleared, and a sad smile appeared. "And *that* is my concern."

Izzy pursed her lips but said nothing.

"I have the feeling, Izzy, that things like this, minor though they be, tend to happen often." His look became more searching. "Am I correct?"

Her heart began to pound unsteadily, and not in a pleasant way. Moments from several years of her life flashed before her, things she had never argued with her family, had never even brought up, but had somehow collected into small piles of bitter seeds within her. She'd simply accepted it as the way things would be, and there was nothing in there that was truly worth the trouble of arguing or contending over.

But the collection…

"You are," she whispered, struggling to find her voice. "But I don't think about them. I don't argue the point, I don't refuse, and I don't disagree."

"When?" he inquired, his voice soft.

She swallowed with difficulty before she was able to speak. "When I am asked to do something, when I am told to do something, when my sister or one of my brothers speaks harshly… I am silent, biddable, and obedient. I always have been."

Sebastian sat up in his seat, turning more fully to her. "You can't stand up for yourself?"

Izzy shook her head. "No. I'm too out of practice, and it's too late to start. And when I have done, I am overcome with guilt for whatever I said, and apologize for it."

"And would they apologize in return?"

"No. Because it was my fault for taking offense."

Her answer hung in the air between them, and he did not look particularly pleased by it. Not exactly angry, but unsettled somehow. As if he had known her long enough to approve or disapprove of anything or have any opinion at all on her life or her manner.

And yet…

She wanted to know his thoughts. She wanted to know how he felt about this. She wanted to confide in him about many things and hear him share with her. She wanted to hear about his days in the army, his days at Lindley Hall as a child, and what he spent his time doing.

Suddenly, his thoughts mattered. His feelings mattered. His wishes mattered.

He mattered.

And he thought she mattered enough to stand up for herself and not be so nice. It was a confusing and intimidating thought.

Izzy smiled a little at him, now that the silence had stretched enough to become blatant.

He returned it easily, and whatever moment he'd had with her description vanished with it. He drew his knee back up and returned to sketching, leaving Izzy to her solitude.

She did not go back to her writing right away, though. She watched him sketch, fascinated by the way his hands moved, though she had no idea what he was sketching. She could see him process whatever it was he was drawing in his face, the way it shifted and changed with each moment. His eyes danced across the page, and the color of them was indistinguishable in the dark of the room, but she knew how blue they could be. Not quite to his sister's intensity and brightness, but only a shade or two behind them. He was a handsome man, she had always known that, but there was so much more to him.

And she was only just coming to know that.

A reserved man who apparently did not tease, but had no problem teasing her whenever the occasion arose. A proper man who did not want Izzy to be biddable or submissive. A gentleman who could sit in a room with a young woman without any chaperone in the middle of the night and not take the slightest advantage of the situation.

A man who had secrets without hiding anything at all. Such as his ability to sketch.

But then, it was entirely possible that he was not that skilled at it, and only drew for his enjoyment. Rather like her writing.

With that in mind, she turned back to the incomplete story with a wince and tried to recall what adventure she had put Molly Moose through with Rose. It was difficult to remember, considering Rose had chimed in with suggestions throughout most of it, some of which Izzy had actually taken and included. If only there were a way for someone to record the details of the stories as Izzy told them so as to avoid all this trouble later.

Izzy tapped her pen absently against the parchment, closing her eyes to focus, taking herself back to only a short time ago in the nursery when she'd told this story.

She did not have time to be without inspiration or productivity. She had to bring more stories with her when she met with Cousin Frank and be ready to answer about more of them. She did not think he would want to continue indulging her without some sort of promise in the future. Her inability to recall the stories her imagination had conjured up so effortlessly was going to get in the way of a newfound dream coming to life.

The fire crackled in the room, Sebastian's pencil scratched against the page, and Izzy... couldn't stand the silence and secrecy one moment more.

She whirled in her seat and clutched the chair tightly. "I'm writing stories for children," she burst out.

Sebastian's head lifted with a jerk, his eyes wide. "You're what?"

Izzy nodded, giving him a wobbly smile. "I tell stories to my nieces and nephews, and now I am writing them down."

He blinked once, then his mouth curved up, and he set his drawing aside. "I heard that you tell stories to the children, but no one told me that you write them down."

She giggled helplessly and bit her lip. "That's because they don't know! Well, Catherine asked me to write a story down for Rose because she was fussing about it, but she doesn't know about this. No one in my family knows, and none of the Spinsters know. I haven't told anybody."

"Except me," he pointed out, laughing once.

Izzy paused then grinned sheepishly. "Except you."

"Why?" Sebastian asked with a tilt to his head that made him look rather charming and relaxed.

Her face warmed at once. "Why you?"

She prayed that wasn't what he wanted to know, because there was no easy answer to that question. Mostly because she didn't know herself, and she could not explain not knowing.

"No," Sebastian laughed again, shaking his head. "No, why doesn't anyone know?" His eyes widened, and he gaped. "Wait, when you say write, Izzy, do you mean..."

Izzy grimaced but giggled still. "I mean that I have a meeting with my father's cousin, who is a printer, and we are discussing the possibility of publication."

"What?" he cried, his voice rising with excitement.

"Shh!" she hissed, looking towards the door.

He clamped down on his lips, then waved for her to join him on the couch.

She scrambled over and sat beside him, folding her shawl more tightly. "I have no promises of anything," she told him in a rush. "He's only read the few that I've sent, and he sees potential, but..."

"That's amazing, Izzy!" Sebastian interrupted, shaking his head. "How did this happen?"

"Well," she allowed with a rough exhale, "he's the one who prints the Spinster Chronicles, so he already knew that I could write a little, and he had taken a chance on us there, which has proven to be beneficial."

Sebastian nodded thoughtfully, smiling still. "I'd say so. I see the Chronicles everywhere these days."

Izzy wrinkled up her nose in delight at that. "I know, it's gone beyond anything. And it's becoming so fun to write more and more articles."

"So, he is actually likely to take another chance on you?" Sebastian pressed, turning more serious for the first time.

"I don't know," Izzy sighed, rubbing at her brow. "It's possible, I suppose, but there is no guarantee that he would truly publish a collection of children's stories by a woman."

Sebastian raised a brow at that. "When he has already published a newssheet written by several women?"

"Anonymously, remember." Izzy shook her head slowly. "Everyone knows who we are, it's true, but they do not know which of us has written which article. And there is no real way to tell if we actually wrote them. The secrecy saves us. This would be different."

Sebastian made a soft sound of understanding, but nothing further.

"And…" Izzy trailed off, looking up at him with hesitation. "There is still the possibility that they are not good enough. That I am not good enough."

"Izzy," Sebastian murmured in an almost scold, reaching out to cover her hand. "Do you really think he would be entertaining the idea of publication if you were not good enough? I've never heard you tell a story, but your family spoke of it while we waited for you, and it captured my attention and imagination just hearing them. I can only imagine that the true story from its author would be much more captivating."

Izzy smiled with such intensity that her cheeks ached with it. "Really?"

Sebastian wet his lips, then turned to pick up his notepad once more. He glanced at her, then turned it around. "Really."

Izzy gasped at the sketch, grinning involuntarily.

A dog with a holly and ivy hat walked beside a small cat with a bell on its tail down what was so clearly a London street, which was dotted with snow.

And it was a very skilled sketch.

She looked at Sebastian in wonder. "This is incredible!" She looked down at the picture, then grinned up at him. "Is that...?"

"Petunia Puppy and Kitty Kitten," Sebastian answered sheepishly, his smile boyish. "I couldn't help myself."

Izzy giggled, then stared at the picture again. "Petunia is actually a spaniel, though. And Kitty Kitten is white with black patches."

Sebastian groaned and took the picture back. "Well, if I had heard the story properly, I would know such things, Isabella," he grumbled playfully under his breath, widening his eyes.

"I can fix that," Izzy assured him, settling in against the couch.

"Really?" he asked, glancing back at her out of the corner of his eye.

She nodded, unable to help smiling. "One fine Christmas Eve, Petunia Puppy paid a call upon her unlikely friend, Kitty Kitten..."

Chapter Ten

Whoever said fear is a great teacher has clearly never had the experience of being truly afraid.

-*The Spinster Chronicles, 8 January 1817*

Her fingers were numb, and yet they trembled.

That seemed an odd thing to notice at a time like this, but when the day was mild and there was no cause for extremity numbness, it did register as out of the ordinary. Of course, when combined with the racing heart, flushed face, bouncing knees, and dry throat, one could surmise that Izzy was anxious.

Which, of course, she was.

She clenched her trembling fingers inside her muff as she sat in the waiting area of Cousin Frank's print shop, trying her best to steady their tremors and focus on her breathing. What was it that Prue always said when she was overwrought? Something about breathing in and out, and fear going in and out?

She wasn't necessarily feeling fearful just now, simply... apprehensive. There was nothing to fear from Cousin Frank. He would tell her exactly what he thought and avoid all hints of flattery, and she would know once and for all if she had any chance at publishing her stories. If he would not do so, she wasn't sure any other printer in the world would.

And then what?

She could not, and would not, pretend that she had always

dreamed of being a writer or that she had always been writing down stories in journals or acted them out or anything of the sort. It had just somehow happened upon her, and now it was one of the chief focuses of her life. But she'd had no dreams or aspirations, and nothing would be ruined by a refusal to publish. She would simply have to go on just as she had always gone on, especially when life had not turned out the way she had expected it to. She had certainly learned by now that expectations were never quite meant to last, and it was best to let them go the moment that realization had struck. But she could not deny that her life was running out of meaningful paths, and that *did* tend to make her fearful.

Which was why she sat here.

Alone.

Waiting.

"I am so sorry to have kept you waiting, Izzy," Cousin Frank said as he came into view, his full face wreathed in a faint sheen of perspiration that was matched by the same on the top of his head. "The life of a printer. Please, come into my office."

Izzy smiled up at him and moved into the room as he indicated.

It was a well-furnished room, but with more clutter than she would have expected from a man of business such as he. Still, it all seemed to be related to articles and printing matters, and the bookcases were filled to the brim, so she could not fault him for that.

He came around her to pull out a seat at a well-worn table in his office, and she caught sight of the ink-smudged sleeves on his equally well-worn grey coat.

For some reason, that made her smile.

Not just a businessman, then. He had started out as his own printer years ago with only two assistants, and she imagined such a beginning stayed with a person. She wondered faintly if he ever laid out the Spinster Chronicles settings himself just to have the experience.

Cousin Frank moved back around the table to sit opposite her and took his seat with a grunt of satisfaction. He smiled at her rather pleasantly, folding his hands over his growing girth.

"You look well, cousin," he told her, his tone almost fatherly. "I haven't seen you in some months, but I must say you look very well."

Izzy had the good sense to blush modestly. "Thank you, cousin."
He chuckled as she ducked her chin. "Still not able to take a compliment, eh?"

She shook her head, grinning now.

"Ah, well." He sat forward and rested his folded hands against the table. "How is your mother? Harriet was asking after her only yesterday, and I was embarrassed to not be able to properly answer her."

Izzy managed a wan smile. "Mama is perfectly well, thank you."

Cousin Frank smiled knowingly, a twinkle in his eye. "Is she really, Izzy? I've never known your mother to be perfectly well in all the years I've known her. There is always something."

"She is well enough," Izzy admitted, her smile relaxing a bit.

"That seems to be more apt." He tilted his head, eyeing Izzy carefully. "And I do not mean to imply that your mother is bent on bemoaning her state in any way. I only mean her mind is often fixed on one topic or another, and it does tend to infiltrate her conversation."

Izzy bit back a retort that would have enhanced his kinder account of her mother's nature, and only smiled as an obedient daughter would. Then she carefully managed, "It does, yes."

Cousin Frank chuckled at that. "Always kind, Miss Izzy, and always so sweet. I wonder very much what would happen if you ceased biting your tongue."

A helpless giggle escaped her, and she could tell it delighted him.

"Well," he said with a heavy sigh, his fingers drumming against each other, "I suppose you would have me dispense with the politeness and get on with it."

Izzy shrugged one shoulder. "That would depend on what it is you have to say."

Cousin Frank laughed again. "Too right. Well…" He cleared his throat and sobered, though there was still a warmth to his gaze. "I read over your latest three stories."

The formality in his tone gave Izzy pause. What could that mean? Was he simply indulging her whims as a relation and not seriously as a publisher? Her fingers clenched in her lap, and her stomach echoed the sensation.

Her cousin's thin lips curved to one side. "They are wonderful, Izzy."

The pit of her stomach burst into a shower of warmth and she exhaled a rough, gasping breath. "Really?"

He chuckled, nodding repeatedly. "You are a talented writer, my dear, and quite skilled. That you should have already surmised from the Spinster Chronicles."

There was no way to answer that in the affirmative while maintaining any shred of modesty.

Izzy managed a shy smile. "Well, I did hope…"

"Hope no more, my dear," he told her as he reached over to pat her hand. "As a professional, and as your friend and cousin, I will tell you that you are very good."

"For a woman?" Izzy suggested wryly.

Cousin Frank gave her a hard look. "For anyone, regardless of sex."

Now Izzy blushed fully and looked down at her trembling fingers. "Thank you."

"I was already fond of the ones you had sent previously," Cousin Frank went on. "And I wondered how you would respond to the query for more of them."

Izzy allowed a rueful grin to cross her lips. "I was terrified and intimidated, to be sure, and worried that I had not yet proven myself capable enough."

Cousin Frank was shaking his head before she finished. "You had, but I wanted more. Not necessarily more in quality, but to see what you could do. You see, two short stories, adorable though they may be, could only be published in a news sheet or a journal of sorts. It would hardly garner you the attention or the funds that you are undoubtedly looking for."

His words shocked Izzy with a jolt of surprise, and her cheeks flushed. "Oh, but I am not…" She began unsteadily.

"But of course you are," Cousin Frank overrode in an almost gentle fashion. "For all our nobility and airs, we writers want to be paid for our efforts. We may write for love of it, and for the sheer pleasure of putting pen to paper and producing extraordinary adventures and sweeping romances, or, in your case, entertaining and

111

admirable creatures, but when it comes down to it, we want our name out in the world for the masses to adore. And we are the tiniest bit mercenary about that. In the noblest sense."

Izzy laughed breathlessly, just once, then nodded. "I'm afraid I do want that. A little."

Cousin Frank snorted softly. "Don't be afraid of it, Izzy. We all do. Nothing to be ashamed of. Now…" He smiled at her, drawing out the moment. "I expect you are wondering about my decision, yes?"

"Yes," Izzy said on a rough exhale, not bothering to hide her relief that they had come to it at last. "Yes, I am."

He chuckled and leaned back comfortably, clearly at ease with Izzy's uneasiness.

Impertinent relation.

"I won't insult your intelligence by bandying about," Cousin Frank told her. "I have too much respect for you to engage in such foolery and could never understand why other men in the world of business do such things."

"I appreciate that, thank you," Izzy replied, wondering when he would get on with it instead of only talking of getting on with it.

Cousin Frank seemed to sense the more cynical side of her thoughts and smiled a little more broadly. "Izzy, I would love to publish a collection of your stories."

Her heart rammed against at least seven ribs in a strange ricocheting dance, and it took her a moment to breathe properly. "Cousin Frank, thank you, that would be…"

"But…" he interrupted with the utmost gentleness.

The dance of the ribs came to a complete standstill, and her lungs paused in their function.

Never had one word been more hated in her entire life.

She wet her lips carefully, swallowed, then forced her face to be less arrested. "But?"

Cousin Frank now looked rather sympathetic. "But I need more."

"More," she repeated uncertainly. "More… stories? More quality? More… variety?"

He nodded at every answer. "All of the above, though your

quality is already wonderful. I need at least twenty, if not twenty-five stories, if we are to truly make this worth my time, your time, and the cost of publication. You need a full collection, Izzy, not a pamphlet."

Izzy let go of years of comportment training and slumped back in her chair with a rough exhale. "More."

"Yes, my dear. More. Any publisher in the world would agree with me, progressive, stingy, or otherwise."

More. It was an incomprehensible thought. She had already stretched her mind as far as she could recall just to give him a few stories more, but the idea of creating twenty all told…

She was only ever able to create stories for the children, making them up for herself was far less amusing and entertaining. Least of all because the creatures wound up being rather spinsterly and wished for a romantic partner, which would not do at all.

"And then there is the matter of illustration."

Izzy looked up at that. "Illustration?"

Cousin Frank returned her look with surprise. "Surely you don't intend to publish a collection of children's stories without some sort of illustration. It would never work."

"Another expense, then."

"I am afraid so, yes. But as your publisher, I would be more than happy to assist in the cost of an illustrator." He smiled in encouragement. "I am sure we can find someone who will be amenable to negotiating the price."

Izzy wasn't nearly so sure. What sort of artist would be willing to do children's illustrations in a collection of stories for something undoubtedly far less than a proper wage for it? There could hardly…

Her mind trailed off of its own accord as a new and rather intriguing idea entered her mind. So intriguing, in fact, that she sat up straighter in her seat, her brow knitting deeply in thought.

"Izzy?" Cousin Frank pressed, sounding more curious than concerned.

She raised her eyes to his and felt her lips curve into a smile. "What if I have an illustrator already? And one who would be more than unusually accommodating for us both?"

Cousin Frank grinned in response. "I would say bring me concept art so that we might see where this leads."

Izzy nodded thoughtfully, her smile blossoming. "I can do that. I most certainly can do that."

She most certainly could *not* do this. Every fiber of her being was suddenly straining against it, and she couldn't breathe a word of it to a single soul.

She had never felt this particular choking sensation. It encapsulated her entire chest, her throat, and her tongue all at the same time. And it seemed to be making her eyes impossibly dry, so her frequent blinking was doomed to give her distress away, if anyone were to notice.

She swallowed with great difficulty, and raised a hand to her brow, which was not as damp with perspiration as she had expected it to be. In fact, it wasn't damp at all, which was a bewildering observation, given her frantic state and the sudden warmth in the carriage.

How could she not appear as distressed as she felt?

"Darling, don't fret," her mother's voice intoned in a would-be consoling tone that did absolutely nothing it was intended to. "Miss Morton will be perfectly fine this evening. You saw how she did with our family."

Izzy managed a wan smile in the general direction of her mother but had to laugh silently. Yes, she had seen how Kitty had done, and if she had not been so perfectly obsessed with fear about her current situation, she might have been equally as terrified about Kitty this evening. But that had not even been close to the forefront of her mind, and it was a shameful thing for a mentor to admit.

Kitty could not possibly be more afraid than Izzy at the present, and the pair of them would be utterly useless to each other and to everyone else.

But her mother did have a point, she had to admit. She could not be so selfish as to focus so entirely on herself that she completely neglected the girl who was relying on Izzy as her source of strength and comfort in all this.

However foolishly placed it was tonight.

She could do both. She could take care of Kitty tonight as well as potentially risk her reputation and her future. And do both with subtlety.

She could.

"I believe it would do you some good to help Kitty Morton," her mother said suddenly, adjusting her gloves. "While you may not have had success in the marriage front of Society, you do tend to navigate things well, and everybody always speaks so highly of you."

Izzy turned to her mother in surprise, smiling. "Thank you, Mama."

Her mother looked up and scowled a bit. "Oh, don't sound so surprised, Izzy. I know very well you are a sensible girl with good manners and training, I would never raise a fool."

The blustering defense didn't rankle Izzy in the slightest, and she smiled more fully. "You love me, Mama," Izzy teased.

"Well, of course I do," her mother protested playfully. "What sort of mother does not love her children?"

"Mine," Izzy's father retorted with a laugh from his side of the carriage.

"Oh, hush!" his wife scolded, kicking at his shins half-heartedly. "She did too."

He laughed more and shrugged, sitting back with his arms folded and winking at Izzy.

Izzy only shook her head and looked out of the window, feeling somehow marginally better for laughing with her parents. Her loving parents who had no idea what she was about, and whose possible reaction to her secret gave her pause.

She straightened as they pulled into the drive of Charlotte's home, knowing that if she showed any hint of her distress, Charlotte would pounce upon it the moment she saw her.

No, she had to get through the politeness of greetings and venture into the ballroom, exchange pleasantries, and eventually wander to the Spinster Corner, as it was called here, before she could relax her features into whatever state they needed to be in.

By then, she would be well on her way to accomplishing her task anyway,

Hopefully.

They unloaded from the carriage and made their way up to the house, shedding their cloaks and wraps before moving into the receiving area.

Charlotte had gone to her usual extravagances in appearance, particularly when her family hosted, but she seemed to pay very little attention to it, now that guests were arriving. She never fussed or fidgeted with her appearance in public, not due to any sort of proper behavior or comportment training, but out of sheer lack of concern. She simply couldn't be bothered by something so trivial as her appearance when she was so busy making conquests she would never do anything with.

Mr. and Mrs. Wright beamed at Izzy, which they usually did, and Charlotte defied all protocols by hugging Izzy soundly, though they had seen each other only days ago.

"Save me," Charlotte hissed through a perfect smile. "I can't bear a single moment more of polite greetings."

"I can hear you, dear," her mother informed her with a knowing smile. "We are almost through here, Miss Lambert can wait for you in the ballroom."

Charlotte groaned even as Izzy laughed and allowed herself to be released. "Fine," Charlotte grumbled, "but I do so hate politeness."

"We know," her brother Charles assured her without reserve. "But it takes longer if you moan about it, so let's get on with it, eh?"

Charlotte looked ready and keen to argue with her older brother, but her father intervened with a quick, "Enough, Charlotte."

It settled her, but only just.

Izzy clamped down on her lip as her parents escorted her into the ballroom.

Events with the Wright family were so very entertaining.

"I don't know what anybody sees in that girl," Izzy's mother mumbled as they moved into the fine and very full ballroom.

Izzy jerked to look at her mother. "Mama! You adore Charlotte!"

Her mother met her gaze without concern. "I know. And I have no idea why."

Izzy chortled a laugh and nodded to her parents as she parted from them, moving towards the small cluster of her friends already gathering.

Kitty and Sebastian were not here yet, as far as she could see, and she was grateful for it. She needed time.

Tony and Georgie suddenly crossed her path, and she beamed in delight at them.

"Nobody is ever that delighted to see me but you," Georgie informed her as she kissed her cheek. "It's always so refreshing."

Tony coughed once. "I beg your pardon? You find my reactions to seeing you somehow lacking?" He turned to Izzy and winked. "Good evening, cousin." He kissed her cheek as well.

Izzy laughed and patted his arm. "I am sure you greet her very well indeed, Tony."

"I should hope so," he retorted gruffly, giving his wife a sidelong look which she ignored.

Georgie looked around the room, then back at Izzy. "Where are the Mortons? I am so wanting to see Kitty again, and Tony says he will dance with her if she will be comfortable."

"I never said that," Tony broke in easily, "though I will gladly do so."

His wife rolled her eyes. "Then why bother saying you didn't say that, when you just did?"

"Because order of events is important."

"Not here."

"In some places."

"Name one."

Tony got a fiendish look in his eye. "Well, for one…"

"Please don't," Izzy laughed, waving her hand. "But I am sure Kitty would appreciate a dance, if she is comfortable."

Georgie sobered and nodded once. "Do you think she will be?"

Izzy sighed and shook her head. "I don't know, honestly. We have spent so much time having her grow comfortable with us that I haven't had time to explore just what it is that makes her so timid and fearful." She ducked her chin a little and looked at her gloves. "And I am a little worried that her continued association with us will only label her a spinster."

"With or without a capital S?" Tony asked playfully.

Izzy gave him a hard look, then laughed. "Either. Both. I don't suppose it matters."

Georgie shrugged. "Not really. But don't worry. She's associating with you, and you're the favorite anyway."

Izzy rolled her eyes and shook her head. "Ridiculous. You two go and dance, I'll go look for the Mortons, or at least Lady Hetty."

"Watch out for Miranda," Tony warned as he took Georgie's hand, "if she comes this evening. She's got a fiendish desire to meet Kitty. And see you."

"God save us," Izzy muttered, moving away.

Miranda Sterling was the last thing they needed on a night when she and Kitty would be entirely out of their comfort, and while she was much adored by all the Spinsters, it was an adoration rather like her mother's regard of Charlotte. They were none of them quite sure why it existed.

Lady Hetty Redgrave sat in her usual chair, and Izzy moved to sit by her, smiling fondly.

"Before you sit down, Isabella," Lady Hetty said, holding out a hand, "would you mind terribly asking if my wrap might be fetched for me? There is a draft tonight, and I find myself too chilled."

Izzy nodded, taking the older woman's hand. "Of course, Lady Hetty. I'll only be a moment."

Lady Hetty smiled with surprising warmth. "You are a dear. You must sit beside me when you return. I cannot abide the others."

"Yes, you can," Izzy laughed, squeezing the hand she held.

Lady Hetty gave her a dubious look that made Izzy laugh again.

"May I bring my friend Kitty Morton to sit with us?" Izzy asked. "It's her first Season, and I'm to mentor her. She is a very sweet girl, but so very timid."

"Oh, the poor chick," Lady Hetty clucked softly. "Yes, indeed, bring her along. I should be happy to assist you there."

"Thank you, Lady Hetty." She turned and quickly made for the door where a servant stood, only to suddenly see Sebastian and Kitty Morton entering.

Kitty looked utterly terrified but brightened considerably at seeing Izzy. "Izzy!"

Sebastian smiled and bowed in greeting.

"Oh, don't you look perfectly charming!" Izzy praised, taking

Kitty's hands. "You are radiant, Kitty!"

Kitty blushed on the spot and averted her eyes, though she smiled.

"Ah, I've made you uncomfortable," Izzy said gently, trying for apologetic. "I am sorry, dear, but praise must be expected."

"That's what Sebastian says," Kitty all but whispered, smiling up at her brother.

"He is right," Izzy confirmed. "In this case, at least."

Sebastian raised a brow at her. "In this case?"

Izzy shook her head. "Sweeping declarations are for children, Mr. Morton, not adults," she retorted, glancing at him quickly. She returned her focus to Kitty. "Take a seat by Lady Hetty over there. Your brother knows her and may make introductions. I am fetching her wrap, and I'll only be a moment."

"You?" Sebastian asked with a curious tilt to his head. "Not a servant?"

"I mean to have a servant do so," Izzy said quickly, moving past. "I only mean to inform them."

She hurried to do so, not bothering to see if they did as she suggested. The footman at the door was more than usually accommodating, and assured Izzy he would bring it to Lady Hetty himself.

Clearly, the Wrights had rather intelligent servants.

Her duty done, Izzy hurried back to her corner, eager to begin her evening with Kitty and get on with her own business.

"Miss Lambert."

She bit back a groan as Charlotte's brother stepped into her path, smiling with his usual friendliness. "Mr. Wright."

"I wonder if you might do me the greatest of favors," he began, clasping his hands behind his back.

Izzy exhaled, her shoulders drooping, and she nodded. "Of course. What can I do?"

Charles's smile spread. "Charlotte had nothing to drink between greeting our guests and gathering her followers, and our mother is concerned. I would take something to her myself, but I am promised to dance with Catherine Burns, and you know how impatient she can be."

Izzy opened her mouth to reply, but Charles was already gone, turning to the dance floor, Catherine Burns flocking to his side.

There was nothing for it, then.

Fixing her most pleasant smile on her face, Izzy moved across the ballroom, getting jostled momentarily by a few over-exuberant would-be dancers, and found a footman bearing a tray of beverages in a corner.

She plucked one off with a nod at him and hurried as quickly as she could over to Charlotte, pushing through her admirers gently. Only one, Michael Sandford, paid Izzy any attention, and he smiled very warmly and helped her get through the throng.

Charlotte beamed at her without reserve, which made the rest of the men consider Izzy with a new light. "My dear, sweet Izzy! What a thoughtful creature you are! I am so very parched, and none of these idiots thought to bring me anything at all." She scowled at the men around her, and took the glass from Izzy, drinking deeply even as the men began to protest and apologize as one.

"Funny how we should think of such things when she never says so," Michael murmured for Izzy's ears alone.

She fought a giggle, giving him a quick look. Michael had been a friend of the Wrights for ages and was always so kind and considerate with the rest of the Spinsters. It puzzled her that he should have said 'we', including himself, when, as far as she knew, Charlotte had never given him the slightest encouragement. Yet, the pair of them were thick as thieves when it suited her, and their friendship had been a constant throughout her years of shameless flirtation. It seems Charlotte only felt friendship for him, however.

Poor man.

"I say, Miss Lambert," one of the others said. "You're a good sort. Fetch me one, will you? I'll lose my spot if I go myself."

"And I, Miss Lambert!"

"I would not mind a glass."

"Now, see here," Michael tried to interject, but the others paid him no mind.

Charlotte rolled her eyes. "She is not my servant, you fools. She most certainly will *not* go…"

"I don't mind," Izzy managed, her cheeks flaming. "Truly. It is a short walk, and Mr. Graves does have a decent position at your left arm. He mustn't give that up."

The others chuckled, and Charlotte looked pained through her smile.

Izzy ignored it, and Michael's gentle hand upon her arm, and moved back to the footman. She took three glasses from him, ignoring his gaze, and returned to the group.

Who then requested another four drinks, which sent her back to the footman, who now followed her, for which she was most grateful. She could carry three, but four could have been catastrophic.

Charlotte widened her eyes meaningfully at Izzy this time, and Izzy took the hint, ducking away before anyone else could request refreshment of her. Michael nodded his approval, and Izzy nodded in return.

"I say, Miss Lambert..."

Izzy pressed her tongue against her teeth as she stopped and turned with a smile to Mr. Greensley, who had always been particularly kind to her, if a bit dismissive. "Mr. Greensley."

"I hate to trouble you," he said with the same polite smile everyone else wore around her. "Miss Sophia Chambers has grown quite overheated in this room and has no fan to relieve her. I wonder if you might speak to the Wrights about the heat. I do not know them well enough to express any complaints, and..."

"Of course, of course," Izzy replied at once, her irritation turning to concern. "Is she all right? Is there anything I can do?"

Mr. Greensley smiled further. "Oh, if you wouldn't mind, I think..."

"Miss Lambert, I am sorry to say, is dancing the next with me," a low voice interrupted beside them, "and the time has come to begin. I believe you will find a servant not ten feet behind you, and they would be perfectly willing to do as you bid."

Izzy turned quickly to see Sebastian there, looking barely polite.

Mr. Greensley swallowed uncomfortably. "Of course. My apologies."

Izzy's face warmed, and she removed the fan from her wrist. "Take this to her, Mr. Greensley. It will help."

His smile returned, and he nodded as he took it. "Thank you,

Miss Lambert."

Sebastian put a hand at her elbow and turned her away from him, moving quickly towards the dance.

"Why do I suddenly feel as though I have done something terribly wrong?" Izzy muttered, her eyes squarely ahead. "And that I am about to be scolded?"

"It is not in me to scold you," he responded, his voice tight. "Though I would be so inclined."

Izzy scowled up at him as they lined up with the others. "For what? Doing a service?"

"Becoming a service," he corrected, bowing with the others. "I saw the entire thing, Miss Lambert, and the abuse of your goodness irritates me."

Abuse? Izzy coughed in surprise and began the first movements of the dance. "There was no such thing! I like being nice, Mr. Morton."

Sebastian gave her a curious look. "And do you like everyone and their aunt taking advantage of you?" he asked, his tone mild.

"They don't..." she protested.

"They do," he overrode. "They quite literally just did."

Izzy felt an unusual curl of anger in her stomach, and she raised her chin in defiance. "They didn't do anything differently than what you did."

Sebastian chuckled, seeming truly amused by her accusation. "Oh, I know I blatantly took advantage of you, and you should have told me to go to the devil."

Now she frowned. "But I don't want you to go to the devil."

His eyes rolled as they joined for the next movement. "It's a phrase, Isabella. For heaven's sake, you are not this naïve, I see it in your eyes."

No, she was not. She knew very well what she allowed and how it tended to grow the more she gave in.

"I'm sorry," she murmured, lowering her eyes as he turned her.

"Don't apologize, for God's sake," he told her softly, bringing her eyes up to his.

His smile encouraged her to smile back.

"I only wish you wouldn't be quite so biddable," he continued.

"You and Georgie both," Izzy laughed, the tension within her easing slightly.

"I knew I liked her." He smiled more fully and parted from her as the dance continued.

Izzy bit the inside of her lip, then steeled herself when they met once more. "I wonder, though, Mr. Morton, if you might consider doing me a favor, given that I did not tell you to go to the devil…"

Chapter Eleven

A daring venture must be carefully considered from all aspects. There is absolutely no sense in rushing into something that may prove fraught with risks. Then again, there is something to be said for trusting an impulse...

-The Spinster Chronicles, 2 March 1816

It was the most bizarre idea he'd ever heard of.

Truly, there was absolute madness in it. So why was he actually considering it?

Sebastian shook his head to himself, his brow furrowing as if to further scold. It wasn't *that* bizarre, really. He'd already engaged in it before the suggestion had been made, and so, from that side, he could clearly see the logic behind it. Well, what little logic there was to it, at any rate. And he would never have told a lady that her notion was incredulous and nearly foolhardy.

But...

An illustrator? Him? His artistry only extended as far as his imagination, and frequently fell short of it. Oh, he could sketch roughly without much disappointment, right enough, and his mother had always asked him to draw things for her, but he had always considered his mother to be particularly biased where his abilities were concerned.

He almost never drew for others to see, and those who had seen had made little enough comment on it.

It was really more of a hobby, a habit, something to alleviate stress and engage his mind.

But to put such a thing to use in a way that could help another, and, in fact, earn himself a wage…

Not that he needed a wage, but if all went well, and according to plan, he could earn some slight wage, and there would certainly be a use for it, either in Kitty's pin money for frocks or some other aspect of their life that could benefit. If he were to be doing more drawing and illustrations, the wages could just as easily be put back into further supplies.

He'd have to take far greater care with his drawings, if they were to be widely published and seen by so many.

Provided he did this at all, which was still up for debate.

He could tell that his answer hadn't pleased Izzy, but as he had not refused her outright, she had not murmured a word of complaint, or looked so very disappointed. Not that she would have complained anyway, as it seemed she never did, but surely there would have been some sign of distress or disheartening.

But no, all he had done was tell her that he would have to think on it, and her recovery had been expertly managed.

"Of course you do," she had said almost at once. 'Almost' because there had been a delay, a hesitation that spoke of disappointment. But these books were her dream and not his. So logically, it should only follow that he would not have the same level of enthusiasm or excitement as she did.

It had occurred to Sebastian that an apology for her disappointment might have been warranted, but before he could properly formulate such a thing, Izzy had continued.

"Of course," she'd said again. "And it is only right that you should. I only ask that you consider it, and send me word of your decision?"

Her expression had been so innocently eager, despite her expressed understanding of his hesitation, that he had almost given in that very moment. Instead, he had agreed and insisted he would do so as soon as possible.

It had been two days, and he was still at war with himself. Much longer and it would be unfair to Izzy. Surely the indecision was an answer itself, was it not? To be without definitive answer after days of consideration must speak of a lack of sufficient interest in the proposed venture.

And yet...

The thought of illustrating Izzy's delightful stories sent his fingers tingling with a strange excitement, and an accompanying a warmth spreading through him. He needed no occupation other than the army, and had no wish for it, but the idea of something else to divert him, and a part of him that satisfied him so, was a rather tempting one.

Why, then, should he hesitate?

He knew the answer, of course. He was not in the habit of giving in to his own pleasure when it did not provide logical and definitive reasoning in a way that would benefit his future.

And this had no promise whatsoever.

Other than spending more time with Isabella Lambert, which, while neither logical nor definitive, seemed a good enough reason.

"Sebastian?"

He looked up, breaking out of his reverie, to find his sister standing in the doorway of the drawing room, looking somehow both older and younger than she should. Her recent forays into Society had given her as much excitement as they had anxiety, though she still had yet to speak more than a handful of words. He had hope that soon she might break out even a little more and give herself more of a chance for enjoyment.

Izzy had already been the means of great improvement there, and for that alone he would be grateful and should accept her offer.

But gratitude was not appreciated when it led to indebtedness rather than true motivation of a deed, and he respected Izzy too much to treat her so.

"Good afternoon, Mouse," Sebastian teased, setting his sketchpad aside. "Come in."

She smiled and came into the room, sitting in the chair beside him. She eyed his sketch briefly. "What are you drawing?"

He glanced at it, then back at her. "A duck in a pond, strangely enough."

Kitty wrinkled her nose up and held out a hand. "May I see?"

He shrugged and gave it to her, then crossed a leg over his knee,

126

his hands folding over the top. "It's not done, obviously. I need to work on the wing a bit more."

"Shh," Kitty scolded without hesitation, smiling softly.

Sebastian chuckled and held up an apologetic hand.

His sister's wide blue eyes rose to his, her smile growing. "Sebastian, this is delightful!"

He matched her grin. "Really?"

"Yes!" she insisted. She scooted to the edge of the chair, her hands gripping his pad. "Yes, really! You know how talented you are, surely."

Again, he shrugged, reaching for the book. "I know I am better than some, but as to talent…"

She rapped his hands with the book, then handed it to him. "Sebastian!"

"What?" he replied in the same screeching tone she had employed, making her giggle.

Kitty sobered quickly, giving him a pitying look she could only have learned from their mother. "Do you remember when you were at school and you would send me sketches?"

Sebastian sat back, smiling to himself, surprised at her recollection. "I do, but I had forgotten until just now."

"I still have them," she told him in the soft tone she usually employed during one of her shy moments.

She could not have stunned him more had she told him she had sung an aria for a roomful of guests. He stared at her with wide eyes, unable to do anything more than blink, and even that was unsteady.

He fought for a swallow, then cleared his throat. "Do you really?"

She blushed and nodded, looking away and tucking one of her dark ringlets behind her ear. "I do. Up in my chest. It's where I keep all my precious things."

His drawings for her were precious? Were treasured enough to be kept and valued above other possessions?

It touched him more than he had ability to express.

"Refresh my memory," he finally managed to say. "What did I draw for you?"

Kitty smiled and looked back at him. "Me. As a mouse."

Now Sebastian laughed in earnest, the memories flooding back. "Ah, yes. For my little mouse of a sister, I turned you into a mouse."

"And quite well, too, I might add!" Kitty proclaimed. "You even gave me ribbons and bows and frilly dresses. There was one with a pinafore to match the one I wore at Christmas when you were home."

Strangely enough, that one he remembered. It had taken him ages to recollect the details properly, and he had been sketching Kitty as often as he could when he was home that Christmas. She had been so proud of her new pinafore and how it had swished and spun when she twirled and had shown it off to Sebastian repeatedly. As he recalled, their mother had had a trying enough time getting Kitty to take the thing off at night and not to wear it again the very next morning.

If memory served him right, Kitty had won that battle.

One of the very few she cared enough to fight.

"I don't think I could draw you as a mouse now, Mouse," Sebastian told his sister fondly, reaching out a hand to her.

She placed her hand in his and gave him a teasing smile. "No?"

He shook his head slowly, returning her smile. "No."

"Why not?"

"In truth, you're far too pretty to be a mouse."

Kitty scoffed softly and rolled her eyes, yanking her hand out of his hold before smacking his arm lightly. "I am no such thing."

Sebastian gave her a severe look. "If I am not permitted to be modest about my artistic abilities, then you are likewise forbidden to be modest about your looks. You are a beautiful young woman, and that is as plain a truth as ever I lived."

Now his sister blushed and looked down at her hands, which sat tightly gripped in her lap. Then she surprised him by raising her gaze to his with an almost steady expression, her color still high. "And you should know that were you not determined to be a soldier, you could be an artist. And before you call me biased, do recall that I have spent a good while surrounded by brilliant works of art in our gallery and was instructed in many more. I do know what artistic talent looks like. And you have it, brother."

Her tone was so firm, so confident, and so stern that he could only stare at her for several heartbeats. Where had this measure of strength come from?

It suited her. And it suited her well.

Kitty smiled at him again, then sat back against her chair. "And it is wonderful to see you drawing so much again. I haven't seen you do so since I've come to London. I was worried that perhaps you no longer did."

"Well, I won't pretend that it is a frequent occupation of my time anymore," he told her, returning to the sketch, "but I do find it relaxes me."

"The way my playing relaxes me, I suppose," Kitty mused aloud, drumming her fingers on the armrest of her chair.

He nodded in thought as he worked on improving the wing of the duck. "Very possible, yes." He glanced up at her, grinning quickly. "I did happen to hear a bit of your practice today. It's getting very good."

Amazingly, his sister didn't blush any further, but she did stare with wider eyes before swallowing and dipping her chin. "Thank you," she half-whispered.

Sebastian chuckled to himself and shook his head. "You're getting better at accepting compliments, Mouse. Still not quite accomplished at that, though."

"No, and I think it would be a mark of good breeding not to be," she shot back.

"Perhaps you're right." He returned once more to the sketch, focusing with greater intent.

It was crucial that he get this right, that he provide work that was accomplished and could enhance the stories Izzy would tell.

It had to be good enough.

It had to.

And therein, he supposed, was his answer.

He paused in his sketching, then looked up at his sister. "Kitty… I have something to tell you, but it is a matter of the utmost secrecy."

He was going to refuse her.

She knew it, she could feel it in the pit of her stomach, and it kept reverberating in her mind like the sound of a bell.

Actually, her mind rather felt like a bell these days. The inside of one, anyway. Thoughts bounced off of the edges and caused almost painful vibrations with their pounding, and she was quite sure she would go mad sooner or later.

It had been three days, and she hadn't heard from him. Surely that was time enough, and a lack of response spoke volumes. She knew it. She knew she had been too forward to ask Sebastian to illustrate for her stories, too presumptuous to take advantage of a skill she knew he possessed. What if he didn't wish people to know he had artistic abilities? What if he was too private to share such matters with the world?

What if he simply did not want to participate and didn't have the heart to tell her? He was too polite to leave her with nothing. He would respond eventually, but the longer it took, the more dread she felt.

She didn't know anyone else who would be willing to illustrate for her and not charge an exorbitant fee.

Granted, she hadn't mentioned anything financial with Sebastian during their dance, as it seemed a poor place to discuss something so mercenary, but it was entirely possible that he might wish for more specifics there before committing.

Whatever his reasoning, he was surely entitled to them, and she had every reason in the world to be embarrassed. The fact that she was already feeling embarrassed in a room filled with her best friends who knew nothing of her embarrassment was only making things infinitely worse. Thankfully, the room was filled with conversation, and she did not need to participate for the time being.

"All I want to know," Elinor was saying in her rather juvenile way, "is why Kitty Morton can come and go as she pleases with us but isn't being recruited as one of us."

Izzy glanced over at her quickly, grateful Kitty hadn't arrived yet. Elinor hadn't quite grown comfortable with Kitty joining them, and they were all aware that Elinor was struggling, and failing, to hide the jealousy that she was no longer the only young member of their group. And Kitty happened to be more likable than Elinor, which she knew all too well.

"Elinor, I am not going over this again," Charlotte snapped without patience. "Kitty Morton has been temporarily adopted by us until she gains her footing. Then, I have no doubt, she will find better friends and possibly even a husband and will have no further need for us. She is *not* a spinster, and she will not *be* a spinster at any given time."

Elinor sniffed haughtily. "With or without a capital S?"

"Either!" at least three of them said.

Georgie rolled her eyes and sipped her tea, then sighed. "Oh, bless you, Izzy, for having the tea made properly. It is just what I needed after this morning."

Prue tsked sympathetically. "Were you i-ill again, dear?"

"Every morning," Georgie answered with a shudder. "I do so hate being ill. But I hate to say it, I am growing accustomed to the routine."

Charlotte made a face and munched on a biscuit. "If I am going to be ill when I am with child, I will not be populating this world in any remarkable way whatsoever. I will do my duty to my husband and his ancestors by providing necessary progeny, but only an heir and a spare. Perhaps not even the spare, if the heir is hale enough."

Georgie looked at Charlotte in amusement. "Somehow, Charlotte, I highly doubt that you will have control enough to limit yourself thusly."

Charlotte returned her look in utter bafflement. "I beg your pardon, I am the most controlled of all women."

Snickering filled the room, and Charlotte glared at them all, before returning to Georgie.

"I will have you know, Georgiana," Charlotte insisted with all prim firmness, "that it will be quite simple. One and done. No need to continue on as though we intend to breed like rabbits. There can be nothing my future husband could do that would induce me to allow myself to be subjected to such suffering."

"I could think of a few things," Prue muttered under her breath, smiling to herself.

Georgie looked at her in outright delight and the two shared a knowing look, and a grin, both of their cheeks flushing.

Izzy coughed in surprise at Prue's comment, but as she had no

131

basis for understanding, she could not add anything to the conversation.

More's the pity.

Charlotte blessedly missed Prue's statement, but did not miss the look between the two married women in the room and eyed them suspiciously.

Edith, Izzy noticed, did not have anything to share on the topic, either.

Curious.

"Is Kitty joining us today?" Grace asked of no one in particular, straightening her already perfect posture into an almost unnatural stiffness, though her smile could not have been more natural. Or perfect.

Such was the way of Grace Morledge.

Izzy swallowed and nodded once. "Yes, she ought to be. I've been thinking we might want to introduce her to some other young women her age, if we know any that might suit."

Elinor raised her hand, widening her eyes in obvious suggestion.

"Suit, dear," Charlotte reminded Elinor in a would-be sweet tone. "Young ladies that would *suit*. You can't decide if you're jealous of the dear or not. She's a mouse, you're a cat. You most certainly would *not* suit."

"Why not?" Elinor demanded, slapping her formerly raised hand on her leg. "I like her, and I am perfectly suitable!"

"Amelia Perry?" Prue suggested without a stammer in a surprisingly loud voice, keeping her gaze on Izzy.

Elinor stared at Izzy in shock, while Charlotte beamed like a proud mother.

Izzy nodded gratefully. "She would be lovely. I was also thinking of Alice Sterling. Georgie, what would you say to that?"

"It may be difficult to say," Georgie replied with a slight wrinkle to her nose. "She's rather outspoken compared to Kitty, and it might..."

"Begging your pardon, Miss Lambert," Collins intoned from the doorway.

Each of the Spinsters turned to him, which had to be an unnerving prospect for the older man, but he did not react in the slightest.

"Yes?" Izzy replied, sitting up straighter.

"Miss Morton has just arrived and will be here momentarily," Collins went on. "But Mr. Morton would like a word before he leaves."

The room went utterly silent, and Izzy could feel the stares of the others upon her.

"He *what?*" Charlotte suddenly blurted.

"Oh my," Grace said, eyes wide. "What could that be?"

"Surely, it's about Kitty," Georgie assured them.

"Kitty would likely *be* there for that," Elinor insisted.

"Thank you, Collins," Izzy murmured, her face flaming. "You may put him…"

"He is in the blue room, Miss Lambert," Collins gently overrode before nodding and leaving the room.

This was it. This was where he would tell her he could not do this, and she would somehow have to hide her disappointment. She'd never been very good at that.

She rose and tried to hide the fact that her breathing was unsteady.

"What," Charlotte began without any hint of discretion, "could Mr. Morton want with you, Izzy?"

"What aren't you telling us?" Elinor demanded in chorus.

"A word?" Grace asked with a bemused smile. "What *kind* of a word?"

"Likely about Kitty," Edith insisted, widening her eyes meaningfully. "Honestly…"

"Izzy," Georgie murmured gently, her voice somehow clearer to Izzy than the others. "A chaperone?"

Izzy looked at her cousin for a long moment, then lifted her eyes to Edith. "Edith, would you mind?"

Edith smirked a little and glanced around at the others. "Do I have chaperone branded across my forehead?"

Charlotte snorted softly. "You're a widow, dear. Chaperone is inherent in the title."

"I wish I'd known that before I became one," Edith muttered as she shook her head, rising to join Izzy.

"Why?" Grace laughed. "Would you have changed things?"

Edith gave her a bewildered look. "Oh, Lord, no," she said at once, her brogue rolling out proudly. "I would simply have found a second husband straightaway."

The room snickered as Edith took Izzy's arm and led her from the room.

"I am so sorry, Edith," Izzy whispered when they were alone. "I don't mean to cause you grief. I know I'm being a bother, but..."

Edith sobered at once and held Izzy's arm tighter. "Not even a little bit, lass. I was only trying to give them something else to blather on about. The only person I would hate to chaperone is Elinor, and only because I would likely have to bodily restrain her from striking the poor man, and I would hate to be so engaged."

Izzy breathed a sigh of relief and managed a smile. "Thank you."

Edith nodded in an almost regal fashion, then leaned close. "Do *you* know what Mr. Morton wants?"

Izzy nodded quickly, swallowing. "You can't tell anyone."

"Of course," came the simple reply.

But it wasn't that simple.

Which was why she had chosen Edith. Edith wouldn't feel the need to discuss it much further and would not be extreme or excitable about any of it. Georgie would have been the natural choice, as her cousin and best friend, but Georgie knew her too well, and would have too many opinions and expectations.

It would be too easy to let her down.

Kitty passed them as they moved to meet Sebastian, and she smiled and waved at them, but said nothing else. No hint of shyness or nerves, and an air of excitement about her.

Edith and Izzy shared an amused look. Clearly, Kitty Morton was coming along well.

They entered the drawing room and Sebastian rose the moment he saw them, a fixed smile of politeness on his handsome features.

Handsome? Oh dear, she could *not* think such things just as he was going to refuse to help her. It would only make things worse.

"Lady Edith," Sebastian murmured with a polite bow. "Miss Lambert."

They both curtseyed in response, and then Edith released Izzy's arm. "I'll just sit over here for propriety's sake and leave you to it. Ignore me, please."

Sebastian watched her with furrowed brow as she moved to the chair she'd indicated, then glanced at Izzy. "Does she know?" he asked in a very soft voice.

Izzy shook her head quickly. "But she will soon, I trust," she managed, somehow avoiding any squeaks of nerves. She folded her hands before her in what was hopefully a calm manner. "If that is what you came to discuss."

Sebastian nodded once. "It is. Izzy... Miss Lambert..."

"Izzy will do, as I've said," she reminded him gently, though her heart lurched with it.

He nodded again, his mouth curving in a smile. "I've thought about what you offered, and thought it deserved all due consideration."

She felt her head move in a nod, but her heart filled with dread.

Here it would be. Here would be the most polite refusal known to man.

"And I find that I do want to provide the illustrations for your stories."

Izzy blinked once, then blinked again.

That did not sound like a refusal to her ears. She played it again in her mind, then stilled as the words sunk in.

He *what?*

He *wanted* to do her illustrations? He wanted to help her chances to be published? He wanted to risk failure in a wild scheme with her?

He couldn't... could he?

"You do?" she eventually gasped, far later than she should have. "You really want to?"

Now his smile turned real and genuine, his eyes brightening. "Yes, I really do. I didn't even realize I'd wanted to until... Well, I was drawing ducks, of all things, and I wondered what kind of stories you had with ducks."

"I have a few," she assured him quickly, her nerves vanishing in the face of outright excitement. "And I can do more. Ducks are very popular."

He laughed once and nodded. "I know you have a meeting of

the Spinsters now, so I won't take up your time by getting into details, but... Perhaps I can work up some particular concepts of certain animals, and we can see what styles you like?"

"Yes!" Izzy cried, laughing now herself. "Yes, I would love to see that. Thank you, Sebastian. I... Well, I thought you were going to refuse me, honestly."

"I don't see how anybody could refuse you, Izzy," he told her, his tone taking on a gentleness that warmed her toes.

Her breath caught, and she stared at him far too long. He *was* a handsome man. Very much so. And when he smiled like that...

Sebastian cleared his throat and stepped back. "Excellent. I will leave the two of you to return to whatever it is you Spinsters do when gathered *en masse*. I'll be back to fetch my sister in two hours, if that will be sufficient?"

"It should be," Izzy assured him, still giddy. "It won't take long. Whatever it is."

He grinned swiftly, then bowed once more. "Lovely to see you, Miss Lambert. Lady Edith."

Edith waved a hand at him. "Good day, Mr. Morton."

Izzy would never admit it, but she would swear that she saw him wink at her as he passed. She waited until his footsteps were no longer audible, then sighed again.

"Well," Edith said slowly, rising and coming over to her.

Izzy glanced at her, wary and worried.

Edith beamed. "You're writing stories? That is the most enchanting thing I have ever heard. And Mr. Morton is illustrating? How delightful! I am so pleased for you, Izzy!"

"Truly?" Izzy took Edith's hand and squeezed hard. "Truly, Edith?"

"No, I just said that because it's polite, and he is handsome," Edith retorted with a soft snort. "Yes, lass, truly." She hugged her quickly, then pulled back. "I won't say a single word. But you may confide in me, if ever you need."

"Thank you." Izzy exhaled slowly, then turned for the door. "Let's go back, although I have no idea how I will keep them from asking me what it was all about. Or how my heart will stop racing."

Edith hummed a laugh. "Leave it to me, Izzy. Give me a topic to distract them with."

Izzy paused in thought as they moved to the room. "Alice Sterling. She's to be at the Staffords' party on Wednesday."

"Perfect." Edith tossed her dark hair, then strode with Izzy into the parlor again. "Are you sure Alice Sterling wouldn't rather get away from her brothers at the Staffords'? Surely we can take her under our wing, too. If only to get her away from Hugh."

"Capital idea!" Elinor chimed, sounding almost as though she were snarling at the thought.

Izzy didn't need to answer, as everyone else had an opinion, and she sat carefully in her seat, ignoring how Georgie stared at her.

He hadn't refused her. He'd *accepted*.

She couldn't look delighted now, but her mind was already whirling with possibilities. This could work, she thought to herself. This could actually and truly work.

And there was no knowing what possibilities that could bring.

Chapter Twelve

———— ❦ ————

One's guest list should never be as extensive as one's ambitions. There is nothing worse than an overcrowded room, unless one wishes to be unobserved. Many eyes make for many missed things.

-The Spinster Chronicles, 19 August 1817

"Lord, did they invite *everyone* in London for this?"

Izzy grinned at Charlotte as they entered the Stafford ballroom, which was tastefully lit and simply decorated, no doubt to accommodate more guests. The music was already playing, and the room was bustling, though dancing had yet to begin.

"The Season has not started yet," Izzy reminded her as she adjusted a coppery ringlet that was destined to fall from its curled state by the end of the night.

Charlotte snorted softly. "Tell that to this room."

"There aren't *that* many people in London, by comparison," Izzy mused aloud, glancing about the room. "I think the ballroom is smaller than others, so it only looks more crowded."

"Annabelle Stafford would do anything in the world to make it seem as though she were inestimably popular," Charlotte retorted with brusque swiftness. "It would not surprise me in the least if she pushed the walls of this room together herself for this event to cram everyone in. They'll call it a crush, and she'll be delighted."

Izzy shook her head, amused against her will, and sighed. "Well, that does not mean we cannot enjoy ourselves."

Charlotte gave her a look. "I always enjoy myself. But it will make things infinitely more difficult for a certain sweet girl we both adore."

That sobered Izzy at once. Kitty would certainly be intimidated by a room quite literally bursting with people, most of whom she didn't know. She was doing so well with the Spinsters, but she had yet to be tested at an event of this magnitude.

"We'll close ranks, if we must," Izzy assured Charlotte, nodding to assure herself as well. "I am sure Annabelle would accommodate whatever we need."

"I am not at all sure she would," Charlotte muttered with a dark look. "I've never liked Annabelle Stafford, and I don't intend to start today."

"Why in the world did you accept her invitation, then?" Izzy laughed.

Charlotte raised a knowing brow. "Because she glares in outright jealousy at the attention I collect so easily, and it's the most charming sort of fun. I can never resist. And I have it on good authority that her brother George finds me utterly irresistible." She quirked her brows before gliding away with an emphatic swish of her gold skirts, the way parting before her, as it tended to do.

Izzy covered her mouth on a giggle, then turned the opposite way to find one of the others.

Annabelle Stafford had truly made a life for herself, and it was plain to see. While Charlotte did not care for her at all, Izzy had once been rather close with Annabelle. Before her wedding to the promising and dashing Mr. Stafford, of course. Back then, Annabelle King, as she had been known, had been widely considered a fair catch for any man, despite only a middling fortune. There had been some concern for her being a social climber, but what young woman was not eager to improve her station in life and her standing in Society? Those were all forgiven her, as she was so engaging as to make disliking her nearly impossible. Except for Charlotte, it seemed.

No surprise there.

Even Charlotte had tolerated her in the beginning, however, though not with any good graces. And then after what had happened between Annabelle and Izzy… Well, Charlotte had not been particularly forgiving, despite the minor nature of it all, and refused to view Annabelle in any favorable light after all that.

It was silly, even Izzy didn't think about it anymore.

Most of the time.

Lady Hetty sat in a chair near a large window, her dark gown nearly the color of the night sky, and Izzy smiled warmly as she approached her.

"Lady Hetty," she greeted with a curtsey. "I didn't expect to see you here this evening."

The elderly woman harrumphed and tapped her walking stick against the ground. "Where else should I be, Isabella? 'Tis not yet time for my deathbed, or so Dr. Folsom informs me."

Izzy chuckled and sat down beside her. "And until it is, you will go to everything, is that it?"

"Not everything, surely," Lady Hetty protested as she watched the people about her. "I cannot stand some people and will never attend on them."

"But you will attend for Annabelle Stafford?" Izzy pressed.

Now Lady Hetty sputtered loudly. "Not at all, I cannot abide her."

"Yet here you are."

Lady Hetty's mouth curved. "I had to see for myself what sort of people the girl would bring into her home, and how she would parade her handsome husband about. People are a spectacle, Isabella, and I adore the view at times."

Izzy laughed in surprise and leaned closer to the older woman. "Then I should request some tea cakes be brought to you so that you might eat your cake and have your cake as well."

A wheezing, cackling laughter erupted from Lady Hetty, and she grinned at Izzy without reserve. "Well done, my dear, well done indeed. I do so love my cake."

"I do hope you will leave some cake for me," a pleasant male voice said near them.

Izzy turned in her chair to see Lieutenant Henshaw standing behind them, smiling warmly. "Lieutenant Henshaw! What a delightful surprise, we have missed you dreadfully since you went away."

He bowed in acknowledgement. "And I have missed my

delightful friends in return, Miss Lambert. Alas, the army does not care so very much about my feelings and my friends, and much prefers my fealty instead."

"A well put turn of phrase, Lieutenant," Lady Hetty praised, her chin dipping in a rare sign of approval.

He bowed to her as well. "Thank you, my lady. I do hope it has impressed you to the extent that you will dance with me this evening."

"Oh, you silly rogue," she protested, waving a lace kerchief at him. "Dancing at my age, indeed."

Henshaw grinned without shame. "I will have a dance one day, Lady Hetty, and you will allow me."

"Only if you're dancing me to the grave, sir."

"You will undoubtedly outlive us all, my lady, and well I think you know it." He gave her a friendly wink, then bowed as Grace approached them.

"Good evening, Lieutenant," Grace greeted, looking radiant in cream silk and blue ribbons. "Lady Hetty. Izzy." She heaved a sigh and sat beside Izzy, her shoulders drooping.

Izzy peered at her with concern. "Something wrong, Grace?"

Grace's dark eyes met Izzy's, and a slight wrinkle appeared between her perfect brows. "My father wrote to me. He is most distressed that I have no suitors and no prospects for matrimony. According to him, there must be something lacking in my behavior to account for this, and it must be remedied at once."

Lady Hetty rolled her eyes and mumbled under her breath, while Izzy only reached out and took her friend's hand.

"Preposterous," Henshaw insisted, his brow darkening. "And I invite you to tell him I said so. That's Lieutenant, as in an officer, and Henshaw, one N, no E at the end."

Grace looked up at him wryly. "Unless you are willing to back that up with a proposal, Henshaw, I doubt my father would care."

Henshaw smiled gently and bowed again. "The honor would be mine, Miss Morledge, but I do not have the prospects worthy of you, and it would likely only cause more of a difficulty for your father."

Grace heaved a sigh. "I know. But some days, I think it would be quite lovely to elope and be cut off."

"If you get in such a fit and are sincere in your consideration, I humbly volunteer," he told her with a surprisingly benevolent air.

"As the bridegroom or my escape driver?" Grace asked, perfect lips curving in amusement.

Henshaw shrugged. "Whichever serves your purpose best."

"Very noble, I am sure," Izzy muttered good-naturedly.

Henshaw chuckled and started to respond when another voice spoke.

"If Henshaw is anything at any time, you can be sure it is noble."

Izzy prayed her cheeks would keep from flushing as she turned with the others to see Sebastian and Kitty arriving to their group, barely managing to keep her smile contained.

He looked marvelous in the finery of eveningwear, and it did nothing to help her sudden weakness in the face of his handsomeness, which she had often reflected on since they had spoken last.

She quickly turned her attention to Kitty, whose timid smile made her ache. The girl was a picture of loveliness in a pale pink that perfectly matched the color of her cheeks at the moment. She would attract a great deal of attention tonight, if she were not mindful.

Izzy rose and smiled at them. "Mr. Morton, Miss Morton, it is wonderful to see you both."

"You always say it's wonderful to see everyone," Lady Hetty pointed out.

Grace snickered and Izzy turned to the older woman in exasperation. "I do not!"

"Yes, you do," the majority of the others said.

Lady Hetty gave her a sympathetic look. "It's a lovely habit, but it does tend to lessen the significance of it."

"I believe Miss Lambert to genuinely be pleased to see my sister, Lady Hetty," Sebastian told her with a polite incline of his head. "I am quite sure it is only polite to include me in her stated pleasure as well."

Izzy glared at him playfully, but the others laughed.

Henshaw, oddly enough, was rather quiet for the moment.

Then it occurred to Izzy that he might not know Kitty, despite being such great friends with Sebastian.

"Lieutenant Henshaw," she said at once, turning more towards him, "do you know Miss Morton?"

He shook his head, smiling very softly. "No, I have not had the pleasure."

Sebastian glanced at his friend quickly. "Apologies, Henshaw." He stepped slightly away from his sister and smiled at her proudly. "Kitty, may I present my friend, Lieutenant Edward Henshaw?"

Kitty's smile wobbled, but stayed, and she curtseyed prettily to Henshaw. "A pleasure, Lieutenant Henshaw. I've heard a great deal about you."

Izzy grinned at Henshaw, waiting for his response eagerly.

But Henshaw only bowed, the same smile on his face, and said, "And I about you, Miss Morton. Delighted."

Izzy did her best not to frown. That was it? There wasn't anything impolite about his answer; indeed, it was the gentlest, most pleased sounding response she had ever heard. But to not tease her about her brother? To not boast about whatever stories she might have heard?

Grace noticed as well and gave Izzy a quick look.

How curious.

"Oh, good, you're all gathered together," Georgie announced as she came to them all, looking a little pale.

"Georgie? What's wrong?" Izzy asked, looking around for Tony, who was nowhere to be seen.

Henshaw snapped out of his solitude and moved to take Georgie's arm. "Come, Georgie, let me get you a chair."

Georgie slapped at his arm. "Nonsense, I won't be but a moment."

"I thought you weren't coming," Izzy stated simply, smiling in polite concern.

"And I wouldn't if certain relations had kept to our arrangement," Georgie told her in a huff. "I wouldn't have had to set foot in the home of the one person I tend to despise on the same level as Eliza Davies, but it can't be helped. I shall leave the moment it will not reflect badly on me to do so." She turned suddenly and smiled with real warmth. "Come on, dear, you'll want to meet them."

"I want to meet everyone, Georgie, so that doesn't signify," came the response. A pleasant looking young woman stepped forward, her hair the color of aged gold and neatly coiffed, her dark eyes dancing with a mischievous light that Georgie would know all too well.

Georgie rolled her eyes, then sighed. "Alice Sterling, may I present, in order of position and not rank because it's too tiresome, Mr. Morton, Miss Morton, Lady Hetty Redgrave, my cousin Miss Lambert, Miss Morledge, and Lieutenant Henshaw." She exhaled roughly, smiling for effect.

"Don't forget me!" cried Charlotte as she hurried to them.

"And Miss Wright," Georgie finished without any enthusiasm whatsoever, "who is incapable of being left out of any situation at any given place or time."

Charlotte grinned a devious grin. "Only because I add so very much to everything."

Lady Hetty snickered, and Kitty stared at Charlotte as though torn between fascination and amusement.

"Right, duty done." Georgie looked at Izzy with a pleading smile. "Izzy, would you mind seeing to Alice while you're here? Francis and Janet couldn't come, I'm not particularly well, and all of us agreed Alice shouldn't come with Hugh."

Charlotte snorted without reserve, the rest of them nodding.

"So," Georgie went on, "now that introductions have been made, might I abandon Alice to your care, dear? Just this once?"

"Delighted to be so burdensome," Alice chimed in, not looking particularly upset by any of this.

"I'll see to it," Izzy assured her. "Go home."

"Where's Tony?" Charlotte demanded of Georgie. "Surely he…"

"He will be here as soon as he can," Georgie overrode. "And he will take her home."

Alice smiled, looking slightly abashed. "I'm afraid I rather insisted on not waiting for him. I didn't want to miss a single moment of the evening. The Season hasn't started yet, and I wanted to take advantage of that by meeting as many people as I could before then. I'm sure that will help me better succeed."

Izzy looked between Alice and Kitty, who were approximately the same age, but could not have been more different in looks or temperament. Kitty looked terrified of Alice, and Alice seemed terrified of nothing.

Charlotte took Alice by the arm at once. "My dear girl, if it's introductions you want, allow me to be of as much assistance as I can." She steered her away, and they began chatting as though old friends.

The rest watched them leave, then Georgie speared them all with a hard look. "So help me, if Alice becomes Charlotte's pet, I will loathe all of you for eternity." She nodded, then turned and left the way she had come.

Izzy exhaled slowly and shook her head, glancing at Sebastian out of pure instinct.

Amazingly, he was smiling as his eyes met hers.

Then he laughed.

Then they all were laughing, and it occurred to Izzy that Sebastian was even more handsome when he laughed.

Would he never be able to steal a moment with her?

There were people absolutely everywhere in a room that was clearly not designed to hold such a number, and he could not manage to get Izzy away from the rest of them.

Nor could he venture particularly far either.

Kitty sat unattended by any new faces, which did not seem to upset her in the slightest, but it would not do her any favors, either. Staying within a new comfort, no matter how expanded by comparison to former levels, would still keep her from the potential she could have.

If only he could break her free somehow, but then he would have Kitty on his arm, and still be unable to speak with Izzy.

Henshaw seemed content to talk with the group rather than dance or socialize with anyone else, which was very like him, but Sebastian could hardly expect him to entertain the entire group of women without him.

Not that Sebastian was adding much of anything to the conversation at hand.

Charlotte and Alice Sterling were nowhere to be seen, which certainly ought to concern Tony whenever he arrived, but it was certain that so long as Alice was in the company of any one Spinster, she would be as safe as can be, no matter the circumstances. Elinor had appeared, which had the potential to irk him, but as all young men seemed to stay far from their group, she was fairly well-behaved.

None of them danced, which seemed strange. It was certainly not the reputation they deserved, having danced with every one of them at least once. But he had never fully comprehended what an influence their Chronicles had on Society, and the less-than-pleasant feelings that their name tended to evoke.

Sebastian wasn't one for gossip, but he knew enough to know that it was mostly fabrication.

Mostly.

Elinor and Charlotte seemed to fill the mold better than the rest.

He couldn't stop looking at Izzy this evening, much as he knew he ought to. She might not have had the obvious beauty that Grace or Charlotte, or even Alice Sterling had, let alone his sister, but she had a warm and pleasing countenance that drew one to her regardless. And she was loveliness itself, in the most natural, engaging ways. Somehow, she seemed to grow more beautiful with every glance.

If he glanced any more this evening, he might just be blinded by it.

Steady on, he scolded himself, shifting slightly where he stood. It would not do to be so overwhelmed by sudden observations of a woman he was about to do business with.

Let alone one he could count as a friend.

"What's this? A lovely young woman on her first foray into London, and she sits here in a chair?"

Sebastian turned to see Tony approaching, grinning directly at Kitty.

"Careful, Tony," Grace teased, smirking in response. "A number of us still consider ourselves lovely young women."

"I don't," Henshaw quipped with a shrug.

Kitty bit her lip on a giggle, and Sebastian nearly sighed with relief.

Tony bowed deeply to Grace. "That is why I specified 'in her first foray', my dear Grace. Never fear, I will shower you with appropriate compliments later."

"Please don't," she laughed with a dismissive wave.

Tony turned to Kitty, extending his hand. "If it will not trouble you, dear Kitty, will you dance with me?"

The entire group held their breath, including Sebastian.

Kitty knew Tony better than any man in the room but himself, and that was not particularly well at all. Would it be enough?

Izzy murmured something to Kitty that Sebastian couldn't hear, but whatever it was made Kitty smile with real warmth and place her hand in Tony's gently.

"I'd be delighted," his sister whispered, sounding pleased despite her abject fear.

Tony's hand closed around hers, and he winked at her as she came with him.

Sebastian exhaled roughly, satisfaction hitting him squarely in the chest. Tony would set her at ease and have her comfortable in moments. Kitty loved to dance, but Sebastian was a poor partner for her. He'd dance with her at some point, surely, but could not bring himself to be first. Now he wouldn't have to be.

Henshaw echoed his exhale, then moved to stand before Grace, bowing. "In lieu of eloping with me, Miss Morledge, would you favor me with this dance?"

Grace tossed her head back on a laugh. "Oh, why not?"

The two of them moved off to join the dance, and Sebastian's breath caught in his throat. If he asked Izzy to dance…

He glanced at her, and she glanced at him, then they both glanced away.

They couldn't dance and discuss their project. It was too secret, too private a conversation to have among other dancers.

To dance with Izzy, or to talk with Izzy… or to stand here trying to decide what to do with Izzy.

Then suddenly, Izzy got up from her seat and started moving away from the group. He watched her for a moment, then looked at the others, none of whom were paying any attention to him.

What had he missed? Had he been so distracted in his thoughts that he had somehow not seen a signal she had given him? Was she running an errand for someone?

Lady Hetty suddenly speared him with a knowing look, then

tilted her head pointedly in Izzy's direction.

Of all the potential allies in the world, he hadn't expected that one. He inclined his head in gratitude, then strode as nonchalantly as he could after Izzy.

He saw her destination straight away and moved quickly to intercept her.

"Izzy," he murmured near her ear.

She jumped and whirled to face him, her hand flying to her chest. "Oh!" She exhaled in a rush of air, smiling up at him. "Oh, Sebastian, you startled me so."

"Apologies," he said with a quick smile. "I only wanted to take the opportunity while I could. I thought we could discuss our venture while away from the others."

Izzy looked over at the others, then up at him. "Oh, I would love to. But I'm to fetch a drink for Lady Hetty."

Now Sebastian grinned outright. "Well, she is the one who indicated I should follow you, so I do believe we have a few moments to spare."

"Did she, indeed?" Izzy narrowed her eyes in the direction of Lady Hetty, then smirked up at Sebastian. "Very well. Come over here."

She hurried away from the punch to a column of the room, sliding behind it. He followed and found that there was space enough for a discussion, and due to the lack of visibility of the dance from it, space enough for privacy.

"What did you think of the drawings I sent over?" he asked, allowing the excitement and nerves he had felt for days to be expressed.

Izzy's eyes lit up, and she beamed at him. "They were perfect! It was as if you already knew the stories and the style I wanted! They were realistic while still holding the charm of childhood imaginations, and I can easily see how they can be adapted to story specifics." Her smile turned distinctly impish. "The lark with the bonnet was adorable."

Sebastian grinned without reserve, pleased beyond measure that she thought so. "That was my favorite as well. I don't know if you have a lark in a story yet, but may I suggest Lucinda Lark in the very near future?"

"I think we can arrange a story for her," Izzy told him, the corners of her eyes crinkling in a rather charming way.

"So, now what?" Sebastian asked, folding his arms and leaning against the column. "Where do we go from here?"

Izzy blew out a breath in thought, making a bit of hair at her brow dance. "I think we had better take your concept art and go to Cousin Frank. He will need to approve it, and I would hate for you to put in so much effort before we know if it works."

He shrugged at that. "I wouldn't mind working up a series of drawings for a particular story. In fact, I'd love it. And it might help your cousin to see how it would play out together. It could give us a better chance. Send one to me as soon as you can, and I'll see what comes to mind." A sudden smile curved Izzy's lips, and he stared at it in wonder for a moment. "What?"

She wet her lips carefully, then looked up at him almost sheepishly. "Us. You said us. I'm not used to having someone else along with me in all this." Her cheeks colored, but she kept his gaze. "I like it."

There was nothing he could think of to say to that. He liked it too. He liked it a great deal. He felt himself smiling, couldn't bring himself to look away from her, and if her breathing, and his, were anything to go by, there was nothing resembling politeness in her statement.

Or his feelings.

Suddenly, he was looking at her lips again, neither too full nor too thin, and now slightly parted. He had the sudden urge to touch them, to stroke that fuller bottom lip with the edge of his thumb, to even press his own lips to them for a taste.

He blinked and inhaled roughly, dragging his gaze back to her eyes, which did not seem as safe as they had before.

Had he leaned closer to her? When? How?

A loud laugh broke whatever spell Sebastian had suddenly come under, and he straightened with a jerk, clearing his throat quickly as he moved to look for the source of the laughter.

Izzy sighed beside him, the sound a resigned one. "It's Annabelle."

He glanced down at her quickly. "Who is?"

She indicated their host and hostess currently strolling about the room. They were a captivating couple who had clearly spared no expense for their gathering or their ensembles. They were all smiles, seemed to know everyone in the room, and were apparently delighted by the sight of them all.

"I've met her once," Sebastian murmured to Izzy, "and that was apparently enough to garner an invitation for Kitty and myself this evening."

Izzy nodded, pursing her lips in a strained way. "Annabelle has always loved people. And the attention from them. She dearly loves playing hostess."

There was a tense note in Izzy's voice, and Sebastian turned fully to look at her. "What is the story there, Izzy? Why do Charlotte and Georgie hate her?"

"It's nothing, really," Izzy assured him, though she would not meet his eyes.

"Why don't I believe that?" He moved back behind the pillar and pulled her with him. "Come on, Izzy. Out with it."

"It won't serve," she whispered, ducking her chin.

He reached out and lifted her chin with his fingers, waiting for her eyes to clash with his. "I don't care," he told her with the utmost gentleness. "Please, tell me."

She hesitated, her eyes searching his, then she closed her eyes and nodded. She moved slightly, her position now squarely behind the pillar, out of sight of anyone but him.

"Annabelle and I were friends in our younger years," Izzy murmured, her eyes somewhere on his waistcoat. "She married Mr. Stafford fairly young and told a small group of us that she wanted us all to dress similarly for her wedding, despite not being attendants. A way to honor her friends, and have them honor her, as it were."

It wasn't a common request of friends of the bride, but Sebastian supposed that was neither here nor there. He leaned in to listen a little more closely, Izzy's voice nearly lost amidst the general murmuring and the music.

"I went to Annabelle after and inquired as to the color or style she wished for us, and she was kind enough to tell me." Izzy swallowed harshly, her eyes shifting towards the dancing. "But when the day of the wedding came, I arrived to find the other girls not only wearing gowns different than what I had been told, but all were bridesmaids. No one else was wearing anything like what I was. None of the guests knew that I should have been among them, and none of the others had any idea of my torment."

Sebastian watched Izzy as her cheeks flushed, then slowly returned to their normal shade. There was pain still in her words, and clearly in the memory, but he couldn't hear a single bitter note in it. And she was here, attending this woman's party, apparently without any concern at all.

"I was mortified," Izzy whispered, shaking her head. "I was hurt and confused, and I couldn't say or do anything about it. I endured the wedding celebration for as short a time as would be considered polite, and then I returned home. I never wore that dress again." She looked up at him, smiling with some sadness. "So. That's the story. It was all very silly and inconsequential, and really a selfish thing for me to be so concerned with."

"And yet it still pains you," he pointed out.

She shrugged a shoulder lightly. "Embarrasses me, rather. As I said, it was selfish and conceited of me to be so concerned about myself in that situation, and on her wedding day."

It was absolutely nothing of the kind, and it irked him that she would write herself off so easily.

"Are you still friends with them?" he asked. "The girls that were all together in this."

She seemed surprised by his query. "Of course. Though, admittedly, not as close as we were."

"Of course?" he repeated incredulously. "What does that even mean, Izzy? You shouldn't be friends with people who can barely remember your existence."

Izzy's brows rose, though her expression showed no hint of naiveté. "If I did that, I would have very few friends."

"Then so be it!" Sebastian cried in as low a voice as he could, given the crowd of the event. He leaned closer and hissed, "You deserve to have real friends, Izzy, not the ones who have to force themselves to recollect you."

"No one intends to neglect me," she insisted, averting her eyes. "They just… can't seem to remember me. They forget to remember me."

"And that makes it all right?"

Again, one shoulder lifted in a shrug. "It's not intentional."

Sebastian was silent for a moment, and then reached out to take her hand. "Izzy, look at me."

She did so, and he could see the embarrassment swirling in every one of her features.

"I want to add a condition to our arrangement," he told her gently, squeezing her hand. "I would like to help you to become less biddable and accommodating."

Her eyes widened. "I beg your pardon?"

He nodded once. "Not to make you less likable or warm or anything else that is so prevalent in your good nature, but in the hopes that you will be able to stand up for yourself. That your voice will be heard. And that you will find that as valiantly as you defend others, you should also defend yourself the same."

Izzy stared at him, her lips parted once more, and he could measure the length and depth of her breathing with his eyes alone. "Why?" she finally asked, her voice as timid as Kitty's ever was.

Sebastian smiled at her then, unable to do otherwise, and he ran a thumb over her hand. "Because I am your friend, Isabella Lambert, and intentionally so. And I care enough to see things change."

Impossibly, she smiled at that, and he felt a rush of air escape in a sigh.

"Is that smile an acceptance?" he asked with a laugh.

"Nobody has ever said anything quite so lovely, Mr. Morton," Izzy told him with an impish tilt to her head. "I accept. Provided I may also claim the dance you owe me this very moment."

He chuckled again and bowed slightly. "Nothing would give me more pleasure, Miss Lambert."

"What if I trod your toes?" she asked as they moved to join the next dance.

"I'm quite sure it would be a very pleasant trodding, indeed."

And it was.

Chapter Thirteen

———— ⟨∽ ∞⟩ ————

Familiarity is a blessing and a curse. We bless it, we curse it, and once you have it, there is no going back.

-*The Spinster Chronicles, 1 February 1816*

"I cannot *believe* he agreed to take us on!"

Us. She'd said only a few days ago that she liked the sound of that, and it had pleased him. Now to hear the same from her sent a curious sensation of warmth racing into the center of his chest, where it spread out to the tips of his fingers and toes.

Us. The word seemed magical, alight with twenty thousand stars in the sky, twinkling in all their majesty.

He blinked away the sudden yearning he felt rising and pressed his lips together in a firm line, swallowing. "I was convinced he wouldn't."

"So was I!" she gushed. "He was so very long about his decision, and you know he was playing with us for his own amusement."

Sebastian took the chance to look at Izzy, and the wild grin on her face produced one on his own. Helpless laughter escaped, and he straightened, turning towards her. "Well, Miss Lambert," he said, still grinning, "do you think you could bear to put up with a partnership with me in truth?"

Izzy nodded in an almost frantic way that he found utterly charming. "I think I could manage that, yes, Mr. Morton."

Her exhilaration was contagious, and he had the most bizarre urge to sweep her up and twirl her around, to hear her giggle incessantly over their success, and to express his own complicated emotions. He was thrilled for her, he was eager for himself, he was breathless with anticipation for the future, and he wanted...

Izzy was suddenly at his side, seizing his hand, eyes widening. "How are we going to manage this? I can't call upon you, and you can't call upon me without someone suspecting something. And we must be able to meet face to face about this, it cannot all happen by post."

That was true, and he'd been thinking about that for some time. They both glanced at Kitty, who was too busy daydreaming as they walked to pay much attention to them. "Easily," he assured her, the thrill of their success finally fading. "You are mentoring my sister, and this is known by several. You will be calling on Kitty, not me. And Kitty, accompanied by me, will call upon you. Everything can be done smoothly and quite properly, and no one will be any the wiser."

Izzy's lips twisted in a slight smile. "Except it does leave Kitty without much by way of mentoring. I cannot spend all of my time with you and abandon her entirely."

No, she couldn't, but the idea had merit, in his mind.

"Of course not," he said quickly, shaking his head. "We'd manage both. Kitty is fine, Izzy, I promise. She's actually very excited about being an accomplice to our secret arrangement."

"Oh, Lord," Izzy muttered as she looked up at him. "I've been allowing her too much time with Charlotte."

A dramatic shudder rode down Sebastian's spine, and it made Izzy laugh.

"Please," she protested with a half-hearted smile. "Charlotte isn't that bad."

Sebastian looked at her but said nothing.

His silence amused her, he could tell.

"What?" she asked suspiciously.

"It would be ungentlemanly to contradict you, or to suggest otherwise of Miss Wright," he informed her stiffly. "Under the circumstances, I will remain silent."

"Not that again," Izzy groaned. "The next thing I know, you'll refuse to call me Izzy, and never smile, and stop talking, and all of the effort I put into loosening you up will be for naught."

Sebastian tilted his head at her, well aware that she was teasing him, but finding a prickle of truth in it. Worse than that, he didn't know how to respond to her. He couldn't tease her in return, not in the same way. He was too much of a gentleman.

Much to his disappointment.

Izzy sobered at once. "I'm sorry if my teasing makes you uncomfortable," she murmured, concern wrinkling her brow. "Kitty may have mentioned that you aren't fond of such things. I should have listened."

"It isn't that," he replied quickly. "It's only that I am out of practice." He gave her a small smile, a sort of apology, he supposed, for not being as congenial as he ought to have been.

As he could have been.

Should have been.

An impish smile curved Izzy's lips, and the maddening urge to kiss them flooded his system.

"So… you don't mind if I help you practice?" she asked with hope, still teasing him.

He needed her teasing. He needed to smile and laugh, to feel alive instead of simply pressing on. Izzy did that for him.

What else could she do for him?

"No," he told her in a low voice, smiling at her. Just for her. "No, I don't mind at all, Izzy."

Her fingers brushed against his, and it was only then that he realized he still held her hand. He stared at them, marveled at the perfect fit, and how he could have held her hand for so long without realizing it.

Shouldn't he have been fully aware of it every moment?

Slowly, he raised his eyes to hers, and even slower, he brushed his thumb along the back of her hand.

He heard her breath catch, sending a thrill of satisfaction into him, and suddenly this whole venture seemed an even greater idea than it had before.

More time with Izzy, more chances to make her smile, more opportunity to have her tease him, and more moments of this pulling sensation that tugged at his heart.

If he wasn't committed to this project before, he most certainly was now.

Izzy blinked her wide, captivating eyes, and her finger twitched against his.

He felt that more than he had ever felt anything in his entire life.

"Come here, you two," Kitty said, waving them up to her, effectively breaking the moment. "Come and see this!"

Their connection broke as Izzy hastily moved to his sister, leaving Sebastian in his place, now rubbing his own fingers together.

See this? Yes, he rather thought he did want to see this.

And he was damned curious where it would lead.

"You didn't invite all of them, did you?"

"No, dear, I did not."

"Not that I would be ungrateful, because it would be very kind of them..."

"Kitty, you're turning into a chatterbox. Are your anxieties so much that it changes your nature?"

Kitty blushed and tightened her hold on Sebastian's arm. "No, of course not."

Izzy took pity on her and looped her arm through her free one. "I'm teasing you. I know better than to throw everyone at you. Only Grace and I will be joining you. I invited Georgie, but she is unwell again."

"Oh dear," Kitty whimpered, giving her a worried look. "Is there anything to be done?"

Izzy smiled at the girl's question, innocent though it was. "Not for several months. Then it will be right as rain, I expect."

Sebastian snorted a laugh, then coughed to cover it.

Kitty looked up at him, then at Izzy in confusion before understanding dawned. "Oh," she said softly, eyes wide. Then she giggled, her cheeks coloring. "You must think me silly for not being aware that..."

"I think nothing of the sort," Izzy interrupted firmly. She inhaled, then sighed, smiling around at their surroundings. "I do love

London on brisk days."

"Do you?" Sebastian asked, looking over his sister's head. "Why?"

Izzy shrugged, smiling in delight. "I don't know. It reminds me more of the country." She looked at Kitty, who was watching her with interest. "I am quite envious of you and your time in the country."

Kitty smiled softly, then returned her gaze forward. "It was lovely, I suppose. But it was lonely."

Izzy heard Sebastian's intake of breath and saw him stiffen out of the corner of her eye.

Kitty felt it and looked up at him, her face hidden from Izzy. "Oh, Sebastian... I didn't... I didn't mean..."

"Miranda!" Izzy called, waving in outright relief to see Miranda Sterling in an open carriage near them.

Miranda saw her and waved gaily back. "Isabella Lambert, you are a glorious sight!" She rapped her hand on the edge of the carriage. "Stop at once."

Izzy very nearly hauled Kitty over to her, separating her from Sebastian before any further awkwardness could ensue.

Miranda smiled with her usual benevolence. "Izzy, dear, you are the breath of fresh spring air we all wish would come soon."

"Just a few more weeks, Miranda," Izzy reminded her, rolling her eyes at Kitty, who smiled, but had returned to her more timid self.

"Yes, yes," Miranda sighed, shaking her head. She turned away for a moment. "Darling, don't fret, you may sit up and see for yourself."

"To whom is she talking?" Kitty whispered beside her.

"Rufus," Izzy said at the same time as Sebastian, who ambled up to them.

Kitty turned to frown at her brother. "Who?"

On cue, Miranda's beloved bloodhound raised his head, moaning sleepily and licking his snout. He yawned, then turned his bleary eyes to Kitty.

"Oh!" Kitty exclaimed in surprise, blinking at the dog.

Miranda giggled to herself. "Yes, Rufus has that effect." She cupped his face and made several loud kissing noises, before scratching his head and turning back to them. "And who, pray tell, is this delightful girl?"

"Kitty, this is Miranda Sterling, Tony's stepmother," Izzy explained with a smile. "Miranda, Miss Catherine Morton."

Kitty curtseyed prettily, her smile less hesitant. "Delighted, ma'am."

Miranda eyed her with the sort of speculation Izzy had learned to mistrust, before beaming. "Kitty Morton, it is a pleasure. Your first Season, is it?"

"Yes, ma'am," Kitty replied meekly.

Miranda hummed, flicking her gaze to Sebastian. "A bit like you in that regard, is she, Morton?"

"Yes, Miranda," Sebastian answered without hesitation. "Kitty has always been a timid creature, more inclined to reserve, as I am. Miss Lambert has been kind enough to help Kitty there."

"Izzy would," Miranda simpered, giving Izzy a pitying look. "Such a good heart."

"I'm no candidate for sainthood, Miranda, and you know it," Izzy retorted.

Miranda speared her with a look. "You're closer than any human I know, Isabella Lambert, and I would vow the same in any church without the slightest fear of damnation."

Sebastian coughed a surprised laugh, which spurned Miranda's smirk.

Izzy scowled at him. "You are not helping, sir."

He only shrugged.

Miranda hummed again, then opened the carriage door. "Kitty Morton, come ride with me a while. I should like to know you better."

Kitty paled at once and looked to Izzy for help.

"Miranda, I don't..." Sebastian tried, jumping to his sister's defense.

"Oh, stop that," Miranda snapped as she waved at Sebastian. "I won't bite her, Morton, and neither will Rufus."

Izzy sighed and stepped back, gesturing for Kitty to get in. "We are due at Bolton's shortly. Miss Morton must have some new gowns for the Season."

"Oh, delightful," Miranda exclaimed, helping Kitty into the carriage. "Put it on my bill."

"No," Sebastian insisted firmly. "Miranda, I can afford to dress my own sister for the Season."

"Don't grow indignant with me, Sebastian," Miranda scolded, giving him a sharp glare as Kitty situated herself. "Izzy may be your sister's mentor, but I shall be her sponsor."

Izzy gasped, looking between Miranda and Kitty in bewilderment. "Miranda..."

Miranda tossed her head. "None of that. The dresses go on my bill, Sebastian, and I will procure a spot at Almack's for Kitty to open her first Season with flare. And as she is so timid a creature, it will be the most dignified and understated flare that ever was. Drive on!"

The carriage rolled on, and Kitty stared after them with wide, terrified eyes.

Sebastian heaved a sigh and shook his head slowly.

"What?" Izzy asked, smiling at Sebastian's suddenly resigned countenance.

"That may be the last I ever see of my sister," he told her, giving her a wry look.

Izzy giggled and turned towards Bond Street. "Come on, we'd better get to Bolton's before Miranda shows up with your sister."

Sebastian turned to walk with her, clasping his hands behind his back. "This is improper, you know. Being unescorted."

"Oh, please," Izzy retorted with a soft laugh. "There's a footman ten paces behind us."

"A footman is not a chaperone, Miss Lambert," Sebastian told her, his tone taking on a formal edge.

"I have no need of a chaperone," Izzy shot back. "I am out shopping, for which purpose a footman is perfectly suitable."

"Not when I'm in attendance," came the reply, amusement seeping into the formality.

Izzy peered up at him with a smirk. "Then go away."

Sebastian chuckled once. "No, I don't think I will."

"Oh, not so gentlemanly, then. I approve," she teased. "Besides, you sat with me in my parlor without a chaperone. Here, we have any number of passersby who would be witness to any impropriety. We are perfectly safe, are we not?"

"If you say so," he muttered, then looked at her for a long

moment as they walked. "Do you find me very ridiculous, Izzy?"

She shook her head at once, her heart dropping to her stomach. "No, not at all. No, I think... I think you might be the least ridiculous man I know, Sebastian."

Her words seemed to take him by surprise, and he looked away, but not before she caught sight of a smile.

At last!

Her heart hadn't been quite steady since Cousin Frank had told them he would take her stories on, and it had only gotten worse when Sebastian had been as relieved about the whole thing as she was. The breathless smile he'd given her, and the moment where their hands had clung so tightly... It had been all she could do to avoid throwing herself in his arms, and taking his hand seemed a rather restrained version of it.

How could she have known that holding his hand might have done more to unravel her than anything else?

And now she would have to thank Miranda for giving them this time alone.

But that would only give Miranda more fodder for her mischief making and nobody needed that.

"And you are..." Sebastian began, his voice low, "far kinder and more generous than I ever anticipated."

Izzy couldn't bear to look at him and found herself holding her breath. "Is that bad?"

She felt his hand on her arm, and he pulled her to a stop.

She swallowed, then forced herself to meet his eyes.

He smiled at her, a caress in his lips, his eyes, even the gentle crease at the corners of his eyes. "No, Izzy. It most certainly is not bad."

She went from holding her breath to losing her breath all in one moment, all by the power of this man before her. This quiet, reserved, complicated, incredibly handsome, and gentle man, whose smiles she was coming to crave with increasing frequency.

And he was going to be spending more and more time with her.

She had better get used to breathlessness, then.

What a peculiar thought.

Izzy cleared her throat and started towards Bolton's. "I can hardly believe we succeeded today," she said in a rush. "There is so much to do, and so much to think about. And the cost... I don't know where we are going to get the money, but surely we can find a way."

Sebastian chuckled, and the sound warmed Izzy more than anything in recent memory. "Yes, indeed. We have quite a task before us. Can you bear to have your dreams come true, Miss Lambert?"

She nearly gagged at the anxious pain in her chest and throat. "Lord... In truth, I don't know. Now it is upon me, I..."

"Izzy!"

Izzy jerked to see Grace descending from her carriage, and realized they were just outside of Bolton's. And she had been brushing arms with Sebastian.

She took a step away and forced a smile for her friend, though the distance between herself and Sebastian suddenly felt cold and gaping.

Grace smiled for them both and turned for the store. "Where's Kitty?" she asked as they turned in.

"Miranda absconded with her for the chance to know her better," Sebastian told her, widening his eyes for effect.

"Oh my," Grace murmured. "The poor dear. Well, it was bound to happen sooner or later."

That was undoubtedly true.

Izzy smiled as Sebastian looked around the shop, clearly uncomfortable.

"Miss Lambert! Miss Morledge!" a bright voice called.

They turned to see Amelia Perry rushing towards them, her dark hair bouncing in perfect curls.

"And Mr. Morton, too! What a delight!" Amelia gushed. "What brings you all here?"

"Mr. Morton's sister is preparing for her first Season," Izzy explained as they moved towards the back.

Amelia peered around for Kitty, then looked at Izzy with confusion. "Where is Miss Morton?"

"Coming," Grace assured her. "You know, I think the pair of you should meet. You would be great friends."

Amelia brightened at the idea. "Oh, lovely! Then I must stay to meet her." She sat in a nearby chair, apparently content. "I am always looking for friends, and if you approve of her, I am sure I will as well. And we shall help her find some new gowns, indeed we shall."

Sebastian groaned as if in pain, and Izzy turned to him, laughing now. "You don't have to stay, Sebastian."

He brightened at once. "Really?"

Izzy looked at the others dryly. "Such hope." She turned back to him. "No, you really don't. You can leave. We will see Kitty home."

He frowned slightly. "But you're all alone."

"Oh no, Mr. Morton," Amelia chimed in. "My parents are coming to fetch me. I assure you, we will be quite safe."

That seemed to satisfy him, and he nodded to them all, quickly making his escape.

Izzy shook her head, watching him go, and sank into a chair, Grace sitting beside her.

Then Grace leaned over. "Sebastian?" she murmured out of the corner of her mouth, her eyes flashing with interest.

Izzy's face flamed, and she looked down at her hands.

Grace giggled very softly, but said nothing else, straightening once more. "Now we wait for Miranda and Kitty. Should we pray for the child?"

Amelia laughed, and Izzy tried to, but in truth, she would rather pray for herself at the moment.

Lord knew she would need it.

Chapter Fourteen

Choosing battles is a difficult business. It must be strategic and wise, beneficial to the task at hand, and, most importantly, provide an opportunity for improvement to one's opposition. The breadth of such opportunity is entirely up to the battler, of course.

-_The Spinster Chronicles, 25 July 1817_

"Yes, yes, just like that. Oh, it's perfect!"

"Hardly perfect, but I do think it works."

Izzy threw Sebastian an amused look. "Correct me if I am wrong, but the idea is for you to put down on paper what I am envisioning in my mind, yes?"

Sebastian smirked and pushed at his rolled sleeves. "Yes…"

She tapped the sketch before them meaningfully. "This is what I envisioned for Molly Moose, bow and all."

He returned her look, his smile rueful. "You imagined a pale blue bow that unravels the more the story goes on?"

Now Izzy laughed and withdrew her hand, rolling her eyes. "Fine, I might not have imagined that exact specification, but I think it is in keeping with the theme of the story!"

He chuckled and slid the Molly Moose sketches across the table, pulling out some of the others he'd spent time on, though they weren't as finished as the rest. "Fair enough. What would you say to these for the Lucinda Lark story?"

Izzy leaned closer, eyeing the sketches, then nodded. "I think that could work out well. Perhaps give her home a bit more of a parlor feel?"

"With embroidery on the cushions?" he queried, smiling at her.

"Oh, why not?" she replied in a playful tone. "Lucinda is clearly a very accomplished lark."

"Ah, then she must have a harpsichord," Sebastian insisted as he turned to lean against the table. "All accomplished animals play the harpsichord."

"Do they really?" Izzy hummed another laugh and pushed a coppery strand of hair away from her face. "How lovely." Her brow creased for a moment as her eyes shifted.

"What?" Sebastian asked, familiar enough now with Izzy's expressions and ways to know when she'd had a thought.

She glanced up at him, beginning to smile. "I've had another idea."

He chuckled wryly and folded his arms. "Yes, so I gathered. Let's hear it, then."

She whacked his arm with a scoffing sound, then laughed to herself, her eyes dancing. "A harpsichord."

Sebastian lifted his brows in surprise. "We're writing about inanimate objects now?"

"No!" Izzy shook her head, turning back to the table, her mind clearly whirling with the ideas. "No, what about... Henrietta Hippopotamus? Who plays the harpsichord, and hits all the wrong keys?"

The idea sprang into his mind, fully formed, and he threw his head back and laughed. "Oh, I can see so many possibilities for that one, Iz. Henrietta could be an eternal optimist, and finds great joy in making music, no matter how poorly it is done."

"And she is self-taught," Izzy went on, grinning at him. "It is difficult to find a harpsichord instructor for a hippopotamus, after all."

"Indeed, those would be hard to come by," Sebastian agreed as he turned to pick up a pencil. He grabbed a blank sheet and began to roughly sketch. "But perhaps her neighbor..." He glanced at Izzy to go on.

Izzy leaned over the table in thought, pressing her forearms into the wood. "Cressida Crane."

Sebastian shook his head in wonder. "Brilliant." He continued with his sketching. "So, Cressida could be skilled in the viola, perhaps, and they create their own music lessons."

"Yes!" Izzy cried with a laugh. "I can see the music recital for all their friends now."

They shared a smile, and Sebastian found his attention drawing to her lips, as they tended to do when she was close, and he wrenched his gaze back to the sketch.

They were quite a pair, and their meetings had grown more and more productive as their ideas grew more aligned. He knew her tastes and she knew his abilities, and their collaborations became more and more exciting. They'd managed ten stories with sketches in various stages of completion, as Izzy had so many prepared before he began providing the artwork, and Frank had suggested they go for twice that many to complete the collection.

The first volume, at any rate.

It was a staggering thought, multiple volumes of her stories and his artwork, all to be published and sold in stores around London, and potentially in other cities as well.

Izzy hadn't spoken about her ambitions for this venture beyond the actual publication, and he suspected she hadn't considered it herself.

If the collection were half as successful as it had the potential to be, she would have to begin considering such things. But he couldn't tell her that, not now. He couldn't push her, couldn't take over this project simply because his nature led him to think beyond the here and now. He didn't want their meetings to grow formal and businesslike, couldn't bear to have these delightful sessions of ideas and sketches turned into something less vibrant.

Whatever he'd begun to feel for this woman beside him before this was paling in light of what was now brewing.

It was not easily defined, nor was it easily thought on. All he knew was every moment with Izzy made him want another, and the strict behaviors and manners he had developed over the years were growing less and less structured.

There was comfort and ease with Izzy, in her nature and in her air, and one could not be with her and not feel such things seeping into them as well.

He hadn't been so relaxed in ages, if ever.

"Izzy?"

Kitty's voice interrupted Sebastian's sudden pondering with a gentle stroke, and they both turned to face her.

His sister smiled warmly, a journal in her hand. "You will want time to get home and change before we're all expected at the Sterlings' this evening. I think Lady Sterling expects finer attire than our day dresses, don't you?"

Izzy brushed off her skirts, sighing to herself. "Yes, I suppose you're right. Much as I would like to spend all of my time in comfortable calico, I don't think it would be appropriate to attend their evening in it." She pushed away from the table and looked up at the grandfather clock in the drawing room they'd rearranged to be their workroom. "Goodness, I had no idea we'd been at it so long." She looked at Sebastian with an embarrassed smile. "I've taken up hours of your time."

"I didn't mind," he admitted with a shrug, putting his pencils down and rolling his sleeves back down. "Never do."

"And you were with me before that," Kitty reminded them both. "We might have to make up a room for you in our house, Izzy, you're so often here."

That made Izzy laugh, and she shook her head very firmly. "That would not be wise at all, Kitty. I would pester Sebastian far too much were I always underfoot, and he would never get anything done but the drawings I would insist upon."

Kitty flicked her eyes to Sebastian, a teasing smile playing at her lips. "He never does anything but your drawings anyway these days, so I'm not sure much would change."

Sebastian coughed a startled laugh at his sister's jest, bewildered and delighted by the change in her. She was almost as timid as before when in large gatherings, though she was improving, but in a more comfortable setting such as this she was lively and vivacious, and it pleased him beyond measure to see her so happy.

"I get everything done that needs to be done," he informed his sister with a definite sniff. "Nothing is in any way lacking just because

I sketch more now."

Kitty lifted a shoulder in a helpless shrug and turned from the room, holding her journal to her chest.

Sebastian watched her go, then turned to Izzy again. "She teased me."

Izzy nodded like a proud mother. "She did, indeed. And it's about time, too. Someone should keep you on your toes when I'm not here."

"Just what I need," he muttered, hiding a smile as he collected up his sketches.

"Yes, I suspect it is," Izzy retorted. She heaved a sigh and glanced at the clock once more. "I love the Sterlings, I do, but I wish I didn't have to attend tonight."

Sebastian grunted and set the pile of sketches at the corner of the table. "I can understand that. Lord Sterling is excellent company, and his wife is a perfect match for him, but it is likely that one will have to endure Hugh Sterling when in their home."

Izzy nodded, folding her arms, shrinking in a bit by doing so. "Exactly. And Hugh is so vile towards the Spinsters now, sometimes quite vocally. You remember how he was with poor Prue at Georgie's garden party last year?"

"I do," Sebastian said, frowning at the recollection. The younger brother of Tony's cousin was a passionate protestor of Izzy and her friends, somehow finding their actions to be infringing upon his more profligate way of life, though in truth, the Spinsters hardly affected anyone directly at all. Sebastian had never been on any great terms with Hugh Sterling, and he saw no reason to change that.

"I worry for Alice," Izzy sighed. "He is her brother, so one cannot intercede there, but I don't want her to hear his version of things rather than the truth. And if he sees Kitty too much in our company, he could make things difficult for her as well."

Sebastian was shaking his head before she finished. "Don't worry about Alice and Kitty, Iz. They'll be all right. And Hugh Sterling can't do much by way of injury for two girls fresh in their first Season."

Izzy made a soft noise of disagreement. "I think you underestimate just how violently he is against the Spinsters, and the lengths he will go to for our humiliation."

She might have been right there, but he couldn't see how anyone could feel that way. Still, he was not about to argue the point. "Will it be horrible?"

"Well, it depends on whether Hugh is intoxicated or not. The drink loosens his tongue and makes everything worse."

"Will he come after you all?" he asked, cocking his head in consideration.

Her chin dipped in a nod. "Most likely. And he'll prod at me. It's a new pastime of his. Mostly harmless, but..."

Sebastian straightened at once. "What does he say?" he demanded roughly, a flash of irritation hitting his gut.

Izzy looked at him, giving him a humorless smile. " 'Miss Lambert won't bite back,' " she mimicked. " 'Miss Lambert is a good sort.' 'Sweet Isabella, always a good girl doing what she's told.' 'She won't say a word.' " She tried to brighten her smile but failed. "What everybody else thinks, but doesn't say, I expect."

He didn't care for that one bit, either that it was thought or that Hugh said it.

"So, don't," he told her simply.

Izzy frowned at him. "Don't what?"

"Don't be a good girl. Say something. Bite back. Don't let him do that."

"It's not that important," she protested without energy, shaking her head.

Sebastian gave her a hard look. "It is. To me, it is."

His words surprised her, he could see, and he only hoped she would consider them for what they were. That she would take them to heart. That something might change for her.

"This is the difficult part of defending yourself, Izzy," he murmured as gently as he could. "You risk discomfort and embarrassment, and possibly giving offense. But you need to remind those who have forgotten that you are, in fact, human, in possession of feelings, opinions, and thoughts, not a drapery to be assessed, criticized, or debated about. You don't simply exist to enhance the surroundings or dress whatever window someone wishes to look through. You are flesh and blood, and ought to be respected as such."

Izzy was silent for a moment, then smiled just a little. "You sound like Georgie."

He laughed once. "Take that back."

Her smile grew and she shook her head. "No, I won't. And besides, you said it much better than she usually does."

"Did I?" he asked, pleased despite the ridiculousness. "Wonderful."

"You did," she assured him. "Very eloquent and very refreshing." The smile deepened, causing a peculiar tug in his chest. "And incredibly kind."

He made a soft noise of acknowledgement, keeping his attention on Izzy, everything within him already attuned to her. "I will always be kind with you, Iz," he heard himself murmur. "I find it impossible to be anything else. And you deserve no less."

He watched in wonder as her complexion turned rosy, heightening the near perfect cheekbones he'd never quite noticed before, the quivering edges of her smile he wanted to touch, and the brilliant shade of her eyes that captivated him.

Were she closer, he would have taken her hand, would have run his fingers over the delicate skin, would have tried to ascertain if her pulse raced at this moment the way his seemed to. But alas for distance, though it was undoubtedly better, he could only do the best a look could manage.

He prayed a look could be enough.

"I must go," Izzy murmured, averting her eyes, which made him smile. "Or else I will be late to the Sterlings'."

"We can't have that," Sebastian sighed, pushing off from the table. "Tony would be offended on behalf of the family, and it might take a great deal of groveling to make up for it."

Izzy almost laughed but refrained in favor of a tight smile. She curtseyed quickly and hurried to the door, then paused, looking over her shoulder. "Sebastian?"

He hadn't bothered to look away from her and smiled. "Yes?"

Her eyes suddenly rose to his in a rather frank manner. "I really like it when you call me Iz." Then she was gone.

His breath vanished in a swift rush of air, and he leaned back against the table for support. He ran a hand over his face, laughed, then found himself grinning madly. He hadn't even realized he had given her a new name, it had felt so natural, and now to discover that she enjoyed it...

She liked his name for her, did she?

What a delightful revelation!

He pushed away from the table again, whistling jauntily to himself.

Suddenly, a night at the Sterlings' seemed like a very good idea.

Francis and Janet Sterling were tasteful, sensible people, and possessed a measure of elegance that many people would spend their entire lives striving for, which was why it was all the more bewildering that Hugh Sterling was so clearly the opposite.

Izzy watched Hugh for a moment as he lingered along the far wall, leaning as though the wall alone held him up. He bore the bleary eyes and disheveled appearance they had all come to accept as his usual one of late, which could not be good for the Spinsters.

He had glared at each of them individually as they came in, though he had yet to approach or say anything.

Small mercies.

Now Izzy sat beside Lady Hetty, as per usual, and found herself growing a trifle sad watching Hugh be disgruntled and miserable.

"He wasn't always like that," Izzy murmured aloud.

"What's that, dear?" Lady Hetty asked, leaning closer.

Izzy indicated Hugh where he stood, though he was frowning at the improvised dancing that had begun. "Hugh Sterling. He wasn't always that way."

Lady Hetty grunted and tapped her walking stick against the floor. "No, but that isn't saying much. He didn't have much to recommend him before he lost his better judgment." The older woman looked at Izzy sharply. "Why are you giving a moment's thought to Hugh Sterling? Surely you aren't fond of him."

"Of Hugh Sterling?" Elinor chortled as she came near them, plopping herself into the seat beside Izzy. "Heaven and angels forbid. What a waste of name and space."

"Elinor," Izzy scolded softly, smiling as Amelia Perry walked by. The girl gave her an utterly superior look. "What, Izzy? You object?"

"As a matter of fact, yes, Elinor," Izzy snapped as she focused on adjusting her gloves. "I take no pleasure in seeing what he is doing to himself, and I feel sad for him."

"You are kinder than he deserves, Isabella," Lady Hetty told her with a would-be gentle pat to her hands.

Though she knew Lady Hetty meant well, the gesture felt pitying and condescending.

Why must everyone find her inclination to sympathize something to be pitied?

"I'd be less hateful towards him were he less vile towards us," Elinor muttered, shifting in her seat. "His hatred fuels my own."

Izzy rolled her eyes, shaking her head. There was no explanation for Elinor's vindictive streak, nor her strange passion for spinsterhood. She was barely twenty years old, and there was nothing remotely resembling a spinster about her, apart from the miserly attitude one generally associated with unmarried women of a certain age.

She'd wind up a spinster in truth through her own efforts, if she were not careful.

Izzy well knew that it wasn't something to be sought after.

"W-what's wrong, Izzy?" Prue's voice asked nearby.

Izzy turned and saw her friend approach on the arm of her husband, Camden, and both were watching her with concern.

Elinor snorted softly. "Izzy was just defending Hugh Sterling."

"I was not," Izzy protested looking at Elinor in disgruntlement. "I neither defended nor excused him."

"I should say not," Cam scoffed, looking over at the man in question. "Nothing worth defending or excusing."

"Amen to that," Elinor muttered.

Prue still watched Izzy, frowning slightly. "Then w-what was it?"

Izzy didn't think she could bear trying to explain it again, not with Camden there. He had once blackened Hugh's eye for what he had said about Prue and Georgie, and he was undoubtedly more inclined to take Elinor's view than Izzy's.

171

Yet she found herself looking up at Camden, his attention back on her, his eyes seeing too much.

"Ah," he murmured in a low voice. "I see your mind, Isabella Lambert, and the good heart you possess."

"Don't tease me, Camden," she tried to retort, though it was weak.

Camden shook his head once. "I'm not. Having been a villain a time or twelve, I think you'll find I understand the journey well. You feel bad for him."

Izzy chewed the inside of her lip, glancing at Hugh again. "In a way."

"You know how he once was," Camden went on, lowering his voice further still, "and what he is now. And you are sorry for it."

Now Izzy nodded, swallowing a little. "And for his family. I cannot be angry so much as sad. I know he may not deserve it, but..."

Camden interrupted her with a soft laugh. "Trust me, Izzy, we villains are most grateful for that which we do not deserve."

Izzy smiled as Camden leaned down to kiss Prue's cheek with the gentlest of caresses. Prue's cheeks flamed at once, but she gave Camden such an adoring look it made Izzy ache inside.

No matter how different Camden and Prudence Vale were in personality and temperament, they were the most devoted and envied of couples.

If only Izzy had such a love herself.

Something sharp and hot seemed to bounce about in her chest, and a too-familiar, handsome face swam in her mind's eye.

Sebastian.

She shivered and wrenched her thoughts away from him, determined not to be one of those silly creatures that would think more on a man and his behavior towards her without any certainty of its intention. Sebastian was a wonderful man, a kind man, and a gentleman. He would never intentionally make her feel and hope for things that he did not intend to give, but in their familiarity of late, it would be only too easy to mistake his warmth for more than friendship.

Much as she might begin to wish for it.

"Oh, Lord, someone save her."

Izzy jerked at Charlotte's voice, only to find her friend staring in Hugh's direction. She followed her gaze, and saw Alice next to her brother, listening to whatever he was saying with a furrowed brow. Hugh didn't seem to be scolding her, but he was clearly impassioned about his topic.

Alice didn't appear to be particularly miserable, though it was possible she was as used to her brother's ways as anyone else and simply tolerating it. But a girl of her age could be quite impressionable, and if she were spending more of her time with Hugh and less with Francis, she would be listening to the less sensible of the brothers.

"Is it necessary to steer her away from her brother?" Izzy asked of the group. "It's not as though he's a danger to her."

"Yes," almost everyone around her said, and she glanced around to find that Grace had joined them, as had Georgie, who groaned.

"I've only just arrived," Georgie whined, shaking her head, "and already I'm forced to intervene."

Izzy made to rise. "I can go."

Georgie stopped her with a look. "She's my relation. I'll go." She sighed and smiled at Camden. "Cam, if I introduce you, will you dance with her? The less time she spends with Hugh tonight, the better."

"Of course," Camden replied with a nod, "if you truly think I am better company."

His dubious tone made them all smile, as usual.

"For the first time in recent memory, Mr. Vale," Georgie informed him as she passed, "you are the lesser of two evils. Congratulations."

He chuckled and moved to stand with Prue beside Lady Hetty, leaning against a pillar. He eyed all the gathered Spinsters, then looked around the room. "No Edith tonight?"

"No," Grace sighed with disappointment. "I tried to convince her, but she would not."

Camden frowned, shaking his head. "We have got to draw her out somehow. This is not a great Society event, though the Sterlings are surely Society. It would have been a good event for her."

"And yet she would not," stated the low, pleasant voice of

173

Lieutenant Henshaw as he reached them. He shook his head and shrugged as he moved to shake Camden's hand. "Much as I tried."

"You've been to see her?" Grace asked, giving Henshaw a curious look. "When? I was only there this morning."

Henshaw returned her look with a smile. "As her unofficial brother in London, I call upon Lady Edith once a week. We must have crossed paths today, Miss Morledge. May I ask what you were doing there?"

Grace's lips curved into a rueful smile. "Edith and I were commiscrating on our shared experience of being daughters who disappoint their fathers." She fluttered her lashes playfully, but Izzy could see the strain in her features. There was real pain in her father's disapproval.

Izzy held out a hand and Grace took it, squeezing tight.

"I've met your father once," Charlotte told her slowly, coming around the chairs to Grace, "and I was not particularly impressed." She kissed Grace on the cheek and wrapped an arm about her waist. "I think you'd best be disappointed in him rather than the other way around."

Grace hummed a noncommittal noise, her smile tight.

"Come on, Grace," Camden said, striding out from the pillar. "Best solution for disappointed fathers is a lively dance. I should know, I made a living out of disappointing my father."

"You had a father?" Charlotte asked Camden with derision.

He pulled Grace away and gave Charlotte a sardonic look she was only too pleased to return.

Sometimes, Izzy wondered if Camden and Charlotte were siblings, despite their legitimacy in their respective families.

"Izzy…"

Prue's hesitant, warning tone brought Izzy up, and she looked where Prue indicated.

Sebastian and Kitty had apparently arrived, and while Sebastian made polite conversation with Francis and Janet, Alice Sterling had somehow escaped Georgie and commandeered Kitty, who was now being introduced to Hugh.

"Where did Georgie go?" Izzy asked of anyone.

"Miranda has her," Elinor reported at once, "and Tony's over by

174

Francis."

Izzy grumbled and rose to her feet. "This will be pleasant." She started forward only to find Henshaw accompanying her. She glanced up at him in surprise and amusement. "I don't recall requesting reinforcements, Lieutenant."

He smiled politely at her. "A good soldier doesn't need asking, Miss Lambert. Lead on."

It wasn't much of a comfort to have a witness to whatever was about to commence, but Henshaw might ensure that Hugh was civil.

Hugh saw them coming and dashed that hope rather quickly. "Oh, good, the Spinster and her lackey are come to save the fair maidens."

Henshaw growled beside her, and Hugh barely batted an eye in his direction.

Izzy smiled as politely as possible at him. "I only came to greet your sister, Mr. Sterling, as I had the pleasure of meeting her before, and I had hoped to introduce Miss Morton to you."

Kitty seemed to whimper in distress, eyeing the people around, clearly uncomfortable beside Alice.

Hugh eyed Kitty briefly. "She's as bad as the goat, isn't she? But perhaps more coherent."

"Hugh," Alice scolded, sounding shocked by the venom in his voice, if not the words.

"Miss Morton, I'm to fetch you for your brother," Henshaw bit out, keeping his attention on Hugh. "He'd like to dance with you, if Miss Sterling doesn't mind the deprivation."

Kitty squeaked some sort of answer and moved to Henshaw, who held an arm out to her. She looped her arm through his, her eyes lowered to the floor, her cheeks growing rosier by the moment.

"Hugh, why would you say that?" Alice demanded once Kitty was out of earshot. "Miss Morton is very sweet, and what will Miss Lambert think?"

Hugh sneered at Izzy. "Miss Lambert thinks nothing. Miss Lambert is always so good and kind, she would never rise to the baiting. She is above the wounds of mortal man. She will save any young woman she can from a depraved soul like myself. Oh, yes, Miss Lambert is a saint among we poor sinners, and we are blessed by her benevolence, are we not?"

Alice stared at her brother in horror, blinking her wide eyes that shifted to Izzy in outright confusion.

Instinct told Izzy to tamp down the bristling, to rise above such childish prodding, and to ignore it and move on, as she had always done. What could be served by responding?

A movement nearby caught her eye, and she saw Sebastian, now standing near them, his hands balled into fists at his sides, his eyes on her. He dipped his chin in the barest hint of a nod.

Right. Defense.

Izzy slid her gaze to Hugh and forced her smile. "I was feeling sorry for you earlier, Mr. Sterling."

He blinked at her words, obviously not what he had expected her to stay.

"Not because I am a particularly benevolent person, but because I am a human one." She swallowed the rawness in her throat and the sudden burning there. "And I see at this moment the pain in your sister's eyes at what you've said. Yes, I know very well what you think of me, and of my goodness, but I wonder what you think of hers. I wonder why you feel you may attack an innocent young woman purely because she associates with me." Heat began to seep into her cheeks, and she fisted her hands. "I have never done you wrong and have only held sympathy for whatever trials you face that lead you to behave in such a way. I have grown used to your attacks on me, and you are right, I never rise to them. But you are gravely mistaken if you think I do not feel the wounds inflicted upon me." Her eyes burned fiercely, but she could not blink now. Not if she wanted to get through this. "If you wish to sink yourself into whatever pit you think to find comfort in, be my guest, sir. But perhaps if you were a little more like the good and a little less like the depraved, you might see that the wounds you inflict hurt more than only your target. Excuse me."

She swept away, her knees shaking with a fear she had not expressed, and her breath a little panicked for what she'd said.

It had felt so good, so exhilarating, and yet so unnatural.

What had she done?

"Iz," Sebastian murmured, his voice sounding awed and pleased as she passed him.

She shook her head, despite the pleasant tickle his nickname stirred within her. "Dance with your sister," she told him quietly. "Don't make Henshaw a liar."

She didn't wait to see if he did so and kept moving.

She had to.

Defense of herself did not come easily, and it did not sit well, for some reason. Had she said too much? Had she gone too far? Should there have been more? She left matters such as this to the bold and secure, not to herself, who was so submissive by habit and insecure in all things. She would replay it over and over in her mind this evening and into the night, likely not sleep well, and the urge to write out an apology and send it before the morning post would come crashing down upon her shortly.

Lord, if her mother were to find out...

"Miss Lambert."

She drew up short, manners and politeness reigning supreme. "Yes?"

Lord Sterling stood there, extending a hand, his features arranged in contrition, if not outright pleading. "Will you let me have this dance?"

She stared at him, dying beyond anything to refuse, yet seeing his need for her to accept.

One could have too much willfulness in a single evening.

She nodded quickly. "Of course, my lord. Of course." She turned and put her hand in his, letting him lead.

"I don't know what was said, Izzy, and I don't care," Lord Sterling murmured in a very low voice, his smile fixed in place. "I beg you to forget it and let me apologize for him."

"I don't hold you to any part of it," she told him, trying for the same sort of smile. "I know better than to think he reflects any of you."

"You are generous."

She gave him a look. "No, I'm not," she said flatly.

His smile was suddenly more natural. "If you think this doesn't feel generous to me, who is quite ashamed at the present, you are sadly mistaken." He leaned closer and whispered, "And you have to know that Janet and I know very well you aren't nearly as good as everybody thinks. Better than most, but hardly perfect."

Izzy laughed and felt the tension within her ebb away a touch. "I don't think you could have said anything better."

"Good." He straightened and cleared his throat. "Now we had better make this a fine dance indeed, Miss Lambert. Mr. Morton is dancing with his sister, and I feel quite sure he would trade her for you as partner if I give him an inch."

At once her attention turned to Sebastian, who was fixed on her with an intensity that clutched at her chest. Pride, concern, and warmth shone in his countenance, even with his reserve and discretion. She could see all of it clearly, and it moved her.

"Oh…" she eventually said as they took their place.

Lord Sterling raised a brow. "Should I give him an inch, Miss Lambert?"

Izzy stared at Sebastian for a moment longer, let her lips almost curve, then turned her attention to her partner with a full, teasing smile. "Not even half of one, my lord."

Chapter Fifteen

Retaliation is a sword that is swift and sure. Few who wield it know how, and those that do know better.

-_The Spinster Chronicles, 23 September 1815_

Her pen flew along the page, the words coming to her with clarity and purpose beyond anything she'd experienced yet. Description and prose formed with remarkable effortlessness, pristine in its creation and pure in its flow. Her fingers would be smudged beyond anything she'd experienced yet, her haste in not waiting for the ink to dry leaving its evidence clearly.

She didn't care.

Couldn't care.

Finally… _finally_ she felt her imagination magnifying itself and showing her the extent of its expanse. The worlds it could create, the characters it could wield, and all the glorious beauties within its scope.

It was perfect. Absolutely and unimaginably perfect.

"What in the world can be that exciting about Fashion Forum?"

Izzy snapped her head up and looked wide-eyed at Georgie, sitting nearby and sipping her tea.

Her cousin seemed mildly amused by Izzy's response, but wildly curious about what she had been engaged in.

Fashion Forum? Was that…?

Izzy paled as she looked around the room and realized that in a room filled with Spinsters, she had been caught up feverishly in her new story.

She hadn't said a single word about anything fashion related, unless one considered the brooch that Belinda Beaver had purchased in the tale as something worthy of mention. As that particular brooch happened to be made from honeycomb, Izzy highly doubted it would count.

"Oh, Izzy's quite passionate about the tartan calico that has become so popular of late," Edith smoothly commented from the corner where she worked on the lead article. "We talked all about it just the other day, didn't we, dear?"

Izzy nodded fervently, smiling at Edith, who was nodding emphatically at her. "Yes, we did."

"What, because Edith's Scottish?" Charlotte asked, looking up from her Quirks and Quotes draft. "That Highland bit of her?"

Edith looked at her ruefully. "Bit of me? Charlotte, that bit is the majority of me. I'm from Inverness, lass, and you don't get much more Highland than that."

Charlotte waved a hand at her. "Yes, yes, dear, I'm quite aware. That lovely brogue of yours reminds me at every turn."

"Yes," Izzy said again, wondering if Charlotte would venture into Scottish and English relations over tea and cakes. "I thought I would get Edith's perspective on the recent trend, given all that history."

"What history?" Kitty asked, looking between Edith, Charlotte, and Izzy in turn. She sat next to Prue, helping her with the Society Dabbler and sipping tea quietly.

Edith set down her pen and turned towards Kitty with a kind smile. "Och, lass, 'tis a murky muddle of political and social matters that we really needn't explore in such a genteel setting as this. But suffice it to say that the wearing of clan tartans was outlawed in Scotland during the last century, and it's all permitted now, as is the Highland culture, in a way, but recently tartan has become a popular print of calico. Even those with no Scottish ties are wearing it."

Kitty's eyes were round, yet her tea never so much as quivered in her hand. "Does that offend you?" Kitty whispered.

Edith smiled with more than a hint of humor. "Not in the least, lass. Unless Charlotte wore my clan's tartan."

"I beg your pardon!" Charlotte laughed in delight.

Izzy quietly returned to her desk, discreetly sliding her story under other papers, and pulling a fresh sheet out.

Apparently, she was writing an article about tartan calico and the consideration one ought to take with such things.

Lovely.

"I love the tartan calico myself," Grace offered from her chair near the window. "It can be so flattering,"

"Maybe for you, dear," Georgie scoffed, reaching for another biscuit. "It does nothing for me, I can assure you."

Izzy glanced over at Edith surreptitiously, and found the woman watching her with a bemused smile.

She nodded her thanks, and Edith acknowledged it with a dip of her chin. Then she winked at Izzy and went back to her article.

Edith was so delightful an ally, and Izzy had never imagined such a thing.

She would have to tell her the good news.

"DISGRACEFUL!" bellowed a voice down the hall.

Charlotte groaned, put down her pen, and covered her face. "Oh, good. Elinor's here."

Kitty giggled a laugh, then covered her mouth.

Charlotte dropped her hands and grinned at the young woman. "I knew I liked you, Kitty Morton. You have excellent taste."

Kitty giggled again, and Prue patted her knee fondly, sighing. "You'll g-get used to Charlotte, dear."

"Don't encourage her," Grace muttered, straightening up and facing the doorway in anticipation of their new arrival.

"MONSTROUS! SHAMEFUL, APPALLING, AND SO REPREHENSIBLE!"

Elinor appeared in the door, indignation as high as her color, her hair barely containing itself in whatever form she'd left home in. She stood there, glaring at them all, chest heaving as she fumed.

"Did you swallow a dictionary, Elinor?" Charlotte asked dryly as she picked up her tea, making a face when she sipped it. "Lord above, Izzy, why would your mother...?"

"What a mess, what a mess," Izzy's mother suddenly said as she appeared behind Elinor.

Charlotte coughed quickly, setting aside her tea. "Mrs. Lambert! What a pleasure."

"Oh, my dear girls," Izzy's mother simpered, looking around at all of them. Her gaze fell on Izzy, and immediately filled with tears.

Izzy turned in her chair completely. "Mama?"

"Aunt Faith, you're frightening me," Georgie told her as she folded her shawl more tightly around her.

Elinor glared harder at Georgie. "*I* wasn't frightening you?"

"You frighten me out of my wits, child," Charlotte scoffed, waving her into the room. "On a daily basis. Mrs. Lambert, on the other hand, never has."

Elinor threw up her hands, then pulled a paper from her reticule. "I do believe Mrs. Lambert and I are upset over the same thing." She shoved the paper at Charlotte, then sat down roughly on the sofa. She reached for the tea, then hesitated, glancing up at Izzy's mother, before wisely changing course and reaching for a cake.

Charlotte's eyes flew over the page, her brow furrowing further and further as she did so. Then she looked up, scowled, and slammed the paper down on the table. She screeched a sound through clamped lips, then looked down at her hands as they clenched painfully together in her lap.

Izzy looked at Georgie and found her cousin wide-eyed and curious, then they both turned their attention to Charlotte.

"Is she all right?" Izzy's mother asked, wiping away a tear.

Charlotte smiled tightly, blinking twice. "As well as can be expected. I was only restraining my less ladylike exclamations so they would not sully your ears and make you think less of me."

Impossibly, Izzy's mother smiled. "My dear, I have three sons, two of whom have been known to exclaim all sorts of things, and I still consider them gentlemen. Under the circumstances, I would have thought it mildly appropriate." She looked at Izzy again, and her smile turned more tender, and then she moved back out of the room.

Charlotte stared at the door, then at Izzy, shaking her head slowly. "Now I have seen it all, Isabella Lambert."

Izzy shrugged, then indicated the paper. "What is it?"

Charlotte plucked up the paper, then looked at it again. "Let's see if I can find a bit worth reading." She hummed in discontent, then cleared her throat. " 'The bitterest, most reviled of women, they consider themselves to be above any and all company, which their unmarried state would surely disprove. According to one such Spinster,' with a capital S, I might add," Charlotte told them all, interrupting the reading.

"Continue, please," Grace told her tightly.

Charlotte nodded once, then looked back to the page.

" 'According to one such Spinster, who is considered by all to be the kindest of the lot, this writer is depraved and injurious to those around him, simply for wishing to meet a young woman and warn her against the dangers of such company. What hope is there for any innocent young woman if the Spinsters descend upon her and turn her into one as cold and jaded as they? For they truly wish all women to remain as unmarried and without purpose as they themselves are. They have even put a respectable lady into a compromising position that they might be the heroines to save her, thus projecting their own self-importance into the attention and notice of Society. They must be stopped, and our innocent misses saved.' "

The parlor was silent as Charlotte finished, and the sound of the paper rustling against the table as she replaced it seemed deafening.

"Who would write such a thing?" Grace murmured weakly, looking a little pale.

"Two guesses," Elinor replied with a stiff voice. "And it rhymes with Hugh Sterling."

Izzy could barely hear them over the sound of her heartbeat pounding in her ears, as her entire body began to fume with indignation. Odd that she could not see the steam rising from her, even as she could feel it doing so. Heat and tension filled every part of her in equal measure, extending all lengths and breadths of every limb and appendage.

She could not even feel her face anymore.

Just heat.

"Why would he write such horrid things?" Kitty asked, her voice sounding like that of a child.

Elinor laughed darkly and sat up, facing the younger girl with venom in her eyes.

"That's enough, Elinor," Georgie said before the girl could start on a topic from which they would never recover her.

Izzy blinked and somehow it pained her.

She had been the one Hugh had written about. She had been the one to enrage him to this degree. She had stood up to him and told him how he injured others. She had...

She had offended him defending herself.

Now he had written something for all of London to see, slandering them in every way, except by name, though anyone with a basic insight into London Society and gossip would know exactly who was being spoken of.

Everyone would know he meant her.

And all they had tried to do would come to nothing because of her.

Izzy shot to her feet, hands clenching and unclenching at her sides.

"Izzy?"

She didn't know who asked, and she didn't particularly care.

She moved out of the parlor, walking swiftly and stiffly, her arms swinging just the smallest bit by her sides, hands now balled into tight fists. She paced out in the corridor, willing her heart to quiet itself, for her temper to abate, for some semblance of her calmer, kinder self to reappear. After so many years of being generous and gracious and biting her tongue, now one act of defiance uprooted all of that?

Her pacing picked up, more frantic, just as her heart did.

Something needed to give, something needed to burst, something...

"Izzy, come here."

Her arm was grabbed, and she felt herself tugged along, and she didn't resist. She inhaled and exhaled roughly through her nose, tears burning at her eyes.

Then suddenly she found herself in the library, among the books and the solitude that had always accompanied this room.

She exhaled once, then turned around.

Sebastian stood there, watching her, his expression curiously blank. She'd forgotten he was in the house, that he would have made himself comfortable in the library, as he tended to do when Kitty was there with the Spinsters. She'd forgotten that he would have been able to hear her pacing, that he would be aware, that he…

She shook her head and held out a hand. "Sebastian, I have just had some distressing news, and I'm not entirely calm at the moment. It would be best if you would leave me be."

"Good."

She blinked at him in confusion. "What?"

He lifted a broad shoulder, his gaze squarely on her. "I said, 'Good.' You should be angry and upset, and it should drive you to distraction. I'm pleased you could admit as much aloud, let alone to me."

Izzy began to shake where she stood. "Why are you so delighted by my reaction to…?"

"To Hugh Sterling's article?" Sebastian finished with a knowing look.

She bit down on the inside of her lip, her fingers rubbing against each other hard. "I'm beginning to wonder if you sent it in for him."

Now Sebastian smirked, though there was a coldness to his look. "Just because I am pleased with your response, Iz, doesn't mean that I take delight in what happened, or that I had anything to do with it. Quite the contrary, actually. I'm considering riding over to fetch Camden Vale, and perhaps Tony, and paying a visit to Hugh Sterling to let him know exactly how we feel about it."

Izzy widened her eyes at that and swallowed once.

"The only reason I have not done so already," Sebastian went on, perfectly calm, "is that I fear taking Vale along would mean I would not have opportunity to get in a single blow, and that would not do for me at all."

"No?" Izzy asked, wishing she could smile, that she could take pleasure in what he was saying, but the anger still raged within her, and tears were nearing the surface.

Sebastian shook his head, then put his hands on his hips. "Well?"

"Well, what?" Izzy asked through gritted teeth.

He grunted softly. "Don't bite it back, Iz. It's just us. Rage and roar, cry, and scream… I can see the anger and the hurt within you. Let it out."

Izzy whimpered a strangled, growling sound. "How?" she pleaded, her teeth grinding now. "There is so… much…"

"Tell me, Iz," Sebastian told her, taking two steps forward. "Tell me what you're feeling, how it burns, what you want to do…"

Izzy squeezed her eyes shut, exhaling an almost sob. "I want to scream in his face, and I want to tear his nasty article to shreds. I want to eviscerate him in the Chronicles, and I want to tell everyone what really happened, what he's really like. How cruel he was to Prue, and what he did to Georgie, what he…" She swallowed, biting off before she could confess what he'd said about Kitty.

If anything was going to make Sebastian lose his reserve, it would be that.

She had to spare him that much.

"I feel so angry," she growled, pacing again, blinking back the tears. "Angry… and embarrassed."

"Embarrassed?" Sebastian stepped into her pacing path. "Why?"

She rubbed her thumbs over her clenched fingers. "I've spent my entire life being good and quiet and avoiding attracting attention. The Spinster Chronicles gave me some, it's true, but it was still anonymous. I've been nice and kind and giving and obedient… and the one time that I decide to stand up for myself, I bring all my best friends down with me. I was singled out, blatantly so, but it was also an attack on all of us. And it's my fault."

He moved to her quickly, taking her arms. "No. No, no, no, you do *not* get to turn his actions into something to blame yourself for."

"How else can I look at it?" she demanded, looking up at him. "I decide to not stay silent, and it offends him to such a degree that he lashes out publicly."

"That is *his* fault," Sebastian insisted, taking her chin in hand. "Not yours. It's not your fault. Don't waste a single moment of your glorious fury feeling guilty or ashamed. Don't apologize. Don't pity. Don't."

A tear edged its way from the corner of Izzy's eye and rolled down her cheek. Sebastian watched it fall, then gently wiped it away, brushing her cheek again. The path of his thumb left a warm, tingling sensation in its wake, leaving the rest of her skin deliciously cool by comparison. His eyes returned to hers, and she was struck by the impossible color of them. Such a fine, rich blue, and like nothing she'd ever seen in nature or in life.

Only his eyes had that color.

Only he could.

"You're still angry," he whispered, his thumb brushing her cheek once more.

"It's fading," she replied in the same tone.

A corner of his mouth curved, and with it her knees, as they suddenly seemed to sway in that direction, leaving her feeling a bit at sea. "But it's still there, isn't it, Iz?"

Her wavering knees began to buzz, tickling up and down her legs with the name only he called her. And she was helpless to resist him when he looked at her like that. Or called her that...

She wet her lips carefully, her fingers unclenching with just as much force as they had been clenched moments before. "Still there," she told him with real honesty, "but certainly better. I don't know that I've ever raged like that in my life."

He chuckled. "I just wanted you to express yourself, Izzy. I wanted you to let yourself feel the pain he caused, not ignore it or write it off or feel bad for it."

"And I would have, too," she admitted, finally able to laugh at herself. "No doubt in an hour, I will write an apology to Hugh Sterling, given that I upset him so, and wallow in guilt for my anger."

"You should never feel guilty for feeling things," Sebastian told her softly. "It's a natural part of us. And as for Hugh Sterling..."

He reached out and touched her cheek gently, as though she had another tear falling, though she knew full well that there were none.

"He doesn't deserve an apology," he murmured, his eyes trained on hers. "Not from you. You have nothing to apologize for."

"But I feel bad," Izzy breathed as she willed her hands to move, to hold onto him, to do anything but hang uselessly by her sides.

They did nothing.

"Don't." His voice was a hoarse rasp, a ripple that cascaded down her frame, and then his lips were on hers.

Gentle, soft, and sweet, his lips caressed hers, creating sensations and feelings she had never experienced, and had no defense against. Her eyes fluttered shut, and she was lost to the new and bewildering sensations. His thumb brushed against her cheek, the tingling pressure making her gasp against his mouth.

She felt him smile against her, felt the gentle tilting of her face up to his, felt the more perfect fit against his lips this way. Her unresponsive hands suddenly moved, trembling as they went to his coat, not gripping, not clutching, not even holding the material. They simply felt him, rested against him, connected with him.

She had never been kissed in her life, and her inexperience was on display now, sending an embarrassed burn across her skin. She didn't know how to respond, how to be, what to think. All she knew was that she loved this, wanted this, needed more of this…

How? How to ask him, how to show him, how…

He broke off with a soft stroke to her cheek, then his thumb moved to her bottom lip and gave it a brief caress.

She opened her eyes and stared into his, feeling his heart pound beneath her hands.

It matched her own.

Sebastian smiled the gentlest, warmest, most perfect smile at her. "I had to kiss you, Iz. I've been wanting to for days."

Her legs shook with his admission, and she managed to smile back at him. "I'm sorry I didn't know how to go about it."

His hand cradled her face, and he kissed her nose very softly. "Don't apologize for that. I don't mind in the slightest."

"I feel… very much at a disadvantage for it," Izzy told him, sighing in a mixture of delight and apology. "It's maddening."

"Don't worry, Iz," he told her, that maddening smile still playing at his lips. "I'll help you."

She laughed at the offer, and tossed her hair, giving him a wry look. "Are you going to make that one of the conditions of our partnership, too?"

Sebastian grinned, then sobered with a shrug. "Perhaps. It seems a very good idea to me."

Izzy rolled her eyes, her fingers shifting against his chest. "So helpful. Such a gentleman."

Something changed in his eyes, and his smile turned less playful. "Even a gentleman feels things."

She tilted her head at that, curious and wondering. "What do you do? When you're angry?"

He shrugged, his hand moving to her shoulder, rubbing her arm.

"Depends on the situation. I don't have much of a temper, though I certainly have my moments. Actually, my mother first helped me with my emotions."

"Your mother?" Izzy repeated, rearing back.

He gave a soft, humorless laugh. "Yes, when I was a child, and I felt particularly angry about something, but tried not to show it, she took me into a room of breakable things, and told me to pick one. Then, she had me throw it across the room."

Izzy stared, gaping a bit. "You aren't serious."

He nodded. "It was important to her that I be honest with myself about what I was feeling," he went on, his eyes distant and unfocused. "Even if I couldn't express it publicly. I'm a reserved man, but that doesn't mean I'm also impassive or unfeeling. Quite the opposite." His gaze suddenly sharpened on her. "I want you to express yourself, Izzy, and to give yourself the value that you always seem to give to others. Your kind, generous heart needs to be inclined towards you as well. Be kind to yourself. You are too remarkable to be anything less."

She exhaled, touched by the warmth and concern she saw in his countenance, and by the tenderness in his words. "If you keep flattering me," she managed to tease, her throat tightening, "I'll begin to think you have designs."

A very soft laugh escaped him, and a crooked smile appeared. "Perhaps I do."

Perhaps he *what?*

She hastily cleared her throat. "Do you... still throw things?"

He stepped away, though his eyes seemed to give her another tender caress. "No, that was the only time. Cleaning things up seemed a poor use of energy." He smiled gently. "You'd best get back to the Spinsters, Iz. They'll likely send out a search party."

She nodded shakily, her feet moving of their own accord towards the door. Yes, the Spinsters. Her friends. Her article. Her story. There was much to be done, and here...

Here...

She turned to glance back at him before she left the room and found him watching her.

She couldn't help it; she grinned at him.

And her heart soared when he grinned back.

Cheeks flaming, she turned and started down the corridor.

"The library, Izzy dear?" her mother asked as she suddenly came into view.

Izzy nodded, praying her cheeks were not as red as they felt. "Yes, Mama. I wanted to be sure Mr. Morton was all right. The article, you know, may distress people, and I didn't want him to worry for Kitty."

Her mother took her hand, smiling lovingly. "I'm not worried for Kitty. Or for any of you."

"You're not?" Izzy asked, surprised in spite of herself.

"Not at all," her mother replied easily. "I am sorry for it, of course, but I know none of it to be true. You are all such fine young women, and do not deserve this."

"Then you..." Izzy swallowed and felt tears threaten again. "Then you'll stand by me?"

Her mother's mouth gaped for a moment, then she gathered Izzy close. "Of course, my love. Of *course* we'll stand by you. We always will. Nothing will change that."

Izzy hugged her mother tightly, heart soaring, tears burning behind her eyelids.

Her mother sniffled, then pulled back, giving Izzy an encouraging smile. "Now, dear, go back into that room, and put a response in the Chronicles that will make that Hugh Sterling wish he hadn't crossed paths with Isabella Lambert."

"Mother!" Izzy coughed, laughing in delight. "You don't think I should rise above this and turn the other cheek?"

"Oh, certainly, certainly," her mother returned, a twinkle in her eye. "Just find a way to have Christian charity and return fire at the same time." She winked, patted Izzy's arms, and moved past her down the corridor.

Izzy watched her go, jaw dropped, incapable of concise thought.

Then one thought appeared, and her mouth formed a satisfied smile. She moved towards the drawing room with a quick step and grinned at her friends when she arrived.

"I have an idea."

Chapter Sixteen

A bit of mystery is good for a person. And a bit of revelation possibly even better.

-*The Spinster Chronicles, 10 November 1818*

"Miranda has outdone herself. Look at this décor, and for only a simple card party?"

"I think Mrs. Johnston has outdone herself, and Miranda is taking all the credit."

"How well you know my stepmother."

"Well, you told such fine tales of her, Sterling, that it was impossible not to know her. And I find the reality to exceed even your detailed descriptions."

Sebastian smiled a little at his friends and their conversation but saw no reason to take part in it. The room was indeed elegantly furnished, and perhaps overdone for something so informal, but not without taste. The space was filling with guests, but hardly so many as to be overcrowded. All told, it was destined to be a lovely evening, and undoubtedly filled with people he enjoyed spending time with.

But he wasn't currently paying attention to any of that, or any of them.

It had been three days since he had seen Izzy, three days since those exquisite moments in the library, and three days since he had felt a single moment of sanity.

He wasn't prepared for this. Hadn't prepared for this.

Had never felt this.

Izzy brought light to his life, energy to his days, and feeling to his soul. He, who had been reserved for so long, could no longer be so when he was with her. He had to tell her everything, let down all his defenses, reach out when he was more inclined to retreat within.

He was more alive with her. He hadn't known he'd ever become less than that.

Not until Izzy.

Only with Izzy.

He inhaled slowly and exhaled the same. His friends couldn't know. They would make light of it, tease him, pester him until he could come to resent them or his feelings, and he couldn't bear either. He might be more accustomed to teasing now that Izzy was taking up the charge, but it was different with her.

Everything was.

"Did you see the Spinster Chronicles today?" Henshaw asked of them, taking a glass of punch from a passing footman. "Absolutely brilliant."

More keenly aware of anything related to the Spinsters now than ever, Sebastian turned to the others. "Pardon?"

Tony raised a brow at him. "Did you not see the edition that went out?"

He shook his head, looking between them. "No, should I have?"

His friend chuckled and shifted to lean closer. "As a husband of a Spinster, I will always suggest that you read them, and read them well. We thank you for your support."

Sebastian rolled his eyes, which made Henshaw laugh, and scowled. "I usually do, and not just to show support. They're always well written and spot on, in those areas I have interest in. I usually skim the Fashion Forum, rather than read thoroughly."

"I won't tell," Tony swore, raising a hand.

"I enjoy that one," Henshaw commented with slightly pursed lips. "They don't hold back on something they disagree with. It brought up several good points about tartan calico."

Sebastian gave him an utterly bewildered look. "What in the world do you know about tartan calico, Henshaw?"

The look was returned with a marked degree of derision. "I have seven sisters. I know everything about tartan calico, believe me."

Sebastian had one sister, no other siblings, and he could honestly say that he had no knowledge of any calico at all, let alone tartan calico.

No matter.

"Was that what I am supposed to read so intently?" Sebastian asked them, keeping his tone mild, if dubious. "Tartan calico?"

Tony scoffed loudly. "Lord, no."

Henshaw shook his head quickly, chuckling to himself. "No, Morton, I don't give a damn about tartan calico."

"That's a relief," Sebastian muttered. "I was beginning to worry."

Tony gave him a quelling look, his mouth curving into a lopsided smile. "They brought in a guest writer for the first time."

"The Spinsters?" Sebastian grunted softly, considering that idea. "What for?"

"As a rebuttal against Hugh Sterling, surely," Henshaw suggested, looking to Tony for confirmation.

Tony nodded, barely restraining the pride in his eyes. "Georgie could barely contain herself when she told me. Refused to say whose idea it was, not that it matters, as it was unanimous once suggested, but she's absolutely delighted at what they've started."

"Who wrote it?" Sebastian asked him, his interest piqued despite his inclination.

"It's anonymous," Henshaw pointed out. "Same as all the other articles. No names at all."

That made him frown in thought. "Then how do you know it was a guest writer? Is it not possible that it was just one of the Spinsters pretending to be otherwise?"

Henshaw made a face of consideration, then turned to Tony. "That's entirely possible, you know."

"I don't think so," Tony said with a quick shake of his head. "Not with the way Georgie described it. She said that a guest wrote the article in defense of the Spinsters after what had been published, and it would not have the same effect if it had been written by one of them. Surely you see that."

Sebastian sighed and gestured with his hands slightly. "Of course I see that, but surely *you* must see that no one would know if their guest was Lady Edith or Miss Morledge or Camden Vale."

"I think we could safely say it's not Vale," Henshaw coughed, laughing and grinning without restraint. "The language is far too refined."

"The point is," Tony went on, riding right over them both, "that it has caught fire. The entire city is talking about it. The argument, if you can call it that, is sensible and sophisticated, avoids attacking the 'esteemed writer of a recent article', and yet swiftly cuts away every single point of the original complaint." He exhaled, shaking his head. "It's quite a masterful piece. And everyone is dying to know who the guest is."

Sebastian smiled, his mind spinning on the idea silently. The author was clearly someone with skills in writing and language, someone who could clearly and concisely express their thoughts on paper and had no compunction to having their words read by others.

He knew one woman with ties to the Spinsters who fit that description.

Izzy.

It would not surprise him in the slightest if she had posed as a guest writer to send a proper reply to Hugh's slander. Given the glorious manner in which she had allowed her anger to rise and fall in the library, he knew full well how pained she had been.

Had she taken his words to heart and chosen to defend herself in the most comfortable manner available?

His thoughts latched onto the picture of Izzy he had conjured up, and he found himself searching the room for her yet again.

If he discovered that she'd done this marvelous thing, stood up to the tyrannical defamation of her character from a wastrel, he wanted to know. He wanted to praise her.

He wanted to kiss her until neither of them could breathe properly.

He swallowed with difficulty, the idea searing itself into his mind.

He might have to do that anyway.

"My money is on Miss Asheley," Henshaw mused aloud, pointing in the direction of Elinor at the card table.

Tony snorted in derision. "Elinor? Absolutely not, her response to the article would have much more fire and brimstone and possibly some profanity."

Sebastian found himself nodding, then stopped in absolute arrestment as Izzy finally entered the room with her mother.

The conversation around him faded, his frantic heart picked up its pace, and everything within him suddenly became acutely attuned to her. She was across the room, and it was as though he could hear her breathing. Could feel the touch of her skin on his fingers.

Could taste the softness of her lips.

Henshaw and Tony continued to speculate beside him.

"Lady Edith?" Henshaw queried. "I could confront her on my next visit."

"I can't see any of the actual Spinsters posing as a friend offering a different point of view," Tony replied in a doubtful tone. "It must actually be a guest writer."

"Lady Hetty, then."

"No, no, it was far too polite. Sounded young."

Sebastian watched as Izzy greeted Miranda and the Johnstons, as she and her mother laughed at something Miranda said, the resemblance between them never more striking than with their laughter.

Lord, but Izzy was a glorious sight when she laughed.

He ought to make her laugh, and laugh often.

Why was he not more amusing?

"What about your cousin?" Henshaw asked Tony.

"I asked Alice, and she was very evasive about the whole thing. It's a distinct possibility, but I'm not sure."

Sebastian didn't care who had written what or if she were young, old, or markedly scarred upon her face. Someone had come to Izzy's defense, and that was all that mattered.

That was everything that mattered.

Izzy moved from their hosts to the table where Elinor, her sister Emma, Georgie, and Lady Hetty sat playing at whist, and greeted all with a warm, bright smile. No hint of the distress he had seen at their last meeting, and only strength emanated from her.

Strength and goodness, and the sudden need to smile.

That was what Izzy brought.

That was what he needed.

Good heavens, he was turning into a pathetic, obsessive fool.

Izzy looked up then and saw him. Her shoulders relaxed, her eyes softened, and her smile became more gentle, secretive, and quivering at the edges.

Yes... Yes, he was turning into a fool, and it was a delightful sensation.

He smiled back at her, dipping his chin in greeting.

She responded in kind, then moved to greet Kitty, who stood looking out of a window with Lady Edith. Kitty beamed when she saw her, and Lady Edith kissed her cheek quickly, then all turned to the window, looking out at something.

"I see what you're looking at," Tony said softly. "Shouldn't you do something about it?"

Sebastian jerked and turned to look at his friend, only to find Tony speaking to Henshaw, who was also staring shamelessly.

"No, I think not," Henshaw answered, missing the mark on achieving his usual teasing air.

"Come, come, you know she thinks highly of you," Tony went on.

Sebastian prepared to snarl and argue, defend his tenuous position, such as it was, and declare himself in pursuit of Izzy. He'd have brawled with Henshaw in the center of this room, if he had to, and despite Henshaw's size and skill, Sebastian would be the undisputed victor.

"Do I?" Henshaw murmured, his tone strained.

Sebastian's hands curled into fists at his sides.

"You meet with her every week, man, can you not see that?" Tony laughed.

He what?

Sebastian glanced over and saw Henshaw blink and smile more fully. "Yes, I suppose Lady Edith must think highly of me. Or simply suffer the poor fool charged with her care."

Somehow, Sebastian avoided swaying with relief, and his lips moved on a very fast, very silent prayer.

"And?" Tony prodded, sounding more like one of the Spinsters might than a well-trained army man.

Henshaw turned to Tony, smirking smugly. "And I have no

desire or need to share my secrets with you, Sterling. Excuse me while I go and flatter your stepmother." He bowed and strode over to Miranda.

Tony stepped closer to Sebastian, chuckling. "I will find out his secrets, mark my words."

Sebastian made a noncommittal sound and willed his unsteady heart to calm, letting his attention fall on Izzy again.

Never mind Henshaw's secrets. Sebastian was having trouble enough with his own.

"Sweet Miss Lambert, it is so good to see you here."

Izzy smiled at Lady Castleton as she moved to sit beside her. "My lady, it is a pleasure to see you as well."

Lady Castleton patted her hands gently, her eyes filled with a strange sheen of pity. "I trust you have heard of my daughter Beatrice's engagement."

"I did," Izzy replied with a bright smile for effect. "And to Mr. Hale, I trust? Such a fine man, I hope they will be very happy."

"Yes, yes, we are delighted by the match," Lady Castleton told her, still smiling in an almost condescending way. "Though I was loathe to make it known to you. You and Beatrice were so close as children, you were as an older sister to her."

Izzy looked at the older woman in surprise. "Yes, which is why I am so very pleased. And proud."

Lady Castleton simpered loudly and squeezed Izzy's hands. "You are so good. You are too good, my dear Isabella. I cannot fathom for the world why you are unmarried."

"The question of the age, I am afraid," Izzy answered as she rose from her chair, curtseying politely before moving away.

She couldn't stand another discussion about her marital state, particularly not as the target of pity or sympathy.

She was a spinster, she wasn't dying.

Apparently, there wasn't much difference.

"Dearest Miss Lambert," greeted Mrs. Johnston, Miranda's sister, as she approached.

She was a warm, generous woman, like her sister, but without Miranda's eccentricities. Izzy liked her very much indeed, but sensed she was in for another sympathetic word.

"You just look a picture," Mrs. Johnston praised, looking over Izzy with fondness. "You are far too pretty to be a spinster, though you do wear it well."

"Do I?" Izzy murmured with as kind a smile as she could manage. "That is good to know."

Mrs. Johnston missed the meaning behind Izzy's words and moved onto other guests, thankfully leaving their conversation at that.

Izzy looked for Sebastian but found him deep in conversation with Kitty and Edith, which she was pleased to see. Edith almost never went out in company, and thus had very few friends or connections outside of the Spinsters. It would do her good to associate more and escape from her loneliness.

"Izzy dear, come listen to this," her mother said, holding out a hand to her. "Come and listen to what Mrs. Larkin says about you."

Biting back a groan, Izzy moved to take her mother's hand, grateful that Lady Hetty was among the group gathered there. If this were as interminable as conversations with Mrs. Larkin ever were, at least she would not be alone in her endurance.

Mrs. Larkin, a rotund and ridiculous woman, fluttered in apparent delight at Izzy's arrival. "Oh, my dear girl, dear Isabella, I was only just saying that there is something absolutely and adamantly wrong with the men of this world."

"Is there?" Izzy asked, keeping her tone as mild as possible.

"There's a surprise for us," Lady Hetty cackled, tapping her walking stick on the ground.

"Especially in light of the fact that none of them have offered for you, dear girl." Mrs. Larkin clucked in discouragement. "I quite despair of the lot of them. Why can none of them see you for the treasure you are?"

Izzy smiled very tightly, exhaling slowly through her nose.

"You are so kind, Mrs. Larkin," Izzy's mother said with all the kindness a mother can possess. "We wonder the same thing about our Izzy all the time."

They all looked at Izzy for her reaction, and yet Izzy had none. It had all been said before.

Mrs. Larkin seemed to sense it was not something Izzy wished to discuss and clucked again. "Well, do not let it discourage you, Isabella. I am quite sure it will happen very soon, and then you will be happy."

Now Izzy's mother appeared to be forcing her smile, and she quickly took Mrs. Larkin to inspect a painting on the Johnstons' wall. She paused only briefly to give Izzy an apologetic look over her shoulder.

Left with only Lady Hetty, Izzy let her face relax, and ceased pretending at politeness.

"Very good, child," Lady Hetty praised as she took a seat. "Now cease biting your tongue before it bleeds."

That made Izzy smile a little, and she moved to stand against the wall.

"Are you all right?" Sebastian asked, suddenly at her side.

Izzy nodded her head, the wallpaper scratching audibly with the movement.

One look at him told her he did not believe that, and she shifted to shaking her head.

"I heard what was said," he told her, lowering his voice further still. "I hope that…"

Izzy waved a hand, silencing him. "Trust me, Sebastian. I have heard it all before. I am quite used to it."

"We all are," Lady Hetty added with a meaningful look. "It's all very helpful, as you can imagine."

" 'You'll find your husband somewhere,' " Izzy mimicked, keeping her voice soft. " 'Why aren't you married, child?' 'Someday it will be you.' 'I can't imagine how difficult this wedding is for you.' "

Sebastian leaned against the wall beside her, facing her, listening and watching with an intensity that emboldened her.

She closed her eyes and tapped her head against the wall once. "I am perfectly capable of enjoying the good things in the lives of others without feeling desolated about myself. Why does everyone around me assume that a woman must have a husband in order to have a fulfilling life?"

"Is that what they said?" Sebastian asked sharply, a defense audible.

"Never in those words," Izzy said, releasing a sigh, "but the meaning is clear."

"So, you are opposed to matrimony, then."

Izzy's eyes sprang open, and she looked at him in anguish. "No! No, not at all, but everybody always assumes that. I think it would be perfectly lovely to be married and to have children, to run a house, and everything else. I want that for myself more than I can dare express. But can nobody see that until that comes, if indeed it comes, I am simply trying to do the best I can?"

"I would never have suspected it troubles you this much," Sebastian murmured, shaking his head. "Or pretend to understand why you aren't depressed or even melancholy. You just smile and continue on."

"You think I am always happy?" she asked, looking up at him. "That I fall asleep at night with a smile and wake with one in the morning? I have been through a more desolate wilderness of feeling than most people will ever understand. Days and days of being utterly useless to anybody not because I wallow in despair, but because I wander through my life without a set purpose or true joy or real interest." She looked away, her throat burning and raw. "My private moments have been filled with agony and tears, and just because I refuse to show that to the world does not mean I have not felt it. But I cannot live in that misery, so I will smile and speak kindly and fill the world with optimism publicly while the pain of lost wishes and foregone hopes remains my private torment."

Sebastian surprised her by reaching out and squeezing her hand, a comforting gesture that weakened and strengthened her at the same time. She looked back to him and found a gentle, encouraging smile upon his lips, and the sight warmed her considerably.

"I'm going to fetch you a drink," he murmured, his eyes caressing her face. "I think you've earned it."

Izzy smiled in gratitude, nodding at him, feeling strangely bereft when he moved away and their hands parted.

Lady Hetty thumped her walking stick again. "You will get such things every day of your life, my dear, until you are either married or dead."

"I know," Izzy sighed, watching Sebastian walk away.

"And it is only because they do not know what to say."

She looked over at the older woman, her smile turning into one of understanding. "I know that, as well."

Lady Hetty's eyes speared her and held her attention. "And when they have known the joy that can come from love and marriage and children, and they see a woman they care enough about and think so highly of, they desire nothing more than that she, too, should know such joy in her life."

"But must they express it?" Izzy asked her, not bothering to hide her irritation. "It reminds me of all that I lack in that regard. I am trying to go on with my life, and though I am not an heiress, I would like to think that should I remain a spinster forever, my life might still have meaning and purpose."

"Gentle heart, it already has," Lady Hetty insisted. She smiled with more gentleness than Izzy had ever seen from her. "If I had been more like you in my youth, perhaps I would have been blessed with a love to sustain me and matrimony to keep me from loneliness. And I do not say that to join the ranks of those who are not helpful in their remarks, I only say so because I believe very firmly that there is nothing lacking in you to such a degree that you are unworthy of the love and situation you seek."

Touched beyond measure, Izzy found her throat clogged with emotion that she struggled to swallow down. "Thank you," she eventually managed.

Lady Hetty nodded, her eyes turning almost misty. Then she looked away, apparently surveying the card room. "I never married, as you know, and I was never in a position where I needed to for my own security. My family was wealthy and powerful, so an heiress I was, and my position in life secure. And I never found a love that would persuade me into matrimony, risking everything I already had for the sake of my heart."

Now it was Izzy who was leaning closer, transfixed by the raw confession of this terrifying woman she had come to respect and admire, if not fear, in a way.

"I'll never know if I would have done it," Lady Hetty went on.

She turned in her chair to look up at Izzy, her gaze serious indeed. "I have no regrets, and my life has been full. A woman can be complete on her own and in her own merits. But in this day and age, child, even that is rarely good enough. Make your plans, stay your course, and trust that the path of your life will make itself known, one way or the other."

"And if I never marry?" Izzy dared to ask, smiling for effect. "My family is not wealthy, my lady, and we have no position. I will be a burden upon them all my days."

Lady Hetty held out a wrinkled hand to her, and Izzy took it. "Come be my burden, dear, if that comes to pass. I can always use a companion, and it would be good to have another spinster inherit."

It was a kind offer, and terribly sweet, but there was no possibility of Izzy taking up Lady Hetty's offer, or her inheritance. If it came to it, Izzy would retire to a cottage in the country and live out her days in solitude. If her publications were successful, she would have funds enough to sustain herself, and while it would not be the sort of independence any woman might hope to achieve, it could be enough to avoid poverty, or the need to rely on her family for support.

But she smiled and nodded anyway, if only to assure the older woman that Izzy had heard her words and taken them to heart.

Sebastian returned to her then, drink in hand, and gave it to her. "Here, Iz. I don't know what Miranda has done to it, so be careful."

Izzy chuckled at that, sipping cautiously. "One never knows with Miranda." She hummed at the taste and grinned at him. "Seems to be quite all right."

"Give it time," he assured her, more relaxed than she had ever seen him in company. "Some of the strongest drinks have the subtlest effects."

"Are you a connoisseur of strong drinks, Mr. Gentleman Morton?" Izzy teased, sipping again.

He laughed to himself and his eyes traced her features. "No, Miss Lambert, I leave that unfortunate habit to men like Henshaw and Sterling."

Something he saw seemed to amuse him, and Izzy tilted her head at him. "What? What do you see?"

His mouth curled into a tender smile. "So much." He exhaled very softly. "I missed you, Iz. I didn't even know how much until I saw you come in."

Izzy's heart skipped a beat, and she stared at him with wide eyes. "It's been three days," she whispered, her voice barely audible even to her.

Sebastian heard it, and his smile grew. "I know," he whispered back. "I counted every one of the hours."

"You're flattering me," she scolded weakly, smiling despite her current breathlessness.

He shook his head very slowly and again reached for her hand, hiding it between them so the other guests wouldn't see. "No, I'm falling in love with you."

She gasped and swayed into the wall, her eyes searching his for any sign of teasing or insincerity.

She saw none.

"I thought you needed to know," he told her, his smile wavering uncertainly. "I hope you don't mind."

"I don't," she admitted in a rushing, gasping breath. "I don't mind at all."

He squeezed her hand again, and it was as though he had taken her in his arms and kissed her again. She grinned up at him, giddy and feeling rather reckless at the moment.

Perhaps she should kiss him anyway, public or no public.

"Izzy, come and be my partner," Georgie called, waving her over. "Mr. Morton, come and partner Tony."

Without a word, they moved to the card table, releasing hands and avoiding looking at each other. They sat in their respective chairs next to each other, and once settled, commenced with the game.

Heart pounding wildly in her chest, Izzy did her best to focus on the game, but found nothing to steady her until she slid her foot across the top of Sebastian's. He turned his foot more towards her, then let it remain beneath hers.

And it stayed there for all six rounds of cards.

Chapter Seventeen

One can always trust Almack's to be stuffy, overcrowded, and
overheated, not to mention overinflated with the self-importance of its
attendants and its guardian committee.

-The Spinster Chronicles, 9 May 1817

"Ah, it is most refreshing to be in company with only the most
important and well-respected members of London's high society."

Izzy looked at Charlotte in surprise, grinning at her friend's dry
remarks. "Aren't most of your suitors outside of the Almack's circle?"

Charlotte nodded eagerly, eyes bright. "Less than a quarter
received vouchers. Do you know what this means?"

"That you will be nearly unaccompanied for the first time in six
years?" Izzy suggested with a mocking note of hope.

"Please," Charlotte sputtered with a laugh. "It means that I have
a chance to improve my list of suitors, and potentially actually find
one worth keeping!"

Izzy shook her head. There was just no understanding Charlotte
at times. "Well, let me know if any of them might do for Kitty. I can
only imagine how terrified she will be tonight."

Charlotte was instantly sympathetic. "Oh, poor lamb. Her first
Season, and so many new faces and experiences… Almack's can be
so dull at times, but that's just from our perspective. It's lost its luster
for spinsters like us." She smiled wistfully at Izzy. "Do you remember
when this was all exciting for us?"

"Barely." Izzy threw her a wry look. "It was ages ago."

"You are twenty-seven, dear," Charlotte reminded her. "Not in the grave."

"No?" Izzy asked, smiling and nodding at acquaintances nearby.

Charlotte sighed heavily and looped her arm through Izzy's. "It does feel as though we are ancient at times, doesn't it?"

Izzy opened her mouth to answer when Amelia Perry suddenly rushed to them, face alight. "Miss Lambert! Miss Wright! How delightful is Almack's?"

"Depends on the day," Charlotte muttered through a smile.

"Shush," Izzy scolded. She brightened as she looked at Amelia again. "Miss Perry, you look lovely. Blue suits you."

Amelia blushed prettily and brushed at her skirts anxiously. "You are too kind, Miss Lambert. I am all aflutter. I can scarce believe it Almack's!"

"Steady on, dear girl," Charlotte told her in the driest tone Izzy had heard her use yet. "It's only the usual husband hunt on a more selective field."

"Charlotte!" Izzy gave her an exasperated look, then turned an apologetic one to Amelia. "Excuse her, please."

Amelia shook her head, smiling just as warmly as ever. "I find it entirely refreshing. And I know I am probably ridiculous, but there is no hope for me."

"Well, as long as you are aware of it," Charlotte offered, now smiling herself. "So, Miss Perry, anyone we should be looking out for tonight in your honor?"

Amelia's blushes turned rosier, and her smile turned sheepish. "Not really."

Charlotte grinned her usual devious grin. "That is not a no, my dear."

"I don't even know if he received a voucher," Amelia admitted with a wrinkle of her nose.

"Ah, questionable as to his societal endorsement, are we?" Charlotte nodded in approval. "Good girl. Keep a weather eye open, and if you need any assistance, you only have to ask."

Amelia nodded quickly, then turned to go before whirling back. "Oh! I forgot!" She stepped closer and whispered, "I've been asked by at least a dozen people if I am the guest writer in the Chronicles. I presume you wish to keep the author anonymous, so I have been entirely ambivalent about the whole thing. It really is a shocking amount of fun." She beamed and whirled back around, darting gracefully off to another part of the ballroom.

Charlotte watched her go, then hummed to herself. "You know, I find her sunshine a bit much to take, but I think I like her better than Alice Sterling."

Izzy looked at her friend in shock. "That's surprising. I thought the pair of you were getting on rather well."

"Only initially."

"Why?"

Charlotte exhaled, then looked over at the girls in question, now ironically standing near each other. "Amelia is genuine. Alice is a bit of a social climber who doesn't listen to anyone, not even Francis."

Izzy was startled by that, as she hadn't spent enough time with Alice to know that much about her, or to characterize her nature so.

"Really?" she asked, less doubtful than surprised.

Charlotte nodded, smirking a little. "Perhaps she's more like Horrid Hugh than we thought."

Izzy shuddered at the thought. That would be all they needed, a female version of Hugh. Yet Alice hadn't seemed so poorly behaved when Izzy had conversed with her, and during Hugh's outburst, Alice had seemed truly distressed.

She couldn't be so bad in truth.

Izzy's more sympathetic side prevailed, and she considered the two girls herself. "Alice is only young," she suggested to Charlotte.

Her friend turned to face her, one dubious brow raised. "Even young people are entitled to eyes and sense, if they know where to obtain either." Charlotte gave her a meaningful look as she strode away, purposefully choosing to venture into the opposite side of the room from Amelia and Alice.

Izzy shook her head, mumbling under her breath. "Wonderful, Charlotte. Lovely of you to help me with Kitty."

"I believe I can be of assistance there."

Izzy grinned and turned to smile at her cousin, looking more radiant and like herself than she had in weeks, her gown a brilliant shade of green that enhanced her eyes. And Tony looked beyond pleased with himself to have her on his arm.

"I didn't know if you'd come," Izzy told her cousin, taking her hands. "Are you feeling well enough?"

Tony rolled his eyes and tugged Georgie closer. "I asked her the same question fourteen times before we arrived, and the answer got more and more vicious with each subsequent asking."

"And yet, the questions kept coming," Georgie quipped, smiling at her husband.

"Well, if you hadn't been ill just this morning, I might have believed you one of the first thirteen times," he retorted. "But the kick to my shins on number fourteen was convincing enough."

"In short," Georgie said, turning to Izzy again, smiling broadly, "yes, I am well enough."

Izzy giggled and linked arms with Georgie. "Good. I seem to be attracting all sorts of spinster pity of late, and I cannot swallow one more word of it."

Tony chortled and looked around Georgie at Izzy as best he could. "Who are you and what have you done with sweet Isabella?"

A smug smirk lit Izzy's lips and she wished Sebastian had heard that. "Sweet Isabella has learned the value of her voice," Izzy informed him primly, "and is growing accustomed to the sensation of speaking it."

"Brava, cousin," Tony praised with a nod, walking with both women around the edges of the room.

Georgie hummed once very softly. "I suspect that the cause of this sudden change in your voice's volume, which has never been as sweet as anybody thought, is due to a certain friend of yours."

"Georgie…" Izzy warned, her cheeks coloring.

"What's this?" Tony teased, missing nothing in his quick glance. "Does Izzy have a secret suitor?"

Izzy bit her lip and looked away, her face positively flaming now. Men.

"Tony, if you cannot behave yourself, I will not tell you my suspicions," Georgie scolded sternly.

Appropriately apologetic, Tony stepped in front of Izzy, plucked up her hand, and kissed her glove quickly. "Izzy, I apologize. I only meant in fun. I would never embarrass you for my own amusement."

Izzy nodded, managing to smile as her cheeks began to settle. "I know, Tony. It's just… Well, I cannot say there *isn't* a secret suitor, but I cannot say how certain his suit is…"

Tony laughed at that, then gave her a serious look. "My dearest Izzy, if he hasn't made that perfectly plain, you need to find yourself a more decisive suitor, secret or not."

His words stopped Izzy short, and she had no response for the moment.

Perfectly plain, he said?

I'm falling in love with you…

Izzy swallowed once, her skin suddenly growing cold and tingling with an odd sensation. That seemed perfectly plain, did it not?

And yet…

"Tony," Georgie murmured, her eyes trained on Izzy, "be a dear and go find your friends. My cousin and I need a moment alone."

Ever the obedient husband, Tony nodded, kissed his wife's cheek, then left them.

Izzy met Georgie's gaze, fighting a smile, despite an overwhelming embarrassment filling her. "Well?" she asked when her cousin said nothing.

Georgie's lips quirked and she tugged Izzy along to walk further still. "Don't rush me. I want to relish the feeling of uncertainty, knowing you have formed an attachment that I know nothing about and cannot confirm."

"Georgie!" Izzy laughed.

"Does anybody know?" Georgie pressed, her voice eager. "Anyone at all?"

Izzy bit her lip on a laugh. "Not a soul. Only me and only him."

"That is most certainly as it should be." Georgie eyed her, a mischievous curve to her lips. "You never blushed before, Izzy. That's what gave you away. Oh, you've surely been embarrassed, and ashamed, and every other such emotion, but never love. Never that."

"Oh, I don't—"

"Oh, I think you do," Georgie interrupted firmly, though her tone was still gentle. "And I think you know it. Or shortly will."

Izzy looked away, her mind and heart seeming to whirl at an

impossible speed. She was suddenly lightheaded, though her feet were perfectly sound where they stood. The ends of her hair seemed to burn with a pleasant fire upon her head, and her chest seemed to expand its capacity to breathe by threefold.

Love?

He had said he was falling in love with her, but she hadn't... She'd never...

The memory of the two of them sitting by the fire at her home suddenly sprang back to life in her mind's eye, and her heart swelled at the sight. It was a comfortable yet intimate scene, him sketching while she told him a story, and she felt a sudden yearning for more of the same. An eternity of such things, if she could bear it.

She gasped with the newfound pangs, fit to bursting with joy and exhilaration and wonder.

Love...

She loved him.

Izzy slowly turned back to look at Georgie, whose eyes were suddenly misty even as she smiled.

"There it is," Georgie whispered.

Izzy giggled again, covering her mouth "I didn't... I'd never..."

"You know what?" Georgie overrode with a laugh. "Don't tell me. I don't want to know who it is yet, I am enjoying this far too much."

"You promise you won't tease me?" Izzy asked, giving her cousin a look.

Georgie snorted once. "You want me to promise not to tease you? When you're clearly all tangled up inside and giddier than Amelia Perry at any given moment? Not a chance."

Kitty was trembling beside him. Sebastian could feel the tremors in her hand as he held it, leading her into the hallowed halls of Almack's.

He smiled at the sensation.

She was so improved in that regard and in all other ways, and had begun to truly blossom, but tonight she was utterly terrified.

"What are you thinking?" he murmured to her as they entered.

"It's beautiful," she whispered, looking around with wide eyes.

He glanced around, taking in the lavish mirrors, gilded pilasters and columns, and pristine medallions gracing the ceiling, the ornate lighting... He supposed it did have a stately beauty, though had never particularly appreciated it. He eyed the dais at the upper end and indicated it with his head.

Kitty followed his gaze, her eyes widening further still. "Who are they?"

He managed to avoid laughing and leaned closer. "Those, sister dear, are the Lady Patronesses. They decide who enters and who does not, and they rule all."

"I've never met a single one of them," Kitty said weakly, barely blinking as she took in all five women in their finery. "How did I manage to make the list?"

"I put you on it, darling," Miranda assured her as she came up on Kitty's other side. "Believe me, I am well enough acquainted to have influence here. Don't mind them, they enjoy looking down their noses in these hallowed halls. As you can see."

Kitty bit her lip on a giggle, looking up at Miranda with a sort of adoration that Sebastian would have to carefully mind. "Thank you for using your influence on my behalf, Miranda."

Miranda beamed down at her and patted her hand with fondness. "Not at all, Kitty. Now, find Miss Perry and Izzy, and let the gentlemen here see how lovely you look in lace and pearls!"

With such marching orders, Kitty nodded once, exhaled, and released Sebastian's hand as she strode forward, head held high.

He watched her go, pride and worry warring within him. She was pretending at confidence, and he would let her, but the overprotective nature of his relationship with her was currently nagging at him to follow her and keep her safe.

She was a woman now, not a little girl, and this was what he wanted for her.

Supposedly.

"She'll do marvelously, Morton," Miranda told him in a low voice as she came to his side. "She's a wonderful girl, and a credit to you. And you know, her timidity is not nearly so off-putting as you feared."

"That's because Izzy has helped her," he replied, letting his eyes slide to the woman in question, now watching Kitty move about with as much pride as he felt. "She has given her comfort and confidence and friends to rely on. I did nothing. She's a credit to Izzy."

Miranda hummed in approval. "Far be it from me to prevent Izzy from receiving her due praise, but someone raised that girl into the woman she is, and there's only one person who can claim that. And his name is certainly not Izzy."

She squeezed his hand briefly, then moved on, leaving him to stare without shame where he pleased.

Kitty said something that made Izzy laugh, and his heart seized within his chest as she tossed her head back, the glorious copper curls glinting in the light of the room. It made no difference that her brilliant eyes were squeezed shut, the color of her cheeks was enough. The simple gold chain at her throat drew his attention there, and a rosy color spread along the slender column. She was not as fashionably dressed as many other women that he had seen already, but none of them drew his eye as she did.

Only Izzy.

He was falling in love with her, he'd said. He had questioned the wisdom of such an admission more times than he could count in so short a time, given his inclination on propriety and reserve, but it always came back to the truth of the thing.

He *was* falling in love. Dangerously, precariously, but undeniably.

Every moment he saw her, it was as though he had forgotten what she looked like. What she sounded like. How she affected him. For heaven's sake, they had been working together the last two days on more of their stories, and he had just seen her yesterday.

It could have been a lifetime based on how he felt at this moment.

Would it always be like this? Would he always be distracted and breathless when she was around? Would anxieties and insecurities plague him more than in the rest of his life if she were involved?

Would he ever feel at ease again?

He'd barely noticed her before all of this, other than politeness and good manners dictated. He might never have known… never have seen...

As all the rest of the world seemed to.

He would be eternally indebted to her for the help she had been to Kitty, but for him...

Eternity wouldn't be enough.

"Terrified of the gorgons, are we?"

He barely felt the thump of a hand on his shoulder as Henshaw came to his side.

"Don't worry, sir," Henshaw went on, oblivious to Sebastian's current state of distress and delight. "I'm an Army man. No gorgons are beyond my abilities."

Sebastian eyed his friend sardonically. "You sure? Five of the most powerful women in London Society?"

Henshaw looked over at them again, then shuddered for effect. "Perhaps not. You're on your own."

"Lovely." He scoffed softly as Henshaw steered him towards Tony and his cousin, Lord Sterling, both of whom were idly watching the dancing that had struck up.

Tony shook his hand while Lord Sterling merely nodded. "Either of you have ideas about the identity of the Spinsters' guest writer?"

Sebastian nearly groaned. "Not that again."

Lord Sterling chuckled and gave Sebastian a look. "Tired of it, Morton? You're the only one in all of London not agog over the speculation."

"Morton has always tried to rise above such a tiresome thing as gossip," Henshaw assured him, throwing a teasing look at Sebastian, who ignored it.

"It was one article," Sebastian protested. He gave a light shrug. "I see no need to get excitable over it."

"But where there is one, the door is open for more," Lord Sterling pointed out. He heaved a sigh and rolled his eyes heavenward. "Or so my wife informs me."

Tony laughed and nudged his cousin. "Plaguing you about it, is she?"

Lord Sterling nodded. "I've told her to ask Georgie, but she says it would be impolite to infringe upon her privacy. And Janet has received so many inquiries as to whether she is the one who wrote it, which just delights her to no end."

Sebastian managed a laugh, even as his gaze moved back over to Izzy.

She wasn't sitting, which was a refreshing change, but with Lady Hetty not attending this evening, there was no one for her to keep company with. Why she always attempted to attend on the older woman, he didn't know, but she seemed to truly take pleasure in it. So long as it wasn't taking advantage of her good nature, he wasn't going to say anything about it.

And despite Izzy's sudden streak of defensiveness, he suspected she would always be a little too kind and a little too giving.

He wasn't sure he minded that. Particularly if she were too kind and too giving with regards to him. He could use such leniency in his life with his flaws.

Amelia Perry joined his sister and Izzy now, and he had to smile at her restrained eagerness with Kitty. He recalled how much of a help Miss Perry had been with Prue last year, how gentle and understanding a friend, despite her own vibrant nature, and it seemed she was employing those qualities again with his sister. Kitty actually seemed to enliven further with Amelia there, and the pair of them chatted together while Izzy listened, smiling all the while.

It was astonishing how a woman of her quality and nature should be available for courtship and marriage at her age. That she should even be a spinster at all, let alone one with a capital S. But he could also see how the virtues she possessed should be undervalued and underappreciated, given how exploited they were by nearly everyone she knew. Hers was exactly the sort of nature that could have been ignored in a romantic sense when it should always have been vaunted.

He'd heard it said of her that she was a spinster because she was nice. She should have been snapped up because she was nice.

Because she was good.

Because she was warm.

Because she could tease a reserved man into an affable serenity, and coax smiles from him that only a handful of souls had ever done.

He'd never understand why he could fall in love with her, but he would be forever grateful that he could.

"There's a fine pairing," Tony commented, breaking into

Sebastian's rosy reflections.

"What, Miss Morton and Miss Perry?" Lord Sterling asked of no one in particular. He made a soft sound of agreement. "I should say so! Miss Perry will help draw Miss Morton out, and Miss Morton can give Miss Perry a steadying influence. What do you think, Henshaw?"

Henshaw took a moment to respond. "Far be it from me to find the need for improvement in either lady. I think very highly of both, and their mutual association could only benefit each other."

Sebastian glanced at Henshaw, surprised by the respectful nature of his acknowledgement. He was never disparaging of people, and certainly never of ladies, but to avoid any hint of teasing was certainly unlike him.

"That's it?" he asked his friend.

Henshaw gave him a doleful look. "Are you asking me to find fault in your sister, Morton? With you standing within earshot? I think not."

That was all too true, he supposed, but he hadn't exactly considered the other two as disparaging Kitty in any way.

"Lady Edith could be considered a timid creature," Tony mused aloud, eyeing Henshaw with a mischievous glint.

"Not when you really know her," came a new voice. "She's got a sharp tongue underneath that Scottish charm."

They turned to see Camden and Prue approaching them, Prue barely resembling the woman they had known in the past, as she had so altered with her marriage. She met each of their eyes squarely, her hand tucked in her husband's arm, and her smile was as warm as any Izzy had ever given.

"Cam," Prue scolded, looking up at him, but smiling. "Edith is v-very kind."

"I didn't say she wasn't," he informed his wife, returning her look. "I adore her. All I said was that she is not nearly as timid as we think."

Prue rolled her eyes, smiling in exasperation. "He s-says that as though it's a c-compliment."

Henshaw grinned at Prue even as his eyes flicked back to Amelia, Kitty, and Izzy, then bowed. "I shall take it as a very great compliment, Mrs. Vale, if you will dance the next with me."

Now it was Camden who rolled his eyes. "For pity's sake, Henshaw, don't flatter my wife better than I can. She'll never be satisfied with me again."

"Which would be all the better for you, I say," Henshaw shot back, looking like the reckless soldier he'd always been.

Prue put her hand in Henshaw's and blushed a little. "I would l-love to, Lieutenant Henshaw."

Camden let his wife go, watching her with a tenderness that did not suit his nature, then turned to the rest.

Tony was shaking his head. "How in the world did they let you into Almack's, Cam?"

Camden shrugged, grinning irreverently. "Haven't the foggiest. Must be my very proper wife. A reforming influence, you know."

"Right," Lord Sterling said with a snort. "Reforming." He turned to his cousin expectantly. "Should we do a wife exchange this dance? Then I can question Georgie without shame."

"Fine," Tony laughed, pushing him away. "Janet would rather dance with me, anyway."

They continued to bicker as they moved away, and Sebastian returned his attention to Izzy.

He watched as a man approached the group, bowed to them, chatted a moment, then escorted Miss Perry out to the dance.

"Hmm. Nicely done, Andrews," Camden offered with a satisfied sound. "Amelia will be delighted for days."

Sebastian nodded without thinking, watching how delighted Kitty and Izzy were by what had happened.

"Should I ask your sister for a dance, Morton?" Camden asked, nudging Sebastian a little. "I'm a respectable married man now, so the prospects..."

"I see no danger there," Sebastian interrupted, chuckling to himself.

"Yes, but would she care for it?" Camden pressed.

Sebastian turned to look at the man, questioning without words.

Camden shrugged one shoulder. "I know something of timid women, Morton. I don't want to upset her."

Well, well, it seemed Prue was a reforming influence on him after all. But then, he'd long known that Camden Vale wasn't nearly the villain he was painted to be.

"She might surprise you," Sebastian murmured with a smile. "But I think you would be more comfortable than a potential suitor."

Camden chuckled and clapped him on the back. "Safer for you, at any rate." He strode forward and bowed to Kitty and Izzy, then took a moment to speak with Kitty.

Sebastian watched as his sister smiled her usual shy smile as she looked to Izzy quickly. She answered Camden and made him smile in return. And then, as he expected, Kitty allowed Camden to lead her to the dance. It was amazing that he had actually expected his sister to do so when only weeks ago he would have found it miraculous.

He let his eyes linger on Izzy, taking pleasure in doing so, breathing in the experience. Then he was moving, striding towards her with a certainty he hadn't quite felt before.

She saw him coming and smiled the sort of smile that made him desperate to kiss her. "Mr. Morton," she greeted with a curtsey as he reached her. "You look quite splendid, sir, if I may say so."

He found himself unable to grin as freely as he liked, emotion too great for such levity. "Then I have no words to describe how you look, Miss Lambert, as you far surpass anyone I see here."

"Surely not," she insisted, though her eyes danced. "There are many beautiful women here, and several very attractive men."

He swallowed with some difficulty, his heart in his throat. "I see none of them. I see only you."

He saw her breath stutter, saw the color moving into her cheeks, saw how it spread across the paleness of her skin, and watched as she, too, struggled to swallow. Her lips moved, but no words escaped.

"Dance with me, Iz," he murmured, extending a hand.

Izzy exhaled slowly, unsteadily, then placed her hand in his. He led her to the dance, feeling as anxious as though it were his very first dance and all eyes were on him.

"Kitty told me you aren't fond of dancing," Izzy whispered beside him, her hand trembling even more than Kitty's had been. "She said you only tolerate it."

"This is true." He glanced over at her, letting his mouth curve. "Why do you mention it?"

Izzy's eyes shifted his way, but never quite made it. "I'm only curious… do you only tolerate it when you dance with me?"

Her uncertainty amused him and concerned him. Could she not know? Could she not see?

He squeezed her hand as they joined in the dance. "No," he assured her when their eyes met. "No, I find I've never enjoyed dancing more than with you."

Her eyes brightened as they parted in the dance, and he watched her as he moved through the motions, changing partners for brief moments, then returning to her.

"And tonight, I had to dance with you," he informed her as they promenaded hand in hand.

Izzy waited until they were face to face, waiting for other couples to finish. "Why?"

He smiled at her and waited until they were close once more "Because I wish I could kiss you, and this is as close as we will get here."

Her eyes widened and she looked away quickly.

He could feel the skittering of her pulse while her hand sat in his, and he thrilled with the feel of it.

They moved again, circled each other, exchanged partners, then returned to each other. "You are coming tomorrow evening, right?" Izzy asked.

Confused by the change in subject, he gave her a sharp look. "To your home? For the musical evening?"

She raised her eyes to his as she moved away from him. "Yes."

He nodded as they stared at each other across the lines. "I'll be there."

A satisfied light appeared in her features, and her lips curved. "Good," she told him.

When he drew close in the dance, she sighed lightly. "I know all of the secret nooks and crannies. And when we could escape."

Sebastian nearly laughed in his surprise but by some miraculous feat managed to keep his face impassive. "You devious woman…"

Izzy giggled and looked up at him as she circled once more. "You just said you wished you could kiss me," she reminded him.

"I did," he confirmed as she moved back to her line.

When it came his turn to circle, she added, "It just so happens that the feeling is mutual."

Years of practice and experience kept him from stumbling then, but it was impossible to look anywhere but at her, no matter what the dance required. The most intense desire to sweep her up and kiss her senseless had never been stronger, and his better inclination was rapidly losing the battle within him.

Izzy smirked at him when she saw how he looked. "What's that look for?" she teased.

A corner of his mouth lifted in a smile as they came together for the next movement. "I am trying to decide how much of a gentleman I really am. I've never had to properly consider that before now."

She laughed and kept her face forward. "Why?"

He matched her expression. "I've never been sorely tempted to cause a scandal before."

He felt her startled movement in his grasp and fought a grin.

She cleared her throat when she settled. "Scandals aren't permitted at Almack's."

"You see my dilemma."

"Indeed."

"So, what would you suggest?"

Izzy made a soft humming noise that seemed to run the course of his arm and into his chest. "I cannot say, sir. Spinsters never cause scandals."

He bit back a laugh and they parted in the dance, forming into lines again. "More's the pity," he murmured, staring at her with as much frankness as he dared.

And Lord bless her, Izzy stared back much the same, an impish smile on her tempting lips. "Indeed."

Chapter Eighteen

———— ⌒⌯⌒ ————

There is nothing so refreshing as well-performed music. Provided anyone is listening.

-*The Spinster Chronicles, 27 March 1818*

Sebastian had been to a number of musical gatherings in his life, and many of them very fine indeed, but he could honestly say he had never paid as much attention to the surroundings and atmosphere of one. Now that he was illustrating a story about musical animals, such details were suddenly of great interest to him.

Oh, he was a great admirer of music, and would always listen appropriately and applaud politely regardless of the skill of the performers involved, but he had never paid attention to the arrangement of the rooms in question.

Not that there should be anything specific or noteworthy about such things, but he felt it should be given all due diligence for the sake of his art.

It was also serving to distract him from blatantly staring at Izzy. If he stared at her, he would think about her more, and if he thought about her more, he would think about last night, and if he thought about the night before, he would think about her suggestion.

And if he thought about her suggestion, he would start watching her every move on the off chance that she would suddenly disappear into parts unknown of the house for the escape she had promised.

He tugged at his cravat, which was suddenly too tight, and

focused on studying the arrangement of chairs and instruments.

The Lamberts had greeted him warmly this evening, as they ever did, and Mrs. Lambert had asked when they might have the pleasure of he and Kitty for dinner again.

He'd been tempted to reply 'on a night when Izzy wouldn't be sent to eat with the children', but instead, he'd deferred to any night that Mrs. Lambert deemed appropriate.

Kitty had seemed delighted by being invited again, though she was delighted with being invited anywhere, now that the Season had commenced. Each one brought a measure of delight mingled with nerves, and the delight was beginning to outweigh the nerves.

His timid younger sister was growing almost bold.

Almost.

He scanned the room for her, pleased to find her once again with Amelia Perry. He was surprised that Alice Sterling had joined them and seemed to be finding their company quite pleasant. It would do Kitty good to have friends closer to her own age, and ones with similar interests.

Not that the Spinsters hadn't been wonderful for her, but with the fervor that tended to surround them in London as a whole, he worried what a fresh young miss could experience if tied to them so closely.

Elinor was a prime example of such things.

And Elinor was nowhere near those three. She sat by Lady Hetty, scowling at any male who happened to venture too close.

He shuddered at the sight. Though she was still very young, Elinor embodied everything one thought of when they heard the word spinster. He did not envy her parents the task of dealing with that.

A movement off to his right caught his attention and he turned to see Izzy's sister and her husband joining the group of Lambert siblings that had gathered not too far from him.

Izzy smiled at her sister, then looked at her more carefully before giving her a bewildered look.

Catherine laughed merrily, fluffing out her skirts. "Izzy, I borrowed your blue silk for the evening. I know you don't mind, and it does flatter me so."

William chortled a surprised laugh, while David shook his head. "Catherine, you don't even live here."

"Hush, David," she replied with a scolding look. "Izzy never minds when any of us do anything."

Sebastian's brows shot up at that, and he watched the group more carefully. Izzy's mouth was set in a tight smile, while the brothers laughed again.

"This is true," David agreed. "She never minded when William stole her dolls, or when we all complained about the meal and had it changed. Where we slept in the nursery, when we made her stop playing the pianoforte, when we needed another person to play with us in the fields…"

"See?" Catherine cried, flinging out a hand towards her sister. "Izzy never minds anything, as I said."

Sebastian eyed Izzy, who had looked down at her hands, where her fingers laced with each other.

Come on, Iz, he urged in his mind. *Come on, say something…*

Why it was so crucial that she suddenly do so, he could not have said, but knowing her inclination to say nothing, particularly with her family, he could not bear to see her endure such teasing without a word, however innocently it was meant.

"She doesn't even mind being a spinster all that much," William pointed out, laughing to the rest. "She just patiently bears it, same as she does everything else."

Sebastian hissed softly through his teeth, knowing how such an accusation would sting. It was meant to be praise, he knew, but it would have quite the opposite effect on Izzy.

And she deserved to say so.

Izzy raised her eyes slowly, her smile less forced, but her eyes hard. "Of course I mind it, William. No one wishes to remain unmarried and be a burden upon their family or the brunt of Society's pity and scorn. I do patiently bear it because I have no other option. I don't require anyone to feel sorry for me, nor do I expect to be treated with more gentleness because of my unmarried state."

The words were said in the kindest tone imaginable, but the recoil in the expression of each member of that group told a different story. Her response was as unexpected as it was overdue.

221

She looked around at her siblings, her eyes softening even as she swallowed with difficulty. "And that's not all I mind. In fact, I minded all of it. I hated being stopped from playing, and I hated being dragged out to play in the field when I wanted to stay inside and read. I despised when you changed the menu because it was usually something I had wanted."

The brothers looked at each other in outright bewilderment, then seemed to consider Izzy in a new light.

Izzy turned to her sister and took her hand. "I do mind when you borrow my clothes, Catherine, because you never return them."

Catherine's mouth began to work, but her husband put a hand on her arm, keeping her from replying.

"I couldn't complain about the nursery arrangements because it upset all of you so much when I did," Izzy confessed, the words coming easier now. She shrugged helplessly. "I mind a great deal more than anyone ever expects me to. I never said anything because I didn't think confrontation and contention would solve anything. It wasn't worth the effort."

Her eyes filled with tears, even as she smiled with love at her siblings. "But make no mistake, I felt everything. Even a spinster feels things."

There was silence among the group, even as the general murmur of the rest of the room continued.

Sebastian held his breath, delighted beyond words and prouder than he knew was possible. Izzy seemed to glow with her confidence, a tower of strength and power, yet without any of the spite that anyone else might have done.

"I'm sorry, Izzy," David said with surprising gentleness, a sad air about his manner now.

Izzy turned to her oldest brother with a fond smile. "You don't need to be. I know that no harm was ever meant. I just needed you to know."

Her brother smiled in return, then leaned over to kiss her cheek, making Izzy's smile quiver as a tear or two escaped.

A lump formed in Sebastian's throat as he watched the scene, and it faintly occurred to him to look away, to let them have this private moment. But he continued to stare, unable to take his eyes off of Izzy.

Her brothers laughed and wiped her tears away, and even Catherine seemed to be smiling at her sister with an increase of warmth and understanding. Izzy said something Sebastian didn't catch, but it made them all laugh, and she stepped away from them, moving towards the refreshments.

Which Sebastian happened to be standing beside.

He watched her come, knowing he should look away, be less obvious, have some of the reserve he was known for.

He couldn't manage it.

She kept a small smile on her face, one that told him she was secretly pleased with herself, though he knew she had to have been fairly terrified by taking such a stance with her family. Her cheeks were rosy and there was no trace of the tears from moments ago upon them. Her gown was of purest white and seemed to float with the effortlessness of clouds, which made the rich color of her hair seem more vibrant by comparison.

Had she been encompassed by rays of light she could not have looked more angelic to him than she did at this moment.

"Iz," he breathed when she was close enough, her name catching almost painfully in his throat.

She paused, looking up at him, the brilliance of her eyes striking him to his very core.

He shook his head in disbelief, in wonder, in adoration. "You're magnificent."

There was a slight widening of her eyes, and her throat moved, but other than that, her expression didn't change. She cleared her throat, then came to the table beside him, focused on the task of getting herself punch.

Would she say nothing? Would she leave him standing here after such a confession and…?

Her hand brushed against his, confounding his breathing in a shockingly effective manner.

Had she meant to do that?

He kept his attention forward, surveying the guests, not truly seeing a single person or detail as every fiber of his being was suddenly attuned to his left hand.

He waited, hoping, not daring to breathe…

She brushed it again, and he flexed his fingers quickly in response.

Out of the corner of his eye, he saw her smile twitch, and felt his lips react similarly.

She stood at the table, glass of punch in hand, and slowly began to sip, her back to the room, her eyes suddenly darting to his. He held her gaze, still facing forward, his heart pounding against every one of his ribs.

Once more her hand brushed his own, and this time he seized it, gripping her fingers without shame.

The cup in her other hand trembled slightly, and her lashes fluttered, her eyes still on his.

Saints above, had anything ever felt so right?

He slowly loosened his hold on her fingers only to feel them move against his, sliding more fully into his hand, gripping and stroking against the suddenly thin fabric of his glove.

He moved his thumb against her own glove, wishing he could wear away the fabric to the skin beneath and caress there until it was red as the glow on her cheeks.

Izzy exhaled shakily, the sound drawing a groan from his chest, which he barely bit back.

Her eyes darkened, and she gave one more distinct brush of her fingers against his hand, the sensation burning as though he'd had the prints of those fingers branded against the skin.

He could only wish for such a permanent mark.

She began to pull her hand back, but he resisted just long enough to press his thumb into the center of her palm, determined to leave just as lasting an impression on her.

Her eyes lowered from his, widening as she took in their hands, then slowly dragging back up to his.

Sebastian dipped his chin in the smallest degree of acknowledgement, and she responded with another tempting twitch of her lips.

He released the pressure against her hand, and she backed away from the table, letting her fingers graze against his until the last possible moment. Then she gave him a faint wink and turned to cross the room, her destination unclear, her pace sedate.

Sebastian exhaled roughly, then swallowed against his suddenly-parched throat.

It now seemed entirely possible that he would not survive the night.

And that was a giddy feeling indeed.

Oh, she was in for it now…

Her hand still tingled and pulsed almost irritably within its glove, but she dared not even look down at it.

She half-expected the glove to be singed away in parts and looking at the evidence would only make things worse.

Heart pounding, breath unsteady, she downed the last of her punch without any pretense at manners, then handed it off to one of their footmen, unable to thank him or acknowledge him or anything of the kind. The liquid almost burned in her throat, though it had been pleasant enough before.

Why had she teased him? Why had she decided she had to touch him?

Oh, because she couldn't have all out kissed him in full view of everyone in her family and friends just because he had called her magnificent.

Magnificent… In all honesty, he was the magnificent one. He, who had encouraged her to stand up for herself, to use her voice, to be more than a well-bred servant to those around her, was magnificent. He, who had given new life to her stories and found just as much of a thrill in their creation as she did, was magnificent.

He, who could leave her breathless with a look or a touch, was magnificent.

And she would swear now that his eyes were still upon her. She could feel them, and every fiber of her being and hair on her head was distracted with the sensation.

How in the world did women in love ever accomplish anything of productivity or sense like this?

She was entirely worthless and helpless at the moment, and she doubted even conversation would be possible.

"Ladies and gentlemen," her father suddenly announced from the front of the room, "we will now begin our performances, if you will kindly take your seats."

Izzy's heart leapt into her throat. Did she want Sebastian to sit beside her or did she want him in the furthest corner away from her? Both would have advantages, though those advantages were starkly different from each other.

Did she want to be with sense or without? Did she want to be coherent or not?

Did she want to escape without being observed or not?

Her face flamed, and she immediately moved to sit beside Prue, taking great care to select the seat on the aisle so as to prevent anyone else from sitting beside her.

Prue turned to smile at her and took her hand. "You look very p-pretty, Izzy," she told her quietly. "I love what you have done with your hair. The white ribbon really is an elegant t-touch."

Izzy sighed, smiling warmly at her sweet friend. "Thank you. Your gown is exquisite. Such a fine shade of lavender, and it suits you well."

"Yes, that's what Cam said," Prue replied, her cheeks coloring very slightly.

Camden took the seat beside his wife and made no effort to hide the fact that he took her hand, lacing their fingers. "What did I say, love?" he asked, raising a daring brow. "I hope it was good."

Izzy snickered to herself, then sat a bit forward to see Camden better. "You apparently said her dress suits her well."

"Did I?" He looked at his wife for confirmation, apparently confused. "I don't recall saying anything so politely. I'm usually far more effusive when giving you praises and compliments."

"Cam..." Prue scolded in a mixture of resignation and delight.

Izzy bit her lip on a laugh, loving how this man loved her friend, and how that love had given her strength.

Cam leaned forward, his eyes warm with ardor on his wife, and whispered, " 'Oh, that I were but a thorn in the garden of such bloom, that mine eyes might be graced by the flowers of this hue. To rest my heart in such exquisite care and die among such petals, so bright and fair.' "

"Oh, that's lovely, Cam," Izzy sighed, squeezing her friend's hand. "Is that what you said?"

"No," he retorted, the moment gone and his levity returned. "I believe I only made weak imitation of sounds when I saw her, and it has taken me this long to properly express what the translation was."

Prue's cheeks were a fervent red now, and Izzy saw her fingers brushing anxiously against Camden's. "Please..." she hissed, her eyes on their hands.

"Steady, love," Camden told her, smiling with gentleness. "I'm all finished." He winked at Izzy and sat back, his thumb moving smoothly over Prue's hand.

Prue turned to Izzy with wide, exasperated eyes. "He's always d-doing that."

"Good," Izzy told her without hesitation. "You deserve to have someone praise you incessantly and sincerely."

Prue's eyes suddenly took on a knowing look. "So do you."

Izzy restrained a smile and shifted in her seat, unsure how to respond.

Thankfully, the first music of the evening began, and she forced herself to listen patiently as her sister played the harp. Catherine was the most accomplished of them musically, but rarely performed in public. Her mother must have prevailed upon her this evening, and Izzy was glad she had.

It would save her the trouble of being asked.

As the song went on, Izzy found herself looking for Sebastian, wondering where he had chosen to sit, and if he had found some semblance of sanity after their little moment.

Little? She might have snorted in derision. She'd nearly come apart at the seams, and there was nothing little about that.

She finally caught sight of him leaning against the east wall near the windows. It was an excellent thing that she had not sat near the front of the room, as she would have had to crane her neck to see him there. As it was, she only had to turn her neck a touch. It would still be obvious to anyone watching her, should she have watched him instead of the performance, but at least it could be accomplished with marginal difficulty.

And she just might wish to watch him instead.

He was currently focused on the performance, as she undoubtedly should have been, so she could observe him freely.

It was strange how she had once been able to consider him handsome without feeling any sort of fluttering, pangs, or nerves. A simple observation of attractive features, and it had been sufficient. Now she could feel a strange keening within her whenever she looked at him, and no other man in the world would ever be as appealing as he was.

His shoulders were broad without being expansive, he was tall without being towering, and his features were well-situated without being striking. He might never draw attention the way blatantly attractive people would, but his was the sort of appearance that one found pleasure in looking at, and the sort that would continue on through time without losing its appeal. A face that one could adore for a lifetime. And a heart even more so.

Lord, she was in love with him, and he desperately needed to know it.

"You know," Prue murmured as the room applauded Catherine, "the t-two of you ought to make your c-courtship official. It makes things so much easier."

Izzy jerked in her seat and twisted to stare wide-eyed at her friend, who was giving her a quietly bemused look, awaiting her response.

She started to deny everything, deny it all, but that look in Prue's eye…

She knew, and Izzy couldn't deny anything.

She swallowed harshly, then stammered, "We aren't courting…"

Prue's mouth curved in a wry smile. "Then p-perhaps you should be."

Perhaps they should, but it wouldn't change anything, other than the public awareness of what they were already feeling.

She enjoyed the privacy and secrecy, apart from not being able to interact the way they would like in public. That would be something to consider, and something they would undoubtedly enjoy.

Perhaps they should. Perhaps they would. Perhaps…

"How did you know?" Izzy whispered as Miranda Sterling

moved to the front of the room to perform next.

Prue chuckled in a low tone. "Oh, Izzy, we all know."

"You *do?*" Izzy gasped, mortified and startled.

A brief dip of her chin was all the answer Prue gave. As Miranda began her aria, Izzy immediately glanced around the room to find the rest of the group.

Grace glanced at her with a slight smile and winked. Charlotte looked directly at Izzy, utterly smug even as she leaned closer to Michael to listen better. Georgie and Tony were both trying *not* to stare at her but seemed close to laughter. Elinor was utterly mournful and did not bother hiding it. Edith's smile was gentle, sad, and loving, and Izzy felt the sudden urge to hug her, though she couldn't have said why.

"Lord," Izzy hissed as she pressed a hand to her cheek. "I had no idea it was so obvious."

Prue patted her knee soothingly. "Don't fret. I d-doubt anyone else knows but us, and it's only b-because we know you so well. We're all supportive, e-even Elinor."

That was surprising beyond anything else. "Seriously?"

Prue's smile turned rather sly for her. "We've always said Mr. Morton is a p-perfect gentleman. Why shouldn't he be s-snatched up?"

Camden coughed a quiet laugh beside his wife and curved his hand more completely around hers. "Indeed, Izzy," he murmured very low. "Snatch away, by all means."

Izzy looked away at once, but not before she heard the faintest thump, which she could only imagine was Prue properly scolding her outspoken husband.

Snatch away.

Oh, she would like to.

Her eyes found Sebastian, almost exactly as he had been before. 'Almost', because now he was looking at Izzy.

Izzy's breath caught at the hungry expression he bore, the intensity with which he looked, and the raw vulnerability in his gaze. She recognized everything she saw there, as she felt the same blend of need and want within herself. She'd never felt such sensations stirring as she had in recent weeks with him, and she was glad for it.

She was glad to have been a spinster and to never have known the taste of love or the scent of desire before this.

It should be new and fresh and exciting for her. It should be only Sebastian that could make her feel this way, bring her to this, stoke this slow-building burn inside. It should be only one man to change a woman so, and only Sebastian had given Izzy the wings for her soul to take flight.

Miranda's rich, soaring vocals suddenly seemed to be coming directly from Izzy's own heart, spanning the room to Sebastian, crying out for his love and his embrace. It seemed to her that he heard it, that he felt it, as she could see how his chest expanded, how his expression softened, how he seemed barely able to remain where he was.

He should fly across the room to her, carried by the notes of Miranda's exquisite voice and his own feelings for Izzy, forgoing any politeness or reserve. She should fly to him and declare herself, leave no doubt of her heart and emotions, ignoring traditional feminine delicacy or demureness.

Yet there they were, remaining in place, despite all desire to the contrary.

She couldn't bear this heat, this pressure, this ache... She couldn't breathe while she stared at him, while he looked at her so, while this music between them drowned out the music around them.

She blinked as the sound of applause met her ears, and she took her chance. She rose from her seat and moved towards the side door of the room, somehow managing not to bolt for it frantically. It just so happened that this was the way to the nursery, as well, so any that asked her would believe that she was only checking on the children.

She kept her eyes on Sebastian until it was impossible to do so, praying that he would know what she wished, see her command, and follow her when he could.

Down the corridor she moved, taking care not to distract any of the guests with sound or speed, and moving into a side corridor when she could.

Then, she waited.

Over the sound of her pounding heart, she heard a new song begin, something almost jaunty in its tone and energy, so different from what they had just heard it would surely attract more attention.

She could only hope it would.

Where was he? Where *was* he?

Then she heard it. Soft steps down the corridor, heading in her direction.

What if it was someone else? What if her mother was coming after her? What if...?

Sebastian suddenly appeared at the head of her corridor, his eyes dark, his breathing nearly as unsteady as though he'd run the length of her house.

"Iz..." he whispered.

She released a shuddering breath, then seized his hand and pulled him further down the corridor, not bothering to keep to a sedate pace now. They had to find a safe place. They had to be discreet. There had to be somewhere...

She wrenched open the door to the parlor they used for the Spinster meetings and tugged him in behind her.

He came willingly, laughing to himself as he shut the door behind her, pressing his back against it and staring at her without speaking.

The music was barely audible now, but that made no difference. This was one song she already knew well.

"Sebastian," she breathed, his name catching roughly in her throat.

He heard the catch and straightened, his eyes fixing on her lips.

She would burn where she stood if he continued to look like that.

Now was the time.

Now.

"I love you," she admitted in a rush of air, losing feeling in her legs as she did so.

He stilled completely, not even his breathing visible.

Her heart pounded in fear as she waited.

One... Two... Three...

Then he was to her, one hand wrapping around her while the other took firm hold of her cheek, his mouth crashing down on hers. His lips pulled at hers insistently, steadily wringing every ounce of pleasure from her. She gripped his coat in one hand while the other slid up to his neck, gripping him as she poured herself into this kiss, into him.

He tilted her head slightly, his fingers pressing against her skin gently, then stroking against her, the kiss growing more ardent and more possessive. She sighed against him, giving herself up to this fire and this need, this delightful onslaught of passion and madness. It was a heady thing indeed to be completely at the center of a man's attentions and actions, to be his whole focus and to feel the same need from him.

He needed her. He *needed* her.

And oh, how she desperately needed him!

She heard and felt Sebastian's growl as he pulled her even closer, as his kiss deepened, and she clung to him as if for her very life.

Was there any feeling in creation as perfect as this?

She broke off with a pant and a sigh, dropping her head back. Sebastian kissed her throat once, twice, then tucked himself there, burying his face against her skin.

Izzy wrapped her arm around his neck, stroking her fingers through his hair, willing her breathing to steady, to calm, but her lungs protested against regulation.

No matter. Overcome in his arms was far and away better than being steady anywhere else.

"I can't feel my knees," Izzy laughed breathlessly.

Sebastian smiled against her neck and kissed her again there. "Knees are overrated," he teased.

She shivered and ran her fingers through his hair again, which drew a warm nuzzling from him. "I think there are several people who would disagree with you."

"Not at this moment, they would not."

Izzy grinned and let him pull back, staring dazedly at him. "You may be right about that."

He leaned forward and kissed her fiercely, lingering enough to make her whimper. "I know I am," he whispered.

She swallowed and tugged his neck, forcing his brow to hers. "Now what?" she asked, not daring to specify what she meant.

"Now," he told her, his nose brushing hers, "we try to remember how to breathe."

She smiled and brushed her lips over his lightly. "Is that so hard?"

His hand slid back into her hair, gripping a little. "It is when every breath makes me want to kiss you again." He did so, twice, before moaning and forcing himself away, exhaling very slowly.

Izzy let him go, but slid her hold to his hand, and gripped it tightly. "We need an alibi before we return."

Sebastian nodded, his fingers rubbing hers in a rather distracting way. "Any thoughts?"

"Any thoughts are impossible when you do that," she muttered even as her cheeks flamed.

He grinned a boyish grin. "Is that supposed to make me stop? Because it isn't."

She rolled her eyes, sighing. "I thought I would say that I checked on the children. Perhaps told them a story. And given that excuse, I would have to actually do it."

"That's certainly believable," he agreed with a nod. "Though I would refuse to return to the music room with the prospect of hearing one of your stories as the alternative."

Of course he would.

She gave him a warm smile, then pulled on his hand and brought it to her lips.

He reciprocated by kissing her lips, and taking far too long a time doing so, considering they were in the drawing room rather than in the music room, where they would be expected to reappear shortly.

Not that she minded his kissing her extensively.

Quite the opposite.

"Right," Sebastian said, breaking off once again. "To the nursery?"

She gave him a wry look. "Why would you be there, love? They are not your relations."

He shrugged and tucked her hand into his arm, opening the door and leading her from the room. "I became lost in the house while trying to take some air. The music room is warm, and I was mistaken in my direction. I crossed your path during your escapade, and you graciously offered to see me back, but then the children clamored for a story. As you are so accommodating, you agreed, and I could not possibly venture throughout the house without my guide, so I patiently waited for you to finish."

Izzy laughed and shook her head. "Should I be concerned by how easily you conjured the tale?"

"Encouraged, I would think," he replied without concern. "Considering we are creating stories together."

"So we are," she murmured, her tone dipping with a wry note, considering their secrets.

He grinned at her then, and leaned down to give her a slow, teasing kiss. "Are we not?" he rasped. Then he straightened again and cleared his throat. "Now, behave yourself, and tell me which story I will be privy to this evening."

Izzy exhaled shakily and shook her head. "I haven't the foggiest. Give me some ideas."

Chapter Nineteen

———⟶❦⟵———

Speculation is a troublesome thing indeed. Nothing gets one into trouble so much as speculation.

-*The Spinster Chronicles, 10 January 1818*

She hadn't been this nervous for a ball since she was seventeen years old, and even then, she hadn't felt this level of apprehension. She'd been filled with excitement more than anything else, and she felt nothing pleasant at all in this moment.

Imagine, Isabella Lambert being nervous for a ball at her age.

It was laughable.

Worse than that, she'd already been here an hour and the nerves were certainly not abating. She'd greeted the Allandales warmly, as she always would, and they'd praised her new yellow gown, though it was nothing of the sort, before proceeding into the ballroom with her parents, who had now disappeared, as they usually did.

The other Spinsters were around somewhere, and they had all greeted each other and dispersed accordingly. Charlotte was dancing with Michael, which tended to happen three or four times a Season, usually when she needed a reprieve from the masses. Georgie and Tony were chatting with Lord Ingram, whose sudden return to London had been a cause for great joy among the young ladies of the ton.

None of that made her nervous. There was only one very particular thing that had her nerves in a tizzy, and they were far from calming.

Sebastian.

After the heat and passion of their last interlude, and her confession of love, she hardly knew what to expect tonight. They'd worked together twice since then, but Sebastian had been entirely focused on business, which drove her absolutely mad. So mad, in fact, that she had spent ages debating on what to wear this evening and how her hair should look.

She was never this ridiculous about that sort of thing, but for Sebastian…

Her thoughts and nerves were interrupted by Kitty darting over to her, her eyes twinkling as she grinned at Izzy. "Have you heard all the fuss about the mysterious writer of the Spinster Chronicles guest column?"

"I have," Izzy replied with a smile, the heat in her cheeks fading. "The praise is effusive, and the curiosity increasing. Everybody wants to know if she will write another, in the hopes that they might more easily guess her identity."

"I know!" Kitty scooted even closer, nearly squealing in her excitement. "The comments and gossip are everywhere!"

"That would be London," Izzy pointed out, the girl's enthusiasm amusing. "And as it is mostly positive comments being said, it is an exciting thing. I can assure you, when all the gossip is the reverse, it is quite dreadful to be in London."

Kitty pursed her lips, then took Izzy's hand, leaning close. "Izzy, what if I *did* write a second article for the Chronicles? I can write up a sample and see if you find it accomplished enough, if you like. I know nothing needs defending, as there hasn't been another attack, but what if I wrote something else?"

It took a moment for Izzy to find words for such a suggestion, but she covered their joined hands with her free one. "I don't need proof of your writing, we have that in the Chronicles already. I'll have to check with the others, but we adored what you wrote last time, so I feel certain they would agree to it. But what would you write upon, Kitty? What topic?"

The girl's smile would have lit up the entire ballroom all on it own. "Why, the Season, of course, and all it's exciting wonders and delights."

Izzy grinned at her. "Charlotte will be thrilled. She might want to write it with you."

"Oh, Lord," Kitty laughed, covering her mouth as she giggled.

"Excuse me, Miss Morton, Miss Lambert," Mr. Andrews suddenly broke in, appearing with a gentle smile. "Miss Morton, if you recollect, I have been promised this dance."

Kitty smiled at him very shyly. "Of course, Mr. Andrews. Do lead on."

He did so, nodding at Izzy as they left, and she grinned as she watched them move away and begin the dance. Kitty's gaze never quite stayed steady on her partner's, and the color never quite faded from her cheeks, which only enhanced her beauty. She was the very picture of an English miss this evening in a cream and pink sprigged muslin, matching pink rosettes in her dark hair.

She would be attracting many more suitors before the evening was out.

"She looks well, does she not?"

Izzy turned in surprise to see Lieutenant Henshaw coming up beside her, his eyes on Kitty as well, expression unreadable. "She does. But then, she always looks well."

Henshaw made a soft noise of assent, his mouth curved in a smile. "Particularly when she dances, I'd say. Do you think Morton knows how it enhances her already fair looks? She'll attract far more suitors dancing than anything else, and he ought to be made aware."

The mention of Sebastian dried Izzy's throat, but she managed a weak laugh. "Then I think you had better tell him. Does she dance as well as she appears to?"

"I couldn't say," he replied, stiffening slightly.

Izzy frowned at that. "You couldn't? Why not?"

"I have no experience in such things."

Now Izzy turned to the tall man beside her, completely incredulous. "You haven't danced with her? At all?"

He met her gaze almost sheepishly. "I wanted her to be comfortable with me before we danced."

"Henshaw…"

"I am a large and imposing man," he overrode with surprising gruffness. "And she is a sweet, timid creature. Despite my association with her brother, she knew nothing of me. I knew no other way to show my respect for her but to respect her comfort."

Izzy couldn't believe what she was hearing. Henshaw, who danced more than any man she knew, who flattered and flirted and teased as a way of life, who was all decency and goodness, had cared enough about Kitty's nature to change his own. Not in any great way, or indeed in any manner that would necessarily have been observed, but enough.

She wet her lips carefully, desperate to avoid smiling at the moment. "Have you asked her?"

Henshaw returned his focus to the dance. "No…"

Now Izzy had to let one side of her mouth curve just a little. "She might have said yes."

He nodded once. "She might. But would she have been able to look at me when she did so?"

It was the sweetest, most considerate thing she had ever heard, and her heart swelled at hearing such a statement. "Henshaw, I think you might be the sweetest man ever born," she told him without hesitation, putting a hand on his arm.

He looked down at her with a wry smile, though he was clearly pleased. He covered her hand with his own. "Don't tell my superiors, Miss Lambert. Sweet officers never get promoted."

She chuckled and nodded, turning back to look at the dance, then stiffening when her eyes clashed with Sebastian's across the room.

He stared at her with the same intensity she felt racing through her body at the moment. He was pristine in his eveningwear, looking almost dangerous as he gazed at her, the color of his eyes vague from this distance, but the power clear.

She wondered if her gown had actually caught fire under such heat, especially given how her skin seemed to burn all the way to the tips of her hair. Between the shade of her dress and that of her hair, she might resemble a flame and feel the effects of such.

Henshaw caught the battle and slid his hand from her arm. "I'm going to leave you, Miss Lambert," he murmured, for once not sounding teasing about something of this nature. "In the hopes that it may preserve us both."

She nodded unsteadily, her hand hanging in the air, the effort of returning it to her own hold too great. "Dance with Kitty, Henshaw," she murmured, her eyes still on Sebastian. "You've earned it."

His answer was lost amidst the buzzing currently filling her ears. *Sebastian.*

They stood, locked in each other's gaze, unmoving even as the room about them swirled and danced and chatted. She needed to go to him. She needed him to come to her. She needed something to happen, anything to break this breathless, writhing tension filling the air between them.

"Izzy!"

She blinked with a gasp and turned, half-blinded towards the voice. "Yes?"

The haze of her vision cleared, and she managed a weak smile at Miranda, who seemed rather determined in her approach. "Miranda! How delightful."

Miranda's mouth curved into her usual smile. "Indeed, everyone says so, yet I never know quite who to believe."

"I think you may safely believe me," Izzy assured her, glancing back towards Sebastian, only to find that he was no longer standing there. A sharp pang of disappointment hit her, but she returned her attention to Miranda, covering the ache with a smile.

"Of course, dear, of course."

Miranda said nothing else, looking out at the dance with some speculation.

Izzy waited patiently for a moment, or would-be patiently, as it happened, then sighed as kindly as she could. "Miranda, is there something I can do for you?"

"What would you say to a potential match for Kitty Morton?" Miranda said without preamble, eyes narrowing slightly.

"A match?" Izzy repeated. She watched Kitty, still dancing with Mr. Andrews, then looked back at Miranda. "With whom?"

Miranda sputtered a little and waved her hand. "Why, Andrews, of course. Look at the pair of them."

Izzy did look, and while they would have made a striking couple in appearance, there was nothing at all in their behavior while dancing that would have lent itself to speculation or flirtation. Kitty's cheeks were faintly colored, and Andrews wore a very small smile, but nothing that had not been seen before with other partners.

"He would make her a fine husband," Miranda said with satisfaction. "And it would be such a favorable match. Morton would undoubtedly be pleased by it, and Society would be so drawn to them. She would be so popular!"

The thought made Izzy blanch, and her throat dried in an instant. Swallowing with difficulty, she glanced at Miranda with a hesitant smile. "You forget, I think, that Kitty is shy, Miranda. She would hate to be popular, or to be the center of any particular attention at all. Why, the fact that she is even dancing with Andrews is…"

"Yes, yes, Izzy," Miranda overrode impatiently. "We shall ensure it is a very subtle sort of popular. Nothing overwhelming or distressing, I assure you. I am not so scheming as to abuse my sweet friend's nature so. I only intend the best, and I daresay Andrews might be it."

Izzy hesitated, biting her lip. "I think," she said slowly, "there might be someone else to whom Andrews might be drawn. And, perhaps, someone else who might suit Kitty better."

Miranda seemed to consider that. "Perhaps… perhaps, indeed. I shall think on it. I stand by Andrews as an ideal, but there is no need for haste." She tapped her fan against her lips, humming to herself, then swept away.

Izzy watched her go, shaking her head in bemusement. Miranda was truly a wonder in so many ways.

"Izzy!"

"Oh, Lord, now what?" Izzy muttered under her breath, turning yet again.

Georgie was suddenly there, eyes wide. "You'll never guess. Tony's just come to tell me. Alice Sterling has been nearly compromised."

"What?" Izzy gasped, gripping her cousin's arms.

"They've only just retrieved her," Georgie rushed on with a nod, wringing her hands together. "She was with that Delaney fellow, thought he was in love with her and that he would propose in the orangery, but instead . . ."

A shudder coursed over them both, and Izzy felt tears rising. "What can I do?"

Georgie shook her head. "Nothing, they've got her and are going home. Tony and Morton are going with them, and they'll see them right. Tony said he's never seen Hugh look so distraught and enraged. He truly had no idea that…"

"Iz…"

Izzy froze, looking behind Georgie, heart pounding in a way it had not done all night. Georgie was quick to move away, but Izzy barely noticed.

Sebastian stood there, hands rubbing together, his expression open, tension in his frame. "May I… call on you soon?"

Her heart swelled, pounding more profoundly now. "Yes," she whispered with a nod. "Yes, please do."

He almost smiled as he returned her nod, then turned around, heading back to the corridor beyond.

"Well, well," Georgie mused behind her, sounding less distressed now. "I wonder what that could be about."

Izzy ignored her, watching Sebastian go, barely restraining a sigh. *Soon*, Izzy thought with delight. *Soon, my love.*

She turned back to Georgie, clearing her throat. "We need to tell the others about Alice. She needs our support. Come on."

Georgie smiled all too knowingly. "Indeed. Lead the way."

It was all Sebastian could do avoid whistling as he strode along the streets of Mayfair.

He'd decided against taking his carriage home from his solicitor's office in favor of walking, as the day was so fine, and he was in a well enough mood to do so without complaint.

After days of details and meetings, poring over reports, and driving himself into a sort of anxiety he had never quite experienced before, not even as a soldier, he finally had resolution, and a decision. Finally, he could move forward, and could do so with confidence. No need for anxiety, no more problems to solve, and nothing at all to cloud his mind.

All that was left was to do it.

Perhaps there was some anxiety needed.

But only a little.

He grinned to himself as he strolled down the street, nodding and smiling politely at passing people, though he didn't think he'd be able to recall just who he had seen. His mind was too occupied with other thoughts to recollect such minor details.

What a change he'd undergone of late! He hardly recognized himself, truth be told, and yet he was quite sure that he had never been more himself than he was now.

Izzy had done that for him. She made him worry less and live more. She made him a better brother to his sister, and he'd never found himself lacking before. She made him better in every respect.

Which was why he would now go to her father and ask permission to marry her.

Or should he ask Izzy first and then go to her father?

He'd never actually asked anyone about the specifics or the order in which things should occur.

Given that he and Izzy hadn't formally entered into a courtship, he supposed he ought to do that first. He'd tell Izzy what his plan was, of course, and see if she agreed to a very quick courtship so they might have a very quick engagement, but he thought she might be in favor of such things.

He had to tell her that he loved her. Had to make sure she was in no doubt of his affection and his respect. She had to know what she did to him, how she had changed him in so many ways, and how complete his life had felt with her in it.

How did a man say such things without sounding like a complete lunatic? He'd never had a way with words, and this seemed a rather lofty occasion to start an exercise in improvement.

Surely, she could not be surprised by what he would say. He'd nearly said something the other night before he'd rushed off to help secure Alice Sterling, and then, in the heat of such a harrowing moment, he'd barely been able to refrain from hauling Izzy into his arms for safekeeping. Some semblance of gentlemanly behavior clearly remained in him, as he'd stood there and politely asked if he could call on her...

He'd been a hair's breadth away from dropping to his knees and proposing, but he hadn't.

Still a gentleman, then.

What a relief.

But poor Alice Sterling... Lord, he'd been terrified on Lord Sterling's behalf. Their sisters were of an age, and it was too unnerving to imagine Kitty in the same situation. She needed to be far better protected than Alice had been, if such cads were able to sway young ladies so easily.

Surely Izzy would have some ideas there.

He was suddenly jostled by an eager young man dashing off somewhere, and Sebastian turned to look after him, more amused than irritated. What in the world would have prompted someone in Mayfair to act so?

He watched as the young man gathered with several others, a familiar newssheet in all their hands.

Ah. That was undoubtedly the cause.

The Spinster Chronicles must have released a new edition today. A rather good one, if the frenzy was any indication.

That was not surprising, as there was always something worth reading in the Chronicles, even if the Society Dabbler struck a little too honest a chord at times. He suspected those were the times when Charlotte had written them. Personally, the Quotes and Quirks segment had always been a favorite of his, no matter who had written it.

The enthusiastic rage around their recent guest columnist had not abated in the slightest. In fact, if anything, the anticipation for subsequent issues of the Chronicles had only increased. It seemed that all of London, if not England as a whole, was trying to ferret out the new writer, wondering if she would be a permanent fixture amongst the group, or if bringing in guest writers would now become tradition.

Sebastian hadn't told anyone, but even he had begun to grow curious about the mystery writer. He'd eventually read her article and found it to be a sound defense in a respectable manner, and not even Hugh Sterling would have been able to find fault with it, which was undoubtedly why no further attacks had ensued. Unaware as to who might have had such a command of language and tone that was not already writing for the Spinsters, he had very few believable suspicions as to the identity.

It was an amusing spectacle, this delirium over a column written by spinsters when most of these people could not decide if they approved or disapproved of them.

Such was London Society, he supposed.

He shook his head, smirking to himself as he turned to continue on his way.

Well, the Spinsters with a capital S would be short one spinster with a lowercase s soon enough, if he had his way.

What would they call their column if they all married?

Not that such a thing was of legitimate concern. He highly doubted that Charlotte would ever settle on a suitor, and Elinor would likely never even have one, given her aversion to the male population as a whole.

Again, he was jostled by someone passing him, and this time he was less amused and more irritated.

"Pardon me, sir," he snapped, scowling after him.

Tony turned around, expression apologetic, then he grinned freely. "Oh, it's you, Morton! Perfect."

Sebastian raised a brow at his friend. "What? Because it is me, you are exempt from offering apology for crashing into me?"

"Something like that." Tony shrugged, still smiling broadly. "Didn't see you, to be honest. The streets are mad today."

"They are indeed," Sebastian remarked, gesturing down the way. "Clearly, the new issue of the Spinster Chronicles is doing well."

Tony's smile shifted to one of disbelief. "You haven't read it?"

Sebastian shook his head, folding his arms. "Not yet, no. I may wait a day or two until the madness fades."

"I doubt it will do so that quickly," Tony replied, his tone rather peculiar.

"Oh?"

Tony's mouth twisted as though he were considering something, then he stepped closer, his eyes darting around. "Morton, may I ask you a rather impertinent question?"

Frowning, Sebastian gestured for him to do so with a quick nod.

Tony's dark eyes held a distinctly sardonic air about them. "Why didn't you tell me that Kitty was the guest writer?"

Sebastian blinked at his friend, not entirely certain he had heard him right. "Excuse me?"

"You could have said," Tony murmured with a warm laugh. "Particularly when she wrote the second one."

Now there was no mistaking it. "Second?" Sebastian repeated, though he wasn't sure how the word had made its way out of his suddenly very tight mouth.

Tony nodded and gestured in the direction of the madness Sebastian had indicated mere moments before. "All of London is obsessed, man. I was nearly accosted in the streets by people demanding confirmation of the lady's identity. As though Georgie would divulge Spinster secrets to her husband." He laughed at the ridiculous thought, clapping Sebastian on the shoulder.

Sebastian was not laughing. Could not laugh. Could not think.

Kitty had... *Kitty* had written...

"How did you know it was her, then?" he heard himself ask while his entire body proceeded to turn very cold indeed.

Tony waved off the question quickly. "Simple deduction and knowing more of the details revealed in the article than the general public would. It was plain as day. Quite a talented writer, your little sister. Marvelous way with words."

"Marvelous," Sebastian managed, his hands forming fists as they sat folded against him. "Will you excuse me, Sterling? I have something I need attend to, and it cannot wait."

His friend nodded, catching his tone this time, and his expression grew concerned, but Sebastian turned away before any more questions could be asked.

He could barely see straight as he walked, his pace turning brisk in an instant. How could this be the case? How could Kitty have been the one writing for the Spinster Chronicles? How could they have *allowed* her to do so?

She wasn't a spinster, and she wasn't part of their Spinster contingent, no matter how they might have adopted her into their ranks. She was a quiet, timid girl in the midst of her very first Season in London, when it would be imperative for her to make good connections and a favorable impression upon any and all influential members of society. She ought not to be parading her thoughts and opinions out in such a public platform like the Chronicles, where all of London would see them, and speculation about her would run rampant.

What if others found the same connections that Tony had? What if Kitty's identity became known as this writer, and she was treated with the same scorn that the Spinsters were?

He could not allow that. He *would not* allow that.

This ought to have had his permission before it was ever engaged in. If this was what the Spinsters had envisioned when Kitty had met them, he regretted ever bringing her into their midst.

He stormed his way up the stairs and banged on the door, grinding his teeth in his fury.

Collins opened the door and bowed politely. "Mr. Morton, sir."

"I need to speak with Miss Lambert, man," he barked, indignation rising further still. "Now."

"Of course, sir," Collins replied, though his eyes narrowed.

He would bowl the aged man over if he had to hear one word that was not expressly related to his seeing her.

He was let in and taken to the drawing room, the very one in which he had first heard her declare her love for him and had then proceeded to kiss her until they were both senseless.

He scoffed at the memory now. If he'd only known then what betrayal had already happened, and would happen, he might have saved himself a good deal of trouble.

Collins said something or other to Izzy and she had risen from her chair, fussing with her mussed hair and drab dress, smiling in encouragement.

He needed none.

Sebastian stepped into the room, bowed, and waited for Collins to leave them.

Then…

"We need to talk, Miss Lambert."

Chapter Twenty

*The unexpected is not always unpleasant, but when it is, it is most
unpleasant indeed to have it be so unexpected.*

-The Spinster Chronicles, 9 October 1817

Miss Lambert?

Izzy's smile vanished as Sebastian's cold and formal tone settled,
his words echoing dangerously in her mind. He did not look like the
man she had been so gleefully loving of late, and the manner in which
he looked at her now informed her quite plainly that he did not see
her that way, either.

"Sebastian, what's wrong?" she said at once, stepping forward
hesitantly. "What's happened?"

He smiled then, a cold and cruel sneer of a smile that startled
her. "What has happened? What has happened, Miss Lambert?"

She flinched as his voice increased in volume, the coldness all
the more chilling for being louder.

Sebastian laughed once. "What has happened, Miss Lambert?
Can you not guess? Did you not plan the thing?"

Izzy stared at him in wonder, her knees trembling with fear and
anticipation. "What are you talking about, Sebastian?"

"Feigning ignorance." He scoffed again, but with more derision.
"So much for the good and honest Isabella Lambert."

Something snapped inside Izzy, and she took another step
forward, her stomach clenching. "I beg your pardon, you have no

right to address me with so much contempt in my own home. State your complaint clearly, as I have no idea what could possibly drive you to be this irate with someone you claimed to be falling in love with. Or had you forgotten that you had done so?"

"I have forgotten nothing," he barked, moving further into the room, but further away from her. "Believe me, I am well aware of the position I have put myself in, and what a mad enterprise that was."

"I am sorry it has left you with such distaste," Izzy spat, her voice catching in spite of her anger. "Now get on with your errand so you may be rid of me all the sooner."

He turned to her, a bizarre sneer still twisting his once pleasant features. "My sister, Miss Lambert, has written for the Spinster Chronicles. Do you deny it?"

He knew.

Her breath caught in her chest, and her anger vanished in the face of bald fear. Of course, she had thought he might find out sooner or later, it was not so expertly disguised as to be completely incoherent, but she thought they would have more time.

Kitty had said she would approach Sebastian about it, that he would be proud of her for expressing herself, just as he had encouraged Izzy to do. It was supposed to make him pleased.

Not this.

Anything but this.

Izzy lifted her chin and clamped her hands together before her, though they shook even then. "No."

"No?" he repeated in disbelief. "No what?"

"No, I do not deny it," she replied, careful to keep her tone as impassive as it had been in her more biddable days. "She has."

"Twice, if I am not mistaken."

Izzy dipped her chin in a nod. "Yes."

Sebastian nodded as well, though his could not have been more different than hers. "And why did my sister write for the Spinster Chronicles, Miss Lambert? That was not part of our agreement."

"Because she asked to," Izzy told him, emphasizing her words with great care.

"And you all just allowed her?" he exclaimed, flinging an arm out. "You, a group of mature, well-educated, well-bred women just let an innocent, naïve, timid girl of eighteen publish an article of her thoughts and opinions in a widely read gossip column?"

Izzy's brow snapped down, and she stepped towards him. "Gossip column? You know full well it's more than that."

"Is it?" he asked, sneering once more. "Is it really, Miss Lambert?"

"Kitty was eager to defend us," Izzy insisted as she felt her heart lurch painfully in a mixture of distress and anger. "When that article came out, I thought we should print some sort of response, and she begged us to let her do it. And I saw wisdom in her suggestion. A writer who is not one of us would hold more weight out there than we defending ourselves. So yes, I let her do it. We all let her write an *anonymous* defense of the Spinsters to the people of London."

Sebastian grunted in some sort of satisfaction. "And yet she was found out. Because I was informed of the identity of this mysterious writer only moments ago on the streets. Imagine my surprise to discover that the handiwork was that of my sister, and that I knew nothing of it. Her brother and guardian, the one tasked with her care, the one who has made it his life's work to provide for her and protect her, and I knew nothing."

Izzy swallowed hard as her cheeks suddenly flamed. "She said she would tell you," she managed, reaching for the chair behind her and gripping tightly. "She said…"

"Don't you dare blame her for this!" Sebastian suddenly roared, pointing an accusing finger at her. "I refuse to hear any argument that this mess is her fault."

"What mess?" Izzy asked him, shaking her head. "What mess? It is only an article in the Spinster Chronicles. I've written hundreds, and I've never…"

"What you choose to do with your unoccupied time is none of my concern, nor is it the issue at hand," he interrupted. "But my sister is not to be any part of it. Had I known you would rope her into your spinster game, I would never have involved you in her care at all. It's no wonder that Alice Sterling was so misguided into trusting such a blackguard as Delaney when she had the leader of such a group for a relation. How many other young ladies have you all been leading into recklessness, hmm?"

Izzy's brows shot up, her pounding heart stopping in her chest. "Recklessness?" she repeated, barely able to say the word. "You think we're to blame for Alice? That somehow we're ruining the lives of young ladies like her and Kitty?"

"What else should we all think?" He gave her a questioning look that clearly did not expect an answer. "A group of spinsters using the attention of Society upon their unmarried state to give themselves a platform? A way to attract notice without scandal or scorn? No one would pay any attention to you all if you had husbands, so why not keep all prospects at a distance? You thrive upon your own independence, now you've had some, and followers of your column may feel themselves emboldened until the proper boundaries of Society have no meaning, and dignity has no place."

This could not be happening. He could not be saying such horrid, hurtful things when he knew the opposite to be true.

Or he *had* known.

Hadn't he?

"Sebastian…"

"Let me make one thing perfectly clear, Miss Lambert," Sebastian went on, overriding her soft use of his name. "My sister is not a spinster. My sister will not *be* a spinster. With or without the damned capital S. I have worked too hard and too long striving for her future for her to be relegated to such a state. She will not associate with any of you outside of the most polite circumstances. I cannot believe that after meeting her, knowing her, bonding with her, that you, Miss Lambert, would allow her to speak out and stand out in a way that will only bring her criticism. Shame on you!"

Tears burned against Izzy's eyes as she listened, as she heard the venom in his tone, her illusions of him shattering one by one. "Have you read it, Sebastian?" she forced herself to ask, even as her voice quivered. "Have you read what Kitty wrote in today's article?"

"No," he informed her without concern. "And I do not need to in order to know that this whole enterprise is entirely inappropriate for her. Nor to refuse my permission."

Izzy nodded very slowly, fighting for control. "Might I humbly suggest that you read your sister's words, Sebastian? Despite your newfound hatred of me, of us, and of all that we stand for, I suggest you read what she wrote, and then make a judgment on what we have done, if you must. Your opinion is meaningless without perspective."

Sebastian's expression hardened, and she watched a muscle twitch in his jaw. "I have said all that I needed to. Good day."

He moved for the door, and Izzy could feel her heart cracking, the deep crevices extending all the way through. "What happened to expressing ourselves, Sebastian?"

He paused, looking back at her. "I think you've expressed yourself quite enough, Miss Lambert."

"Enough?" she cried, her voice suddenly harsh, strident, and rapidly rising in volume. "Enough? I haven't begun to express myself, Mr. Morton!"

Now he turned completely, expression impassive, but superior, daring her to go on.

He would wish he had not done so.

"I object to your harsh accusations, sir," Izzy began, now seeing the man before her as a traitor, an enemy, someone rather akin to Hugh Sterling, only she felt no pity for him. "They rankle and chafe, and I despise the inference that I am somehow less of the woman you originally saw me as simply because you are being petulant and temperamental about being left out of a rather straightforward venture that many people are quite proud of. But we'll leave the defense of myself for another time. Perhaps for another article, if your sister wishes to refute *you* for all the world."

He snarled and made to answer, but Izzy wasn't finished.

"If you were a little less conceited and a little more observant," she went on, releasing the chair behind her and fisting her hands at her side, manicured nails digging into her palm, "you would see that your sister is not a child. She is a woman capable of making her own decisions, and occasionally does so. *She* was the one who wanted to take part in the Chronicles. She begged me to let her write the articles. She wanted to express herself in a manner she was comfortable with, which I thought was something you, of all people, would understand, given that you insisted that I do the same. Apparently, being a gentleman is more about stiffness and propriety than it is about honesty and respect. But I'm not sure what that makes you, Mr. Morton, considering I also have never judged a gentleman to be a

251

hypocrite."

Sebastian stiffened and lifted his chin, eyes flashing. "Hypocrite, madam?"

Izzy smiled without any degree of warmth. "How else should I describe it, sir? You want me to express myself, and yet when your sister does, it offends you. You think it a wonderful thing that I should aspire to be a writer, and yet your sister may not do so. You claim to admire the Spinsters and have no trouble associating with unmarried women of a certain age, and yet you object to your sister being tied to us in any way. You rush off to save Alice Sterling, a sweet girl whose brother you once encouraged me to rail against, and yet I am suddenly to blame for her trusting that same brother and his friend. Hypocrite, Mr. Morton. The very definition."

The room was silent, both of their chests heaving, the air between them heavy.

A traitorous quiver began in Izzy's jaw, and she tightened her face to resist it. She shook her head slowly, swallowing hard. "I don't know how you can live with yourself when you don't even know your own mind."

Sebastian blinked unsteadily and exhaled once through his nose. He stared at Izzy for a hard moment, then nodded. "Very good. That was perfectly executed. Good day."

He turned and opened the door, striding down the corridor quickly.

Izzy waited until she could no longer hear him, waited for the door to close, waited for the house to be silent once more.

Then her legs gave way, trembling with a ferocity she had never felt before, and she crumpled to the floor on a ragged sob. She covered her face with one hand, the other reaching for a chair to steady her. Cry after cry was ripped from her, tearing at her chest, throat, and frame with a vengeance. Tears streamed from her eyes and fell in rapid succession onto her hands and lap, blinding her almost completely.

It didn't matter. None of it did.

The man she loved had destroyed her, and she had lashed out to do the same.

Apparently, she had hit the mark.

Brava for finally learning how to be something other than nice. What satisfaction in her victory.

She curled into herself as the sobs continued, her body aching from top to bottom and inside out, her heart somehow seeming absent after all of that. All of her hopes and dreams lay dashed at her feet, every single one. There was nothing left to cling to, no light to brighten her suddenly bleak and darkened world.

Only emptiness. Only space. A raw void of nothingness.

Nothing.

He'd been avoiding it for over a week.

Avoiding anything resembling it, tied to it, or about it.

He'd had to.

Now, however, he had no excuse.

Sebastian stared at it where it sat on the desk, fully within his reach, yet seeming at an insurmountable distance.

Reaching across the desk would change everything. Giving in would mean moving forward in one direction or another. Spanning that gulf would give him insight he wasn't sure he wanted.

Reading that article would give him answers he'd specifically been avoiding.

But the misery was too much. The silence was too much.

The pride was too much.

He'd been trapped in a vortex of self loathing and anger since he'd confronted Izzy, and he hadn't found a way to escape its current. The anger wasn't directed at her anymore, but it existed all the same. He'd snapped at his sister more times than he could count in the last week, though he'd never directly confronted her about the situation. He'd shut himself up in his study and avoided the room he and Izzy had once worked in like the plague.

He'd avoided anything to do with Izzy, spinsters, and art.

And now he was miserable.

Read your sister's words...

He squeezed his eyes shut against the echo of Izzy's voice in his mind, which had assailed him again and again since that day, never giving him a moment's peace.

The truth of the matter was that he was afraid to read them. He was bloody terrified of doing anything of the sort. Because he knew very well that between the two of them that day, Izzy was by far more likely to have been in the right, and he would be in the wrong.

He knew that already. But how wrong exactly had he been?

That was where he was cowardly.

Still, he could not distance himself from Kitty anymore, no matter what happened between he and Izzy, or he and anybody else. Kitty was his only family, and he needed to mend whatever fences he had destroyed with her. He'd already done his worst with Izzy, and he'd likely suffer an eternity in hellfire for that. He could not do the same with his sister.

He would not.

Mustering the very same courage he'd employed in battle, he exhaled and stretched out for the paper, pulling it to him as his heart leapt into his throat, beating out a bitter tasting cadence that burned him.

His eyes scanned the sheet quickly, the familiar sections passing in a sort of blur.

There. The main article.

Reflections of a First Season Miss.

That would eliminate so many from the mystery at once. They could discover Kitty as the writer fairly easily, in fact, given her association with the Spinsters.

Former association.

She hadn't been in their company for a week. He'd made sure of it. She could see Amelia Perry or any of the other girls she'd met, but none of the Spinsters.

He swallowed and read on, forcing his panic down.

There is nothing like London during the Season, or so I had been informed numerous times before I had ventured into it for myself. I was expected to anticipate every ball, every party, every opportunity to perform or be on display in any way, shape, or form. I was perfectly prepared and had been for some time. I possessed the necessary accomplishments to be suitable, had been trained up by governesses and tutors, dancing instructors had praised my lightness of foot, and my French had been declared exquisite.

But I felt unprepared and unqualified to be entering what has been called the Marriage Mart. I was nothing more than a child, in my own eyes, and a shy one at that. Such timidity may be praised once as demure, but more than that is unacceptable.

I was not simply demure; I was terrified.

How to properly express such things? I was to be representing my family and our reputation by my every action, and yet I could not open my mouth to say how I take my tea. I was destined to be a failure to the memory of my parents, and to the loving elder brother who had sacrificed so much to ensure my life lacked for nothing. He whom I loved better than any creature on earth would be ashamed of me. How could I bear it?

Sebastian gasped at the sudden and searing pain spreading across his chest, the paper crinkling in his hands as he found himself unable to stop the shaking there. He laid the paper on the table, smoothed it out, and cleared his throat as he forced his eyes to trace the words once more.

That same loving brother provided a way. He brought into my life a woman who was gentle, kind, and good. One who had her share of Seasons and was no longer intimidated by them. She took my hand and led me through the motions, just as my dance instructors had done. Her steps were sure, her tread as light as mine, and, step by step, she showed me the way.

In her care, I found comfort, and I found strength. She taught me the value of my voice, and the vision I wished for myself. Because of her, I made the acquaintance of other girls, some in the same situation as myself. I was not alone, for the first time, and I found my way forward.

It has been weeks now, and the Season is well under way. I am still a timid creature, and I find I am content to be so. But I no longer fear these events, I look forward to them. I long to glitter as the candles do, to shine as a jewel, and to find myself liked for the qualities and attributes that I possess. I wish to take part, and to see the world with fresh, new eyes.

Not all of us are born with great confidence, despite our training, upbringing, and heritage, but all of us strive to find our place in the world, and in Society.

I may not have found mine as yet, but with the care of those who love me best, I have found the path I wish to take in order to find out. The Season is more than a Marriage Mart.

It is a training ground. For here, we become who we must for the future that lies ahead, for good or for ill.

Here we find ourselves.

Step by exalted step.

Sebastian sat back against his chair roughly, a suspicious burning behind his eyes.

How could he have been so very blind?

His sister had nothing to be ashamed of in this article, despite what he had feared. This was a glorious testimonial to her growth, which he had witnessed firsthand. She had so perfectly, so poignantly, expressed her growth and maturity, and he felt nothing of the despair he had feared.

He felt a swelling of pride and love for his sister, moved by her tender expressions of love and her fears, and he wanted to hold her in his arms while he told her so.

Gratitude for Izzy washed over him, and a wave of shame rapidly followed. She had given Kitty so much, so very much, and he had been too obsessed with his own need for reserve and what he had considered to be propriety to see it. Kitty had been right; she had been a child when they had brought her to London, yet now she had blossomed into a young woman that could walk with confidence into any room in London.

She had become everything he had ever wanted his younger sister to be.

And he had raged about it.

Worse than that, he'd accused Izzy of sins that did not belong at anyone's door purely out of that rage.

Sebastian buried his face into his hands, then gripped at his hair as a growl of agony erupted from him.

There was no atoning for such an offense.

He was not worthy of either of them, his sister or the woman he loved.

Loved.

His chest seized and his breath caught audibly as the very thing he'd been denying for a week flashed into bright illumination within him.

He loved Izzy still. He loved her more. He loved her beyond words and beyond sense and beyond his own shame. He loved her for fighting against him, for defending his sister, for ignoring her habitual submissiveness to lash out for what she believed in. He loved the risks she took, the criticism she endured, the smile she always wore no matter the circumstances.

He loved everything she was and everything that she made him want.

And he had lost her. More than that, he had shoved her away.

Lord, he was a worthless creature.

Was it even remotely possible that her goodness could extend to him after all of that? Even if she could never love him again, could she forgive him?

He would take the smallest portion of whatever she would extend to him.

If she could.

But first, he had amends to make closer to home.

He pushed himself out of his chair and exited his study, knowing his emotions would be too close to the surface, but willing to sacrifice a little dignity for forgiveness.

Kitty was easy enough to find, sitting in her personal sitting room, wrapped in a shawl, a book in her lap. He'd seen her in this exact position time and again over the years, but for the first time, he saw a woman and not a child. She did not need his edicts and dictates. She was grown now, and it was time he treated her as such.

"Mouse," he murmured, leaning in the doorway.

She looked up at him, her eyes wide. After a moment, she offered a hesitant smile. "There you are, brother. I was afraid I'd lost you."

There was no use pretending he did not understand her meaning. "So was I," he admitted.

Kitty sat up and patted the seat beside her. "Come. Sit."

He nodded and moved to the sofa, surprised when Kitty took his hand the moment he was settled. He looked at their fingers as they wrapped around each other and found himself unable to speak.

Kitty surveyed him through much wiser eyes than he'd given her credit for. "You read the article."

Again, he nodded, swallowing hard.

His sister smiled very gently. "And?"

He squeezed her hand as tightly as he dared. "It's wonderful, Kitty," he told her, finding his voice at last. "Beautifully written, and a magnificent insight into your journey. I am profoundly proud of you."

"Really?" she half-squealed, her grip clenching in her excitement.

Sebastian chuckled and nodded at her. "Yes, Mouse, I am. And I am so very sorry that I have made you think anything else in the last week. I've been battling my own demons and neglected everything else. Especially you."

"Oh, Sebastian…"

Her soft whimper nearly undid him, and he shook his head quickly. "I thought that your writing in the Chronicles would be a source of criticism for you, and I could not bear to have you attacked. The attempt on Alice Sterling affected me far more than I imagined, and I took out my fears in this. I had forgotten what a voice you have, and I doubted you and your friends. I doubted everything I thought I knew. You deserved better than that."

Kitty offered him an apologetic smile. "I am sorry I did not ask your permission before writing it."

"No," he told her at once, covering their hands with his free one. "No, there is nothing to apologize for. You do not need my permission for that. Other things, perhaps, given that I am your guardian…"

Kitty snickered at that but beamed at him in a manner he did not warrant.

Sebastian sighed, shaking his head at her. "You are a woman now, Mouse. And I am not your jailer. I do hope that in the future you will inform me of articles you have coming so that I might be the first to read it. I hope you will tell me of the friends you are making and the gentlemen you are meeting."

"Sebastian," she groaned, blushing adorably.

He chuckled and kissed her hand. "Not because I need to know, Mouse, but because I want to. No matter how old we get, or how fine you become, I will always be your elder brother, and I will always want to know the details of your life."

Kitty sniffled softly, wrapping her arms tightly around him. "I love you, Sebastian."

His own emotions brimming, he held her tightly. "I love you, too, Mouse."

She stunned him by whacking him on the back of the head lightly.

"Ouch!" he yelped, pulling back. "What was that for?"

She gave him a dubious look. "That was for whatever you said to Izzy. Make it right."

He sighed and pulled her close once more. Make it right. Yes, he absolutely had to make it right.

But how?

Chapter Twenty-One

Upon reflection, you may find pain. But where there is pain, there is also healing.

-The Spinster Chronicles, 3 June 1816

"Izzy, dear, I want a word."

Izzy turned to her mother, standing in the doorway and surveying her with open concern. It struck her that she had been left alone for over a week, despite not being herself in all that time, and having that privacy she craved to mourn her loss in peace. It had been a blessed relief, but she knew it could not last forever.

At least now she was enough removed to address the situation without dissolving into tears.

She hadn't cried in two days.

"Of course, Mama," Izzy said, gesturing to any of the open chairs in the room. The Spinsters hadn't arrived yet, and she knew she would have to recount everything for them, given that she hadn't been to a gathering since her fight with Sebastian.

She swallowed painfully as her mother came and took the chair beside her. Even thinking his name caused her grief.

Perhaps she might cry today after all.

Her mother smiled gently at her. "I know that I can be a bit fastidious, Izzy, and that I take advantage of your good nature more than I should, as your mother."

"Oh, Mama," Izzy protested at once, shaking her head quickly, stunned by the admission.

"No, let me," her mother insisted firmly. She tilted her head at Izzy, her smile turning emotional. "I know it must pain you to be a spinster, especially when I remind you of it. You must know that I never mean to cause you more pain."

"I know," Izzy whispered, trying for a smile and failing miserably.

Her mother nodded, folding her hands in her lap. "But above all, my girl, I hope you know that I don't find fault with you or in you for being unmarried. I truly mean it when I say that you are perfectly, exactly as I would wish. It is not only something I say to make myself feel better, or you. I believe it. You are a strong woman, Izzy, and I don't know where you learned how to be so. I don't believe I could bear with the life you have with as much grace or integrity, and I sometimes wonder what I can possibly offer you as your mother."

Tears sprang into Izzy's eyes, and one began to make its way down her cheek. "Mama…"

Her mother reached out and smoothed the tear away, stroking her cheek gently. "I don't know what has happened between you and Mr. Morton, Izzy, but I pray it will soon be mended. I could see in your eyes how you adored him, and he looked at you much the same. I didn't say anything because I wanted to let you have your privacy, but I always wanted you to find someone to look at you that way. And even if what has passed is the end of it, I believe you to be exactly as you should be, and I pray that never changes."

Izzy leaned forward and hugged her mother tightly, her heart swelling at the comfort of being in her arms, rather as she had as a child. "Thank you, Mama."

Her mother nodded against her, then kissed her cheek before rising, surreptitiously wiping at her own eyes. "Now, chin up, love. Your friends will be here in a moment, and that Charlotte Wright will pounce upon the first sign of tears she sees, and never let you have a moment's rest until you confess all."

Izzy laughed and sat back in her chair. "How do you know that?"

The comment earned her a wry look, and her mother adjusted the lace cap on her head with a sniff. "Her mother was exactly the same way. It drove us all quite mad." She widened her eyes meaningfully before turning from the room.

A rough sigh escaped Izzy, and she sniffed back the last evidence of tears. Her mother was quite right, Charlotte wouldn't settle a bit if she knew Izzy had been crying.

Then again, none of them would.

Interfering busybodies, the lot of them.

And how she had missed them.

Only Georgie had come to see her, and she knew all now, but she'd had no comfort to give. Still, her presence had been comforting enough.

Now she needed the rest of her friends, and she prayed they would understand.

"Oh, lass, there's a sad look."

So much for hiding her emotion.

Izzy turned a smile to Edith as she came and sat next to her. "You weren't supposed to see that."

Edith nodded in understanding, her dark hair bouncing with the motion. "I'll forget all about it, don't you worry." She rubbed a soothing hand over Izzy's back. "What did he do, lass?"

There was a question. "We both did it," she admitted, shaking her head and looking up at the ceiling. "There is enough blame to share."

Edith made a soft scoffing sound. "What could you have done to cause a strain between you?"

Strain? They were broken, possibly irreparably so. Her emotions were strained from overuse, but she and Sebastian had been destroyed.

"I may have lashed out at Sebastian," she admitted with a wince.

"Good heavens," Edith murmured, her hand pausing on Izzy's back before continuing. "Well, I'm sure it was a very quiet lashing. You're not vindictive."

Now the wince was accompanied by a loud hiss. "Well…"

Edith's hand vanished. "Izzy?"

Izzy turned to look at her friend, smiling in embarrassment. "I think you'd find that episode proof enough that I have been spending far too much time with Charlotte."

Edith's emerald eyes went wide as saucers. "Oh, Lord…" she

breathed.

There was nothing more to be said than that, and Izzy only nodded slowly, letting the truth sink in.

"I'm sure he deserved it," Edith eventually said, though her tone was not at all convinced.

Izzy wasn't sure of that. Not even a little bit.

She'd been over the argument time and time again, and while there was certainly reason for her to be upset, he had also given some valid points. The only thing she could say was that they had both behaved badly, and she would never accuse him of being purely at fault for what had happened.

Whatever good nature she'd cultivated over her life, it had vanished in that moment, and she feared he would only remember her in the throes of temper.

She needed to be more than that to him, even if she only lived in his memory forevermore.

Lord, how she missed him. It seemed incomprehensible that she could miss a man who had made her feel so very dreadful, and at whom she could have been so angry, but the truth of the matter was that she ached to be with him. She was desperate to apologize, and willing to forgive, if he could do so.

Surely, they could find a way to resolve it. Surely, there could be hope for them.

Surely, he could love her again.

"Oh, Izzy, you look so much better than I thought you would," Grace commented as she entered the parlor, smiling with warmth and tenderness that only made her look more perfect than she already was.

A loud snort echoed in the corridor. "How did you expect her to look, Grace?" Charlotte called. "The face of wallowing and despair?"

"I believe the phrase is *in* despair, dear," Georgie added as she and Charlotte came into view. "And Izzy never wallows." She winked at her cousin and moved to the divan, sinking onto it with a sigh.

Charlotte rolled her eyes and took an open seat with an ungraceful flop. "Everybody wallows." She smiled at Izzy, waving her fingers in her direction. "Wallow away, dear. You deserve it."

"Do I?" Izzy laughed, folding her hands together in her lap. "Marvelous, I'm so out of practice."

"In what?" Elinor asked as she burst into the room. "Sorry I'm late, I was visiting Alice Sterling with Kitty Morton and Amelia Perry." She rolled her eyes quite dramatically.

Charlotte eyed Elinor curiously. "When did you and Alice Sterling become friends? Let alone the others."

"We're not," Elinor admitted with her usual bluntness. "I happened to be walking this way when Amelia and Kitty made me go with them to see her. And Alice wasn't engaging at all, it was miserable."

"Steady on," Georgie muttered with a dark look. "She is my relation."

"By marriage," Elinor shot back. "Izzy is your relation."

"For my sins," Izzy quipped with a sigh, flinging a grin in Georgie's direction.

Prue gave her a bewildered look as she entered, taking the seat beside Edith. "What sins are those? I'm not aware of any."

Izzy groaned loudly and looked at Prue with as much severity as she dared. "We all have sins, Prue. Nobody is perfect."

"I have loads of sins," Charlotte admitted freely, widening her eyes for effect. "I sin with flare."

"I am sure the Lord quite despairs for you," Georgie told her with sympathy.

Prue looked concerned for the topic and crossed herself quickly.

"And I'm quite sure Alice has a reason for being in low spirits," Grace reminded Elinor, her expression severe. "Don't criticize her."

"Hear, hear," Edith murmured.

"There's something I don't understand, Izzy," Charlotte mused aloud, giving her a speculative look.

Izzy looked at her friend expectantly, though she knew there was no preparing for anything where Charlotte was concerned. "Yes?"

Charlotte's brow furrowed, which it rarely did. "How did you and Mr. Morton grow so close that you could have such a tremendous falling out? Surely not just in your aiding Kitty."

"Charlotte Geneva Wright!" Georgie exclaimed, glaring murderously.

"I told you not to ask her that!" Grace shrieked as her hands flew to her mouth.

Charlotte glanced at Grace with a shrug. "Apparently, I don't listen well. Surprise." She returned her focus to Izzy. "Well?"

Izzy stared at her, waiting for her heart to resume its proper function. When it did so, she swallowed once, then asked, "How did you know?"

Her friend smiled in fond derision. "Dear girl, it was rather simple. We all knew the two of you were infatuated with each other, and then suddenly you were not attending our gatherings and not seeing anyone. There was a falling out, and it was disastrous, and I don't understand why."

"Why we fell out?" Izzy tried, hoping she could avoid revealing absolutely every secret she possessed.

Charlotte stared at her without speaking, clearly not willing to let this go.

There was nothing for it, then.

Izzy heaved a sigh and glanced at Edith, who nodded in encouragement. "I suppose it is long past time to tell you all what I've been doing. What *we've* been doing."

"Wait a moment, I am determined to be present for any and all confessions."

Every Spinster in the room turned to the doorway in shock, knowing that voice all too well.

Miranda Sterling was in the doorway of the parlor, dressed in the smartest walking dress Izzy had ever seen, the rich grey emphasizing Miranda's brilliant blue eyes to perfection.

Georgie was the first to recover and rose to greet her. "Miranda, what are you doing here?"

Miranda kissed her cheek, then moved into the room, keeping her gaze trained on Izzy. "Kitty Morton sent me a note, and I came to see Izzy. I had no idea you'd all be gathered, but no matter." She sat in the chair as though it were a throne.

Charlotte grinned at Miranda, drumming her fingers on the armrests of her chair. "Where's Rufus, Miranda?"

"Downstairs in the kitchens," Miranda replied, still staring at Izzy. "He hates large gatherings."

Charlotte snickered into a hand, as did someone else, but Izzy couldn't look away from Miranda.

"Go on, Izzy," Miranda encouraged with a warm smile. "Tell us."

Slowly, her face flaming the entire time, Izzy told them everything. Her first letters to Cousin Frank, his encouragement to try, and her desperate attempts to record as many stories as she could think of. She told them about her anxiety in keeping the secret, in succeeding or failing, and in being good enough. She mentioned her meeting with Frank and the need for an illustrator to enhance the story properly.

Then she spoke of Sebastian and his ability to capture the stories perfectly with his art, and how he had agreed to work with her on this. She told them how excited they had been to have Frank take them on, and how they'd used nearly all of the moments they should have spent with Kitty to work on their collection. How Sebastian had encouraged her, emboldened her, and her fears that this rift between them might destroy her dreams, along with her heart.

"And then there is the cost," she admitted at last, her throat nearly raw with so much talking. "Cousin Frank isn't a publisher of novels, strictly speaking, and so the costs will be more, which means I have to pay for a good portion of the process, and there is no money to be had for such a venture. So, it's irrelevant anyway. Unless I tell my parents, at any rate, and there is no reason for me to think that they will give me hundreds of pounds to publish the collection the way I would like."

She looked at her friends in turn, and each stared at her without much by way of expression.

"Well?" she finally asked of any of them.

"Why didn't you tell us from the start?" Prue shook her head, smiling in her gentle way. "Of course, we w-would have supported you. It sounds perfectly l-lovely!"

"Yes!" Grace echoed, turning towards her. "I would have loved to help you with any of it."

Izzy sighed, torn between relief and embarrassment. "Thank you."

"So, you fell in love with him through all that," Charlotte stated

266

in a surprisingly soft voice.

Izzy's eyes filled with tears as she looked at one of her oldest friends, and then she nodded, swallowing the lump that had formed in her throat. "Yes."

Charlotte smiled sadly and said nothing further.

"Well, I can certainly resolve one of the issues at hand," Miranda said, her voice choked.

Izzy looked at the woman in surprise. "What?"

Miranda wiped at her eyes delicately, then sniffed. "I insist on funding your publication, Izzy. All of it. Whatever you need."

"Miranda!" she gasped, shaking her head quickly. "No!"

"I don't understand that word," Miranda replied, making Charlotte hoot a laugh. "So, you had best not say it. I *am* doing this, and you *will* have the best of all materials. I will call upon your cousin Frank tomorrow and settle it all."

Izzy gaped at her, mouth working soundlessly, then glanced around at her friends for help.

They had none to give.

"Thank you," Izzy finally managed, squeaking awkwardly.

Miranda dipped her chin in a regal nod. "Delighted, love. I cannot do anything about your Mr. Morton, I'm afraid. You will have to manage that one on your own."

Izzy nodded frantically, smiling in helpless delight. She had no idea how she would resolve that, but she would find a way. She could make things right between them somehow, if only given a chance. She refused to believe that all would be lost, that there was nothing to save between them.

She still loved him, and while she loved him, she would work to do all she could to save them.

"Begging your pardon, Miss Lambert," Collins suddenly intoned from the door. "Something has just been delivered for you."

Delivered? What could possibly have been delivered for her when she had purchased nothing of late?

"Ooh, presents!" Charlotte applauded politely. "Bring it in, Collins."

Georgie shushed her, and thankfully Collins ignored her, keeping his focus on Izzy.

Izzy swallowed once. She had no secrets from them anymore, so there was nothing to be gained by further secrecy. "Bring it to me, please, Collins."

He nodded, disappeared for a moment, then returned with a scroll of sorts on a platter, tied with a blue ribbon.

Fingers trembling, she picked up the scroll and untied the ribbon, setting it in her lap.

No one in the room spoke, and she so wished they would.

Her breath caught as she opened the scroll, no more than plain paper, but upon it had been drawn a scene that stole her breath.

It was of a warm and cozy parlor, a blazing fire roaring in the fireplace to one side. A small rocking horse sat in the corner next to a chest with various toys stacked around it. A woman was in a chair, sitting right at the edge, her hands and arms waving in a dramatic fashion. At her feet sat four children, the youngest barely more than an infant, all in their nightclothes. They were riveted upon her, hanging on her every word, eyes wide as saucers.

The woman was Izzy, that was plain, and the children all resembled her in some way. And on a sofa at the edge of the drawing, cradling an infant, was Sebastian. Smiling at her.

"What is it?" Charlotte demanded in excitement.

Izzy couldn't speak, could barely breathe. Sebastian had captured every aspect of the life she had imagined. No matter what he had said or done, this alone spoke volumes.

"It's an illustration," Edith told Charlotte in a firm tone intended to end the discussion.

"Oh, for the collection?" Charlotte went on, missing the hint entirely.

Miranda hummed very softly. "I don't believe that is for the collection at all, Charlotte. And I further believe it is a private matter. Now, speak of something else, or I shall insist we all take Rufus for a walk."

"Well," Elinor chirped brightly, "does anyone want to hear my news?"

"I doubt it will top Izzy's news, but why not?" Charlotte said with a wave of her hand.

Grace rolled her eyes and huffed. "Really, Charlotte…"

"Mr. Andrews may have developed a fondness for someone we know," Elinor told them all, ignoring the other two.

That sparked the interest of the group, but Izzy lost track of the conversation and stared at the illustration in wonder. How could he have known she needed this? That this would renew something within her, rekindle what she had thought lost? How could he have known her so perfectly?

He loves me.

She gasped very softly to herself, afraid of the truth, of believing…

She looked up and her eyes clashed with Miranda's. She smiled with the utmost gentleness at Izzy and winked before going back to the conversation.

That wink sparked something within her, something she hadn't felt in days, and feared she never would again.

Hope.

Sebastian was shown into the Lambert home without any fuss or ado, and without a single scowl from the butler, who surely had to know what had happened the last time Sebastian had entered the place. Yet the older man had taken him up just as easily and efficiently as he had any other time Sebastian had called.

Strangely, that gave him a bizarre sense of hope.

He'd sent a note asking to see Izzy today, and was astonished that he received a favorable reply. His nerves at their extremes, he'd wondered at least a dozen times on the ride over if he should have waited longer. Spent longer making amends and making restitution. Courting Izzy's forgiveness before appearing for judgment.

Ultimately, he could not wait.

He could not wait one day more.

He was shown into the drawing room, and Izzy was ready for him, standing by the window, her dress simple, yet elegant.

And she was smiling.

He wasn't sure she had ever been more beautiful.

Collins' footsteps disappeared down the corridor and faded to nothing.

Still Izzy watched him, her expression warm, but hesitant.

"How is Alice Sterling?" he asked without any preamble, unable to think of anything else to ask. "Kitty tells me you've all been to see her."

He watched her throat work on a swallow. "Recovering. It will take time." One of her brows rose quickly. "I believe Hugh may be more distraught at the moment."

"So he should be," Sebastian replied, completely unapologetic. "It's unforgivable what he did."

"Is it?" Izzy asked with a mildness that stole his breath.

The irony was not lost on him.

"Perhaps not," he managed, averting his gaze. "He is her brother, after all. And he clearly did not mean to lead her so far astray."

Izzy cleared her throat once, drawing his gaze back. "Brothers do the best they can for their sisters, do they not? Even if at times they do so wrongly?"

He opened his mouth to speak but found no words.

No excuse.

"Is it to be faulted if they meant no harm?" she pressed with such gentleness it weakened him.

Even when she was not defending herself with a fire, she was magnificent. Her goodness was just as magnificent as her strength. And he loved her just as much for that, if not more.

He inhaled slowly, then exhaled in a rush. "Izzy, I... I need to apologize."

She didn't respond, which made him want to smile.

"Profusely," he added with feeling. "Repeatedly, and extensively. And you know that. I overreacted in a way I didn't think I was capable of. Not only were you right to tell me to read what Kitty wrote, but you were right about everything. I was a hypocrite. I *am* a hypocrite. It was difficult to hear, but it was absolutely the truth."

He shook his head, shame and revulsion filling him, paining him still as he faced her this way. "I became one of those critics who turned against you, only I couldn't see it. I was blinded by ignorance and a puffed-up sense of propriety. All that I had been encouraging you to do, and suddenly I took it all back. I proved myself the worst sort of friend; the kind that cannot weather the storm. The disloyal one. The one without honor. But you…"

He broke off, his voice hoarse with emotion. He cleared his throat quickly. "You've always been exactly who you are. You're steadfast and true, you're kind and good, and you understand the confines of the human heart more deeply than anyone I've ever met. You see what we all should, and yet you aren't blind to anything. You are a wonder, Izzy. Something of a miracle."

Izzy made a soft sound of denial, but he stepped forward, holding out a hand.

"Please, let me finish," he begged. "Please."

She clasped her hands and nodded once.

Sebastian sighed bitterly. "I cannot take back what I said, though I dearly wish I had that power. I cannot pretend that I will always be this humbled or clear, but I can vow that I will be the stalwart friend you deserve, Isabella Lambert, and from this day forward you will always have my support and loyalty, no matter what. All I ask is for a chance to atone, and to eventually be forgiven, and to prove myself worthy of your friendship."

Izzy stared at him for a long moment, her wide, incomparable eyes surveying him with such depth he would vow she had seen his soul, but she said nothing.

In agony, he waited. Hoped.

Despaired.

"I don't want another friend, Mr. Morton," she eventually murmured, her voice barely reaching him. "I have so many, and we both know most of those are only of convenience."

His heart crashed into the pit of his stomach, and he blinked at the shocking pain of it all, lowering his head.

"What I am in desperate need of is the man I love."

Stunned, his head shot up, and he stared at her in wonder. She smiled at him with such tenderness, he could scarcely breathe.

"For I've missed him," Izzy went on, her voice growing in strength and fervor. "Very much. And I cannot bear to see him hurting so when he is so very treasured."

He was *what?*

His feet were moving before he knew what was happening. "Izzy…"

She laughed, the sound more like a sob, and reached for him as he came to her. He hauled her into his chest, her arms twining around his neck tightly. He inhaled the scent of her, the beautiful fragrance of warmth and laughter and home, drinking it until it filled every part of him.

"I love you, Iz," he breathed, gripping her hair in desperate fingers. "I love you so much. I'm so very sorry."

Izzy shushed him, stroking the back of his neck. "I'm sorry, too. I shouldn't have said what I did to you, should never have accused you of such horrid things…"

He pulled back and gave her a severe look. "Stop apologizing," he ordered, leaning down to kiss her, savoring the taste and feel of her lips against his.

"I must," she insisted, breaking away. "I have to apologize. You deserve it."

He kissed her again, more fiercely, taking great care to silence her. "No, I don't," he rasped against her mouth, dusting his lips across her cheeks and nose. "I don't need your apology. You have nothing to apologize for."

"Yes, I do," she whispered, her lips grazing his cheek in a way that sent fire into his toes. "I was so rude and angry, and I should have listened."

Sebastian chuckled as he nuzzled her gently, letting her hair slide through his fingers, pins scattering in every direction. "You're being nice again."

Izzy sighed and dipped her head back, exposing her neck and throat to him, which he took advantage of. "Of course I am. I'm always nice."

"Yes, you are," he agreed, layering kiss after kiss along her neck.

"I was so… so horrible to you," she whimpered, the first sounds of real distress making their appearance.

He tipped her head back up, and held her chin in one hand, forcing her to meet his eyes. "Yes. And I was as proud of you as I was upset by you. Don't ruin it."

Her eyes searched his in an almost frantic manner. "Proud?"

He nodded as he stroked the underside of her chin. "So proud. You were taking charge of the moment, even as I was railing against you, and you flung it back in my face. You were bold and breathtaking and beautiful. It terrified me and thrilled me. Magnificent creature."

Izzy shook her head, her hands gripping at the back of his neck. "I couldn't be so bold but for you. I couldn't... I love you, Sebastian. I love you."

He leaned down and kissed her softly, tenderly, with all the burning in his soul. "Be as bold as you like with me, love. I'll love you just as you are and just as you wish to be, nice or cruel, sweet or spiteful, and you can yell and scold and hurl breakable things, if you like, and I'll only love you more."

That made her chuckle and she gave him a coy, teasing look that undid him. "Are you sure? I have a fairly good arm."

"Positive," he insisted, nudging his nose against hers. "Toss all the crockery you want. My thick head can take the beating so long as my heart is in your keeping."

Izzy hummed a delightful, low sound and her expression became almost slumberous. "It's there. And I'll keep it safe."

Sebastian grinned, toying with her now loose curls. "I know you will. So, will you marry me?"

A slow, tender smile crossed her perfect lips, and her hands slid into his hair. "Marry a perfect gentleman, sir? But I am a spinster."

"You are *my* spinster," he told her hungrily, kissing her yet again. "And I'm not giving you up."

She sighed a laugh and nodded, arching up to kiss him once. "Then I'd best marry you, sir. A spinster never causes a scandal."

"How very nice of her," he murmured with a suggestive lift of his brows, placing a very soft kiss at the corner of her lips.

Izzy hummed again and winked at him. "Isn't it just?"

Epilogue

———— ⚬⚭⚬ ————

A daughter has two purposes: to represent her family with honor, decorum, and discretion, and to make a good match that will bring to her family honor, decorum, and discretion. What, then, of the daughters who accomplish the first but not the second? Are they, and we, to be faulted for our incomplete state; our unfulfilled purposes? Are we doomed to be considered failures in our term by something, which, through no fault of our own, may never be? Oh, the disadvantage to the unmarried, flawed, purposeless daughters of England, and what luck to those that have managed to escape such things, and do their duties without fault.

-The Spinster Chronicles, 9 April 1819

"We are quite the dreary lot, are we not?"

Charlotte's voice was dry and teasing, as usual, but the truth was plain for all to see.

They *were* dreary.

But it couldn't be helped.

"This room is dreary," Elinor informed her with a sniff, never one to let Charlotte be the only one speaking her mind.

"I won't tell my mother you said so," Charlotte shot back. "She thinks the grey is a lovely shade and accentuates any adornment with great effect."

Elinor glared at Charlotte with a strained superiority. "Then your mother's tastes in décor align rather nicely with Mrs. Lambert's tastes in tea."

Grace winced audibly and glanced at Edith and Prue just near her. They each had similar expressions.

Charlotte's eyes widened as she straightened in her chair, and she leveled the younger woman with a murderous look. "You take that back."

"My aunt's tea is not the issue," Georgie said irritably from the sofa opposite, where she was lounging almost inelegantly. "Nor is Mrs. Wright's, who has excellent taste, and deserves better than your insults to the contrary, Elinor. She is our hostess, now that Izzy is gone from our original place of meeting, and if you cannot treat her with respect, I will send you home to your sister and give you leave to explain to her why we cannot have you any longer."

Elinor gaped at Georgie in horror, her mouth working soundlessly.

Grace quickly looked over at Georgie, whose pregnancy could no longer be hidden, desperate to change the subject. "How is Alice, Georgie?" she asked with as much gentleness as she could.

Georgie smiled at her, irritation fading. "Well enough, though it took her a good while to be able to confess the whole story to Francis and Janet. She believed Mr. Delaney to truly love her, as he had claimed to her in private. But then when she was alone with him at the Allandale ball, when she thought he might propose…" She shook her head, turning somber and resigned, leaving the rest unsaid.

"I only heard the basics of the affair from Izzy before she left," Grace told her, shaking her head in sympathy. "Poor Alice."

"How could we have been so mistaken in her?" Elinor asked, scoffing in disparagement. "To willingly be in company with Simon Delaney at all is sheer folly!"

Prue sighed loudly, giving Elinor a scolding look. "Alice Sterling is not to b-be criticized for trusting the wrong man, especially when we d-did not take her into our c-confidence on such matters. Despite what you m-might think, Elinor, we are not the soldiers of all feminine virtue against m-men with vile designs."

"Hear, hear," Edith murmured, looking rather worse for the wear. "The lass was duped, and there it is."

"But how?" Charlotte frowned in thought, shaking her head. "I cannot see how she was so duped. Francis and Janet surely knew

Delaney was not to be trusted, and they would have…"

Georgie sat up quickly, wincing with the sudden motion. "They didn't know," Georgie insisted. She sighed and rubbed at her back. "They didn't know. Alice was manipulated by Hugh to consider all his friends as men of honor, and that there was an unfair prejudice against them."

"Unfair?" Elinor cried with a laugh of disbelief. "Unfair, is it? I could provide a list of women…"

Edith cut her off with a sharp slash of her hand. "This is not a debate session in the House of Commons, Elinor! Kindly temper your tone and your opinions for the present."

"Yes, please," Charlotte added, her eyes wide as she took in Elinor as though she were a deranged child. "Calm yourself."

"I miss Izzy," Elinor grumbled, folding her arms across her chest and looking rather petulant. "She would make it right."

Georgie sighed and tried to look sympathetic. "We all miss Izzy, dear, but you know if she were here, she would ask us to pity Hugh as well."

"Not bloody likely," Elinor said with a rough snort.

"I could pity him," Prue broke in, her voice trembling with uncertainty. "As I understand it, he has been betrayed by a man he considered his friend, however misplaced that friendship was. Even you, Elinor, cannot believe that he would have sacrificed his sister willingly."

There was a moment of silence from them all, not only to appreciate the perspective, but the fact that Prue had been able to express her thoughts so perfectly and without any stammering at all.

Elinor made a face as though to consider the thought, then reluctantly nodded. "I suppose even Horrid Hugh must love his sister."

Georgie managed a wan smile. "He's distraught. Beyond consolation. Tony says he has never seen him like this."

"Good," Elinor grunted, sniffling without concern.

Edith was far more sympathetic. "What will he do?"

"He's going away," Georgie told them, gradually reclining back on the sofa. "I can't recall where, some relation's estate. He has much he feels he needs to atone for, and he cannot face anyone until he is recovered."

"Small mercies," Elinor scoffed.

Grace shook her head, looking towards the window. While she might not particularly care for Hugh Sterling in any way, she could certainly sympathize with shame so great that one could not face it. Or indeed face one's self in the looking glass.

She knew that all too well.

"When are Izzy and Sebastian due back?" Edith inquired of the group, changing the topic once more, and into much safer realms.

Prue chuckled a knowing laugh. "N-not for some time, I should hope. They deserve some time alone, away from all of London. I am glad they were able to marry so quickly."

"As am I," Georgie laughed, relaxing at last. "And so is Aunt Faith. She has never been so pleased in her entire life."

"Yes, I am sure having a spinster daughter marry must be quite the relief indeed," Grace murmured, swallowing with some difficulty.

Edith looked at her in surprise. "That is rather cynical for you, Grace. As was your last article, come to think. What's the trouble?"

Charlotte's attention suddenly centered on Grace as well. "Yes... You've been avoiding events of late, Grace. I know you were at Allandales', but then I did not see you at the end of it."

Grace managed a smile, though it would not have convinced anyone in truth. "I was unwell that evening, I fear. An appearance had to be made, and so it was." She glanced at Georgie in apology. "And I am most dreadfully sorry I was unable to assist with Alice in all of that."

Her comments were waved off with a dismissive hand. "We behaved with a minimal amount of fuss at all, and no one else was brought in. No one knew outside of the Spinsters, and they were told after the fact. Truly, there was nothing you could have done."

She knew that, but it only added to her current feeling of uselessness.

Of being found wanting.

"That was ages ago," Elinor groaned as she reached forward for one of the biscuits on the tea tray before her. "Do we have *anything* else to talk about? It's been weeks since the Allandales', and Georgie says that Alice is recovering. Hugh is gone, Izzy is married and reportedly blissful…"

"She ought to be," Charlotte scoffed, grinning at no one in particular. "She can have no true complaints as Mrs. Morton. I wouldn't."

"Yes, you would," several of them replied at once.

Charlotte coughed in mock-effrontery. "I would not!"

"Give her Lord Ingram," Elinor suggested merrily. "He is new to London after all. I am sure he could take it."

"No!" Georgie shook her head emphatically. "No, I like him far too much! Not Lord Ingram!"

Grace reacted to the name without meaning to, then prayed the flinch would go unnoticed by the rest.

She could not be the center of gossip and speculation, not now.

The gentle ribbing of Charlotte's nature continued, as well as the objection to certain suitors of high caliber to be tossed her way, and Grace exhaled silently, pleased to no longer be the focus of attention.

She'd have enough of that to come.

"You don't seem well, lass," Edith murmured very softly, leaning close to do so. "What can I do?"

Grace smiled at her friend, though she felt it waver on her lips. "I'm not sure yet, Edith. But when I am, I will tell you."

Edith nodded, squeezing her hand, and was quick to join in the teasing of Charlotte, leaving Grace to her thoughts.

She did not wish them for company. They were too much in concert with the focus of the most recent letter from her father.

Yet she feared these thoughts and this focus would rule her life all too soon. She shuddered involuntarily. There was no telling what might be in store for her when they did.

Coming Soon

My Fair Spinster

The Spinster Chronicles
Book Four

"Oh, what a beautiful Spinster."

by

REBECCA CONNOLLY